KT-361-904

The A to Z of Everything

DEBBIE JOHNSON

HARPER

Harper
An imprint of HarperCollins*Publishers* Ltd
The News Building
1 London Bridge Street
London SE1 9GF

www.harpercollins.co.uk

A Paperback Original 2017
1

Copyright © Debbie Johnson 2017

Debbie Johnson asserts the moral right to be identified as the author of this work

A catalogue record for this book is available from the British Library

ISBN: 9780008150198

This novel is entirely a work of fiction.
The names, characters and incidents portrayed in it are the work
of the author's imagination. Any resemblance to actual persons,
living or dead, events or localities is entirely coincidental.

Typeset in Birka by Palimpsest Book Production Ltd, Falkirk, Stirlingshire
Printed and bound in Great Britain by Clays Ltd, St Ives plc

All rights reserved. No part of this publication may be reproduced, stored
in a retrieval system, or transmitted, in any form or by any means,
electronic, mechanical, photocopying, recording or otherwise,
without the prior permission of the publishers.

MIX
Paper from
responsible sources
FSC C007454

FSC™ is a non-profit international organisation established to promote
the responsible management of the world's forests. Products carrying the
FSC label are independently certified to assure consumers that they come
from forests that are managed to meet the social, economic and ecological
needs of present and future generations, and other controlled sources.

Find out more about HarperCollins and the environment at
www.harpercollins.co.uk/green

The A to Z of Everything

Debbie Johnson is a best-selling author who lives and works in Liverpool, where she divides her time between writing, caring for a small tribe of children and animals, and not doing the housework.

She worked as a journalist for many years, until she decided it would be more fun to make up her own stories than to tell other people's. After trying her hand at pretty much every genre of writing other than Westerns and spy dramas, she has settled on women's fiction that seems to make people laugh and make people cry, often at the same time.

Her books include *The Birthday That Changed Everything*, *Pippa's Cornish Dream*, and *Summer at the Comfort Food Café*, all published by HarperCollins. She also ghost-wrote model and presenter Abbey Clancy's debut novel, *Remember My Name*.

Follow her on Twitter @debbiemjohnson, or at www.Facebook.com/debbiejohnsonauthor – but be warned, she mainly talks about dogs.

B000 000 020 9424

ABERDEEN LIBRARIES

Also by Debbie Johnson

Cold Feet at Christmas
Pippa's Cornish Dream
Never Kiss a Man in a Christmas Jumper
The Birthday That Changed Everything
Summer at the Comfort Food Café
Christmas at the Comfort Food Café

For my mother – five years gone, and part of me still expects it to be her when the phone rings late at night.

PART ONE

The Stage Is Set

Prologue

Andrea

Forty years have passed since my own mother died, and yet I can still remember it like it was yesterday. I can still recall the sounds and the smells and the way her tiny hand felt in mine as she finally gave up the fight, as the light faded from her eyes.

I can remember the hollow feeling inside me as I made my way home to my own children, crying on the bus and ignoring the kindness of strangers as the double-decker trundled across London.

Walking through the door to our flat, overwhelmed with the need to bundle them up and keep them safe and love them so much that no harm would ever come to them. Protect them from the cruel torments of the world.

Four whole decades later, it is still so vivid. When it comes to the people you love, and the people you lose, the passage of time is irrelevant – some things simply stay with you forever.

I'm thinking about this so much more now, because this morning I was told that I am dying. Not in the slow and certain way that we are all dying – but in a two-months-if-you're-lucky way.

The look of practised sympathy on the consultant's face as he explained was enough to kick-start my stiff upper lip, and I silenced him with a smile. I've been an actress for the whole of my life, and I've done many a death scene.

Now, I've got to decide how to play my own – and what good can come out of it.

My last diary entry was a reminder to tell my friend Lewis that his ancient dog, Betty, needed a flea treatment, pronto. The one before that seemed to revolve entirely around buying a new hat for our trip to the races.

Funny how quickly things can change.

Now, I have a few weeks left – and I have to make them count. I have to scheme and work and plan like I've never schemed and worked and planned before. In those few weeks, God willing, I will be directing my own play – and performing a minor miracle.

Because, of course, I couldn't actually bundle up my own children for the rest of their lives – no mother can. I couldn't keep those two girls safe, and I couldn't protect them from the cruellest torment of all – the way we can hurt the ones we love.

If it's the very last thing I manage, I am determined that I will make the impossible happen. I will bang my daughters' heads together, and make them whole. I will do as much as I can to heal them, and their future, as I have time to do.

Because they're going to need each other, so very much. One day, very soon, they are going to wake up to a world without their mother – and, like I say, I still remember how that feels.

Her tiny hand, holding mine.

Chapter 1

1984 – Farewell to Templeton Peck

Dead goldfish are pretty revolting items, thinks Andrea, as she lovingly wraps up the body of the late, great pet known as Faceman. Once a delightful creature dashing through his fake coral reef and pirate castle, he's now slippy and cold and far too reminiscent of three-day-old Chinese food that's starting to disintegrate.

Once he's enveloped in tissue paper, he is placed in a shoebox, which the girls have decorated in the style of the little Corvette that *The A-Team* character drives around in. It's a masterwork of red felt-tip pen and blobby white paint that is barely dry, so some of it has smudged pink.

Patch, their cross-eyed Jack Russell terrier, is yipping and snapping at her ankles, desperate to get at the box. It's just food to him, and Andrea shoos him away. He disappears to the side of the garden, and starts digging a hole in the flowerbeds.

Poppy is sobbing uncontrollably, her wild dark hair plastered to the tears running down the sides of her cheeks. Seven years old and already a drama queen. Rose is hugging her, making soothing noises to try and calm her down. They're both barefoot, still in their nighties, and look impossibly small and forlorn as they traipse through the dew-soaked grass of the cottage garden.

It's easier for Rose to be calm, of course. Her fish, B. A. Baracus, is still happily swimming around in the bowl, calling people 'fool' and looking tough. Poor Faceman has lasted less than three months. This is their first encounter with death, and emotions are running high, in the way that they do when little girls are involved.

There is a small hole, which Andrea dug earlier that morning, and a cassette player next to it, running on batteries. Andrea hands the shoebox to Poppy, who drags herself out of her hysteria long enough to accept it with tiny, shaking hands. Andrea reaches out and strokes her face clear of tears. Her skin is clammy and pale and moist, and although at least some of the performance is for effect, Andrea knows her baby girl is genuinely devastated.

Next time, she thinks, I'll get them a pet with a longer shelf life. Like one of those tortoises that live for a hundred years.

'Go on, Popcorn,' she says gently, gesturing to the hole. 'We need to say goodbye to Faceman now. Would you like to say a little prayer for him?'

'I c-c-c-an't!' she stutters, trembling so much the box starts to shake as well. Andrea has visions of the goldfish making a bid for freedom, flying through the sky and landing on the head of one of their garden gnomes. This, for some reason, amuses her, and she fights to keep her face straight. She can't laugh. Not now. This is a big, serious thing. The way she plays this will affect their outlook on the Grim Reaper for the rest of their lives. She has to at least try and get it right.

'I'll do it,' says Rose, who is two years older and already displaying the kind of alarming maternal instincts that make Andrea think she might end up as a grandma by the time she's 40. She'll have to lock her in the broom cupboard before long, or make her take a bite from an enchanted apple.

Poppy nods, and leans down to place the box in the ground. It tilts as she does it, but luckily no goldfish corpses slosh out and scare them all. Patch is watching them from the hole he's now sitting in, and Andrea silently says her own prayer: please do not let that stinky little dog gallop over here and run off with the dead fish's body.

They stand back respectfully, and place their hands together in the prayer position they've been taught at school. Andrea's not at all sure she believes in God, or the afterlife, but it's certainly useful where small children are concerned. Much more comforting than the alternative.

'Dear Jesus,' says Rose, bowing her head so her brown curls swing around her chubby face, 'please take this wonderful fish, Faceman, into heaven. He was a good fish and we all loved him. Please give him a nice bowl to swim in, and lots of other fish to play with, and let him know that we will *never* forget him. Amen.'

It is a lovely prayer, simple and heartfelt and innocent, and Andrea feels tears filling her eyes. They are so precious, these two beauties. These two grubby angels who have enriched her life beyond belief. In moments like these, she can forget all her worries: the bills, her lacklustre acting career, the sheer exhaustion of being a single mum in a world built for couples. She can ignore it all, and focus on what matters – her Rosehip and her Popcorn. Best girls in the world.

Poppy looks up at her big sister, and offers a small, tremulous smile.

'It'll be all right, Pop,' says Rose, reaching out and holding her hand. 'Heaven is a beautiful and perfect place, and Faceman will be happy there.'

Poppy frowns, and Andrea recognises her Thinking Face. It's the look that usually goes before a very tricky question – like Where Do Babies Come From? (said very loudly in the park after seeing a lady with a pram), or Why Is That Man Bald? (said very loudly on the bus behind the town's answer to Kojak), or her particular favourite, Why Don't I Have A Dad? (said very loudly at Parents' Evening).

'Mummy,' she says, with a voice far firmer than her tearful expression, 'how does Faceman get to heaven? If he's buried in a box in a garden? And is there a different part of heaven for everything – you know, like a Sheep Heaven and a People Heaven and a Goldfish Heaven, all in separate bits? Because sheep would need grass, and fish would need water, and people would need the pub . . .'

Again, Andrea bites down on her lip to stop herself from laughing. The *pub*? That's what she thinks people heaven would be like? She's clearly been on one too many trips to the Farmer's Arms . . .

'Well it's all a bit of a mystery, my love,' Andrea replies. 'Nobody has ever come back from heaven to tell us about it

– because they're just too happy there. Personally I think that angels will come down and fly Faceman up with them tonight, while we're asleep.'

As she says this, she sees Rose's face also screw up into a thoughtful frown. Oh no, she thinks. They're too old for such an outrageous fib. They don't believe me, and now they'll want to dig up the bloody box again tomorrow and check if he's gone. That's my night sorted – a glass of red wine and an impromptu goldfish exhumation.

'But do they always fly to heaven?' asks Rose, her gaze flicking back to the house. 'Because B. A. Baracus hates to fly, you know that, don't you?'

It's actually an easier question than she'd anticipated, which is a relief. This whole thing is a minefield.

'Well, when B. A.'s time has come, we'll . . . flush him down the toilet? And then he can swim to heaven.'

'Goldfish heaven?' asks Poppy again, obviously not letting go of her idea of a compartmentalised afterlife.

'Exactly. Now,' says Andrea decisively, keen to avoid any more of the Junior Tag Team Spanish Inquisition. 'Shall we play the music?'

Both girls nod, and their mum presses the button on the cassette player. *The A-Team* theme music blares out, echoing around the garden and drowning out the birdsong and the sound of a lawnmower in the distance and the faint rumble of traffic heading into the village. They all stand to attention, singing along and doing the 'duh-duh-duh-duh' noises at the right places. It's their favourite TV show, and is a fittingly rousing end to Faceman's short, soggy life.

With the final ritual completed, Andrea reaches out for both their hands, hoping that they'll be happy and not too confused by all of this mortality nonsense. The three of them walk together towards the cottage, winding their way through the maze of potted lavender and garden gnomes and buzzing bees.

Just as they're about to go back inside and hopefully settle down for their usual Saturday morning cartoons, Poppy pulls on Andrea's hand, and comes to a halt.

'Mum,' she says, in a tone that means business. 'What will happen to us when *you* go to heaven?'

Andrea kneels down on the cracked crazy paving, and takes both girls into her arms. She feels small hands and skinny limbs wrap around her, and squeezes them as hard as she possibly can without popping their ribs. Like she never, ever wants to let them go.

'Oh, darling – don't worry about that. There's a very long time before your mummy goes to heaven.'

She pulls back, still on her knees so she is at eye level with the children, keeping one hand on each of their shoulders. She looks from face to face, and sees the way that Poppy's hand has already crept into Rose's; sees their strength and their wonder and their potential. How did she ever create two such perfect creatures?

'And even when I do,' she adds, giving them both a re-assuring smile, 'you'll always have each other.'

Chapter 2

The Present Day

'I know you're aiming for Scarlett-O'Hara-on-her-deathbed, darling, but with those earrings, you're landing closer to Pat Butcher leaving the Queen Vic in a black cab.'

Lewis is perched on the end of the bed, trying to ignore the machines and the wires and the dreaded drip stand. He's feeling a little queasy because of the smell. That unmistakable hospital smell: that hideous combination of death and disinfectant.

He can hear the nurses outside, chatting away about their night out at the weekend, and has a deeply uncivilised urge to run through the door and clang their heads together. He realises it's unfair – God knows, if anybody is entitled to a life-affirming booze-up, it's people who care for the dying. But still. A little decorum wouldn't go amiss.

Andrea manages to kick him, though it barely registers – she is very weak, and his behind is very well padded. It's like a gnat biting a T. Rex. He pats her foot beneath the green blanket, and gives her a smile.

'I hate you,' she says, 'with an absolute passion.'

'Careful, my sweet,' he replies, noticing that she is removing the gaudy drop earrings with shaking hands. 'You could pop your clogs at any moment. Would you really want those to be your last words?'

'No,' she answers, throwing the jewellery down, ignoring the fact that the fake ruby drops skitter across the floor, one disappearing beneath the bed and another taking up residence under the cabinet.

'If they're going to be my last words, I'd make it "an absolute *fucking* passion". Now, are you ready? How's the lighting? Honestly, you'd think they'd spare more thought, wouldn't you? A few gentle spots instead of all this . . . fluorescence?'

'Spare more thought to lighting? In hospital? I suppose they're concentrating on more important things.'

'Ha! I've reached the stage where there is no more important thing. Lighting makes all the difference, you know. There was this time, on set, with John Nettles . . .'

'Oh lord!' Lewis exclaims, standing to his size-12 feet and throwing his arms in the air in a gesture that is half pleading, half surrender, 'if you tell me another story about bloody Bergerac, I swear to God you won't get the chance to die naturally – I will take that pillow and *smother* you with it!'

She manages a smile, but it is a sad thing. Like her skin doesn't have enough life left in it to give it any conviction. She's always been slim, as long as he's known her, but now there is barely anything left.

Within the space of six weeks, the disease and the drugs have ravaged her like a Viking horde, leaving this grey, skinny streak of a human being behind. He'd do anything to pass on some of his solid bulk, but apparently the boffins haven't yet come up with a way to transplant the health and vitality of a 68-year-old man to his dying friend.

He feels like crying, and gives himself a stern talking to. There will be time for self-pity later – right now needs to be all about her.

'Maybe you should, Lewis,' she says, rooting around in the make-up bag that sits on her lap. 'And I can't say that I'd mind. I'd much rather say my farewells to this cruel world with a handsome man in my bed . . .'

'Well,' he replies, fussing around with the camera, 'I'll pop out later and see if I can find you one, then. What do you fancy, Daniel Craig? Or something a bit more old-school with a lot of chest hair, like Burt Reynolds?'

She's not listening now, he can tell. She has her little compact mirror out, and is inspecting her reflection. The grimace on her face implies she's not entirely delighted with what she sees. With a shaking hand, she tries to grip a brush, dip it in powder, touch herself up for her final scene. It is pitiful to watch, and he can't bear it.

He puts the camera down, lumbers towards her, and sits at her side. There is, sadly, plenty of room for both of them. He takes the brush and the powder, and goes to work. He adds some blush, and a touch of colour to her lips. They are cracked and thin, dehydrated. Like her body is rejecting anything that will sustain it.

Patiently, she endures his fussing without a single word of abuse. She must be feeling bad, he knows, to miss an opportunity to mock him for his make-up skills. All those years in the village amateur dramatics have not been wasted.

'Are you done, Max Factor?' she says, her head lolling back on to the pillow, as though holding it up has drained her of all energy. 'How do I look?'

He reaches out, and smooths down her hair. It is a dazzling shade of silver-grey, closely cropped to her skull in one of those boyish styles that only the very beautiful can carry off. And Andrea is beautiful – or at least she had been. Now, the once-stylish cheekbones – the type his mother always said 'aged well' – are poking out like wires, and her skin is stretched taut, like the world's worst facelift.

Her eyes are clouded by pain – she's refused to take any medication this morning, saying she needs her wits about her – but are still the same striking shade he will always remember. Such a deep blue they are almost violet. Elizabeth Taylor eyes.

He's seen Andrea in many of her TV roles, from back in her heyday, and she was what they would have called a 'stunner' back then. She was never a star, and hasn't appeared on screen in anything new since 2005, but she still occasionally gets fan mail, or an invitation to appear at a convention. A lot of people would recognise her – those eyes. That face. All the roles she played in the 1970s and 1980s, usually as someone's love interest, or a feisty barmaid, or what she called Posh Totty.

Never quite the leading lady – but then again, interesting roles for women were sadly lacking then, and she had two kids to look after as well. These days, she'd have smashed it, he thinks - been a Keeley Hawes or a Rachel Weisz or a Kate Winslet. Still, even when she was playing the Tart with a Heart on *The Sweeney* or a Sexy Alien Sidekick in *Doctor Who*, she was always good. Always stupendously glamorous. Always unforgettable.

In fact, the only people who seemed to have been able to forget Andrea are the two people she loves the most. The two people she's about to record her final message for, after weeks of preparation. Of field trips for him. Of rooting through photo albums, making cassette tapes, emptying out bin bags, setting up video-sharing accounts, drawing on maps with red pen, pilfering from scrapbooks. Pillaging their past, in the determined hope that she can change their future.

He has no idea if it will work. He has no idea if he even cares – they're not real to him, Rosehip and Popcorn. He's never met them, and has no real desire to. She banned him from contacting them to explain that she really is ill this time (from that, he deduces that Andrea may have tried to scam them with dramatic hospital visits before now, just to get their attention), and that suits him just fine. He's been friends with Andrea for more than ten years and never been introduced to them, which says it all.

Partly, he thinks, looking on as she sucks in breath, eyes closed, fingers weakly clinging on to the blanket with her coral-painted nails, she didn't want them to see her like this. Reduced to skin and bones held together with sheer force of will. Partly, she is so focused on this crazy plan of hers that it has now become more real to her than anything else, clinging to it and pinning all her hopes on it.

She is convinced that this is her legacy. That this will work. That she will be able to achieve in her death the one thing she was never able to achieve in life – bringing her daughters back together again.

As far as Lewis is concerned, those two deserve less of a second chance, and more of a good whipping – so caught up in the past, in their own petty bitterness, that neither of them could see what it was doing to their mother. It had been destroying her, from the inside out, just as surely as the cancer, and neither of them seemed to notice or care.

She's seen them, of course – there have been weekends away, trips to their homes, nights out at shows in London. But never at the cottage. Never in the same room. Never *together* – and that's what did the damage. That's what caused the internal injuries that all the MRI scans in the world wouldn't show up.

He still has no idea what the two of them were even feuding about – Andrea has always cast a dramatic glance skyward, and uttered something vague. But surely it wasn't serious enough to cause this – to leave their own mother spending her last weeks on this earth coming up with some crazy plan to reunite them?

Maybe, he thinks, she is right not to have told them. She wants to be remembered as she was, not as she is. And perhaps, deep down, she doubts that even a call to her deathbed will bring them together, and that would be more than she could bear.

His motives, his reasons for being grateful for their absence, are less pure. Lewis thinks they simply don't deserve her. But what does he know? He's never had children. It would be possible now, in this day and age – he'd find a nice lesbian couple and come to some arrangement, or even do an Elton John and David Furnish and maybe adopt. But back in his era . . . well, confirmed bachelors didn't become fathers, simple as that. And from what he's seen of Andrea's life, he's quite glad about it.

He reaches out and takes one of her hands in his. He has huge hands – he is built like a grizzly bear – and hers are tiny. Her skin is fragile, like the dusty paper in an antique book, and he holds it gently, scared it might disintegrate and fly away with the slightest touch. He feels her fingers twine into his, and is grateful to be there. She might not have her daughters, but she is not alone.

'Is it all sorted, do you think, Lewis?' she whispers, startling him from his thoughts. He'd assumed she was on the verge of another fitful bout of sleep.

'Do you think I've done enough?' she says, her fingers clinging to his, looking for reassurance.

'Darling, it is all beyond sorted. I have never seen you display such organisational skills as I have in the last few weeks. It will be enough, I promise. So don't worry about a thing – I know what to do. Everything is ready, and I'll play my part to perfection.'

'Ha! That'll be a first, then . . .' she murmurs, sarcastically. Ever the critic. Just because once – *once* – he dropped the bloody skull during his am-dram *Hamlet*.

She tries to sit up, and he sees she is struggling. He helps her move forward, and adjusts the bed so she is propped upright. He casts one last glance over her – the hair as neat as it can be, the make-up done, the dreaded earrings gone. She's insisted on wearing 'proper clothes', even though her cream-silk blouse is now hanging off her shoulders, and has doused herself in Chanel Coco, as though the girls will have some kind of sniff-o-vision when they watch this.

'Okay,' she says, drawing in a big breath. 'I think I'm ready. I can practically see a man with a scythe lurking in the corridor by the vending machine, my love, so we'd better get on with it. The show must go on. All set?'

He nods, and switches the camera on. He's never been much of a one for technology, and he's had to learn fast. Now, if he ever tires of playing the Solid Rural Lawyer, he can become an internet whizz-kid instead.

'Testing, testing, *uno-dos-tres* . . .' Andrea says, her voice high and firm; stronger than he's heard it for days. What a trouper.

He adjust his angles, knowing that she will insist on reshooting this if it doesn't meet her high standards, and gives her the thumbs-up.

She turns those brilliant eyes towards him, and smiles into the lens. It's a perfect close-up, and she plays it exactly right.

'My darlings. Rosehip, Popcorn, my only true loves. Not to be too Hollywood about this, but if you're watching this tape, that can mean only one thing: I have shuffled off this mortal coil . . . and you two are going to need each other more than ever. You need to set aside your differences, and look out for each other – just like you always used to.'

Chapter 3

Beacon C of E Primary School, 1986

'I'm going to rub your nose in that dog poo, you stuck-up cow,' says Jackie Wells, holding Rose's face down on the grass by the scruff of her neck.

It's Rose's last year at little school, and she has committed the cardinal sin of being clever. She's won all the prizes; she's pretty and popular and even good at netball. Of course Jackie Wells hates her.

'You don't even have a dad, and if you did, my dad would beat him up,' adds Jackie, sitting on Rose's back. Rose has no doubt about that; Jackie's dad looks like a Tonka truck.

She struggles, trying to throw her 11-year-old nemesis off her back, but only succeeding in wriggling ineffectually on the school playing field. She glances ahead, sees flat green grass and, not very far away, a lovely pile of dog mess is buzzing with flies.

If she was on her feet, she might stand a chance against Jackie – but unfortunately for her (and for Jackie), the child takes after her father and already weighs as much as that baby hippo they saw on the school trip to Chester Zoo.

Naturally enough, there are no teachers in sight, and the small circle of kids gathered around the spectacle seem to be enjoying it. The ones that aren't – Rose's friends – look twitchy and embarrassed and worried, but too scared of Jackie to intervene.

Rose tries to remind herself of her mother's oft-repeated words, the ones about jealousy being the mother of all aggression.

That might be true, Rose thinks, but it's not much of a consolation right now. Not when her uniform is covered in grass stains and her face is smeared with soil and she'll be eating poo for lunch.

She flails around, trying to kick Jackie with her Clark's shoes, but can't manage it. All that happens is that Jackie presses her face even harder into the ground, and for a terrifying few moments, she can't breathe at all. She can hear jeers and shouts and the brave, solitary cry of her best friend, Tasmin: 'Leave her alone, or I'll fetch Miss Cunningham!'

That is followed by a small, sad yelp, so Rose has to assume that Tasmin has paid the price for her courage.

Jackie pulls her head up, using Rose's long, curly ponytail like a handle, and slams her face back down into the damp ground. She feels soil smash between her teeth and into her mouth, and again panics as the world goes dark.

Just as she is about to give up and accept her early death, there is an ear-splitting screech, and Jackie's hefty weight is suddenly gone.

Rose takes a brief moment to suck in air, then rolls around so she can see what is going on. Poppy has arrived, in a blur of violence and fury, and is holding Jackie down while she punches her in the head. Rose has no idea how she is doing that, as she is not only two years younger than Jackie, but most of a baby hippo lighter.

'Don't!' she yells, punctuating each word with a blow from her screwed-up fists, 'Ever! Touch! My! Sister!'

Obviously, it's at that point that Miss Cunningham arrives, and the group of spectators magically all disappear off to play football or collect ladybirds or talk about Zammo in last night's episode of *Grange Hill*.

Miss Cunningham physically drags Poppy away from Jackie, who is left cowering and crying and, yes, Rose notices with some satisfaction, covered in smears of the exact same dog poo she was threatening her with just moments ago.

Poppy is trembling with anger, her long, scrawny body vibrating with emotion. She looks over at Rose, who is getting to her feet now, and is instantly calmed by her big sister's smile. The smile that tells her that everything is okay, that it will all be fine, and that there is nothing to worry about.

Rose knows that Poppy is going to get into trouble for this. But she also knows, deep down, that she wouldn't have it any other way. Rose might be the one who seems to look after them both – but when push comes to shove, it's always Poppy who is willing to rush right in and batter someone. She's her avenging angel, and anyone who crosses her pays the price.

Rose dusts herself down, and prepares the case for the defence. As soon as she is upright, Poppy flees from Miss Cunningham's lecture, and throws herself into her arms. She's so skinny, and she's crying, and her hair is all messed up, and she looks a bit like a tramp.

Rose hugs her, and smooths her hair down, and whispers into her ear: 'Thank you, Popcorn. And don't worry – it's all going to be okay.'

'Mum's going to kill me . . .' Poppy mutters, the reality of the situation starting to sink in as Miss Cunningham prowls towards them, hands on hips and scowl on face.

'Mum,' replies Rose, 100 per cent sure this is true, 'will completely understand. And she'll probably take us out for tea to celebrate.'

Chapter 4

The Present Day

Lewis is sitting on a traffic bollard, a few feet outside the hospital foyer. It's not very comfortable, despite his bulk, and he wishes there was somewhere more pleasant to sit. Maybe he'll donate a bench, he thinks, in memory of Andrea.

The Andrea Barnard Memorial Bench. It would welcome the arses of the cold, the lonely, the ill, the desperate. She'd absolutely hate it, he decides, and the thought of the look of contempt on her face makes him smile. If there's a heaven, she'll be shaking her fists and uttering dire threats. 'Something with a bit more class, please, darling,' she'd say. 'A nice little tequila bar, perhaps? God knows these poor people need a drink!'

It's late now – somewhere after 10 p.m. on what has been a very long day. By now, he'd usually be tucked up in bed with an episode of *Antiques Roadshow*, or reading a good Barbara Cartland.

It's a Friday, so he'd have a nice lie-in the next morning, before taking a brisk constitutional in the valley. Maybe he'd persuade Andrea to come with him. Perhaps, if the weather was good, they'd go for a paddle in the lake with his ancient springer spaniel, Betty.

For Lewis, and for poor old Betty, there will at least be another morning. Another sunrise. Another chance to wonder at the world – not that it looks very impressive when all you can see is a neon-drenched hospital car park and frazzled paramedics on a fag break.

For Andrea, there will be nothing. No more sunrises. No more tequila. No more *Antiques Roadshow*, unless she's been shown Downstairs, where she'll be taunted by scary-looking dolls and ugly pottery for all of eternity.

She's gone, and he's struggling to believe it can possibly be true – that somehow the world continues on as normal. There should be a black hole in the sky; a swarm of shooting stars to mark her passing, a murder of crows lined up on the bus stop cawing her name. Not just this . . . mundane reality.

She made her film, and he had marvelled at her. At her strength and her resolve and her determination. He knew how ill she was, how much pain she was in – but you couldn't tell from that video. She somehow managed to be loving and firm and even funny. Quite frankly, it had been the performance of a lifetime.

He'd been the liability, not her, with his shaking hands and constant need to blink tears from his eyes. Pathetic. He was a mess – she was a powerhouse.

Once she'd done it, though (one take, miraculously making it sound spontaneous even though he knew she'd rehearsed it), it seemed like whatever life and energy she had left drained out of her. It was her last hurrah, and within minutes of filming that one last close-up, her grey head dropped back into the lumps and bumps of the pillow as she fell into a long, staring silence.

There'd been a few sniffles after that, a few quick, breathless questions asking how she'd done, but he knew – he knew that it was all she had left to give, and she'd given it to her daughters. After that, it was silence and morphine all the way to the end.

It was a strange experience, seeing someone die. He wasn't even sure she'd gone when it finally happened, after several false alarms.

On one occasion, she went what felt like minutes without drawing in a breath, then when he went to check on her, she suddenly opened her eyes and made him scream like a big, fat girl. At least that provoked a laugh – albeit one that ended in a coughing fit.

Almost an hour ago, though, it ended. It all ended. That glorious life, that wicked sense of humour, that vigorous bundle of vitality. Sixty-five years of love and laughter and experience – all gone. One papery hand fell away from the blanket to dangle loosely over the edge of the bed, coral nails vivid against the white sheets, and the other – clutched into his – became limp and lifeless.

He waited, and waited, and waited some more. Part of him had been desperate for this moment – for her to be put out of her torment. But part of him felt like he had simply died with her, which wouldn't have been the world's biggest tragedy. He'd wanted to crawl into that bed, pull the sheets over them both, and just stop breathing. Stop existing.

A world without Andrea was, right then, too terrible to even imagine.

Lewis had made a lot of friends during his long, rich life – but none of them had ever come close to Andrea. She was like a beacon of energy, a rainbow shining into a grey world, a blast of dazzling light scattering away the darkness. She was his soul mate, his true love without being his lover, his partner in crime.

He'd first encountered her when he moved to the village years ago, and their eyes met over a crowded giant vegetable stand at the annual fete. They'd both been staring at the same collection of ridiculously large marrows, and they both had the same raised eyebrows and 'oo-er missus' expressions, straight from a *Carry On* movie.

That had led to coffee. Coffee had led to a night in the pub. And a night in the pub had led to an unshakeable friendship, based on a rude sense of humour, a love of banter, and, if he was entirely honest, on mutual loneliness.

And now she was gone, and he was sitting with a concrete bollard up his bum, and it was dark and cold and rainy. The height of the inglorious English summer. He'd left his mac on the back seat of his car, his tweed jacket was soaked through, and he knew his shirt would be plastered to his skin in ways that were far from flattering. She'd be thoroughly shocked at him showing off his man boobs in such an unbecoming way, he was sure.

His fingers were shaking and his carefully combed hair was wet and flat to his skull, letting all the bald patches peek out.

Somehow, though, he just didn't seem able to care. All his life, he'd done the right thing – been properly turned out, played his part, done what was expected of him. Now, he wouldn't be bothered if he was naked, covered in woad and speaking in tongues. Everything felt heavy, and useless, and empty. Especially him.

None of it felt real yet. He'd done some paperwork, accepted sweet tea and sympathy from kind nurses who never really knew her, and been forced to eat some over-buttered toast. Eventually, after 'giving him some time', they gently suggested he needed to leave the room.

It was only decades of training and conditioning and pure English politeness that stopped him from yelling at them. From kicking them out, and barricading the door with his recliner chair, and wailing like those Middle Eastern ladies you see on the news.

He understood now, for the first time, how grief could make you wail like that. How pain could be so pure and so livid that it took on a life of its own, a small, furious animal that wanted to howl at the top of its lungs. To scream and scream and scream until the whole world shattered with the sheer force of its misery.

His own parents had died after long, full lives, and they were never especially close anyway – they were merely the people who visited him at boarding school, and insisted he became a lawyer. It had hurt when they passed on, but nothing had prepared him for this.

For the rawness. The agony. The inability to accept that she was really gone. That it wasn't some silly trick of hers, that she hadn't faked it all, and any minute would sit back up, tears of laughter in her magnificent eyes, proclaiming: 'I well and truly got you that time, sweetie! I completely Reggie Perrin-ed you! Fancy a G&T on the way home?'

But no matter how long he waited, it didn't happen. She just refused to stop being dead, damn her. And now he is here, in the rain, fishing around in his jacket pocket for his phone and his cigar box. The cigar that she'd bought for him – a limited edition Montecristo that, under normal circumstances, he'd be looking forward to smoking.

He'd enjoy it on the terrace of his small garden, along with a nice glass of ruby port, listening to the night-time sounds of nature all around him, bathing in the starlight.

This, though, is slightly different. There are no sounds of nature, just sirens and screeching tyres and shell-shocked-looking people, standing in small, damp clusters as they wait for taxis. The starlight has been replaced by the flickering yellow signs of the hospital, and the glow of hundreds of tiny lights shining from hundreds of tiny windows. The car head-lights are reflected in dark pools of oily rain on the pitted tarmac as they zoom past, and he can hear a horribly loud drunken argument going on somewhere nearby. It is far from idyllic.

He waits until the downpour slows from its previous let's-all-build-an-Ark levels to a mild drizzle, and pulls out his cigar box. He's left his cutter at home, so he commits the blasphemous act of simply tearing off the end. He lights it, and takes that first, glorious puff, white smoke billowing out in front of his face in a fragrant cloud. He realises that he is sitting next to a 'No Smoking' sign, but nobody else seems to be taking any notice.

The cigar tastes and smells divine. A rare treat. She'd made him promise that he'd do this – that he'd do lots of things, in fact, but especially this. A quiet cigar, all alone, just for her. After a few tipples, she'd often filch one from him, and chug away on it while wiggling her eyebrows at his scandalised expression. Andrea often tried to shock him by doing un-ladylike things, and still somehow managed to remain the classiest woman he'd ever known.

After a few moments of enjoying the aroma and the sweet, woodsy taste in his mouth, Lewis looks up to see a man in a wheelchair parked in front of him. He looks about ninety years old, and only has one leg.

His wizened face is wrapped up in the hood of a fur-lined parka, and closer inspection shows that he isn't anywhere near ninety – he's much younger, but prematurely aged by some addiction or another.

Lewis has spent enough time in courts to know that the missing limb is likely to be a related condition, and even in their relatively quiet patch of the country, drugs have ravaged the lives of many. He'd usually make his excuses and leave, overwhelmed by that peculiar mix of sympathy and disgust that men of his age and background tend to feel for the heroin-afflicted.

Andrea, of course, was never overwhelmed by any such thing. She gave money to everyone who asked for it, had enough back copies of the *Big Issue* to wallpaper her whole cottage, and was ever empathetic with the lost souls of the world.

'We all have our demons, darling,' she'd say, passing a fiver to a shabby bloke with a dog on a string, 'it's just that some people's are more obvious than others'.'

He decides he's not going to budge, not tonight. Not while he's smoking his magical Montecristo, and still debating whether he should run back into the hospital and take Andrea back home with him. Perhaps he could mummify her and prop her up on the sofa, so he still has someone to talk to. He's convinced that Andrea mummified would still be better company than most people alive.

'Smells good,' says the man, sniffing the air appreciatively. 'Have you got a spare, mate?'

'I'm afraid not,' replies Lewis, shuffling slightly to try and relieve the numbness in his nether regions. 'This was a gift from a friend.'

'You must have some good friends,' his visitor replies, tapping dirt-encrusted fingertips on the arms of his wheel-chair. 'I don't have any left.'

I wonder why, thinks Lewis, uncharitably, before reminding himself that Andrea could be watching right now. Hovering over his shoulder, a shimmering diamanté wraith telling him that he could afford to be 'just a tiny bit less of a snob, don't you think, my love?'

'I'm not sure I do either,' Lewis eventually answers. 'The best one I ever had just died, in there.'

Actual tears well up in the man's eyes, and Lewis immediately feels like a shit for silently despising him. He has no idea what his story is, or how he ended up here, or what his demons are. He knows nothing about him, and has no right to judge.

'That's rubbish, mate. I'm so sorry for you. Been there, done that, got the T-shirt. They say that time heals and all . . . but I'm not so sure. Sometimes time seems to stand still, as far as I can make out. Anyway, good luck to you. I'll say a little prayer for your friend.'

He gives Lewis an abrupt nod, and starts to wheel himself away, his hands slipping on the wet frames as he turns, the wind blowing his parka off his shaven head.

'Hang on!' says Lewis, standing up, and immediately feeling a shooting pain fly right up his spine. Ouch. He recovers, and follows the man in the chair, handing him the cigar. He's lost his appetite for it now, anyway.

'Her name was Andrea,' he adds, as he backs away towards the car park. 'And I appreciate your prayers. I'm sure she would too.'

The man mutters his thanks and waves at him as he leaves, watching Lewis head towards his car, an old Jag he's had for donkey's years. He glances back, and all he can see of his new friend is the orange glow of the cigar tip moving around in the black night, like some kind of aromatic firefly.

He opens the car door, and sinks into the passenger seat in a soggy, crumpled heap.

He's smoked his cigar. He's increased his karmic brownie-point count. And now he has to do what he's been dreading for the last hour. He has to do what Andrea asked him to do. What he promised her he would.

He has to start the process that she hoped would put all her daughters' broken pieces back together again.

He knows he needs to be strong. To help the girls and, in

31

doing so, help Andrea. But he doesn't feel capable of putting their pieces back together, when his are all scattered and shattered and shed.

He feels like Humpty Dumpty, and has no idea how he is going to find the strength to do what he needs to do.

Call Rosehip and Popcorn, and tell them that their mother is dead.

Chapter 5

It's almost 11 p.m., and Joe is in bed. Rose is under no illusion that he's actually asleep. He'll be on Instagram, or playing Xbox Live, or doing whatever else it is that 16-year-old boys do when their mum isn't around. She decides she's probably better off not pondering that one, and walks into the kitchen.

She sees a blurred reflection of herself in the stainless-steel fridge door, and hastily pulls it open. Nobody needs to see that, especially her. She's wearing a baggy old dressing gown and stripy bed socks, and her hair desperately needs washing. Or possibly shaving off entirely so it can have a fresh start, and stop impersonating a neglected badger – her mass of curls is now pure frizz, the dark brown streaked with premature grey.

She stares into the fridge, bathed in the yellow glow of its light. She inspects the shelves, already knowing what is there, and knowing that she wants to eat none of it.

She went to Tesco on the way home from work, and there is practically a whole farm crammed on to the shelves. Fresh rocket and carrot batons and a cucumber big enough to qualify as a deadly weapon on an episode of *CSI*. Salmon fillets and a quinoa salad and green juices in trendy glass bottles. Her fridge is leaner than the entire British Olympic cycling team in pre-camp training. Surely some of that vitality will be absorbed into her just by looking at it, through some kind of environmental osmosis?

She roots around, sighing. She's bought all of this for her new health kick, walking round the supermarket full of hope and resolve as she packed the trolley with overpriced superfoods. She'd been shamed into it by Joe, who pointed out that him being forced to eat a broccoli stir-fry in one room while she stuffed her face with cream cakes in another wasn't exactly setting a good example. Plus there were never any cream cakes left for him, which wasn't fair.

Rose didn't really need him to point this out to her at all. She was already painfully aware of it, and he didn't even know the full extent of the problem. At 16, he was out a lot. He had friends to see and parties to go to and parks to hang round in. And while he was out, she didn't even need to hide – she could binge to her heart's content.

Except, of course, her heart probably wasn't all that happy with it. Multipacks of Wotsits and microwave sticky-toffee pudding in pots are never, ever to be seen on those healthy food pyramid charts they have pinned up in the school where she works. They are the renegades, the outcasts, the bandits of the nutritional world.

They are also, Rose thinks, shutting the fridge door a lot harder than she probably should, the only things that make her feel even marginally better about life.

She walks over to the cupboard under the stairs. The one Joe never goes in because it is the place where she keeps a strange combination of the Hoover, printer cartridges, empty cardboard boxes that once contained long-gone appliances, and random presents for other people.

It's known as the Present Cupboard, a throwback to a time when Joe was much younger. When he was at primary school, and there seemed to be a party every weekend. When life was dominated by the local soft-play centre, and coming up with some £5 toy to stick in a gift bag. When teachers needed novelty mugs for Christmas, and toiletry sets for the end of term.

It used to contain a cornucopia of delights. Cheap games and craft jars and wrapping paper and boxes full of cards with pictures of cuddly bears for the girls and pirate bears for the boys.

All of that faded out as Joe got older, when the tenner-in-the-envelope replaced the tat on birthdays. Now, his mates don't have the kinds of parties that involve climbing frames and ball pools – they have the kind that involve deliveries from Domino's Pizza and illicit booze smuggled into the garden in Coke bottles and someone plugging their phone playlist into speakers.

But for some reason, after all these years, they still both call it the Present Cupboard. And Rose does in fact still keep some presents in there – for colleagues, for neighbours, for those odd occasions when she just needs to say 'thank you' via the medium of chocolates or wine.

That's what she has in mind now, as she rummages through

the empty backpacks and the battery tin and the cardboard box brimming with mysterious chargers for equally mysterious items.

She eventually emerges victorious, brandishing one of those big, round, plastic tubs full of Cadbury's Heroes. She bought it in the run-up to Christmas, along with about five others. This is the sole survivor. The rest have taken up permanent residence on her thighs.

Rose checks the sell-by date, sees that all is good, and retreats back to the living room. She slumps down on the sofa, and sighs when she sees she's left the remote control by the telly. Heaving her too-big body up again, she retrieves it, and flicks through the channels until she finds something bearable.

This takes longer than it should considering the fact that they have about 8 million channels. She settles on a repeat of *Poldark*, which is pretty much the equivalent of a big box of chocolates in visual form, and leans back into the cushions.

Just one episode, she tells herself. And just a few chocolates. It's Friday, after all. She's had a busy working week, and she deserves it. She'll start her health kick tomorrow, and soon she'll be all spry and limber, like Demelza, skinny enough to frolic through the waves on a Cornish beach in summer instead of hiding her despicable calves in leggings and encasing her bingo wings in cardigans.

She hears a bumping sound from upstairs, and deduces that Joe is on his Xbox. His game chair is rocking around, and he'll probably be getting over-excited as he shoots things. At least it's the start of the school holidays, so it doesn't matter how late he stays up. Or her, for that matter. Six weeks stretch ahead of them – six weeks of fun for him, and six weeks of boredom for her. School holidays feel different when you're 42 than when you're 16.

At least she'll be able to catch up on all those jobs she's had piling up around her. Clean the car out. Unblock the drain in the shower. Many other exciting tasks.

She makes a mental note to call her mum in the morning – that needs to be top of the list. Her mum sent Joe a gift voucher to celebrate the end of his GCSEs, which of course he's already spent. It turned up weeks ago and they both keep forgetting to phone and thank her.

Now she comes to think of it, she's not spoken to her mum much recently at all. She usually called a lot – or at least what feels like a lot, when it's your mum.

She shrugs, deciding her mum must just be busy, and uses her untidy fingernails to tear off the tape around the lid of the box. Why do they always make these things so difficult to get into? Why is it that the carrot batons are just there, all washed and ready to go and simple, and the good stuff like the chocolate takes an engineering degree and a blowtorch to break into? Life just isn't fair sometimes.

Rose shoves a handful of miniature Caramels into her mouth, and hides the wrappers in the tub. If they're right at the bottom, it's like they don't count. Nothing to see here, nothing at all.

She looks on as Poldark takes his top off again – quality television – and wonders if this is all she has to look forward to now. Quiet nights in with a box of chocolate and Aidan

Turner. Which wouldn't be so bad if it was the actual Aidan Turner, here in person and scything her back garden for her, but it's not. It's a teeny-tiny-TV version, which is nowhere near as satisfying.

She also wonders what Simon next door is up to. She saw him doing his own gardening earlier, also with his top off. Not quite Poldark, but enough to make her blush. He's probably asleep, she thinks, or chatting to supermodels online. And I'm turning into a horny old woman who needs to get her own life, instead of living through other people's.

Joe is starting sixth-form college in September, doing his A-levels. He's excited, and hopeful, and bright enough to do well. The world is at his size-10 feet, which is where it belongs – because he really is a great lad. He's not had it especially easy, between his dad and his dad's new family and what she suspects has been her increasingly morose presence, but he's always stayed upbeat. Confident. Secure.

She remembers those days when everything felt possible. The days back home, when mum was still acting and they all lived in the cottage, and She Who Shall Not Be Named was still in her life.

It feels like a million years ago, she thinks, getting to work on the miniature Wispas.

Chapter 6

Forest Hills High School
Christmas Disco, 1991

Rose collapses down on to one of the benches, drenched in sweat. Poppy stays on her feet for a while longer, trying to tempt her back up to Chesney Hawkes singing 'I Am the One and Only'.

'No chance,' says Rose, wiping her forehead clean and grinning at her younger sister. 'I hate this song anyway.'

Poppy pulls a face, and sits down next to her. She's on a mission tonight. A mission to have the most fun humanly possible at an event held in a decked-up school sports hall.

It's their last Christmas disco together, and she wants to make it count. Rose is 16 now, and will be going off to sixth-form college to study hideously science-y things in September. Poppy will have to face the rest of high school alone, and can barely tolerate the thought.

She's boiling, and would like to follow Rose's lead and wipe her face clean, but she knows all her foundation will come off as well. Then her spotty forehead will be revealed to the world like the devil's own logo. She hates spots almost as much as she loves Rose, and her battle with acne has already taught her a very valuable lesson: life just isn't fair.

Rose comes from the same genetic material (as far as they know) as her, lives in the same house as her, and eats the same food as her – but has that kind of milky-white skin that they use to advertise Simple cleansing lotion.

Poppy, who actually uses Simple cleansing lotion, has a face full of crusty blisters that make her look as if she's re-invented smallpox.

Rose looks at her sister, and sees her skin glistening under the disco lights. She pulls a tissue from her pocket, and gently dabs the moisture away.

'It's okay,' she says, quietly, as Poppy starts to mutter in distress and tries to knock her hand away, 'I'm being careful. The slap will remain in place, I promise. Just trust me.'

Poppy settles immediately. Of course she trusts her. Rose would never leave her exposed to the taunts of her alleged friends, and the insensitive gaze of the Bastard Boys. Rose would never call her Spotty Poppy, like they do.

All cleaned up, she feels better. It's hard to see properly with sweat dripping off your mascara-laden eyelashes. Not that Rose knows that – she never wears make-up. Never needs to. She has mum's gorgeous eyes, and that perfect skin. She's an *English* Rose, as their mother always says.

Poppy's not quite sure what she is – an Ugly Duckling, with any luck, who might magically transform into a beautiful 14-year-old swan sometime soon. She might even grow boobs, which Rose has already managed. Not that she appreciates them – she says they're more trouble than they're worth, and keeps them hidden away under baggy sweaters. If Poppy had them, she'd probably start walking around topless just for the thrill of it.

'I can't believe you're going to leave me here . . .' says Poppy, sighing as she looks out at the dance floor with disgust.

Everyone seems way too interested in members of the opposite sex, and what everyone else is wearing, and being cool. Madonna's 'Vogue' has come on, and they're all busily making squares with their arms. It's not very co-ordinated, and it kind of looks like they've all been possessed by a jerky-limbed demon.

'I'll only be at the college on the other side of town,' replies Rose, nudging her so hard she almost falls over. 'You'll still see me every morning and every night and every weekend. Besides, you've got friends here. It's not like you're Little Orphan Annie, is it?'

Poppy gives her a sideways look, and nods. Technically, she's right. The college is only on the other side of town. But she knows it's The Beginning of the End. After her A-levels, Rose will apply to universities, and they most definitely won't be on the other side of town. They might be on the other side of the country. Everything is changing, and she's not happy about it.

And while Rose is right again, she does have friends, she's not especially close to any of them. High school seems to be ruled by teenaged tribal warlords, and she hasn't quite found her faction.

She's not slaggy enough to be in with the Hot Girls, and not nasty enough to be in with the Mean Girls. Not weird enough to be part of the Geek Gang. She's not sporty. Not musical. Not especially good at anything at all – other than being Rose's sister.

Rose is excited about college, and Poppy wants to be excited for her. But she can feel everything . . . sliding away. Slipping and changing and wriggling around her. She'd quite like to keep things the way they are – the two of them together – but the world seems to have other ideas.

'I know,' she says. 'You're right. I'll be fine, of course I will. It just won't be quite the same without you.'

She feels sad as she says this, and then feels guilty for sucking at pretending to be happy. Rose is two years older than her, and there's nothing she can do about that. If she carries on being a sourpuss, she'll spoil the night for both of them.

As she plasters a huge smile on her face, determined to fake it till she makes it, the lighting makes a sudden change from flashing neon strobes to something more subdued, and the music changes with it. Poppy looks up at the clock on the sports-hall wall, and sees that it's almost 10.30. Kicking-out time – which also means it's Slow Dance time. Eeek.

The girls look on as couples pair up and move apart, as hearts are broken and dreams are crushed. It's painful to see the rejects slink off to the corners, and downright funny to see the loved-up duos shuffle round the dance floor to Sinéad O'Connor singing 'Nothing Compares 2 U'. There is snogging and groping and a few concerned looks from the teachers lurking on the edge. Maybe, thinks Poppy, there will even be a Christmas Disco Baby in nine months' time.

She giggles at the thought, and amuses herself by trying to guess who the lucky couple could be.

A shadow falls over them, and she looks up. Uh-oh. It's Him. It's Marcus Pemberton. He's in Rose's class, and he's been chasing her for what feels like years. Rose smiles at him, shielding her eyes against the lights, and he looks as though he might melt in a puddle of Levis at her feet.

Marcus is one of those boys who is on all the teams, and has his name called out in Assembly for his latest sporting triumph practically every morning. He's the Head Boy to Rose's Head Girl, and if *he's* ever had a spot, Poppy has never seen it. His hair is floppy and blond, and his expression as he stares at Rose is completely ga-ga. Poppy totally and utterly hates him.

'Would you like to dance with me, Rose?' he says, shuffling a bit on the spot, hands in his jeans pockets. His face is in shadow, but Poppy knows he will be blushing madly.

She stays quiet, but notices the way her sister is looking at him. Like he's a giant Freddo and she feels like a snack. She steels herself, ready to sit this one out, hiding away on the bench and pretending she's fine with it.

It's Rose's last disco, after all. If she wants a giant boy-shaped Freddo, she deserves one, and Poppy won't get in the way. She stares at her fingernails, wondering when it was she chewed them down to the stubs, and tries very hard not to exist.

'Thanks Marcus,' says Rose, 'but I'm already taken. I'll see you at the weekend, though, all right? Maybe we could go and see the new *Star Trek* film or something?'

Poppy risks a sneaky glance from beneath her clumped-up

lashes, and sees that he is both disappointed and hopeful. She's said no to the Slow Dance, but yes to a date. Probably all a bit too much for a teenaged boy to compute, especially one who plays rugby and regularly gets his bonce battered, but he nods and leaves. Poppy resists the urge to stick two fingers up at him as he disappears into the darkness.

'Come on then, sis,' says Rose, standing up and stretching. She holds her hand out, and Poppy takes it. She's actually already taller than her big sister, a long, lean streak of a girl, not quite grown into her own legs. Her mum calls her Bambi, and Rose just calls her lucky.

'Let's show them how it's done . . .'

Rose leads Poppy on to the dance floor, and the two of them perform the kind of waltz their mum taught them when they were little. The type that involves a lot of laughing, and treading on toes, and counting 'one-two-three' in their heads, even when it bears no relation to the music at all.

They bump into people, and interrupt quite a few snogs, and attract a lot of dirty looks. But they couldn't care less.

For now, at least, it's Rose and Poppy versus the World, as it has always been – and as Sinéad almost says, nothing compares to two.

Chapter 7

The Present Day

Poppy is standing, staring into the fridge, wearing her sweaty gym gear and feeling the familiar and welcome pangs of hunger rumbling through her flat stomach.

There is nothing on her shelves apart from a few sticks of celery and a bar of 80 per cent cocoa chocolate. She snaps one small square from the bar, and places it on her tongue, enjoying the almost orgasmic feel of the chilled chocolate melting in her mouth.

She closes the fridge, and goes to make a coffee. Sadly she's all out, so she pours the boiled kettle water straight into the empty jar, knowing from years of experience that the crusted-on granules will last for at least one more half-hearted effort.

She needs to do some shopping, she thinks, taking the scalding-hot coffee jar into the lounge area and sitting at her desk. It's late, and she's using the Anglepoise lamp as she casts her eye over paperwork and the initial mock-ups from the graphics team. They're all rubbish, and she'll have to go in and do some arse-kicking on Monday.

Poppy is the head of marketing for a pet supplies firm, and it's about as interesting as it sounds. It does, however, allow her to live in her nice flat in Islington, with her own parking space, an en-suite in her bedroom and a gym in the basement. Whoop-di-do.

She's just come up from the gym, in fact, where she spent as much time flirting with Josh, the 23-year-old financial advisor from the floor above, as working out. She half wonders how he can possibly be qualified to offer advice on anything other than doing weights and drinking, he is so young. She certainly wouldn't trust her ISA with him, that's for sure.

She would, however, sleep with him, and already has, on several occasions. He's tall and bulky and fit and energetic, and he doesn't give two hoots that she never wants to stay over. Or that she's 40, even though she's never directly told him that. With her toned body and long, sleek hair, she passes for a lot younger anyway.

It's fun, she tells herself, playing with men like Josh. And carbs are way overrated anyway. At least that's what she tries to explain to her mother, when they're sitting in some Cotswolds tea room on one of their weekends away, and she ends up drooling into her salad as her mum tucks into scones and cream.

Mum never seems to change, no matter how much she eats. After years of borderline starvation to stay slim for her TV roles, her metabolism seems to have adjusted to her twilight years by giving her the gift of consistency. She's fit for a woman in her sixties – she still does yoga and swims and walks in the hills – and looks lean and attractive.

Her last telly gig – playing the feisty-yet-caring secretary of a handsome maverick QC – was a few years ago, but people would still recognise her as Penny Peabody, and marvel at how well she has aged.

Last time she spoke to Poppy, a couple of weeks ago now she supposes, she sounded a bit tired, and a bit less enthused about their planned spa break in Cheltenham than she'd expected.

Maybe, thinks Poppy, sipping the tasteless coffee water straight from the jar, she's just had enough of facials. Maybe they should mix it up a bit. Perhaps she could take her on a wine-tasting weekend, or they could go sky-diving together. Maybe she should put her fiendish pooch plan into action and get her mother a dog. They'd been on a photoshoot for the latest ad campaign for Woof! a few months earlier, and there was a field full of adorable pups. Adorable when they weren't shitting all over the place or trying to hump each other, anyway.

They've not had a dog since Patch, the psychopathic cross-eyed Jack Russell, went to the big kennel in the sky when they were teenagers, and the time could be right now. She's at home all day, loves going walking, needs company . . .

Poppy puts it on her mental list of Things To Do, along with Kick Arses of Graphics Team, Buy More Coffee, and Pick Up Work Suits From Dry Cleaners.

She swills the coffee-and-chocolate water around her mouth, licking it from her perfectly white teeth, and flicks on the TV. She has an hour to fill before she heads out again. She's meeting Kristin for drinks at the wine bar on the corner, and they're likely to be out until the milkmen are doing their rounds. Making meaningless conversation with meaningless people and just possibly indulging in some meaningless sex afterwards. It's a Friday night ritual, one that Poppy tries to persuade herself she still enjoys.

Part of her would just like to go to bed instead of meeting her 20-something partner in crime – but that would be admitting defeat. That would be acting like a 40-year-old, which is far worse than actually being one.

Anyway, apart from the colleagues she works with, it's one of the only times she gets to meet new people. It's not easy meeting people in London.

Everyone is always so busy, either with work or family, battered by commuting and finances and, in the case of the few people she knows with kids, trying to move to an area with a Good School. It had all felt like a lot more fun when she was younger – but these days, as she chats and laughs with people ten years her junior, it feels a bit more . . . desperate.

God knows what will happen when Kristin gets married. It'll happen, one day, she knows – she's already lost most of her party animal pals to the sacrificial altar. They're never the same again once they've tied the knot.

She uses the remote to pass on a Bollywood movie, ignores the news (which always depresses her), and is only marginally tempted by a Steven Seagal film. It's always fun watching a fat man do karate kicks, but she's not quite in the right mood tonight. She finally settles on *Poldark* – something she'd very much like to do in real life. Right on top of him.

Letting out a dirty laugh that echoes around her empty flat, she puts the almost-coffee down in disgust. Maybe she'll go for a nice G&T instead. It's the freaking weekend, baby, and it's never too early to start drinking.

She's not stupid, and appreciates the irony of her lifestyle: going to the gym every day, banning cake, drinking enough water to fill a flotation tank, and then polluting her temple-like body with booze at the weekend.

Well, she thinks, pouring herself a hefty glass, nobody's perfect, are they? And some habits are harder to break than others. She just wishes being a party girl still felt as exciting and fun as it used to, in the Olden Days back in the last century.

Back when she still had a sister.

Chapter 8

Glastonbury Festival, Somerset, 1995

'Okay, that's settled then,' says Rose, lying on top of her sleeping bag because it's too hot to get inside it, 'you can have Liam, and I'll have Noel.'

'That's fine by me. Liam is way sexier. You only want Noel because he writes the songs, and you're an intellectual snob so you think that means he's cleverer.'

'I have to be honest, Pops, I don't think you could call any of Oasis clever . . . If I wanted clever, I'd have to go for Jarvis Cocker.'

'Even though he's so skinny?'

'Even though. There was something foxy about him tonight, don't you think? All those shapes he pulled, and the way he held the microphone? Or is that the marijuana speaking?'

'If the marijuana is actually speaking to you,' says Poppy, passing her sister the item under discussion, 'then I'm going to suggest you drank some of that special mushroom tea the hippy dudes were offering us earlier.'

'No! I didn't, honest!' says Rose, giggling. Everything seems very, very funny, for some reason. Even earlier, when there was a wasp trapped in the tent with them – and she is terrified of wasps – she couldn't stop laughing as Poppy batted it out again with a rolled-up festival programme. Fearless wasp warrior.

'I believe you, thousands wouldn't . . .' replies Poppy, also giggling. 'Hey, I just had a thought. It's a funny one.'

'Go for it. I'm a very receptive audience right now.'

'Okay,' says Poppy, 'you know how the Stone Roses were supposed to be playing, and they dropped out?'

'Yeah.'

'Well, we're lying here smoking up a storm, and instead of the Stone Roses, we have the . . . Stoned Rose! *Rose!* Your name! You get it?'

Rose does get it, and frankly it is the most hilarious thing she has ever heard. She laughs so much she fears she might have some kind of calamitous event going on in her cerebral cortex.

It's Poppy's fault, she decides, with a grin. That she's a Stoned Rose, and that she's almost laughing herself to death. She might be two years younger, but she's a bad influence. Leading her astray.

Rose is in her first year at Liverpool University, studying Biology, with a nice sideline in cheap lager. Poppy is at college doing her A-levels.

They don't see as much of each other now, for obvious reasons, and this has been a glorious weekend. They've watched fine bands, and eaten less fine veggie burgers, and had henna tattoos done on their hands, and witnessed one of the amateur flame-jugglers get taken away to hospital. They've danced and drunk and been hoisted on random men's shoulders and lain out in the sun, listening to the sounds of bongo drums and acid trips wafting past their ears.

It's late now, and they're enjoying their last night together. Even in the early hours, in their tent, they can hear the sounds of festival life going on around them: music and laughter and yet more bongos and guitars strumming and the very occasional vomit.

'Was Andy disappointed you weren't sharing with him?' asks Poppy from out of the blue. Andy is Rose's boyfriend, and he's here too, with a gang of his friends. Poppy doesn't have a boyfriend, just a few lads she snogs when she's been in the Tennyson's Arms on a Friday night.

'I don't think so,' answers Rose, passing back the joint and twisting on to her side so she is facing her sister. Poppy is still long and lean and lovely, and the spots have cleared up now. She's a bit of a babe, but doesn't seem to realise it. Bambi's all grown up, at least in body.

'I think he's happy enough with his mates,' she adds. 'And anyway, even if he wasn't, so what? This is our weekend. We've been planning it for ages. I can see Andy whenever I want – but spending quality time with my adorable little sister is far more precious.'

Poppy laughs, and stubs the cigarette out on the lid of the little tobacco tin she carries everywhere with her. Rose glances at it – it's what they call 'vintage' these days, and the lid is decorated with a naval design. It looks suspiciously like one that used to live in a glass cabinet back in the cottage.

'Did you steal that from home?' she asks, pointing at the tin.

'Well, as it's my home as well, technically I don't think it would be called stealing, do you?'

'Mum would go nuts if she could see us now . . . especially when she realised you had that tin . . .'

Poppy stretches out, her limbs so long her grubby, bare toes touch the end of the tent, and replies: 'Nah, she wouldn't. Well, maybe about the tin. But she wouldn't mind us lying here having a smoke, I don't think. Mum was working in show business in the Seventies, dahling, don't you know? She's probably snorted cocaine off Oliver Reed's arse! Plus she paid for the tickets and everything – I don't think she was under any illusions that we'd be spending the weekend behaving like nuns, do you?'

Rose ponders this, and it takes her a few moments to drag her mind away from the image of her mum and Oliver Reed. Is he on the list, she tries to recall? The list that her and Poppy keep, of names their mother has dropped from her more glamorous days? She seemed to have known – and 'known', she suspected, could mean anything from having met on set to had lunch with to shagged in an orgy – pretty much every big-name actor of her era.

The girls know there is truth in it. When they were younger, they joined her on set in various locations, and found it all pretty boring. To them, it was just what happened when your mum went to work, even if it sounded glamorous from the outside. And to them, Mum was just Mum, even if she did once paint Joan Collins's nails for her.

'No, you're right,' she eventually concedes. 'She wouldn't

mind. Actually, I kind of wish she was here, don't you? She'd be a good laugh.'

'Don't tell anyone,' replies Poppy, whispering conspiratorially, 'but I think she might actually be here. I think she might have been one of those naked ladies with the blue-painted boobs, the ones who were doing yoga around the camp fire earlier . . .'

Rose bursts out laughing at the idea, and Poppy joins in. Everything really does still seem very, very funny. For some reason.

They laugh for what feels like hours, until the bongos finally go silent, and peace falls over their little patch of Glastonbury.

Chapter 9

The Present Day

The phone rings, and Rose is so shocked she physically jumps. The tub of Heroes jerks from her lap, and the shameful evidence of her binge eating spills out on to the carpet in a mass of shiny, multi-coloured foil wrappers. She kicks them under the sofa with her bed-socked feet.

It's the landline. Nobody ever calls her on the landline any more. In fact, nobody ever calls her full stop. Apart from Joe, when he needs a lift or wants to check if he can stay out later.

Joe . . . she reminds herself that he is upstairs, safe, and that the landline call will not be from the police, telling her he's had an accident, or been beaten up by chavs, or fallen down a well. Which means it will probably be some nice man from India worrying about her levels of life assurance cover, or possibly her mother, calling to tell her *Poldark* is on.

Once she's calmed down, she reaches over to the side table, and answers with a cautious hello. She doesn't like to be rude to the nice men from India, they're just trying to make a living after all, but she doesn't want to encourage them either.

'Good evening,' says the voice, too posh and well modulated and elderly and English to be a nice young man from India. 'Am I speaking to Mrs Rose Young?'

Rose mutters yes, and is suddenly, for no apparent reason, gripped by utter dread. Her entire body feels cold and shaky, and she has an almost irresistible urge to put the phone down. To end this conversation – this conversation she is convinced must not be allowed to happen.

'Rose, my name is Lewis Clarke-Smith, and I'm afraid I'm calling with some bad news . . .'

Chapter 10

Approximately 200 miles away, in Islington, Poppy is still trying to muster up the energy for a quick shower, and debating how short a skirt she should wear for tonight's adventures.

She is surprised when the landline rings, and it takes her a few moments to find the handset. Kristin would text her if she wanted to get in touch, so, she deduces, it must be her mother, who tended to stay up late watching re-runs of old TV shows and critiquing everyone's performance. She might have some stern words to utter about that scything scene.

Poppy slings back a gulp of her G&T, and answers.

'Hi, Mum!' she says jauntily, trying not to let any of her borderline maudlin mood seep down the phone lines to Shropshire. Everything in the garden must always be rosy, as far as her mother is concerned, or she'll just worry about her.

'Erm . . . no, I'm afraid not,' comes the reply. It's a man's voice, someone older, deep in tone and precise in enunciation. 'Is that Miss Poppy Barnard?'

'It is,' she says, starting to get annoyed now. 'To whom am I speaking?'

'My name is Lewis Clarke-Smith,' he says, 'and I was a friend of your mother's.'

Poppy barely registers the name, and is no longer concerned with his enunciation. She only hears one word of that sentence: 'was'.

The glass falls from her hands, and spills the remainder of her drink across her Lycra-clad thighs.

Chapter 11

Rose puts the phone down, and automatically reaches for another chocolate. It takes her three attempts before she manages to get the wrapper off, her fingers are trembling so much, and she doesn't even taste it once it's in her mouth.

She's just going through the motions. Giving her brain something to do. Trying to avoid processing what she's just heard.

That her mother is dead. That the great, garrulous bundle of energy that was Andrea Barnard is no longer gracing this planet. That she'd been ill for a while, and not told her. That she'd been diagnosed with stomach cancer a few weeks after her birthday, and for some reason kept it secret.

She doesn't know what she is feeling. It is a sensation unlike any other she has ever experienced. It is a shock, the way she has been told, and that is making her numb. Perhaps it would have been different if she'd been there at her bedside, where she belonged. If she'd been with her. If she'd had the chance to say goodbye.

She wasn't alone, she knows. Lewis Clarke-Smith assured

her of that, in his calm, steady, deep voice. The kind of voice that is used to being listened to, and is used to making itself firmly understood.

Except she didn't understand. She didn't understand any of it. Of course things had been difficult in recent years, but she still thought of herself as having a close relationship with her mother. She saw her as often as she could, making the trip down scenic A-roads from Liverpool to Shropshire, meeting her in Ludlow for lunch or shopping in the markets. Having her here for Christmases. Alternate Christmases, of course, as every other year she went to the home of She Who Shall Not Be Named.

They spoke on the phone, they texted each other. They were present in each other's lives – so why wasn't she present in her death? In her suffering; in her final days?

Rose feels a stirring of anger in the pit of her stomach, mixed in with shock and disbelief. She tries to stamp it down, she knows it's not appropriate – but it's there.

She's angry that she wasn't told. She's angry at the slightly disapproving tone in Lewis Clarke-Smith's perfect voice – just a hint, the barest sneer, but most definitely there. He thinks she failed her mum, and Rose has the sneaking suspicion that he might be right. And that, when it comes down to it, is why she is angry – because she can feel the guilt starting to curdle its way up to the surface.

She has so many questions, and she asked so few of them. The call was unexpected, shocking. The voice on the end of the line delivered the news with steady, practised sympathy, and he sounded so calm that she completely forgot herself.

It was one of those authoritative voices that she could never resist, like the head teacher at her school. He's a complete wanker, but somehow everything he says seems to make sense. It was the same with this man, with this Lewis Clarke-Smith who, now she comes to think of it, her mother has mentioned in the past. She's never met him, but recalls vague stories about am-dram shows and the village fete and borrowing his dog Betty for walks in the hills.

She wasn't paying attention, of course. And she never went back to the village, or the cottage that had been her childhood home. She was too caught up in her own life, her own challenges. In avoiding memories that would hurt too much. Probably, if she's entirely honest, too busy planning what she was going to order from the takeaway that night. And Mum's stories were never in short supply – there was always an anecdote, a memory, an amusing vignette.

She'd taken that for granted, and now it suddenly occurs to her that there will be no more stories. No more tales about her Eighties show-biz life. No more accounts of the size of the marrows in the vegetable-growing contests. No more descriptions of the time she let out a 200-decibel fart during her sun salutation at the village-hall yoga class.

No more Andrea.

It is simply inconceivable, that thought. Her mother, she'd assumed, would outlive everyone. She was a force of nature, a one-of-a-kind, a goddess walking among mortals. She couldn't be dead. It just did not compute.

Rose is now on to her fourth Creme Egg Twisted, and feeling slightly sick for all kinds of reasons. The news. The chocolate. The fact that all of those questions are still swilling around in her head like sour milk sluicing through a sieve. The fact that Lewis had calmly instructed her that she now needed to watch a bloody *video*. That a lot of her questions would be answered, and that it's what Andrea had wanted.

The nausea rolls over her, and she leaps to her feet as fast as she can. She runs into the downstairs loo, kicking aside the various travel brochures she keeps in there, full of luxury holidays she'll never go on.

She falls to her knees, and pukes up an entire tub of Cadbury's. By the time she's done, the toilet bowl is full of thick brown chocolatey liquid, and tears are streaming down her cheeks. She falls back on to her bottom, landing plumply on a Kuoni safari brochure, and lets herself fall apart.

Chapter 12

Poppy strokes her tobacco tin, the one she filched from her mother over two decades ago, tempted to smoke for the first time in years. Instead, she puts it away and slides the desk drawer closed. She picks up her phone, and messages Kristin to say she will definitely be late, and might not make it at all.

Feeling strangely calm, she sends the email from Lewis to her 'incredibly clever TV', as her mum always called it, steadfastly refusing to attach the word 'smart' to any kind of technology.

'Smart means a well-tailored suit and some polished brogues, darling, not a few buttons on a silly device,' she'd always said.

Lewis had answered every question Poppy had thrown at him, as she worked her way through some kind of scarily efficient checklist that had sprung up in her brain during their brief conversation.

She has no idea where it came from – it's not like she had planned for this, or been prepared in any way. But she was used to holding meetings, and being in charge, and she supposes that's what kicked in – her lizard brain was helping her process this new information by turning it into action points. She could practically turn her mother's death into a PowerPoint presentation now.

She had died that evening, in the nearest big hospital. She had stomach cancer. She'd planned her funeral in advance; the arrangements were all made, and there was nothing she needed to do. Lewis, as Andrea's friend and as her solicitor, was taking care of her affairs, and needed to see both her and Rose after the service. Both of them. Together. In the same room.

Jesus. That was almost as much of a shock as the fact that her mother was dead, which didn't exactly make her feel good about herself. Andrea was gone, and she was beginning to freak out about seeing her own sister again – how selfish could one person be?

The gin-infused haze has cleared completely now, and *Poldark* has finished. Her legs are still damp from spilling her drink, and she can smell her own body odour. She needs to shower, inside and out, to scrub her brain clean of all the conflicting emotions she is starting to feel.

Keep calm, she tells herself, tapping away on the controls. Keep calm and carry on. There is nothing to be gained here by having a nervous breakdown. It won't bring your mother back, and it won't help you.

She moves to the sleek leather-and-chrome sofa in front of the television, and presses play with one long, perfectly shellacked nail.

Chapter 13

Andrea is propped up on a hospital bed, her steel-grey hair smooth, her make-up flawless, if a little more heavy-handed than usual. The silk blouse she is wearing is perfectly pressed, and her smile is dazzling. If not for the weight loss and, of course, the location, you'd never know she was ill.

The room is small, dominated by that bed, by the tiny figure lying in it. The cabinet is overflowing with flowers, wilting lily petals drooping down into the open jug of pale-orange cordial, and the lighting is bright.

Andrea does a quick test, and the camera wobbles slightly, as though the person holding it is moving around, or maybe giving a 'thumbs-up' gesture. She nods once, folds her delicate hands neatly on her blanket-covered lap, and begins. Her voice is steady, assured, perfectly poised – she's delivered many a monologue, and this is by far the most important she's ever spoken.

'My darlings. Rosehip, Popcorn, my only true loves. Not to be too Hollywood about this, but if you're watching this tape, that can mean only one thing: I have shuffled off this mortal coil . . . and you two are going to need each other more than ever. You need to set aside your differences, and look out for each other – just like you always used to.

'I know this has all come as a terrible shock, but I make no apologies for doing things this way. The illness came quickly, and horribly and, before I knew what was happening, I was dealing with lovely Macmillan nurses and charming doctors – all of whom had awful news.

'It's only been a few weeks, my loves, and I know that you'll be so sad that you didn't get to spend that time with me. You might even be a tiny bit angry that I deprived you of the chance to be here, at my side – but I had my reasons, and if ever an old lady has the right to be awkward, it's when she's dying, don't you think?

'Part of me was reluctant to let you both see me suffer. You were both too small to remember when my mother died, but it was one of the worst experiences of my life – sitting by her bedside, holding her hand, when she didn't even recognise me. The pain had taken her over, you see, like some kind of demonic possession. I honestly wouldn't have been surprised if her head had started spinning and she talked in ancient Aramaic.

'Pain can do that to a person – it reduces them to their animal state, strips them of everything that makes them . . . human. I spent endless nights in that hospice with her, all alone despite being surrounded by people, and I vowed right then that it was an ordeal I would never put you two through. I have no idea what my fate is – I am hoping for a dignified swansong, with gentle lighting and aromatic oils and possibly some gentle Gregorian chanting in the background. A graceful exit, stage left.

'But the truth is, I might just as easily turn into my mother – become that pain-wracked animal who only knows one thing: that they are dying. She had no clue I was even there at the end, and since then I've always thought the whole sitting-by-the-deathbed thing is simply a steel trap for suffering. It's a consolation, I suppose – as the person left behind, you can always tell yourself you did your best, that at least they weren't alone.

'But honestly? I think we are all alone when we die. We're embarking on a journey that nobody can accompany us on – we don't get a plus one.

'For the people left behind, exhausted and drained, it is an emotional battering the likes of which you can never prepare yourself for. It is an indescribable torment, waiting for someone you love to leave you, knowing that each minute together could be your last, but also knowing that part of them has already gone.

'I simply didn't want that for you two, and I hope you understand – it was a decision made out of love. And I had my poor Lewis with me, I am guessing – I've tried to kick him out on several occasions, but the stubborn old fool simply won't have it, and I suspect he'll be here to the bitter end.

'He's here with me now, helping me make this video, and let me tell you he's one of the finest human beings that has ever graced the planet. But enough of that – I can't have his ancient hands trembling, or him crying, can I?

'Anyway. That was part of my reasoning. I should probably

have discussed that with you at some stage, but it's not an easy one to slip into casual conversation, is it? "I'm having a lovely mini-break, darling, and by the way, I won't be inviting you to my deathbed." It doesn't slip easily off the tongue, so I'm afraid I avoided it. Perhaps I was being a cowardly lion, who knows? But it never seemed relevant. I always felt so healthy, despite all of those little games I played over the last few years.

'And that, I suppose, brings me to one of the other reasons I'm chickening out of seeing you, and leaving this message instead. I love you two, more than life itself – I hope you know that. But I have to be honest – and this is a time and a place for honesty, my sweets – you have broken my heart. Shattered it into tiny pieces, to be dramatic about it – which of course I always like to be.

'Over the years, I've tried everything to bring you two together again. I've organised parties that neither of you attended, for fear of seeing the other. I've performed in dingy small-town theatres in the hope that you'd both come to the opening night – and neither of you did. I've pretended to be rushed into hospital with pneumonia, when I had nothing more than a nasty cold. I've lied and I've schemed and I've shamelessly emotionally blackmailed the two of you – all to no avail.

'No matter what I threw at you, you simply didn't budge. I know you love me, and perhaps right now, watching this, you are starting to realise how much – that is normal, don't worry. It's a punch to the gut that you will learn how to live with, I'm sure. But realising how much you love me now I'm gone doesn't change the fact that in life, you couldn't set aside your differences – not for your sake, not for Joe's sake, and certainly not for mine.

'I'm incredibly proud of both of you – you are, and always will be, my grubby angels. I'm proud of your strength, your resilience, the way you've made your way in the world. But you have both let your bitterness define you. You've both been moulded by this old, tired anger that you cling on to, until it's become an almost physical part of you – like your curly hair, Rose, or your brown eyes, Poppy. What started as something painful seems to have become something you can't live without, and that is what has broken my heart.

'You've both built lives. Have careers. Rose, Joe is a wonderful, wonderful boy, and you've done a brilliant job of raising him. But no matter what you've achieved, or gone on to do in your lives, you've done it without each other – which means that nothing has ever been quite right, has it?

'I know you both like to fool yourselves that you're better off without each other, but you couldn't be more wrong. I raised you to laugh together, to fight together, to protect each other. The world can be a cruel and scary place, and it was always a great consolation to me that there were two of you.

'Bringing you up on my own was never easy. There were all kinds of cracks beneath the surface that you didn't see – which I never intended you to see. I had to make compromises with my career, I struggled at times for money. It was challenging, and it was often lonely – but, I told myself, at least these two precious girls will never face this kind of solitude.

'They will always have a best friend, an ally, someone to

turn to in their hour of need. They won't just be drinking wine at midnight and staring into the log fire looking for answers, like I often was.

'But instead of turning to each other, you turned on each other – and this fight has destroyed our family. Destroyed our chance to be together, the way I'd always hoped we would be, eventually. I never gave up hope that the old wounds would heal, but now I have to accept that if they do, it's not something I'll be around to celebrate.

'I'm not saying this needlessly, to hurt you – God knows that would be the last thing you need right now, after the news you've had. And I know you've both done your best. Rose, believe me, I've loved my visits to Liverpool, and all Joe's Christmas plays and being involved in his life. Getting to play the Glamorous Granny has been one of the best roles I've ever had.

'And Poppy, I do understand how hard you tried – all our holidays, and trips away, and the silly amounts of cash you always spent on my gifts. I've never had so many cashmere sweaters and hand-made leather bags in my wardrobe.

'Time spent with the two of you was never wasted, and I valued every second I had with my two gorgeous girls – but for me, it was always bittersweet. Because I could see, more clearly than you could yourselves, how much damage had been done. Together, you could take on the world. Apart, you're like a three-legged dog, or a tortoise stuck on its back – there will always be something missing. Something holding you back.

'That, I think, brings me to more current events. To the

here and now and the future, even if that is a foreign land I will never visit. To the whole purpose of this video, and the way I've spent my last few weeks. If you thought I'd emotionally blackmailed you before, then this time I'm going for gold in the Manipulative Mother Olympics.

'This time, I'm not going to be subtle. I'm not going to play games, there's no point. I'll state things as clearly as I possibly can: I am your mother. I love you. I am dying. And my one great wish is to see you two together again. I could never achieve that in life, and I am desperately hoping that I can in death.

'Lewis – stop snivelling, Lewis! – has been at my side throughout all of this, and he is your go-to man, as they say in the movies. Listen to him, and do as he says, and buy him a nice cigar, because he bloody well deserves it. Lewis is, so to speak, my representative on earth, and he'll be guiding you through this process.

'I can practically hear the question – "What process?" – so I'll answer it for you. The process of at least trying to rebuild your relationship. The process of putting the pieces back together, and moving forward in your lives – at each other's sides, just like I always wanted.

'Although I am, excuse my French, completely pissed off at being dragged away from life while only in my sixties, it has been a good life. Full and rich and never, ever boring. You two have been both the highlights and the low points, and I'm hoping that the low points will soon be specks of dust on the horizon.

'At the moment, as I record this, I'm not afraid. I'm not

71

afraid of dying, or what comes next, even if I accidentally end up in Goldfish Heaven – I'm only afraid for you two, and what will become of you once I'm gone.

'I know that when my own mum died, I was suddenly swamped with questions that only she could answer. About my childhood, about her life, about the best way to make a steak-and-kidney pie, about everything.

'Your mum is the person you most take for granted in your life and, right now, you'll both be willing to give up your right hand to have one more conversation with me. To be able to pick up the phone one more time. To be able to sit and chat about mindless things, or not-so-mindless things – you will have questions, and that won't stop.

'As you get older, and your lives change, and you face new challenges, there will always be part of you that wants to call your mum and ask her what she thinks. Or to see her, and get a special mummy hug, one of those that makes you feel like everything will be all right in the end – the kind only mums can give, no matter how grown up you are.

'I know that's how I felt, at least. I still do, right now, at this very minute. I still wish she was here, all these years later. Losing your mother leaves a hole that is simply never filled. The pain of not being able to make that phone call, or get that hug, will always be with you, right up until it is your turn to walk in my shoes. It's the cycle of life, just like in *The Lion King*, but without the lovable warthog.

'I'm so sad, for you, that I won't be here to answer your questions, or give you advice – at least in person. I won't be picking up the phone, or just down the motorway, or trying and failing to use Skype, not any more. Believe me, if I could live forever and always be around for you, I would.

'Instead, I am offering you a gift. It's a strange gift, and it comes in many forms. There are videos, and diaries, and letters, and photographs. There are words of wisdom, and words that are undoubtedly lacking in wisdom, and there are small tasks for you to carry out. You know I always liked a good project – and this, my darlings, is my most ambitious yet.

'I've been calling it the A–Z of Everything as a working title, always convinced that I'd come up with something better – but time seems to be running out on me, so I suppose that will have to do. And, truth be told, it's accurate at least.

'There are things in there that will surprise you. Shock you, even. Secrets to be told, mysteries to be shared, stories to be recounted. Don't expect it to be easy – nothing worthwhile ever is, is it?

'I've poured my heart and soul and most of the contents of my attic into this A–Z, girls, so I beg you to take it seriously, and treat it with respect. Lewis has it all for you, and I also beg you to accept this gift in the spirit with which it is given – in love, and in hope. The funeral is all sorted – sorry to deprive you of the chance to plan it all, Poppy – and there is very little for you two to do, other than show up, sit down, listen, and learn.

'This is a project that you need to complete together. I realise that very thought is probably making you both shudder, and that even in this time of shock and grief, you're thinking it's impossible. That you need to find a way out.

Maybe even that it doesn't matter – that I'm gone, so what difference does it make?

'Well, I can't control what you do next. All I can do is ask – as your mother. Your dying mother, not to put too fine a point on it. Come to the funeral. See Lewis. Embrace the A–Z of Everything in the way you'd undoubtedly like to embrace me right now. Think of it as one last hug, and humour me.

'I like to think it's not that much to ask, as I'm at the end of the line here. To borrow a line from Frank, it's time to face my final curtain. But, believe me, if you pull this off – if you see this one last mission through – I'll be somewhere, up there, watching; giving you a standing ovation and clapping until my hands are raw.

'But before then, I have a few final comments, and a task to start you off. First of all, let me say two very simple things – I love you, and I know that you love me. That sounds so simple, but grief has a sneaky way of obscuring those simple truths, hiding them beneath rainclouds of doubt.

'When that happens, when the "I wonders . . ." start to kick in, then kick them straight back out again. I love you, and I know that you love me. Repeat as often as necessary, until it becomes so real you don't ever question it. If you take nothing else with you from all of this, then at least take that.

'Now, the teensy-weensy task I mentioned. I'd like you both to make a list. Poppy, I know you will relish this one, and you probably have some kind of app you can whip out on your incredibly clever phone, but please don't. Do it the old-fashioned way. Rose, it'll take you a while to find a paper and pen – try that little drawer by the telephone table you never use.

'Once you're ready, I want you both to make a list of the things you feel guilty about. Guilt is a terrible emotion. While it serves a purpose – it's our conscience's way of telling us we've done something wrong, and hopefully avoiding a repeat performance – it can also eat away at you like a disease. It sours every drink, poisons every meal, casts a shadow over every joyous occasion. I am not, as you might be able to tell, a big fan of guilt.

'But we all have it. Everyone has regrets, and that nagging sense of self-loathing that comes out to poke at you in bed at night. So, take control of it, my dears – and make that list. Be entirely honest, because nobody will ever see it but you – rest assured that my next instructions are not to post it on Facebook, or whatever you young people are using these days. When you've made it, keep it safe.

'As well as that, I need you both to think about the way things have gone wrong between you. And, just as importantly, the way things used to be right between you. When exactly did everything start to go wrong? And why was the wrong so much stronger than the right?

'I imagine you sitting at home in Liverpool, Rose, pulling a face right now and thinking "Well, that's bloody obvious, isn't it?" And to some extent, yes, it is.

'But if we're honest, the obvious thing that went wrong was only part of it. Nothing could be shattered as thoroughly as your relationship was without there being some cracks already in place. So, I'm asking you, please – much as it might hurt, think about it.

'And now, darlings, I'm going to sign off. I have a date with some excellent drugs, and a nurse is bound to pop in soon to see if I want any jelly . . . plus poor old Lewis looks like he badly needs a hug.

'Remember, I love you both, so very, very much . . . and I know that you loved me.'

Chapter 14

Rose is splayed across the sofa, her tear-stained face hidden by a cloud of frizzy hair. She is in pain, everywhere. Her neck is sore and her stomach is screaming and her swollen ankles are tender. Everything hurts, and she has no idea how to make it stop.

She'd quite like to make everything stop, especially the one thought that keeps going round and round in her exhausted brain: She'd broken her mother's heart.

No matter how much love there was in that video, how much pride, and hope, and humour, this was what had stayed with her: *she'd broken her mother's heart.*

Her wonderful, vivacious, ever-bright mother. Gone. How could it even be true?

Part of her is still refusing to accept it. As pranks go, it would be cruel – but she'd take cruelty over the alternative any day. She'd give anything right now for the phone to ring again, and to hear Andrea's voice.

'Sorry I had to do that to you, Rosehip,' she'd say, apologetically, 'but it was the only way to get your attention.

I'm not actually dead at all, but if I was, how would you feel?'

She would feel . . . destroyed. Completely and utterly destroyed. Wracked with agony. Raw and exposed and empty.

Exactly how she feels now. She's watched the video three times, and the panic has got worse with each viewing. She can feel it now, rising up to choke her, wrapping around her internal organs and strangling the oxygen out of her.

Every moment is etched in agony in her memory. The way her mother smiled. The way she clutched the blanket on her lap. The way her nails were still painted, glamour against the grey. The way she spoke, so calm and deliberate and real. As though she was sitting in the room with her right now, not already dead. Already cold.

The image of her mother in some chilly mortuary in the Midlands grips her, and she can't get it out of her head. Lying on a stainless-steel slab, skin pale, flesh pallid, eyes closed. Fingernails painted, hair done, make-up still on. Looking like her mother, but not her mother – a waxwork model of her mother. She wants to bust in, and cover her up with a fleecy blanket, and keep her warm.

The pain is so intense, she doesn't know quite what to do with herself. Physically, she's a wreck – short of breath, panting, paralysed by shock, aching. Emotionally, it is even worse, and she wants to die. If it wasn't for Joe, innocently upstairs, now quiet, possibly sleeping, his shaggy brown hair curling over his forehead, she probably would.

She wants to reach out for someone, to seek comfort, but has nowhere to turn. Joe's dad Gareth is in London, on to his third wife and fourth child, and dead to her in any way that matters. Any way beyond terse emails about Joe, and the sly digs she knows are intended to hurt and always hit their target.

She has friends, but they're not the kind you call at midnight to sob uncontrollably. She has Joe himself, but she can't use him as an emotional crutch. His granny's death will hit him hard enough – she can at least let him sleep one last night without having to deal with it.

She has a sister, but even thinking about Poppy makes the pain so much worse. It's too big. Too frightening. Too much.

There is nobody to help her. Nobody to console her. And all she wants is her mum. Her mum, who always smelled of Chanel Coco and had the softest skin and gave the best hugs. Her mum, who held her hand when she started school, and lurked across the road in the car on her first date in case it didn't go well. Her mum, who got up at 5.30 a.m. that summer she had a paper round and did it with her just so she had company.

Her mum, who had wiped away so many tears; and always had a tissue handy. Who talked her through the importance of properly burping a baby, and took Joe out for huge walks in his pram when he had colic and Rose was on the verge of a nervous breakdown. Who cleared her entire ironing pile while she zoned out on sleeping pills after Gareth left.

Her mum – who taught her everything she knew about love.

She'd broken her mother's heart.

'Oh God,' she wails, muffling her words into an already

snot-stained cushion, 'please tell her I love her! Tell her I'm sorry!'

God doesn't answer, and, even if He did, Rose probably wouldn't listen – she is lost and alone in her grief and her anguish.

She rolls physically to the floor, and lands on the carpet in an ungainly heap. Crawling first on to all fours, then to her feet, she totters unsteadily through to the hallway. Her eyes are red and raw, and she bounces off walls as she walks.

She pulls open the drawer of the telephone table so hard it comes out in her hand, and she drops it to the floor, spilling its contents: a small torch, a ball of string, a tube of Superglue, a rubber in the shape of Pikachu's head, a Thai takeaway menu, a pedometer.

She kneels down, breath heavy with the effort, and scrabbles until she finds a biro and one of those block memo pads for taking phone messages. Clutching them to her like a newborn baby, she walks back into the living room.

There isn't a desk down here, and she needs something to lean on. She finds one of Joe's hardback books – a *Star Wars* encyclopedia – and covers up Yoda's head with the paper.

Her hand is trembling, and she can't hold the pen properly. It keeps slipping, and making her scrawl, and she's useless. Just utterly, pathetically useless. She can't even do this properly. She stabs Yoda in the eye in frustration, and draws in a long, slow, shuddering breath.

She knows the biology of what is happening to her. She knows she needs to calm down, to regulate her breathing, to inhale and exhale and simply stop bloody panicking. She takes in three long, slow breaths through her nose, tries to let them out just as slowly through her mouth.

She temporarily gives up on the list, and goes to the fridge. She opens the door, sees that the quinoa and the carrot batons are still there, and grabs a half-full bottle of Blossom Hill from the door.

She looks around the kitchen, and there are no cups. No glasses. She is as shitty at keeping a house as she is at everything else. She pulls open the cupboards, and sees only an egg cup. Everything is either in the dishwasher, or festering somewhere in the science experiment that Joe calls a bedroom, buried under layers of mouldy pizza and rigid socks.

She pulls out the egg cup. It has an acid-house-style smiley face on it, and it's just too small. She opens the next cupboard, and pulls out a plastic measuring jug. That'll do.

The wine glugs in, splashing back up to sting already stinging eyes. She looks at the markings on the side of the jug, having a strange flashback to simpler days – days when a laboratory and strange liquids and carefully poured fluids were the centre of her world.

The wine bottle is empty. The jug shows her she has 600 millilitres of anaesthetic to play with, and she takes it back through to the lounge. She picks up the book, the pen, the paper. She tries to rub the ink mark off Yoda, but it's gone too deep, like a weird eyeball tattoo.

Rose drinks, and she breathes, and she swipes snot from her inflamed nostrils with the corner of her already soggy cardigan, the long one that she fools herself covers her arse.

And she makes her list.

Chapter 15

Rose starts with shaky hands, calmer now but still barely able to hold the pen, eyes blurred by tears. As the wine goes down, and the tears dry up, and the words start to flow, it gets easier. And worse. It feels like the List That Will Never Die. The guilt pours out of her and into the pen and on to the tiny white pages. She underlines the title twice, freehand, so the line is a jagged doodle, and she even feels guilty about not using a ruler.

Things I Feel Guilty About
1. That I wasn't there when my mum died
2. That I broke my mother's heart
3. That I didn't see her enough, or tell her I loved her enough
4. That last time she was supposed to come and stay, to keep me company when Joe was at his dad's, I made an excuse about work and cancelled, when really I just felt too depressed to be bothered, and wanted to stay in and eat kebabs on my own

5. That I let my marriage get fucked up and didn't work hard enough to save it

6. That Joe has grown up with me for a mum

7. That I am a crap mum

8. That I sometimes use Joe as my friend instead of having real friends and make him watch *Grey's Anatomy* with me

9. That I eat too much and drink too much and do no exercise; that I don't seem able to stop even for Joe

10. That I seem like a nice person on the outside but inside I am actually horrible

11. That I stole a box of Cadbury Roses from the village shop when I was 11 and told my mum I'd won them as a prize at school, and she was so proud of me she baked a Victoria sponge to celebrate

12. That I dumped Andy by text when I was drunk and accidentally sent it to his best mate instead

13. That I didn't have enough sex with Gareth, because I was always so tired after I had the baby, and maybe if I hadn't been so selfish Joe would still have his dad around

14. That I sometimes secretly wish that Gareth would get hit by a bus

15. That I don't condition my hair or do my nails or take a pride in myself, like mum always did

16. That I messed up my career and gave up on everything

17. That I spend more money every week on junk food than I do on Joe

18. That when Joe was born I thought for a little while that I could never ever be happy again
19. That I was supposed to cure cancer and I ended up as a teaching assistant and that must have disappointed mum so much, not that she ever said anything
20. That I once reversed her car into a tree and blamed the dent on a hit-and-run in the supermarket car park
21. That I hate my job and everyone I work with, even though it's not their fault I'm doing it
22. That I lost touch with all my university friends after I met Gareth, at first because of him and then after he left because I was too embarrassed to admit I'd made a mistake
23. That I once told my mum I hated her when I was 15 because she wouldn't let me stay out any later than 10 p.m. even though Tasmin Hughes was allowed to stay out as long as she liked
24. That when Tasmin Hughes got pregnant and had a baby I never went to visit her, and I know now she must have been really lonely because that's what it's like when you have a baby
25. That I stabbed Yoda in the eye
26. That every year I buy Joe a nice Thornton's Easter egg with his name on it, then eat it myself, and have to buy new ones, crap ones from the newsagent
27. That I once lay on the floor and pretended I wasn't

84

in when the Jehovah's Witnesses called round instead of being polite about them trying to save my soul

28. That I used to pull faces whenever Mum started one of her show-biz war stories and now I'd love to hear some more

29. That I eat Extra Strong Mints before bed because I can't be bothered brushing my teeth

30. That once when Joe was a toddler and Gareth had gone I left him alone in the house asleep while I went to the chippie, and he was crying and terrified when I got back

31. That I am really bad at keeping the house tidy and everything is always a mess

32. That I am now so fat I can barely cut my own toenails

33. That Joe once accidentally-on-purpose forgot to tell me about a Geography field trip to Iceland because he knew I didn't have the money and didn't want me to feel bad, even though all his friends were going

34. That I never bought him a puppy

35. That I have never met this man Lewis, which shows how much I know about my mother's life

36. That I neglected her, and myself, and everything

37. That Joe makes his own packed lunches because I'm too disorganised and lazy

38. That I don't change my duvet cover for months at a time because nobody ever sees it

39. That when the phone rang tonight and I thought

it was my mum, I was annoyed because I had to
drag my fat arse away from *Poldark*

40. That I have spoken to my mum twice in the last
    month and never noticed she was so ill because I
    am too wrapped up in myself – she's a good actress
    but I should have noticed

41. That I didn't remind Joe to call and thank her for
    that voucher she sent

After more than forty stop-off points on the guilt trip, Rose
stops, and looks at what she has done. Her mother probably
imagined a journal, or some neatly written-out pages of A4.
Instead, it's a tear-stained mess; an almost illegible scrawl
with smudged ink and creases and incoherent punctuation.
The memo-pad paper is small and square, and she has filled
more than twenty sheets of it. She'll need to go back and
gather them all up.

She pauses, and finishes the wine; 600 millilitres down, a
new bottle to go.

She knows she has to add one more to the guilt list. She
doesn't want to, though. She doesn't want to acknowledge the
truth she can feel tugging at her, prodding her, whispering
her name like one of those Satanic blond-haired kids in old
horror films.

She watched that video three times, and Mum had asked
her to be honest. To tell the truth. So that's what she has to
do.

Rose wipes her eyes, and picks up the pen again. She winces
because of the blister that is starting to throb on her finger,

a dull ache compared to all the others. She picks up a fresh square of paper, covers Yoda's mutilated face, and adds:

42. That I never gave Poppy a second chance, no matter how hard she begged

Chapter 16

Poppy isn't sure what to do next. She's watched the video, and called this man Lewis, who sent her straight to voicemail, and also phoned around various hospitals until she could confirm that it is all true. Unfortunately, it is.

She needs to *do* something, and decides to take a shower. She ends up sitting on the floor, the too-hot water sluicing over her head and shoulders, burning her skin bright red, steam cocooning her in a smeared glass box. She stays in there until her fingertips are so wrinkled and puckered up they look as if they belong to a witch, and her bottom is numb on the tiles.

When she finally climbs out, the whole bathroom is filled with steam, as though she's in a Turkish sauna. She uses a fresh towel to wipe the mirror clean, and stares at herself.

Mascara is smudged beneath her eyes, and her hair is plastered to her skull, and her body is slightly too thin. Her collarbones are prominent, and the skin around her neck is just too taut to be attractive. There are lines around her mouth from years of smoking, and her long legs are so toned they're almost hideous.

She hates what she sees, even though she has worked hard for it.

She hates it because that face, that body, belong to the kind of woman she never wanted to become. The kind of woman who lives alone and works in marketing and has meaningless friendships and is a complete bitch to everyone who works for her.

The kind of woman who could drown in her own shower and not be found for weeks on end, or until the flat below flooded. The kind of woman nobody really cares about, because the only person who did has abandoned her and selfishly died.

The kind of woman who could break her own mother's heart, and not even notice she was doing it.

She picks up an aerosol can of shaving cream, and takes off the lid. She holds it in front of the mirror, and sprays it all over the glass, until everything is obscured and all she can see is the cream, slowly falling down in white dollops and plopping into the marble sink.

Satisfied at her minor act of vandalism, she puts on a black satin kimono, and goes back into the living room, where she briefly considers getting out her tobacco tin again.

She can still picture it in its original home on the polished shelf in Mum's glass display cabinet. It sat alongside her other accumulated nick-nacks and almost-antique oddities: a giant conch shell she bought from a gift shop in Dorset; her own father's pocket watch and chain; a beer mat autographed by John Lennon when she met him in a pub in Soho in the Seventies; a tiny dragon carved out of jade.

Her memories of that display cabinet are vivid, and it sums up their cottage – eclectic, unpredictable, full of clutter; every item laden with some significance.

There will be a lot to do, she thinks, as she sits down at her desk. A lot to sort through. Things to package up. Things to send to the charity shop, or keep for themselves. They might need to hire a skip for the junk, and call in an antiques expert to appraise the valuables, and it might not always be easy to tell the difference between the two.

She takes a pen, and starts to jot down a few points. Practical stuff. Things that she thinks are keeping her calm, until she realises that she is crying so hard her whole body is shaking in huge spasms, and her handwriting is unreadable.

Her hair is still soggy, and the kimono is getting soaked through as it drips over her shoulders and back, and it feels a bit like she is drowning in snot.

She snatches a tissue from the box on her desk, and angrily wipes her eyes and nose and face clear. She screws the tissue up, and throws it on the floor, to be dealt with later.

She's been making the wrong list, she knows. This isn't what her mother asked her to do in that awful video, looking so neat and tidy and thin.

Poppy picks up the pen again, and turns to a fresh page in her leather-bound notepad. She takes a deep breath, and starts. She's going to be totally honest, just like her mother asked. She puts pen to paper, and it doesn't take long at all.

There is only one item on Poppy's guilt list:
EVERYTHING.

Job done, she slams the notepad shut, and wrings her soggy hair out in a damp ponytail. A small puddle of water builds up on the hardwood floor, and she dips her toe into it, for no good reason other than it's there.

She's made her list, and she's had a shower, and she's cried, and now her whole mood feels as empty as her grumbling stomach.

She doesn't want to do the other thing that her mother asked her to do. She doesn't want to *think about it*. She doesn't want to even let Rose back into her mind, let alone her life. It's too hard, too nasty, too brutal. She might not survive.

For years now, she's closed that part of her life off. Walled it up, like a mad woman in a Gothic novel – left it to starve to death in the hope that it would rot and crumble like an ancient skeleton, and eventually be nothing but a pile of dust on the ground.

It's allowed her to function. To have a life. To have a career. To have fake friends. But she knows that old crone is still walled up in there: wailing, insane, still so, so hungry. If she lets her out, she'll be devoured. If she lets herself think about it, like her mother has asked, she will think of nothing else – and her whole life will fall to pieces, crumpled up like the soggy tissue on the floor.

It's too much, and she can't do it. She won't do it – not right now.

Chapter 17

'Wassup, mum?' says Joe, his usual morning greeting. It is after 11 a.m., and he has just staggered downstairs, wearing stripy pyjama bottoms and sporting a supreme case of bed-head. He's tall, her boy, and is taking after his dad in looks at least.

He towers over Rose as she putters around in the kitchen, emptying the dishwasher. She's barely slept, and when she did, it wasn't what you'd call restful.

When she woke up, she felt normal – until she remembered. She'd had about twenty seconds of peace before the world came crashing down around her, and she disappeared back under the duvet, too exhausted to cry, too wrecked to move.

Since then, she's cleaned the house, hidden her Guilt List, and put the *Star Wars* book away in a cupboard where she hopes Joe will forget all about it. She's still ashamed about going all Dark Side on Yoda.

Joe is reaching for the cereal box on autopilot when he stops, pauses, and looks around at the sparklingly tidy kitchen. He wipes his eyes, and then screws them up, like he's not quite seeing properly. His hair is flopping over his forehead and, despite his height, he still looks impossibly young to Rose. Her little boy, but all stretched out and super-sized.

'It's really clean in here. Are you feeling all right?' he says, giving her a lazy grin to let her know he's joking. 'Should I be calling 999?'

Rose says nothing, but pulls him in for a big, long hug. He lets her, but backs away after a few moments, looking borderline embarrassed. He might be a little boy to her, but he's still 16 in the real world.

She realises she doesn't know how to do this. She doesn't have a clue what to say, or what to do. She doesn't know how to break it to him gently, or how to do it in a way that won't traumatise him, or freak him out for the rest of his life.

It's the first time he's had to deal with death, and truthfully, it's the first time she has as well. Unless she counts the pets, which she doesn't – Mum stage-managed those brilliantly, but this is far, far different.

Her own pain is still huge – a living, snarling beast inside her – but she knows she needs to set it aside, and do the right thing by her boy. Protect him from the kaleidoscope of hell that she's going through, and help him deal with it.

'Joe, come and sit down with me, will you?' she says, gently pushing a lock of his too-long hair away from his face and tucking it behind his ear.

He looks confused, but follows her barefoot into the living room, plonking himself down on the armchair in that exhausted 'I'm-so-busy-growing-I-don't-have-any-energy-left' way that teens have.

'All right, Mum,' he says, when she remains silent. 'I'm sitting down. And I've seen too many TV shows to think this can mean anything good. What's wrong?'

'It's Granny,' replies Rose, staring off into space, her eyes fixating on the motes of dust that are floating in the bright sunlight filtering through the windows. 'I got a phone call last night, and . . . well, she's gone, Joe. Your granny died yesterday.'

She doesn't know what she has been expecting from him. Tears, maybe? Hysteria? The same kind of ridiculous drama she indulged in last night, during her Festival of Snot?

Instead, she simply sees his lower lip tremble slightly, and his frown deepen. She realises that – even at his age – he is trying to be macho.

'It's okay to be upset,' she says quickly. 'I know I was. You don't have to be brave for my sake, sweetheart, honestly.'

He studies her face, as if he's examining her for evidence of lies, and she feels so ashamed. Her beautiful, bonny baby is trying to protect her when, really, it should always have been the other way around.

All those times he stayed in with her when he should have been out with his mates; the way he'd sent her a friend request on Facebook even when it wasn't cool to have your mum as a Facebook friend in anyone's universe; all those occasions when she'd sensed him feeling guilty as he left to go and see his dad in London.

All of it was wrong, and all of it was her fault. She'd relied on him when she should have been relying on herself. That really has to change.

'What happened, Mum?' he says, eventually. 'She seemed really great the last time we saw her, and it wasn't that long ago, was it?'

The tears are there, now; she can see them shining in the blue of his eyes before he swipes them away, as though he's angry with himself for allowing them to even exist.

'I suppose it was just before her birthday, wasn't it?' Rose replies, even though she has absolutely no doubt about when she last saw her mum. She's gone over it enough times. It was over four months ago, hard as that is to swallow – time flies when you're not having fun. She was supposed to visit after that, while Joe was away, but that was when Rose had cancelled on her. Before she was ill, according to Lewis's timing, but still. Unforgivable.

'Yeah,' Joe replies, biting his lip. 'That's right. When we took her out for lunch at that National Trust place with the castle and the fake jousting. She bought some lavender bags in the gift shop and said the chocolate cake was so sinful she needed at least two portions, because there wasn't enough sin in her life these days.'

Rose finds herself, against the odds, smiling at the memory of her mum relishing every last mouthful of both her slices. She never seemed to put any weight on, whereas Rose felt she only had to look at a chocolate cake to gain a stone. Or maybe that was going home and eating her own bodyweight in Hobnobs once she was on her own, who knows?

'That's it, yes. Well, apparently she became ill a little while ago. Six weeks or so, her friend said, when he called last night.'

'Who called?' says Joe. 'Was it Lewis? And why didn't she tell us? We could have visited her, and . . . I don't know, said goodbye properly! I never even thanked her for that voucher she sent!'

His tone pops up a few octaves with the last few words, reminding her of the time a couple of years ago when his voice started to break, and he spent weeks sounding like the frog chorus. She feels his sadness, and his desperation, and his guilt. She feels all of that herself too – but she deserves it, and he doesn't.

'Yes, it was Lewis,' she answers. 'Although I don't remember much about him, even though I know she's mentioned him before . . . and Joe, your Granny wouldn't have wanted you to feel bad about this, okay? She didn't tell us because . . . because she wanted to protect us. Because it was quick, and because she wanted us to remember her the way she was – happy and stuffing her face on chocolate cake, not in pain. That's what she wanted, and that's what we need to try and do for her. Do you think you can manage that?'

He considers this, and swipes more tears from his eyes, and finally nods.

'Well, I'll try if you try,' he says, sounding tired and a little bit scared. 'Will we have to go to her funeral?'

'Of course,' says Rose. 'That's when we say goodbye, and when we celebrate her life, and when we try and remember all the good times. We'll go to her cottage, and you can see where I grew up, and we'll take our time, all right? I know this hurts. And I know we'll miss her, Joe, but we'll get through this, we really will. You can talk to me any time, about any of it, okay?'

He nods again, and starts to frown. Rose can tell he's thinking about something, and waits with some trepidation to hear what it is.

'Will she be there?' he asks, curiosity now mixed in with the sadness. 'Will my aunt Poppy be there?'

Rose grips the arms of the chair, and forces herself to keep her expression calm, and her voice steady, which isn't easy when her heart is hammering away like a steam piston.

'Yes,' she replies simply. 'I'm sure she will be.'

Chapter 18

Rose knows that using her own son as a human shield probably isn't in the *Big Book of Good Parenting*, but she can't help it.

She is struggling to keep herself together, here, bum squashed up on the wooden pew of the village church, feeling like a trapped, wounded animal.

It's a tiny place, dating back to the sixteenth century, and today it is crammed. She risks a quick glance around, and sees that most of the village is here. Mrs Rubens from the post office. Jack Slater who runs the Farmer's Arms, and his counterpart from the Tennyson's. Gloria Lubbock, who used to be the head teacher of the village school.

Fred, whose last name she never discovered and was only ever known as Fred the Milkman. Sergeant Taylor, who'd been the local bobby throughout her childhood, and shooed her out of bus stops on more than one occasion. The farmers, en masse, sitting together in their tweedy suits, looking unnatural without their green wellies.

So many familiar faces – but, at the same time, not familiar.

She's not been back here for so long, and they have aged. Not in the normal, gradual way that people living around you age – but all of a sudden, like they've fast-forwarded in a time machine.

Hair has turned grey; skin has become wrinkled; tummies have grown. The grown-ups she thought of as old when she was a teenager – but were actually only the same kind of age as she is now – suddenly *look* old. Properly old.

As she glances around, she gets some sympathetic nods from people she doesn't even recognise at first. People, she soon realises when she adjusts her mindset and sees them through time-lapse goggles, she was at school with. They, too, look so much older. It's just completely weird, like something from a science-fiction film.

Of course, she knows, they are probably thinking the same about her. They're thinking how much weight she's put on. That her hair is a mess. That she was once such a pretty young thing, and now she's a frumpy 40-something wearing a horrible black dress that she panic-bought from Evans and now hates. It's a hot day, summer finally deciding to kick in, and she's hot and too sweaty and her hair is the size of a privet bush.

They're probably also thinking: haven't seen her for ages. Her poor mother, abandoned in her dotage. Not that 'dotage' is a word that could ever really be used about Andrea, thank God.

Joe squeezes her hand, reassuring her, and she snaps herself out of her fast-approaching self-pity party. She gives him a smile, hopefully one that says 'this is sad but I am fine', and continues to look around.

No show-biz faces, which surprises her. She'd at least expected a few, or maybe her co-star from her Penny Peabody days.

Andrea herself, of course, is providing plenty of show biz – certainly more than this church has ever seen. Big easels are set up all around, each holding one of her beloved head-shots from different eras, blown up so her perfect face is clear for all to see. Young and glamorous in the early Seventies, hair flowing wild and free. Overly made-up and super-coiffed from the Eighties, in a red silk blouse with shoulder pads. Dignified but still gorgeous, Penny Peabody era, right at the front.

Rose stares at that one, to distract herself from the coffin. Every time she allows her brain to even consider what is inside that shining mahogany box, she starts to dissolve in a fizz of agony. Her mother – everything about her mother – is surely too big to fit inside that thing? It defies the laws of physics.

It doesn't feel real, none of it. Even now, over a week later, it doesn't feel real. She feels like she's playing a part in a film: the grieving daughter at the funeral. Playing it badly, as well.

Being back here – with these people, in this place – would be enough of an emotional overload at any time, but at her mother's funeral it's just too much. She just has to get through the next hour; hold on tight until this ordeal is over with, and she has to face the next. One horrific step at a time.

She continues to look around, and gets a small finger-wave from a bleach-blonde lady who is even bigger than she is. She smiles, and waves back, still not sure who it is until it hits her: Tasmin Hughes. It's Tasmin Hughes, her friend from another lifetime, who got pregnant when she was 15 and could well be a grandma by now. Her first thought is that time hasn't been kind to either of them, but then she tells herself off – Tasmin looks happy, at least.

As she scans the crowd, she knows she is only really looking for one person. The person who wasn't there for the sad, traditional procession behind the coffin; the person who left that walk of pain to her and Joe and Lewis. She's probably hiding in her car until she can sneak in, thinks Rose, or maybe she won't come at all.

She is ashamed of the fact that even now – at the funeral – and even after watching that video, part of her is still desperately hoping that that is true. That Poppy won't show up, and she'll be saved the extra anguish of that on top of everything else. She doesn't know if she can cope with anything else. Especially that.

As the vicar starts to move towards the pulpit, and the low-level buzz of chatter clears, she hears the sound of high heels tip-tapping on the stone floor of the aisle. She knows, without a shadow of a doubt, who it is. Who it has to be.

She hears the footsteps getting closer, and stares at her own hands. She is so tense, so tightly screwed up with grief and anxiety and panic, that she starts to tear the skin from the sides of her nails. It hurts, a sharp stab of pain as bright-red blood flows, and it is enough of a distraction to stop her from getting to her feet, and running out of this place screaming.

She senses, rather than sees, Joe look up. Feels him move slightly closer as he shuffles along to make room. She's there, she knows she is. Poppy is sitting next to Joe, and her mum is in that box, and every person she knew in her childhood is staring at her like a gang of gargoyles that has come to life.

She gulps, and tries to breathe, and pulls more skin from her thumb. It's never too late to start self-harming, she thinks, wiping the blood on her dress.

She refuses to look up, and stays deadly still, and completely quiet. As though if she stays still enough, she will become invisible.

The vicar taps his microphone, and the sound echoes around the walls of the church. As the congregation falls completely silent, she hears one sentence being whispered a few spaces along the pew: 'You must be Joe. I'm Poppy. It's so nice to meet you at last.'

Chapter 19

Lewis is, he suspects, ever so slightly tipsy. He has just walked into the corner of his desk, banged his hip, and then laughed about it like a teenaged girl. Sure signs of inebriation.

That, he supposes, is what happens when you start the day with a glass of port, and follow it up with too much champagne at an altogether very jolly funeral reception.

He fully intends to continue drinking for the rest of the day. He might end up stripping naked and running round the green, or climbing the church tower and screaming 'I'm on top of the world, Ma!' at the sheep in the surrounding fields.

He can risk waking up with a hangover – or possibly an arrest record, or a pet sheep – tomorrow morning, at least. Because, by tomorrow, his main part in all of this will be over. He'll still have the legal stuff to do, of course – sorting out the estate, dotting the 'i's and crossing the 't's on probate, finalising all the paperwork and the finances. But he can do that kind of thing in his sleep.

The tricky stuff, though? The family stuff? That, he hopes, will have been well and truly passed on to the two lost souls sitting in front of him, on the other side of his antique desk. They might still need him to answer questions – Poppy, for sure, will probably insist on it; she's that type – but mainly, it'll be over to them to do with as they will.

Then, he hopes, he can get on with the small matter of grieving for his lost and most beloved of friends. He might take a small holiday, or run away to join a commune in the foothills of the Himalayas, or simply lock himself away in his little house and continue to drink himself stupid.

The funeral went as well as these things can, as did the little celebration afterwards. Andrea had choreographed it all, down to the last detail. She'd been quite specific – no actors, no show biz, no old luvvies. Apart from her, of course, the star of the show. And no obituaries to be submitted until after the funeral, as she didn't want Helen Mirren or one of the other dames turning up and stealing the limelight.

He thought she was joking on that one – she'd never mentioned acting with Helen Mirren before – but who knew? Andrea was always something of a mystery. He was secretly disappointed at her insistence – he'd have quite enjoyed meeting the still-famous and the once-famous, and matching their realities up to the incredibly naughty stories Andrea had often told.

But insist she had, and of course he had carried out her commands. In death, as in life, he was her devoted servant.

Now he felt off-kilter – that strange blend of euphoria and sadness that a good funeral can invoke; where the party goes swimmingly until you remember that the guest of honour isn't even there.

Still, no matter how weird he feels, it is clearly nothing compared to what these two are going through. Rosehip and Popcorn – the legendary Lost Girls – finally here, in the flesh.

Between them, he thinks, they have the flesh of two normal human women. But Rose has too much of it, and Poppy doesn't have enough. Rose is perched on the edge of her chair, pulling absently at the skin at the sides of her nail, even though it is already bloody and sore. The toes of her shoes are tapping on the parquet, and she is looking around her as if she expects men with flaming torches and pitchforks to rush out and drag her away at any second.

Poppy is leaning right back in her seat, long, skinny legs elegantly crossed in front of her, dark hair sleek and shining, perfect in a designer suit and stupidly high heels. A woman that tall doesn't need heels, but he knows that for certain ladies, they give a level of confidence he's never quite understood. If he was a woman, he'd be one of the Birkenstock brigade, he thinks.

She's trying to look relaxed, in control. As though she isn't even remotely out of her comfort zone. The only thing giving her away is the constant crossing and uncrossing of the fingers of her right hand, like she needs to be doing something – texting, or writing, or – if everything her mother said about her is true – rolling a cigarette.

Rose is looking around her and twitching, her beautiful eyes – her mother's eyes – taking in the deep-green walls and the framed oil paintings of local landscapes and, of course, the picture of him and Andrea on his bookshelves. It was taken on the day he took her for a hot-air balloon ride over the hills, and she still looks giddy with excitement. Rose's gaze lingers on that longer than anything else, and he sees another tiny strip of skin get torn from the side of her thumb.

In fact, the poor thing is looking everywhere except at the person sitting next to her. She's shuffled her chair a few inches further away, as though she's scared she might catch something – it's like she's physically afraid of being near her sister. She's even more nervous now, because she's been stripped of her bodyguard – Joe (lovely lad) has been left in the waiting room, where he is drinking lemonade and looking forlorn.

Poppy is equally observant, but in a calmer way. At least on the surface. She, though, is taking sneaky sideways glances at Rose, her eyes widening each time, like she can't believe she's real. Like she might be a Rose-shaped mirage.

He clears his throat, and peers at them over his glasses. He actually only needs his glasses for reading, but has decided they give him an air of authority. He's playing a part here – one Andrea wrote for him – and he needs to do it well.

'So, Rose, Poppy,' he says, hoping he doesn't sound as drunk as he feels, 'it's wonderful to meet you both at last. I just wish it had been in more pleasant circumstances.'

Or, he adds silently to himself, any circumstances at all, you selfish young fools. He'd dearly like to give them a piece of his mind, but that's not what he's here to do. He's here to give them a piece of Andrea's mind, and they're bloody lucky to get it.

'There are some estate matters to clear, but nothing too taxing. The cottage is fully paid for, and you two are the sole beneficiaries. Andrea also left a life-assurance policy made payable to you two, to be shared equally. Apart from a few small items which she bequeathed to friends, the contents of the cottage are also yours – and it's entirely up to you to determine what to do with them. I have the keys here, which I'll pass on to you when we're finished. She also left around £30,000 in savings.'

He notices the look of surprise on both their faces, and studies them hard looking for the telltale signs of greed. He's seen that so many times, sitting here in this exact same situation – grieving relatives whose eyes light up with cartoon dollar signs the minute that money is mentioned.

But no, he thinks, after a brief pause, not this time. They are both taken aback – they obviously didn't expect their mother to have saved so much, clearly not being aware of how well Penny Peabody had provided for her in later years – but it's surprise rather than excitement.

'She has asked,' he continues, 'that you use part of that for the special project she has left behind for you – I will be able to advance whatever you need to you until the formalities are sorted – and that the remainder is put into trust to help fund Joe's university education, should he choose to go down that path. If not, it will be made available to him on his twenty-first birthday. Does that sound agreeable?'

Rose, he sees, is starting to lose the plot a little. There are beads of sweat on her forehead, and she is clenching back tears. Again, he's seen that before – people who hold themselves

107

together until something, often small or intangible, simply sets them off.

She seems incapable of speech, wringing her hands and physically trembling, but luckily Poppy – cool, calm, controlled Poppy – steps in.

'That's perfectly agreeable, Mr Clarke-Smith. As far as I'm concerned Joe can have everything that's been left. But I would like to know more about the "special project" now, if you don't mind?'

Her fingers are still crossing and uncrossing, and her right eyelid is twitching, but her voice is very professional. Very polite and business-like, very bossy. She's used to being in charge, he thinks, and this is difficult for her on so many levels. She might not look it, but she's just as much of a Lost Girl as tatty-handed Rose.

'Indeed,' he says, leaning back in his chair and steepling his fingers in front of him. The waistcoat of his suit is a little too tight, and he's itching to pull off his bow tie, but he still has his part to play.

'I believe she called it the A–Z of Everything, didn't she, in that video we made? She wasn't happy with that, but I find it quite a satisfying title. She – we – worked extremely hard collating all the different parts, and it's very much a labour of love. There will be some travelling to do, and some interesting . . . *activities* is probably the simplest word to use. Do be prepared to deal with your mother's sense of humour on top of everything else – I'm sure I don't need to tell you how wicked that could sometimes be.

'Anyway, I have some printed information here,' he says,

sliding sheets across the desk for them, 'and the rest has been emailed to you.

'Once you're at the cottage, you'll find much more. This, if you do it the way your mother intended, will not be a quick rummage through a few boxes – so I'd suggest that unless you have other plans, you both go home, and make arrangements for some time off work, and sort out any domestic necessities. A couple of weeks should do it—'

'That won't be possible,' interrupts Poppy, quickly, 'not right now, I'm afraid. Can this be done later?'

Rose gasps audibly, and Lewis gives Poppy a look that, he hopes, might literally turn her to stone. Then he could smash her to tiny pieces with a hammer.

'I see,' he says slowly, gazing at her over his specs. 'Is there some kind of dog food advertising emergency that you need to sort out? A cat collar campaign that needs overseeing? Heaven forbid that your mother should dare to die at such an inconvenient time. You really should have sent the cancer a memo, then perhaps it could have been rearranged.'

Poppy tries to meet this look with defiance, and Rose stays quiet and shuffles, and for a few seconds the only sound in the room is that of his antique carriage clock ticking on the mantelpiece. It is a battle of wills, and one which he knows he will win – because he is right.

'I'll see what I can do,' Poppy eventually replies, redeeming herself slightly by looking suddenly and unexpectedly tearful. She's just a child, he tells himself – a damaged child. A child that Andrea loved.

'Splendid. I'd suggest you meet back at the cottage in two

days' time – can I say midday, to give you both enough time to make it here from your respective dwellings, and me enough time to give everything a final check-over?

'There are several packages, and the information you have includes all the instruction you'll need, pass codes, that kind of thing. I hope you'll find it illuminating. I know I did – or at least as much as I was allowed to see.'

'What do you mean?' asks Poppy, frowning as she drags the papers towards her with long, painted fingernails. 'I assumed you'd been the one helping her put all of this together? Surely she wasn't well enough to do it on her own?'

There is a slightly accusing note in her voice, and he shrugs it off. It's not him she's angry with, it's herself. And quite right too.

'I helped her with much of it, but some things, she said, were meant only for your eyes – so I respected that. She only had one proviso – that you do this together, or not at all. One of you can't take possession of the items without the other's permission, and all of the various tasks and scenarios that she has laid out for you must be completed in each other's company.

'I know, from what she told me, that this will not be especially straightforward – but I would ask you to respect her wishes. If, after seeing the materials she has left, you decide you cannot go ahead, then simply let me know and I'll arrange for it all to be collected. And destroyed.'

He sees Rose wince at his use of the word 'destroyed', and feels a smidgeon of guilt. He only said it for effect. He wouldn't be capable of destroying anything Andrea had left behind

– he'd even kept her combs and her lipstick and the last crumpled tissue she'd used to wipe the tears from her eyes after she had finished the video.

'Now, unless there is anything else I can help you with, I suggest we adjourn for now. I, for one, quite frankly feel bloody awful, and I'm sure you two have a lot to think about. Please feel free to contact me if you have any further questions, and I will be in touch with regard to the estate in due course.'

He stands – using his six-foot-four height to full advantage – and waits until they follow suit. He can tell that Poppy wants to argue, but can't find anything to argue about.

Eventually, both of them stand, and he passes a set of keys into Rose's shaking hands. He admits to himself that this is childish, and he did it because he knew it would annoy Poppy. But, as Andrea would say, small pleasures, darling, soon mount up.

They both mutter their thank yous, and start to leave, Rose lingering slightly so there is no danger of making any accidental physical contact with her sister. He shakes his head as they go, not at all sure from this initial encounter whether even the warmth of Andrea's legacy will be enough to melt this kind of permafrost.

As she reaches the door, Rose hesitates, and turns back to face him.

'Can I ask you something, Lewis?' she says, voice small and apologetic.

'Of course,' he replies.

'You and my mum . . . you seem to have been so close.

You've obviously been a huge help to her. Can I ask – were you more than friends?'

There is a hopeful note to her question, as though she desperately wants him to say yes. Perhaps it would make her feel less guilty about her mother's final few weeks if she thinks she had a lover by her side, instead of a boring old fart of a solicitor.

'I loved your mother dearly,' he says, fighting to keep his own voice from cracking, 'but no, we weren't more than friends. She wasn't my type, beautiful creature though she was. I'm more of a Jason Statham man myself.'

He enjoys the look of shock on both their faces – he doesn't get to shock people anywhere near enough these days – and finds himself smiling as they leave.

Smiling, and wondering. Wondering what went wrong, all those years ago, to cause such an apparently uncrossable divide?

And wondering if there is any way that a trip through Andrea's sometimes psychedelic alphabet will be able to bridge it.

PART TWO

The Curtain Opens:
The A–Z Begins

Chapter 20

Poppy

I am sitting in my car, outside the childhood home I've not seen for over a decade, waiting for them to get here.

Waiting for my sister, who I haven't properly talked to for seventeen years, and my nephew, who I hadn't even met until the day of the funeral. I have been avoiding thinking, and feeling, and crying, for so long now, I'm not sure I even exist any more.

I am just a blob of a human being, melting on a hot summer's day, confronting a past that makes me cringe and a future I can't even imagine. I've coped until now by keeping busy. By out-bitching myself in the office, and by using up every spare moment of every day drinking or working or sometimes both at the same time. Because that's what hip flasks were invented for.

Everything's been building up to this – to this A–Z madness – and now, I feel like I've been here for hours. My blouse is sticking to the sweat under my armpits, and I have no clue why I still have my leather jacket over my shoulders. Just for show, I suppose, like the stupid high-heeled sandals that are crippling my feet. Heaven forbid I look less than perfect.

I might look it, but I really don't feel it. I'm a nervous wreck, and every time I hear the distant sound of a car engine, one that might be hers, I try and pull myself back together again.

I've planned for this, I tell myself. I've practised my neutral face in the mirror, and my calm speaking voice by talking out loud. I am determined not to start us off on the wrong foot, but . . . well. She's late. And there's nothing like being locked out of your dead mother's house to make you tetchy.

Obviously, I'd arrived early as well, so it's almost an hour I've been waiting now. Walking around the gardens; counting the gnomes; staring through the windows. Thinking about stuff I didn't want to think about.

It was the window peeking that finally did me in. Shielding my face from the glare of the sun, like you do when you're at an ATM on a bright day, and gazing inside at the living room. Seeing the chintzy sofa and the matching armchair, and picturing Mum sitting there, watching a movie or reading a book or on the phone to me.

The little side table next to it, where she kept her glasses – both the type she used to read with, and the type she used to drink wine from. The books on the shelves; the now-empty vase she usually had filled with wildflowers. The brand-new flat-screen TV that I'd heard all about – 'darling, I swear, Richard Burton's head is bigger on my new telly than it was in real life!'

It all looks the same. Apart from the flat-screen. Just like it did the last time I was here, which is way too many years ago. I almost expect to see her pottering around in there, wearing her yoga pants and a nice pashmina, wandering in from the kitchen with a jug of something cool and alcoholic.

It's the knowledge that she won't ever wander in again that breaks me. And when the tears come, they come with a vengeance – as though they're annoyed that I've been avoiding them for the last few days. Holding them back, imprisoning them behind chains made of to-do lists and meetings.

I retreat into the car, with the air con on, and just let them flow. Best to get them out of the way before putting my game face on. At least one grubby angel needs to try and stay strong enough to get through this.

I'm tired, and sad, and I want my old life back – the one where kicking the arses of the graphics team was the most trying thing on my schedule. Or, even better, the one before that. The one where I was a loud, proud angry young woman, preparing to do battle with the world. Preparing to battle with Rose on one side, and my mum on the other – safe in their love and secure in the knowledge that both of them would always be there for me.

Now, I have neither – and I'm finally being forced to think about it. To do like our mum asked, and look back at where it all started to go wrong. This is not my idea of a fun time, and it doesn't help to stem the waterworks.

By the time I hear her car chugging up the lane, I'm a bit calmer, but a lot soggier. I have kept a box of tissues on the passenger seat for exactly this kind of occasion, and clean myself up, inspecting my face in the mirror when I'm done. Not perfect, but good enough under the circumstances.

I get out of the car, and arrange myself carefully, aiming to look fifty shades of okay by the time she actually arrives.

Part of me is terrified – part of me is relieved. She's now forty minutes late, and I had been starting to wonder if she'd decided not to come. If I wasn't worth the effort. If she'd just completely forgotten about me.

Because that, even if she doesn't realise it, was one of the things she got really good at. And that, as far as I can see, is where the rot first started to set in.

Chapter 21

The Cottage, 1999 – Poppy's 22nd Birthday

I am still living at home, after doing my English degree. It's weird being back, but I'm kind of between life choices at the moment. Floating between one stage and the other, like a once-shiny helium balloon running out of puff.

After I graduated, I did some travelling, but got so bored I ditched my friends in a beer cellar in Budapest, and made my way back to the UK. None the worse for wear, apart from the Buddha tattoo on my hip that had seemed like an excellent idea at the time.

Now I'm home, I'm stuck in a rut. An English degree doesn't feel like the most useful thing in the world. I can't go off and build wells in the Third World, or discover a new planet, or cure cancer. I can, of course, quote extensive passages of *Beowulf* in Old English, but that isn't a great consolation.

A lot of my friends are going into journalism, and there's always teaching, of course. That phrase gets repeated so often it should have capital letters – There's Always Teaching.

I'm not set against that, but I don't feel passionate about it either.

Still, it would be a shedload better than marketing, which one of my more ambitious friends has moved into – for a pharmaceutical company as well. I can't think of anything worse than marketing – totally soul destroying.

What I'd really like to do is write a book, which doesn't exactly make me special. Everyone wants to write a book, including our milkman, Fred. But wanting to write a book, and actually doing it, are very different things, I've discovered recently.

Truth is, I don't have much to write about yet. Boyfriends: several; none serious enough to break my heart. Travel: backpacking around Europe, where every hostel seemed the same, and every night seemed to consist solely of drinking cheap local beer. Trauma: luckily, I suppose, very little. Family: oddly shaped, but brilliant.

So far, my books have been big on emotions, and low on action. Pretty much like myself right now, I think, rolling around on my bed and staring at a poster of The Doors. The Blu-Tack on one corner has died, and the paper is curling up on itself, making Jim Morrison look as though he only has one leather-clad leg.

I'm bored, but also gripped with some kind of paralysis that is stopping me doing anything else. It's all just too . . . *comfortable* here.

Mum makes it very easy to loll around at home, pottering in the village and watching crap telly and reading. Mum is glad of the company – she's between gigs herself, as parts for middle-aged ladies don't seem to come knocking that often. Patriarchal bullshit is alive and kicking in the world of show biz, it seems.

One day, perhaps I'll move to London, and live in a Bohemian garret and write stirring literature with a feminist sub-plot – but not right now. For now, this will do – and at least I have the weekend to look forward to.

It's my birthday today. I'm 22 years old, which sounds a lot more grown up than I feel. Up until 21, you get away with things. Your twenty-first is a birthday on which cash still falls out of your cards when you open them. You get shiny metallic-painted plastic keys, and cakes, and parties, and older people look all misty-eyed and reminiscent as they buy you booze.

Nobody expects anything of you when you're 21, not even yourself. It still feels like you're just starting out. Twenty-two, though . . . well, it's a bit of a nothing birthday, isn't it? Nothing, but old.

Still, the one advantage of having a birthday is that Rose will be coming home. She's still in Liverpool, and shows no signs of budging. She's done her degree – got a first, obviously – and her Masters. Now she's taking a year off, working in a lab where they do something frightfully clever with plant cells, and is considering taking on a PhD. So she'll eventually be Dr Rose.

She's already made it very clear that if she does go down that route, she will fully be expecting everyone in the family to refer to her as Dr Rose at all times.

I like this idea, and the ways I could have fun with it:

'Would you like salt and vinegar on your chips, Dr Rose?' 'Pint of lager please, Dr Rose.' 'Was it you who let out that terrible fart, Dr Rose? It smells like a gerbil crawled up your bum and died, Dr Rose.'

She's not quite decided yet, but I hope she does it purely for the comedy value. And, you know, because it would add value to the world. Unlike me, Rose could potentially cure cancer, or at least make coffee for someone who is curing cancer. Rose is brilliant; a huge, clever cake, with awesome sauce and sprinkles on top.

I miss her so much, and I can't wait for the weekend. She came home for Christmas, but then disappeared back up North for the New Year – she invited me to go along, but I didn't want to leave Mum on her own.

Mum had taken me in, cooked my dinners, pretended the tattoo wasn't awful, and lent me the car whenever I needed to escape. Mum had been great.

The least I could do was spend New Year with her. It had even turned out to be a laugh – we downed several chilled G&Ts, made in a jug with cucumber just how she likes them, and then saw the year in with the rest of the village at the Farmer's Arms.

At least, the rest of the village aged over 30. Younger people go to the Tennyson's, where the landlord accepts a library card as a valid form of ID. The grown-ups go the Farmer's, which is all olde-worlde stone floors and exposed brick walls and a blazing fireplace, like something out of Emmerdale but with more adultery.

I could have gone to the Tennyson's. There would still be

people I knew there – but it felt wrong, somehow. The thought of seeing people from school again made me feel melancholy.

Either they'd have fab careers and exciting prospects, which would make me jealous, or they'd be taxi drivers or working at the poultry-processing plant down the road, which would make me depressed. All that gilded youth now elbow deep in turkeys would be too much to handle.

New Year wasn't quite the same without Rose, who was at some super-duper party in Scouseland, but it was fun – especially the part where Mum led a conga round the bar to the soundtrack of Prince singing '1999'.

Now it's the first week in February, which I always think is a totally shitty time to have a birthday. Everyone is skint after Christmas, the weather is always crap, and there's nothing in the whole month worth looking forward to. Unless you count Valentine's Day, which I don't, as I'll only get one card this year. It will be signed 'from your secret admirer', and it will be from my own mother.

Rose coming back for the weekend is the only thing I've had to look forward to for ages. We always spend the nearest weekends to our birthdays together, even when we've been living in completely different parts of the country. Rose would come to my college bar and get drunk, or vice versa. Or sometimes we'd just meet at the cottage, which was kind of in the middle, and Mum would do jelly and ice cream and tell us both how splendid we are.

I roll over so I can play Snake on my new Nokia, and jump when the phone actually rings. I see that it is Rose, and answer it immediately. Happy time is here.

'Hey Dr Rose!' I say, sitting up, cross-legged, absent-mindedly sticking down the corner of that Doors poster as she talks. Poor Jim has enough problems without losing a leg. 'How's it hanging?'

'It's hanging well, thank you,' says Rose, slightly crackly over the phone lines – the reception is pretty rough out here in the middle of the arse end of nowhere.

'In fact, it's hanging in a decidedly Irish way. You won't believe this, sis, but I'm in Dublin. Sitting in a pub in Temple Bar, pint of Guinness in front of me, and a band playing "It's A Long Way To Tipperary" in the background. Can you hear them?'

I can hear them. It sounds like a god-awful racket to me, but that might be the poor phone reception. Or the lack of Guinness.

'That sounds like a most excellent adventure – what are you doing there?'

And why aren't I with you, I think but don't say, instead of slowly vegetating in a village where watching two sheepdogs try and hump each other in a field is considered entertainment?

'Oh . . . I'm with Gareth. You remember, I told you about him? From New Year?'

'I remember you said you'd met someone, which wasn't very specific – I assume you met a lot of people while you were out at a do in Liverpool city centre. Last time I was there, I met about 7,000 people, including several who wanted to open a bar in Tenerife with me. It's that kind of place. So who's Gareth?'

I'm trying not to sound annoyed, but I am. I'm bored and lonely and my whole life feels like some big loose end. And it's my birthday – which Rose seems to have forgotten.

'He's . . . God, Pops, I don't want to sound like something out of a Meg Ryan film, but he's *amazing*. I mean, getting off with someone at a New Year's party is no big deal, right? You probably snogged loads of people that night, didn't you?'

'Erm . . . no. I was at the Farmer's with Mum, remember? I would've been snogging pissed-up granddads wearing their best cords.'

'Oh yeah! I'd forgotten that's where you went . . . Anyway. New Year was when we met, and we've been seeing each other ever since. I'm sure I told you . . . well, I don't suppose I've called that much recently, have I?

'So, it's all been going ace, and then yesterday, he surprised me with this trip. He has family here, and he knows all the best pubs and clubs, and he took me to this brilliant coffee shop, and we saw this brilliant live band at a venue about as big as Mum's kitchen, and we're staying with his friend who has this brilliant flat near St Stephen's Green.'

'Wow,' I say, wondering if I sound as sarcastic as I intend to, 'that sounds . . . brilliant? So, what does he do, this Gareth? Apart from whisk you away on romantic breaks?'

'He works in banking, on a graduate trainee scheme. It's just a stepping stone, he says – what he wants to do is move into investment. I know it sounds really boring, but you'd have to meet him – he can even make finance sound interesting, honest!'

My interest in finance extends as far as rooting round in

the sides of the sofas to see if I can scrape together enough spare change for a packet of fags, so I seriously doubt this.

'Well, I hope I do meet him then,' I say, actually thinking, 'I hope you dump him before I have to.'

There is still no sign of Rose wishing me a happy birthday, or talking about our plans for the weekend, and I suddenly feel very aware of the fact that it's already Thursday.

'How long are you in Dublin for?' I ask.

'Until Monday night,' Rose answers, sounding distracted. There is a scuffling sound and then the noise of glasses tinkling. Sounds as if somebody has just bought another round in. Probably the financial whizz-kid, who is undoubtedly absolutely *brilliant* at getting served at a crowded bar. Tosser.

'I wish we could stay longer,' Rose adds, after a slurpy pause, 'but I have to be back at work by Tuesday. Anyway, look, I'd better go. Gareth's back. Poppy, I can't wait for you to meet him, and he's really excited about it too – aren't you, Gareth?'

'Yes! Hi Poppy! Cheers!' shouts a man's voice down the line. I immediately hate the sound of him, and wish a severe case of Guinness arse in his direction. He deserves the Curse of the Black Poo for ruining my birthday weekend, even if he did know nothing about it.

I mean, it's not that I don't want Rose to be happy. Of course I do. But . . . well, couldn't she have held off on being quite so happy until after the weekend? And even if she's not coming home, couldn't she have at least remembered it was my birthday at all?

'Anyway, gotta go, sis – see you soon. Love to Mum!'

The line goes dead, and the phone goes even deader as I throw it across the room. The battery case comes off, and it all falls apart as it hits the floor.

'This,' I say to Jim Morrison, 'is the crappiest birthday ever.'

Chapter 22

Rose: The Present Day

The drive has been hellish, and the air con in my car is practically non-existent. That's what happens when you drive a 1998 Ford Fiesta held together with duct tape and prayers.

Joe makes it tolerable, and we sing along to Adele songs together, sweating away until he forces me to accept that we need to wind the windows down.

'We're going to dehydrate and die if we don't, Mum,' he says, as a welcome gust of cool air rushes in.

'I know. But I hate having the windows open . . .'

'Don't worry,' he answers, brandishing a copy of a road atlas that has all the country's Little Chefs marked on it in case of pancake emergencies, 'I'll be on wasp patrol.'

I nod, and we sing some more Adele. We even hit some of the right notes.

'It's just like she's here in the car with us, isn't it?' he says, as he skips forward to his favourite track.

'It is. Maybe she'd come to a Little Chef with us, what do you think?'

'Yeah. She'd be cool with that. I think maybe she'd be happy I've wound the windows down as well. How much further?'

I glance through the windscreen, squinting into the sunlight through glass smeared by sat-nav suckers – my window-fluid-squirter thingies aren't too brilliant either.

'Not far,' I say, quietly. The landscape is achingly familiar now, and I am driving around these twisting roads and narrow lanes purely from muscle memory.

I see all the familiar landmarks – the twisted tree stump at the crossroads just before you get to Goldfinch Lane; the metal gate to Hawthorne Farm that once got crushed by the farmer's tractor when he was drunk in charge of an agricultural vehicle; the old-fashioned bright-red postbox on the corner that is almost completely covered in ivy.

Familiar territory, but also a strange land. Strange because I made it so. All these years, I've stayed away – at first because Poppy was still living here, then because of the state of my life with Gareth and a baby, and then, later, purely to avoid being in contact with anything that reminded me of my sister.

Joe is staring out of his window, taking it all in, logging the landscape and the pretty cottages and the scarecrows left over from the annual festival earlier in the summer.

'They look weird,' he says, as we pass one that is sitting on a child's swing, his tattered jean-clad legs swaying in the breeze. 'And scary. This is starting to feel like the start of a horror film. Are we heading to place that is inhabited entirely by demonic children or devil-worshipping farmers who sacrifice passing tourists to ancient fertility gods?'

'Have you been watching *Buffy the Vampire Slayer* again?'
I ask.

'No. I've been watching *Supernatural*. It's about two demon-slaying brothers who drive round small-town America defeating evil. And I think they'd be starting to get worried right about now.'

I laugh, and keep a lookout for the sharp turning that I know will soon be coming up on the right. I'll probably take it by instinct, but I'm not feeling 100 per cent at my most chipper this morning. In fact, on a scale of 1 to 10, with 1 being 'fine and dandy', and 10 being 'absolutely shit', I'm heading for a definite 27.

It has been a busy couple of days, getting Joe ready for his trip to his dad's, sorting the house out, and having a nervous breakdown. That last one especially was pretty time-consuming, and kept getting in the way of the others.

I'd try and distract myself by ironing Joe's boxers – for the first time ever in the history of me and Joe's boxers – and find myself staring into space, crying into a cloud of steam. Or I'd be rooting through the back of my drawers, having a clear-out and throwing away knickers that were seven years too old and several sizes too small to be of any use, and suddenly realise I was sitting on the floor, using the knickers to blow my nose with.

I'd had the urge to call my mother every single night, and on several occasions actually did. She's still there, listed in my contacts, under the imaginative name of Mum. Three little letters, looking so innocent, but carrying so much weight. The most taken-for-granted three letters in the entire world.

I know now how much I relied on her. How much I . . . used her, I suppose. I mean, that's normal – and I am a mum, so I get that. It's not like you want your kids to be going round feeling grateful all the time. But now, I have so many regrets.

Like the fact that I only called her when I either needed her, or felt like so much time had passed that it was my duty to call her. That sometimes I call-screened, doing 1471 to see who it was, and didn't always bother to call back. That other times, when I heard her chirpy voice at the other end, my heart sank – because I knew I'd be stuck on the phone for ages.

That I'd make excuses, come up with a fake knock at the door or say I had something on the stove, when in reality I probably had an urgent TV show to watch, or *Hello!* magazine to read – heaven forbid I should talk to my own mother rather than catching up on the latest news from the Swedish royal family.

Or like the knowledge that our last, final-for-ever conversation was about Nigel Farage. I mean, for God's sake – what a low to leave it all on.

I'd tried not to sink into an alcoholic misery for Joe's sake, but had ever-so-slightly cracked last night, when my neighbour Simon called round with a six-pack of Carlsberg and two Pot Noodles. He's old-fashioned like that.

Joe had told him about my mum, and he was checking up on me. He'd lost his own parents years earlier, and it was good to talk to him. Good to be told that one day, eventually, it would start to feel better. That, in the end, I might actually wake up and not be paralysed by guilt and grief.

I wasn't sure I believed him, but at least he tried. And I am not one to turn my nose up at a man who comes bearing Pot Noodles and beer.

Truth be told, I have a pathetic little crush on Simon. He's a builder, and has hair cut so short he looks like he's in the Navy SEALS, and he often walks round without his shirt, wearing cargo pants and those big belts with tools in them and steel-capped boots. Maybe there's something hard-wired into women to always go a little bit ga-ga about that, I don't know – some kind of primal biological response to being in close proximity to a seasoned hunter-gatherer. Or maybe I just think too much.

Anyhow, he's a nice bloke, and would undoubtedly be horrified that I'd even entertained such thoughts. Not that I was thinking them last night. Last night, I was just panicking. About Joe leaving. About coming here. About seeing Poppy again. About not being able to call my mum and tell her I was panicking about all those things. It wasn't pretty, and the beer and the company helped, especially as Joe was out having one last hurrah with his mates.

I'd even told him a little bit about Poppy, or at least explained that I hadn't seen her for years.

'Why?' he asked, predictably, frowning at me over the lager we were drinking straight from the can.

'Long story, best left untold,' I replied, simply.

'Fair enough. Families, eh? Who'd have 'em?'

And with that, we'd clinked cans, and left the subject alone. Which was genuinely the best place for it.

Sadly, we didn't leave the lagers alone, and they'd taken

their toll on my spirits this morning. As well as my head, which is banging and throbbing and doing all kinds of things I wish it would stop doing.

The turn comes up, and I take it a tiny bit too late, tyres screeching as we go, ending up on completely the wrong side of the narrow road. Luckily, there is rarely anybody else on this particular narrow road, as the only place it leads to is my mother's home – Greenfinch Cottage, the place where I grew up.

It's close enough to the village that you can walk to the pub, and close enough to the main road that you can occasionally hear traffic at busy spells, but other than that it is totally secluded. The nearest neighbour is a farmhouse two miles away, and all you hear from there is the noise of cows and industrial-sized ride-on lawnmowers.

The cottage isn't quite chocolate-box pretty – the white-washed stone and thatched roof are offset by quite an ugly extension that got built on to the side before we moved in, and which Mum always vowed to get rid of for 'committing crimes against my aesthetic sensibilities'. She never did, though, and over the years I suppose we just grew into it – using it to store our bikes and winter boots and boxes of books we never read any more but couldn't bear to get rid of.

The cottage is surrounded by really very, very pretty gardens, and I suck in a quick breath as we approach, bumping down the driveway that becomes less of a road and more of a track as you go. In winter, it fills up with muddy water, and in summers like this one, it becomes so rutted it feels like you're driving over speed bumps.

I had no idea how I was going to react when I finally came back here, back to this place where I spent so many years. Happy years, on the whole, barring the usual dollop of teen-aged angst. Years filled with my small, cosy life; with my delightfully eccentric mother and my little sister and tiny local school, and my village friends. I'd even brought Gareth here, all those years ago, in another lifetime.

Now I'm here, I feel like I am having some kind of out-of-body experience, seeing it all again through alien eyes. I'd expected tears, or that familiar raw, panicky sensation I've been living with for days now, like acid burning away at my insides, but I don't feel that way. I feel like I've come . . . home.

I park the car up, and look around. Some things are the same. The grave-markers for Patch, and the goldfish, and the pets that died before them, at the end of the garden. The jasmine, growing wild on its trellis, and the honeysuckle in glorious shades of pink and white and yellow.

The garden gnome collection has grown even bigger, which makes me smile. She did always love her garden gnomes, my mum; insisted she used to be one in a previous life – 'I was the glamorous garden gnome, darling, wearing diamond earrings and a mink coat.'

Some things, though, are different. I see the barrels she'd told me about, rescued from a nearby farm, and planted with bright-blue trailing lobelia. I see a new bird table, complete with nuts and a little bath, now completely dry in the midday sun. I see a really very lovely carved pinewood bench, and a small matching table, where I can perfectly easily imagine my mother – perhaps with Lewis – enjoying a glass of wine as they gaze out over the hills on a day just like this one.

And, tucked away by the side of the cottage, I see a small black Audi A1. I don't need a million guesses to figure out who it belongs to.

'Damn,' I say, slapping the steering wheel with my hand so hard I accidentally honk the horn and scare up a small flurry of starlings. 'She's already here. I should've known she'd turn up early.'

'To be fair, Mum,' says Joe, grinning at me, 'she's not early. We're late. To be fair.'

'Will you please stop saying the word "fair", Joe?' I reply. 'If life was fair, do you think someone as lovely as Adele would ever have had her heart broken?'

'I think,' he says, winding the car windows back up so wasps don't get in, 'that Adele probably consoles herself by counting her millions, polishing her Grammies and kissing both her baby and her Oscar goodnight, don't you?'

Darn him and his logic. He has a point.

'So,' he adds, looking at me expectantly. 'Shall we get out of the car? I mean, we've come a long way to just stay in it.'

I nod, but know I don't want to. While I'm in the car, I'm still on my own territory. While I'm in the car, I can do ugly crying and nobody will see. While I'm in the car, I don't have to walk into that cottage, which will destroy me. And while I'm in the car, I won't have to deal with Poppy, who is now striding towards us, looking annoyed.

She's perfectly turned out in posh skinny jeans and a fitted blouse, wearing high-heel wedges that I could never drive in, and has a black leather jacket slung over her shoulder. She has her phone in her hand, and is doing her best to keep a murderous look on her face.

The only thing that's spoiling it is her eyes. They're red, and raw, and her mascara is clumping in jagged spikes.

My little sister has been crying, and a part of my heart that I didn't even know still existed begins to bleed for her.

Chapter 23

Poppy

When she finally does park up, Rose doesn't seem to want to get out of the car. Joe is at her side, so tall his head is almost scraping the roof of the battered old Fiesta, and he is looking at me through the window with a great deal of curiosity.

It's only natural, I know – I don't even have a clue what she's told him about us. She's probably fobbed him off with one of those 'it's complicated' comments that grown-ups use on teenagers when they're too embarrassed to talk about something.

The way Mum always did with us when we were young and asked about our dad; before we were mature enough to realise the subject stressed her out so much that we gave up and left it alone. Our mum rarely got stressed – at least on the surface – and it was too painful to see her flustered.

She's switched off the engine and Adele isn't singing any more, so I decide to approach them. Apart from anything else, I am desperate for a wee, and she has the bloody cottage keys – I still can't figure out why Lewis gave them to her and not me. I suspect he was just being bitchy – I recognise the signs. I practically invented them.

The doors to the car finally open, and Joe climbs out, immediately stretching his legs and arms and jumping up and down on the spot. God, he's so tall. I mean, I know he's 16 – and Mum has showed me photos of him over the years – but knowing it and seeing it are two different things. Whatever has happened between me and Rose, I hope I at least get a chance to get to know my nephew. Even just a little bit.

As soon as he was born, I started saving for him, salting away a small chunk each month into an account imaginatively called Joe le Nephew. I had no idea if I would ever get to meet him, and it was the only way I could think of to try and show that I'd always been thinking of him. It's been one of the greatest sadnesses of my life, not being involved in his.

Now, he's here. In the gangly, man-child flesh, and I feel a sudden rush of happiness as I watch him squinting through his fringe.

I'm not quite sure what to do with all my feelings right now; they're tumbling over me like a waterfall – grief and pain at losing Mum; relief and fear at having Rose back in my life; sheer affection for Joe.

Affection doesn't have much of a place in my emotional repertoire, and I'm not sure how I'll fit it in – or even if I'll be allowed to. That, as ever, will be down to my sister, who has certainly made it clear enough over the years that I'm not welcome in her life.

Rose follows him out of the car, and she looks terrible. I

was shocked at her appearance at the funeral, and it is still shocking now.

The Rose I remember was curvy and pretty and had this lovely, wild, curly hair. She was confident and laughed a lot and just had that certain something about her that people automatically liked.

This Rose . . . well, this Rose is almost unrecognisable. Mum had stopped showing me pictures of Rose a while back, after that time we were having afternoon tea in Claridge's, and I burst into tears. I don't know who was more embarrassed, me or the poor waiter, who was hovering in the background not knowing whether we wanted our cucumber sandwiches or not.

She's gained weight, quite a lot of it, and her hair is a mass of grey-streaked frizz, tendrils clinging to the sweat on her forehead and neck. She's still extremely pretty, in a pre-diet Dawn French kind of way, and her eyes have retained their show-stopping glory, but right now her face looks bloated and puffy, not helped by the fact that it's bright red from the heat.

She's trying to arrange her expression into something presentable, but I know her too well, even after all these years, not to see the pain and the anxiety creeping through.

She looks old, and tired, and as if she hasn't laughed in years. It's painful to be presented with the real-life evidence of exactly how much of a train wreck she seems to have become.

I know that at least some of that is down to me. I've always known this, and I spent a long time trying to get her to forgive me – years of my life were consumed by it, until I simply couldn't be both people at once any more. I couldn't be me, and move on with my own life, as well as being the grovelling sister who would do absolutely anything to make things up to her sainted sibling.

I gulp, and hope she doesn't hear me. If I crack, she'll crack, and poor Joe will be left with two hysterical middle-aged women to mop up from the gravel.

'Nice of you to join us,' I say, more sharply than I intended, cringing inside when I see her flinch. Joe gives me a look that says he's not happy, and I realise I am not making a brilliant impression on my long-lost nephew.

'The traffic was bad,' replies Rose, finding enough steel to give me a little glare. 'Tough tittie.'

That almost makes me laugh, the way she says it. 'Tough tittie' – just like she used to when we were kids, and we had a fight about something. I roll my eyes – just like I used to as well – and give Joe a small smile. I'm not evil, or unfeeling, or cruel – I'm just well practised at faking it – and I know I've started this off exactly the way I didn't want to.

'I'm dying for the loo,' I say, bouncing around on my wedge heels as if to demonstrate. 'Could we go inside, do you think?'

She nods, and fishes the keys out of her bag. It takes an age, and I try very hard not to look as annoyed as I feel. It's not her fault I need a wee. It's not her fault our mum is dead. It is, however, her fault that her handbag is the size of a small African republic and just as crowded.

'How are you, Joe?' I ask, as I follow Rose to the front door. He's taller than me, even in my heels, and is at that painfully lean stage where he is only growing in the one direction.

'I'm okay, thanks,' he replies, super-polite, looking at me over his shoulder. 'And she's right. The traffic really was bad.'

I'm being told off, I understand. Gently, but definitely. Good for him.

'I'm sure. There's always a bottleneck near Ludlow. We'll all feel a bit better when we're out of the heat.'

He nods, and we both stand around awkwardly while Rose struggles with the keys. Finally, the old wooden door swings open, and we all walk in.

I see Rose pause in the hallway, and understand why immediately. It's the smell. The smell of lavender and fading fresh flowers and the ghost of puddings past. The smell of our mother, and the life she built for us, and the life she was forced to live without us.

The smell of childhood, and home.

It's the first thing that hits me, and I know from the look on her face that it is the same for Rose. At once so comforting and so painful – we are coming home, but she isn't here. The person who made it a home – who lined the drawers with lavender and picked the flowers and baked the cakes – is gone, and has left behind this vivid sensory echo.

I've never believed in ghosts, or anything even remotely spiritual, but the way that smell makes me feel is exactly the same as if Mum had wafted down from the ceiling, all made of cobwebs.

I feel suddenly woozy, and lean against the wall.

'Going to the loo, I'll be back in a minute,' I say, fleeing up the stairs, practically crawling up them like an animal on all fours, desperate to escape.

Of course, the bathroom is even worse. I shut the door behind me, locking it, leaning back against it and trying to steady my breathing. I look around, and see all the tiny things that make up a room like this: her shampoo, her shower gel, her make-up bag.

I sniff it, inhaling the familiar scents of Chanel and Lancôme and Max Factor, my nostrils flaring as I am transported to a different time: us, as girls, watching my mother put her make-up on, getting ready for a night out or an audition. The skilful way she blended and coloured, the almost magical transformation, the running commentary explaining what she was doing. The way she always used to give each of us a final pat on the end of our noses with her powder puff once she was done.

I see her Pears soap on the soap dish, dry and cracked now, and feel bad for it. As though it is a person, and feels abandoned, untouched by my mother's hand. I see the new Egyptian cotton towels I bought her neatly stacked on the shelves, along with a dozen expensive toiletry sets I've given her over the years – all unopened, still pristine in their boxes. I should have known, really – despite her proclamations of delight at each gift, she remained loyal to certain brands for the whole of her life.

The same soap. The same make-up. The same perfume. Maybe that's why the smell of this place is still so powerful, so evocative – it's like a time capsule for the nose.

I use the loo, and splash my face with cold water. I need to get a grip. I want to sit in here forever, sniffing the used towel hanging on the back of the door, touching her belongings, holding the things that she once held, pretending that none of this is happening. But I can't. I have to go downstairs, and face Rose, and deal with whatever it is our mother has planned for us. I owe it to both of them.

I open the bathroom door, and see that Joe is in his mum's old childhood bedroom. I don't go in there – I'm not quite ready for that yet – but I pause on the landing and give him a little wave.

He waves back, and gives me a sweet smile.

'Mum sent me up here to have a "*rest*",' he says, grinning. 'But I think she actually just wanted to get rid of me for a bit, just in case you two have a cat-fight or something.'

'We won't, I promise,' I reply, sensing his tension beneath the smile and the banter. 'That's not what we're here for. Anyway, you'll have fun nosing round in there. You can try and imagine what your mum was like at your age.'

'Maybe,' he answers, frowning in confusion, 'although I'm still not sure I can take her seriously ever again now I've seen this Boyzone poster on her wall.'

'That was a joke,' I reply, craning my head around the corner to see that yes, for some reason it is still there.

'She absolutely hated Boyzone, so while she was away at college, I covered her walls with pictures of them just to freak her out. All the walls, the entire ceiling, the door – everything. It was one hundred per cent Boyzoned up, took me ages. She

143

ripped most of them down, obviously, but left that one up for a laugh. Don't worry, your mum's not a secret Ronan Keating groupie or anything.'

'Oh,' he answers, possibly looking even more confused. I suppose it's a little too early for him to be able to accept that once, a long time ago, his mother and I were actual, proper, real-life sisters – who wound each other up and played tricks on each other and spent a lot of time laughing. Bearing in mind he only met me for the first time a few days ago, anyway.

'You all right?' I ask, reminding myself that he is just a kid – albeit a huge one – and that he's just lost his grandmother. 'Is this all freaking you out a bit? Being here in Andrea's house?'

'Yeah,' he says, honestly. 'It kind of is. I mean, I've never been here before, for some reason – and neither of them ever talked to me about why, or what happened. And I know you're not going to either, don't worry – but it is weird. And sad. It smells like Granny, doesn't it? Like her perfume, and . . . well, *her?*'

I nod, and do a spot of rapid blinking to get rid of any approaching tears. 'It does. And yes, it's sad. Look, I'd better go downstairs for now – is that okay? Hopefully we'll get more time to chat later.'

'I'd like that,' he says, 'and I think I'll probably have a bit of a rest now anyway, like Mum said.'

He collapses back on to the bed, his Converse-clad feet hanging off the end, and closes his eyes. He looks younger when he does that, and almost unbearably sweet.

I take a final look at that bedroom. Rose's room, the one

I used to hang round in when she was gone, touching her things and lying on her pillows and wishing she was there. Wishing she'd never met bloody Gareth, and wondering if there was a way I could secretly arrange for him to die in a tragic exploding calculator accident and get away with it. Wishing that things would go back to normal.

Wishing everything was different.

I look Ronan in the face, and stick out my tongue. Screw you, Ronan, I think. Screw all of this – especially the past.

Chapter 24

Poppy: September 1999,
Lime Street Station, Liverpool

Rose has forgotten I'm coming this weekend. It's the only reason I can come up with to explain the fact that I'm sitting alone on my backpack at the train station, where I've been for the last hour.

It's just after 7 p.m., and the place is packed. A few lonely drunks are staggering around asking for change, and one man is playing a rousing rendition of 'Let It Be' on a guitar made of cardboard with drawn-on strings.

She was supposed to meet me here just after six, but she never showed. Since then I've been drinking expensive coffee, people-watching, and listening to muffled announcements about platform alterations and the delayed 18.43 service to London Euston.

I've texted Rose so many times I barely have thumbs left, and so far three separate, disgustingly cheerful, middle-aged Scouse men have told me to 'cheer up, girl, it might never happen.'

I give up, and head to the nearest pub. I've been looking

forward to this weekend for ages. Ever since that trip to Dublin, barely a sentence has come out of Rose's mouth that doesn't contain the word 'Gareth', and I'd planned my visit to coincide with him being away.

It wasn't easy, as they now live together. He's been down to the cottage to meet Mum, and they've even adopted a cat from the local rescue centre. They've been on mini-breaks and been to Ikea and been to dinner with his parents. Bleeeugh. I'm sick of hearing about him.

This weekend, he's away at some kind of poncey team-building event in the Lake District. I've got no idea what that means – presumably learning to make better financial decisions about other people's money by bungee jumping off Helvellyn or something. I don't really care. I just care that he's gone, and that I might get my sister back for a few days.

Mum's been all philosophical about it, obviously. When I asked her what she thought about him, she'd just shrugged and said: 'What I think doesn't matter – he's not my boyfriend, is he? Or yours. He seems to make Rosehip happy, and that's all that counts.'

She's probably right, but I can't shake the feeling that there's something . . . *off* about Gareth. Which I know covers a multitude of sins, but I suspect he's committed them all.

I cross the road, dodging black cabs and buskers, and slam the door to the pub open so hard it bangs against the plasterwork. It's an old place, near a theatre, dimly lit and decorated with old programmes and portraits of the stars who have played there. It's also empty enough for me to be able to sit, but full enough for me to be left alone.

I stand at the bar, waiting to get served, and ponder it all. It's not Rose being in love that's bothering me. Or even the fact that I don't especially like Gareth. It's the way she's somehow becoming less and less like Rose as the months go by.

She doesn't seem to ever mention her old friends any more – the university buddies who used to visit for raucous nights out on the town. And she seems to have stopped socialising with the people from the lab where she works, even though she used to adore them in all their geeky wonder. She's given up on the tutoring work she was doing, and seems noncommittal about the PhD idea, and hasn't even been going to the homeless shelter where she used to volunteer.

Running a soup kitchen for people who live out of cardboard boxes was never my idea of a good time, but Rose loved it. And now, she 'doesn't have the time' – not now she has Gareth, and the Cat, and is busy being one half of a couple.

I've never had a serious relationship – just a lot of silly ones – but it just feels wrong that being one half of a couple means that you have to chop off one half of yourself.

I take my Foster's back to a table, and get out a copy of *Harry Potter and the Prisoner of Azkaban* to put anyone off trying to talk to me. I probably look as welcoming as Severus Snape, and set about doing some serious drinking.

I'm on my third pint by the time my phone beeps with a text from Rose: *Where R U?*

Feeling a bit angry and a lot relieved, I tell her, and she replies saying she'll be there in two minutes. I fold the corner of the book over, and concentrate on the relief. So, she's late – it's no big deal. What's a few hours between sisters?

There might have been a traffic jam on her bus route, or an emergency plant-cell situation to sort out, or she might have fallen asleep on the sofa and woken up in a panic. She's coming. That's all that matters.

Every time the door opens, I look up expectantly, grin ready – until, finally, it is her, a whirlwind of crazy curls and flustered apologies. It's her, and then it's Gareth, right on her tail.

I stare at him, open-mouthed, not quite believing what I'm seeing. He's handsome enough, so I can see why Rose fancies him. Tall, broad, dark hair, blue eyes, perfect clothes. But no matter how hot he looks, he might as well have cloven hoofs and horns.

'I thought you were away?' I say.

'I got out of it,' he replies, giving me a wink and sitting down on the stool opposite. 'Threw a sicky, in fact – didn't want to miss the chance of spending some quality time with the famous Poppy.'

'You really shouldn't have,' I reply, gripping my pint glass so hard my knuckles go white. He laughs, like I'm joking, but I mean every word.

'Isn't it brilliant, Pops?' says Rose, still hovering above us. 'Gareth says he can get us into this new club that's just opened, and you can meet the cat, and you two can get to know each other better. My two favourite people in the world. Do you want another drink?'

I notice, as Rose speaks, that her hair is even wilder than usual. That she is blushing. That the buttons on her shirt are fastened up wrong. I deduce from this that the reason my sister was late – the reason I was left fending off drunks and feeling like such a loser at Lime Street Station – is because she was too busy shagging. For. Fuck's. Sake.

'Yeah,' I reply, biting back the sniping words that I actually want to use. 'In fact, get me two. I think I'm on a bit of a roll tonight.'

Chapter 25

Poppy: The Present Day

I leave Joe to his nap, and I walk down the stairs – still rickety, still made of old floorboards that seem to wheeze beneath your feet – and into the living room. The ceiling is low and criss-crossed with dark wooden beams, and Joe will undoubtedly spend his whole time here having to duck, or rubbing the bumps on his head.

One of the walls, which used to be covered in family photos, is now strangely bare, the outlines of old frames and the vivid patches of colour where they used to be hanging there like ghostly reminders.

I find Rose staring at the flat-screen telly, even though it's not on. She is lugging two boxes down from the table, and has tied her hair up into a huge ponytail. I recognise the look on her face – it is the one that means business.

'There's a lot to do,' she says, not even looking at me. 'We'd better get started.'

She sounds bossy, and a bit rude, and despite the fact that I understand how hard this is for her, for both of us, it still makes me bristle. It's the tone she sometimes used when we were kids, and she was trying to get me to revise when I wanted to go out; or when Mum had left us chores to do while she was working, and I made excuses not to do them.

I nod, and deliberately take an absolute age getting the papers Lewis gave me out of my bag. I take even longer unfolding them, and know I am being ridiculous – but, somehow, I can't help myself.

The boxes are sitting at her feet, and looking at them makes me smile, no matter how sad I feel. They're big, old-fashioned wooden crates, one decorated with beautifully painted poppies, one with roses. The flowers are all red and white against a black background, twining green leaves and draping petals and curling stems blending in with each other to create a floral meltdown.

'I remember those . . .' I say, reaching out to touch the wooden sides. 'Our old Special Things Boxes.'

Mum had given us one each when we were little, after spending hours painting them. She told us they were for us to keep precious items in, mementos for the future. I suppose she had in mind school prizes and cherished artworks and baby clothes, but we were too immature to understand that, and instead used them as toy boxes. They'd been stashed in the Hideous Extension, crammed with old Barbie dolls and dried-up Play-Doh and Monopoly with all the hotels missing.

Lost to us, as we got on with our adult lives, but clearly not forgotten. It's only now, as I stare at them both, that I realise how much time and effort she'd put into the painting. How pretty they are. How much love she'd put into them. And how much we'd taken it all for granted.

'Yep,' says Rose, her tone still brisk. 'So do I. Shall we?'

'Okay,' I say, looking at the index. 'It says here that we start with "A" – fair enough – and that A is a letter, which we'll find in the Rose box. Let's get on with it, shall we?'

Chapter 26

Andrea: A is for Ashes

My darlings,

I hope you are both doing as well as you can under the circumstances. I also hope the funeral went swimmingly, and that everyone enjoyed getting drunk in my honour. I know the people in the village must seem like cartoon characters to you girls these days, but I've lived among them for so long, they've become good friends. The least I owed them was a decent booze-up.

If you're reading this, then I have to presume that you are together, in the cottage. That is a very good start, my loves – thank you for at least coming this far. I hope it's not all too traumatic for you both – this place is practically an Aladdin's cave of family history, and I know that might feel overwhelming.

All I can advise is some yoga breathing and possibly a stiff gin. You'll find that in the usual place, assuming I haven't knocked it all back by the time I take my leave. That's always possible; you know I was always a borderline lush!

This is the very beginning of our little project, and I thought I'd start it with a letter. I'm doing that because at the moment, the pain is manageable, and I'm still at home. I'm writing this in my armchair, using that old *Atlas of the World* we have on the bookshelves to lean on. I'm planning on finishing this letter, then spending some quality time with the Beeb. There's a new Dickens coming on that looks like an absolute dream.

So, I thought I'd start with the obvious – A is for Ashes. I believe it usually takes a little while for an entire human being to be burnt to a crisp, but Lewis has promised to get it expedited. He actually does use words like that – 'expedited' – he's such a love! He's going to arrange for my corporeal remains to be delivered gift-wrapped to you as soon as possible – a bit like Amazon Prime, darlings, but without that frightfully handsome Polish delivery man who pops in to see me every now and then.

Check with Lewis, but he thinks about a week in total – so feel free to stay at the cottage, or if that's simply too much right now, take yourselves off home until I'm ready for my big scene.

Just so you know, I decided on cremation for a few reasons. My own parents were both buried, and I always feel guilty about not visiting their grave. It's a long way away, and I never found the whole cemetery chic thing very appealing. There's something very maudlin about standing by a grave, isn't there? Imagining your loved one's flesh rotting and the bones crawling with worms?

Or maybe that's just me, who knows? I was never the same after I did that stint with Hammer.

Anyway, I didn't want that for you. I'd rather this unpleasant aspect of the whole affair be over with, and for you two to be able to say goodbye once and for all. It's just ash, it's not actually me – I will live forever, in a way, because you two will always carry me in your memories. And, by the time I've finished all of this, on memory sticks as well.

Now, with regard to the whole ashes-to-ashes thing, I do of course have a plan.

I'd like you to take me up to Stapeley Hill – you remember, near the Mitchell's Fold stone circle? We used to go there a lot, when we still had Patch. It was the one where the big stone was supposed to be a witch who drained a magic cow of all its magic milk. In which case, of course, it served her right – we should all be more kind to magic cows; you never know when you might need one!

I hope you remember it, and remember it fondly. I've not been up there with you two since you were about 14 and 12, I don't think. Life seemed complicated then, but in comparison to what followed, it was relatively simple, really. A big bottle of water, some ham sandwiches, a few Granny Smiths, and we were all happy. Though I did once take a hip flask with me for a few sneaky fortifiers.

Anyway, that's where I'd like my ashes to be scattered – up on that hill. The views there are wonderful, you can see for miles, and the modern world hardly seems to intrude at all. Take me there – hopefully on a blissfully sunny summer's day – and scatter me to the four winds.

I'd like you to take a picnic – you can use the old wicker basket, it's in the Hideous Extension somewhere – and, more importantly, take your time. Talk to each other. Remember the good times, my angels – because there were so many of them. It's been one of my greatest sadnesses that more recent events have completely over-shadowed the past, and I'd like you to try and focus on how much fun we had together, us three, all those years ago.

I feel a little mean about leaving Lewis out of this one – he has been my Stapeley Hill walking partner in the last few years, after all, along with his old spaniel Betty (who, I warn you, if you ever meet her, is extremely flatulent). So, if it's not too totally disgusting, maybe you could save a bit of my magic fairy dust for him? Scoop a few spoonfuls into an old champagne bottle or some-thing, perhaps? But only if you can face it. He'll un-derstand if not. He's good like that.

And, just to mention, I'd be really happy if you could take a look at B on the same day – all will become clear (don't skip ahead, that's cheating – and Poppy, I'm prob-ably talking to you here, you always were so impatient!). After A is done and dusted – so to speak – you'll need to spend a night in the cottage, so don't be sneaking off to a hotel or anything.

Anyway, I'd better sign off for now. My fingers are a

little tired, and I'm going to need all my energy if I'm going to properly savour this new show. I shall enjoy myself quietly bitching about the quality of the acting, even if it's tremendous – small pleasures.

I am sending you, as ever, all of my heart – and remember, girls: I loved you, and I know you loved me. Everything will be fine. You just have to trust your old ma one last time,

Mum xxx

Chapter 27

Rose

It is boiling hot, and my thighs are chafing. I very unwisely decided on a sundress today, which undoubtedly means I will have lobster-red shoulders by the end of our walk. But that's okay – at least they'll match my face.

I'm feeling down, for so many reasons, and also feel bad because Mum wanted us to remember the good times. Looking around as we traipse up the hill, I can remember them – but those memories are distant, intangible, like faraway scenes from somebody else's life.

We came in Poppy's car, which made sense as mine is on its last legs, and parked down the lane, after a journey spent in stony silence. So far, I feel like we're technically doing what Mum asked – but neither of us seems to have the will to storm the barricades and embrace it in spirit as well. Two days apart, while Lewis sorted out the cremation situation, have only served to make us both even more entrenched on our respective sides of the fence.

Still. We're here, and we're doing it, and perhaps for now, that's all that matters.

Poppy has the picnic basket, which she has filled, and I have the cardboard box, hanging over my shoulder in one of those Bags 4 Life, which is ironic when you consider its current contents.

Joe has been dispatched to London to see his dad and, as ever, I became a morose lump the minute his train pulled away from the platform, waving him off with a fake smile on my face. I try not to let him see how much I will miss him, but he's not daft, and he always texts me the minute he's left.

He'll be gone for three weeks, as usual in the summer, and I hope he enjoys it. It's probably for the best, all things considered – it will give me and Poppy time to get through this, without dragging him through the mire of all our emotional baggage. He'll enjoy himself at his dad's, and is excited about spending time with his range of half-siblings. It's a part of his life I'll never be involved in, and it's good for him to have time away. From me, from our house, from everything that's playing out around him.

Now, we're here, and Poppy is galloping ahead on her stupidly long legs, showing off her superior cardio-vascular fitness levels, looking like a dark, skinny streak as she bounds towards the stone circle. I think she looks a bit too thin – a bit too fit – but that could very well just be jealousy speaking.

She comes to a standstill in the middle, and waits for me to catch up. I do so, trying to hide how hard I'm puffing, and we stand together, gazing around. Some of the stones are small and jagged, poking up from the earth like old grey teeth. Others are smooth from the thousands of bottoms that have sat on them, admiring the views over the hills. The biggest – the Witch Stone – is tall and rugged, and I walk over, laying my hands on it and enjoying the texture.

At the moment we're the only people here, although it's a popular route for dog walkers. We're surrounded by beautiful countryside, hills and valleys in dazzling shades of green, colliding with the vivid blue of the sky. I can hear skylarks singing, and the buzzing of small insects, and the distant mooing of cows. It's utterly and completely peaceful, and I can see why the ancient dudes chose exactly this spot to build their stone circle.

I'm not one for hippy-dippy shit, but this place does feel special – even the touch of the stone beneath my fingers has a certain restful energy to it. I wish Joe was here to see it all, and make a pledge to bring him back one day, under happier circumstances.

Poppy joins me, and places both her hands on the Witch Stone. Her long hair is tied up in a ponytail, and it makes her look younger.

Our fingers briefly touch on the stone, and we both jerk away a little, like we've had an electric shock. All it takes is that tiny contact to unleash at least some of the memories I've subconsciously been trying to avoid. They play out in my mind, still unreal, still tethered in some alternate universe that exists only in the past.

'Do you remember coming here?' I ask, leaning my face against the cool surface of the stone. 'And the way Mum always made us both dance round the stones, making up chants? Something about a picnic goddess?'

She smiles, and I realise that I've not seen her smile for . . . well, years. And I realise that I've missed it.

'I do remember. She sang it like a nursery rhyme, prancing around like a loon: "Goddess Good, Goddess Fair, please don't leave our hamper bare . . ."'

As she chants, I can almost hear my mother's voice, trying to sound serious and sacred, us two giggling on her heels, pigtails flying, feet encased in the jelly sandals that were the very height of childhood fashion back then.

'"Bring us an apple,"' I continue, smiling at the thought, '"bring us a pear, bring us a Mars Bar if you dare . . ."'

'Then wasn't there something about cow shit?' asks Poppy, frowning as she tries to dig up the line.

'Kind of,' I reply. 'Although she was far too much of a lady to use words like that. What was it? Something like "Goddess Good, Goddess Pure, shelter us from cow manure . . ."?'

Poppy laughs, and I can't help but join in. I don't really want to – it is far easier to cling to my protective barrier of silence – but I do. The sound echoes around the stones, blending in with the birdsong and the buzzing, as though it belongs there, hovering in the sun-hazed air.

'She really was a bit of a nutter, wasn't she?' asks Poppy, pulling away from the stone and picking up the wicker basket again.

'Yep,' I reply, reluctantly removing my hands from the Witch Stone. 'She really was. Come on. We still have another hill to climb.'

We continue our trek upwards, interrupted by occasional walkers and one especially intrusive beagle that takes an unhealthy interest in Poppy's crotch. We are both quiet again, as though that one tiny step towards each other has worn us out. Scared us, maybe. Looking at Poppy's rigid expression, the way she is concentrating on the path, I can tell that she is tense, bundled up in the same anxiety that I am, wearing it like a suit of armour.

We pick our way through the paths, weaving around the bushes and patches of flowers that dot the heathland, climbing stiles and crossing bridges and going through gates, passing more stone circles, until we eventually reach the top of the hill. The view, as I make my way up to join Poppy, is spectacular, stretching and tumbling out around us, an ancient landscape that seems to be caught in time. I can't even see the electricity pylons that I know must be there.

I would appreciate the view more, but by this time, I am struggling – even with a relatively gentle climb like this one; my body is complaining, my lungs whining and my legs straining. I've been a stranger to exercise for so long, and it is added to a now very long list of things I am unhappy about.

I'm sickened by my own lack of fitness – and I'm not talking about running-a-marathon or doing-a-triathlon fitness, I'm talking about going-for-a-walk fitness. Liverpool is largely flat, and a gentle stroll on the beach near our home isn't exactly challenging – not that I even bother doing that, these days. I tend to just park the car and watch the sunsets from the Ford Fiesta instead of getting out there and enjoying it.

When I was a kid, we would be all over these hills,

scrambling up and down them like mountain goats in patched jeans, running for the joy of it, shouting into the wind, filled with energy. And when Joe was little, I wasn't too bad – you have to get out and about with kids, or you end up wanting to kill them. But these days, as Joe gets himself from A to B, and I drive everywhere, I've sunk into a pit of inactivity. I don't like it – it makes me feel weak, and vulnerable, and as though I'd be the first to die in a zombie attack.

I suppose, perhaps, that I need to change it. I'll never be like Poppy – I was never as limber or as agile, even when we were little – but I could most definitely be a new and improved version of myself. Maybe, by the time I bring Joe back here, I'll be able to actually enjoy it, instead of wheezing like a vandalised steam engine.

Poppy is standing still at the summit, a few feet away and, as I look up at her, I see a strange expression on her face. I'd expected contempt, possibly disgust, but instead, I see . . . sympathy. For some reason, this makes me feel even worse, and I put on as much of a sprint as I can to catch up with her.

By the time I do, she is opening the hamper, making herself busy – deliberately, I suspect, to give me the chance to catch my breath again. Allowing me some dignity as I suck in air. A small kindness that I don't want to be on the receiving end of.

She pulls the achingly familiar black-and-red tartan blanket out, gathers it into her fists, and sniffs it so hard it looks as if she is inhaling it whole. I screw my eyes shut, and try not to cry. I know what she is doing – she is looking for the lost traces of our mother – and it is like a punch to the heart. I fight the urge to run at her, snatch the bobbled fleece from her hands, and do exactly the same.

She throws it out, and stretches it over the shaggy grass, and starts to unpack the picnic. So much for an apple, a pear and a Mars Bar if you dare – there's practically the entire contents of a posh deli here. Slivers of Parma ham, smoked salmon, a chunk of Brie, cherries, nectarines. Granary bread rolls, pastries, a small glass jar of duck paté. Just as I think she's finished, she produces a box of Ritz crackers and a plastic tub of cocktail sausages. My childhood favourites.

'I didn't know if you still liked these . . .' she says, looking vaguely embarrassed. As though remembering has somehow rendered her less impressive.

'Of course I do,' I reply, lowering myself to the ground. 'You don't get a figure like this without comfort food, Poppy. And I guess I've needed a lot of comfort over the years.'

She looks up at me sharply, and actually bites her lip so hard it bleeds. Like she's snatching back sharp words. Like what I've just said has been perceived as a dig, which I suppose, from her point of view, it could have been. It wasn't a dig – not at her, at least – but I don't have the energy to explain the complexities of my current self-loathing, and instead distract us both by tearing open the box.

We sit, and we eat – some more than others – and we sip the chilled bottles of Buck's Fizz that she's brought with her.

Afterwards, full and very slightly tipsy, I lie back in the sunlight, letting it warm my face, screwing my eyes shut against the glare. I try to pretend that I am alone here, or at least with someone I want to be with, like Joe or my mum, and let my mind wander. Poppy stays sitting, her knees drawn up sharply to her stomach, clasped into the embrace of her own arms. She's wound so tight she could explode at any moment.

'We came up here with Patch, didn't we, on the day he died?' she asks, staring off into the distance.

'Yeah, I think so,' I reply, swatting away a fly and hoping no wasps come and join the party. 'She said it was his last hurrah, and we carried him the last bit. Poor thing was knackered.'

'Then we had one of Mum's special garden funerals, didn't we?'

I nod, and wonder why she's picking on this particular memory. Mum had asked us to remember the good times, and we're here talking about a dead dog. Maybe that's all she can come up with – and I suppose, in a way, it is part of the good times. Mum's garden funerals were always quite the occasion, and Patch's was no exception.

'She read that poem she'd written – an "Ode to Terriers", or something like that,' I say. 'And played "Jumpin' Jack Flash" by the Rolling Stones so loud that all the magpies squawked out of the trees and flew away.'

'But instead of singing "Jumpin' Jack Flash" in the chorus, we all sang "Jumpin' Jack Russell" . . . yeah. Well. As we've already established, she was a bit of a nutter . . . shall we do it, then?'

'Do what?' I ask. I'm feeling so physically wrung out that I am actually starting to relax a little – the walk, and the sunshine, and the food, and the lack of oxygen, have squeezed at least some of the tension out of me. For a tiny second, I had simply been feeling warm and content, lying in the sunshine, losing myself in the moment.

'The ashes thing,' Poppy replies, turning to give me a look that makes me feel about as useful as pickled walnut. As though I've forgotten why we're here, because I'm such a knob, and she's had to remind me. Like she's had to pack the picnic, and drive the car, and sort out the whole shebang. It is a look that immediately drains me of all contentment, and any fleeting sense of relaxation, and puts all my nerve endings back on high alert.

I would quite like to punch her in her perfectly skinny face, but that would not be in the spirit of the A–Z of Everything, I remind myself. I can't fail on A, I just can't. I need to at least hold out until M for Murder if I want to kill her.

I climb to my feet – this takes a while – and nod. I get the box out of the Bag 4 Life, and try not to engage with any potential ickiness. This, as my mother said in that letter, is not her – this is simply what is left of her body. It's not the most important thing about her, and I must not allow myself to collapse at this stage.

I can't stop the tears from filling my eyes, though, as I open the horrible thing up. I look at my sister, and see that she is crying too. She nods once, acknowledging what is happening, not even trying to hide her tears, and takes the box from my now trembling hands.

This is what we came here to do, at least in part – and yet

I still don't feel ready. I don't feel ready to give her up, throw her away, cast her aside. To admit that she is gone.

'Come on,' says Poppy, firmly. 'We can do this. It's what she wanted. We can't take her home and keep her in an urn on the mantelpiece – it's not what she asked for. We're here, and it's a beautiful day, and there will never be a good time to do this, so we might as well get it over with. We'll do this, and we'll save some for Lewis, and then we'll move on to "B".'

'What is "B"?' I ask, not really caring right now but wanting to put off the inevitable. 'Have you looked?'

'It's a recipe, bizarrely. And a card. We'll read it properly tonight. Are you ready?'

She lunges towards me, and I have a momentary panic – maybe she wants to punch me in the face, too – until I realise that she was just swatting away a wasp. She always was good at that; a fearless warrior in my ongoing battle with the stingers.

'No,' I reply, honestly. 'But I don't think I'll ever be ready. So let's just do it.'

Poppy nods, opens the folds of the box, and starts to whirl around, energetically throwing the ashes in all directions, whooshing them into the sky as she spins. I'm glad there's only a gentle breeze, and it whirls away in small clouds, taking what feels like forever. It's actually quite shocking how much there is in there, for such a tiny woman.

'"Goddess Good and Goddess Fair",' chants Poppy, as she whirls, '"we cast our mother to your care . . . Goddess Good and Goddess Fit, keep her out of that cow shit . . ."'

Ah, Poppy. She always did have a way with words. A way of expressing herself that wasn't quite like anybody else's.

Which is one of the things that has always confused me about what eventually happened. Communication was her thing. She was brilliant at it. And yet, somehow, in the run-up to the New Year that effectively ended our relationship, she lost the ability to talk.

Instead, her actions did all the talking for her – and nobody liked what they had to say.

Chapter 28

Rose: New Year at the Disco 2000, the Lake District

I am, to put it mildly, a bit drunk. But at least I'm not the only one – the whole house is full of dancing queens and disco divas and snogging couples.

It's been a brilliant party, completely brilliant. Gareth rented this big old house in the hills above Lake Windermere, totally secluded so we could all see the new millennium in with style.

The music has been awesome all night, and we celebrated the New Year with the perfect song – 'Disco 2000' by Pulp.

It's been so nice to catch up with my old friends – some of whom, I realised as they started to arrive, I've not seen for way too long. Plus Poppy, of course. Such a relief that she agreed to come. I've not seen much of her this year, and there is a tiny part of my brain that feels bad about that. I was starting to wonder if I'd become That Girl – you know, the one who dumps everyone else once they've met a cool boy?

Whenever that part of my brain starts to nag at me, I tell it off. I tell it I've made every effort to bring her and Gareth closer, to merge the two halves of my life. Okay, so there was that time I forgot her birthday . . . that was bad, no getting away from it. But that was almost a year ago now, and so much has happened since then.

A new flat. A new cat. A new everything, really. Mainly a new me – because I've never, ever felt like this before. I'm in love, completely in love, and sometimes it's hard to see beyond that. It's like the lake down there, beyond the terrace where I am sitting to cool off, breathing in chilly night air and taking in the scenery. It dominates every part of the surrounding landscape; it's everywhere you look.

It's kind of the same with Gareth. He's my Lake Windermere. He dominates everything – but in a less creepy way than it sounds. In a harmonious way, like the lake. Especially now Poppy is here, and everything feels better.

The lake – the real one, not Gareth – is beautiful, and I'm enjoying gazing at it from my perch on the table-scattered terrace. It's dark and mysterious and shining in the moonlight, surrounded by snow-capped hills and silent forests.

Well, silent apart from the booming music pouring out from the house. The DJ has moved on to some banging house tunes, those ones with the singing bits in the middle. I preferred the Britpop section myself – dancing around with Poppy to the Stone Roses, doing actions to 'I Am The Resurrection' and pogoing to that Blur song about the boys who like girls and girls who like boys.

It was the only time in the night, truth be told, that Poppy got up to dance. Because while she has at least come, she seems a bit distracted. Off. Like she's there in body, but not in spirit. It's probably just Poppy being Poppy – feeling a bit artistic and tortured, and not really fitting in at a party full of bankers and scientists.

But partly, I suspect, it's because she actually wanted me to come home for New Year instead. She'd tried to persuade me that a night in the Farmer's really would be more fun than this. As if!

Anyway, even if I had been tempted, Gareth had already booked this place. He'd sorted the DJ, arranged the catering, ordered the drinks. I hadn't had to lift a finger – he'd taken complete control, and organised it all. He'd even tried to organise the guest list, but I stepped in at that stage – even I couldn't face a night with just the bankers.

He hadn't included my friends on the initial list, but, well, that was fair enough – he didn't know most of them. And he hadn't objected at all when I added a few in. He'd even suggested we invite Mum, but Andrea had wisely said no.

'Thank you so much, darling,' she'd said on the phone, 'but I must make my apologies on that one. I have a hot date with a jug of gin and a Jilly Cooper. Such a shame that Rupert Campbell-Black doesn't drink in the Farmer's, don't you think?'

It is almost 3 a.m. now, and the party is still going strong – but in that stripped-down-to-the-hardcore way that the best parties have. There are fewer people on the dance floor, but they're giving it their all, and the kitchen is packed with people chatting and flirting and stubbing out cigarette butts in half-drunk glasses of wine.

It's that time of the party where people will start to couple up, or puke up, or come up on the drugs that they might just possibly have consumed.

That doesn't include me – I'm not beyond the occasional toke on a joint, but the rest simply isn't my scene. I stick to booze, because I know exactly where I am with that. The others, though?

Well, I'd have to be blind not to realise that at least a few recreational pharmaceuticals are floating around in there. Scientists and bankers are bonding over little white pills and small foil wrappers. I suspect, though I'm not sure, that Gareth has even been responsible for providing some of it – seeing it as part of his party host duties.

Still, there's no harm, I suppose. Everyone is a consenting adult; it's not like anybody is being corrupted. Even my little sister is a grown-up these days, although she doesn't always act like one.

I'm starting to wonder where Poppy is. After the dancing, she disappeared off to get more booze, and the last time I saw her she was coming out of the kitchen with a pint glass full of Bailey's and a slice of pizza, looking glassy-eyed and slightly unsteady on her long legs. Like Bambi after a night out on the piss with Thumper.

I decide to go and look for her. I've drunk enough champagne already, and I'm starting to feel cold, and now it's occurred to me, I'm a bit worried about Pops.

Setting aside the fact that she's an alleged grown-up, one who has just in fact bagged a traineeship in marketing with a big publishing company, she seems a bit vulnerable at the moment.

She might have brilliantly ferocious one-liners and appear to be as tough as nails, but she's still my little sister. I should find her, and tell her I love her. It's New Year after all – you're allowed to be sentimental.

I head back inside, and laugh as I see a group of people doing a limbo dance to a remix of 'I Will Survive'. I check the kitchen, and the second living room.

I see plenty of amusing sights – and some slightly disturbing ones, as people are clearly heading towards an amorous state of mind – but no Poppy.

I chat to people as I go, repeatedly being told what a great party this is, and head up the winding, wooden staircase. The house is old, and magnificent, but slightly past its best – the carpets are a little frayed, the oil paintings a little grimy, the chandeliers a little dusty. It's a house that's seen better times, and needs some TLC – which is probably why Gareth was able to persuade the rental company to let it out to a gang of party animal 20-somethings for the New Year.

I walk up the steps carefully, conscious of the fact that I've definitely had too much to drink now, holding on to the unpolished wooden rail as I go.

There are lots of rooms up here – it was built in an era when people had big families and big amounts of servants to look after them – and I start to go through them all, knocking politely before I look inside. Heaven forbid I scald my retinas with anything full frontal.

Some of the rooms are occupied, others are empty apart from rucksacks and suit carriers and abandoned make-up bags, still bearing the signs of people getting ready to party. The master suite I'm sharing with Gareth is filled with our clothes and belongings, scattered over the floor, the bed still unmade. I smile as I see the vase full of roses on the dresser – he'd presented them to me earlier in the day, a cascade of fragrant red and white. Gorgeous.

I stroll down the hallway until I reach the room that Poppy is staying in. She's probably in here, on her own, reading something by Hemingway and underlining sections with red pen. Old habits die hard.

I knock, very gently, not wanting to wake her if she's actually managed to fall asleep, despite the din roaring up from downstairs.

I push the door open, and light from the hallway spills into the darkened room.

It floods from the hallway, into the room, and right on to two bodies. One is female, pushed up against a wall, skirt hiked up to her waist, legs wrapped around a man's body, fingers twined in his hair. The man is pounding away, grunting and moaning, his face clasped into the woman's breasts by eager hands.

My first thought is to apologise and run away, but for some reason I squint my eyes to see better.

As soon as I do, the whole world falls away. The sounds

175

of the party disappear, and the cheers of the guests fade into nothing, and the booze fizzing through my veins turns to ice.

Everything changes in that one moment. Everything turns upside down.

Because the man is Gareth, and the woman is Poppy.

Chapter 29

Andrea: B is for Beef Wellington – and also for Bastards

Darlings,

How did it go today? I do hope it wasn't too windy, and I didn't end up as grit in your eyes – how amusing would that be?

Do you like the card, by the way? It's from that set that Joe bought me for Christmas, Rose, with the pretty pictures of British mammals on them. I especially like this hedgehog. He's rather dashing, don't you think? I shall call him Henry.

Anyway, not so much space on here, and I am about to turn in for the night, so I'll keep it brief. Tonight, my sweets, I'd like you to eat a meal together. I've left you a lovely recipe for Beef Wellington, and my Tinkerbell, Lewis, will have left everything you need in the fridge. I opted for ready-made pastry; I don't suspect either of you is in the mood for kneading right now.

No idea how it'll turn out – Rose, you don't seem to cook much any more, and Poppy, you barely seem to eat

– but give it a go. Cook a splendid meal, and eat it in the Posh Room, and drink some bubbly, and talk.

What I'd like you to talk about, specifically, is Bastards. We've all known them, my loves, even me. I had a torrid affair with my former manager when I was barely out of my teens, only to discover that not only was he married, but he was screwing half his other clients as well! Utter Bastard – but he did get me some of my best roles, so I forgave him.

Some, though, are not as easy to forget. Some leave their mark on everyone around them. Some simply destroy everything good that crosses their path – and they're often the ones with the most handsome face, the wittiest of conversation, the most charming of demeanours. They seem full of life and energy, but they're secretly empty – and they try to fill themselves up by sucking the life out of the people around them. Usually women who've fallen under their spell.

I think we all know who I'm talking about here, and it's time it came out into the open. So eat, drink, and be honest – and remember, girls, that Bastards only have power over us if we let them.

And while I'm at it, scoot forward to C now – it's one line on the ever-efficient index that Lewis will have prepared, and I think it sits magnificently with your dinner.

Bon appetit!

Mum xxx

Chapter 30

Poppy

'Looks like she stole this from a magazine,' says Rose, brandishing the laminated recipe sheet and waving it around like a referee's yellow card. 'It's Gordon Ramsay.'

'Does that mean I'm allowed to swear in the kitchen?' I say, wrestling with the bloody pastry in an attempt to wrap it around the beef. The pastry is winning.

I hate cooking. I always did. I never helped out at home when I was younger, and I was one of those students who survived on crumpets, coffee and fags for three years. These days, my shopping consists of what I can get from the deli counter. Usually I just emerge from Sainsbury's with a bottle of gin and a packet of prawns.

I give up on making the pastry look at all presentable, and slam it into the fridge. It's supposed to chill for half an hour, according to Gordon, but I'm not sure I can be arsed with waiting that long.

Rose has been preparing new potatoes and runner beans to go with it, and we've edged around each other warily in the not-especially-large cottage kitchen, both being careful not to collide or make any bodily contact at all. It's been a tough day, and I have the feeling that we both need a hug – but we're nowhere near the stage where we can offer that to each other. At the moment, we can barely offer each other civilised silence.

We arrived back at the cottage late in the afternoon. Rose had taken the whole ashes ceremony hard, and I could tell she was struggling to keep herself together on the drive back. She was deep in thought, and possibly revisiting things I was deeply ashamed of.

I left her to it – there was nothing I could say that would help, and I had enough pain of my own to deal with. I turned up the air con, switched on the radio, and simply got us home.

It was clear as soon as we arrived that Lewis had been over. The fridge was full of fresh ingredients, neatly lined up. Beef fillet, mushrooms, herbs, butter, oil, ready-roll pastry, three bottles of very nice Bollinger.

He'd done his job well, I have to say. In and out while we were at Stapeley Hill, like a huge, bear-shaped Ninja. The fridge isn't the only sign of his visit – he's also mowed the lawn and restocked the bird table. There are a pair of tiny blue tits out there now, I can see, one bathing in the water and the other pecking at the seed wire.

We've both had a shower, carefully timing it so only one of us had to be upstairs at a time, and we've read Mum's card, and we've started cooking. Neither of us has commented on the contents of the card, other than agreeing that Henry the Hedgehog does indeed look quite dashing, because neither of us wants to have this conversation.

In fact, we don't want to have it so badly, we've taken ages in the kitchen. Partly because we're both pretty ineffectual cooks, it seems – and partly because, as long as we're cooking, we're not in the Posh Room. And if we're not in the Posh Room, then we don't have to talk about Bastards. And if we don't have to talk about Bastards, we can ignore the fact that our dear, departed mother, in her wisdom, wants us to discuss Gareth.

Personally, I'd rather poke myself in the eyes with a very dashing hedgehog than talk about Gareth, and I am sure that Rose feels the same. After we read the card, it was as though we both simply decided to ignore it for the time being – perfectly in tune for once.

It's also very strange simply being back in the cottage together. Mum has had a change-round in the kitchen cabinets, so the pots and pans are in unexpected places, and she has replaced all of her china. I don't know why this surprises me – did I really expect her to have frozen completely in time?

Some of the rooms – my bedroom, and Rose's, plus the Posh Room – are pretty much identical to how we left them. Not in a Miss Haversham way – they've been cleaned – but in terms of layout and contents. Other places, there've been subtle changes. The natural evolution of a space well lived-in: new light fittings here and there; a different shade of paint in the hallway; the flat-screen TV.

It's all very strange, and I need some solitude. I live alone, and being around other people for too long in a domestic environment practically brings me out in a rash. I leave Rose to finish off the cooking, and take myself off to my bedroom for a while, with a nice glass of C; the entry for that was simply 'C is for Champagne – drink it as often as you can, life needs a bit more fizz.'

By the time I come back down, having spent a restless half-hour firing off work emails and flicking through my younger self's book collection, Rose has laid the table in the Posh Room, and dinner is ready.

The Posh Room is probably called a Dining Room in estate-agent speak. To us, though, it was simply always the Posh Room – the place where Mum had some of her most precious objects on display; the place where my old tobacco tin used to live. It's a large room, with the walls painted deep red, low ceilinged and beamed, dominated by a massive old oak table complete with silver candelabra.

I sit, and look at the food on my plate. There is so much, I know I'll never get through it all, even though it smells so good. Rose is showing no such hesitation, and is tucking in with gusto. I know she's down on herself at the moment, because of her weight, but I actually envy her appetite.

Perhaps that's why I decide, just as she spears a butter-coated baby spud, to finally start the conversation our mother has asked us to have.

'So,' I say, after a fortifying sip of C, 'shall we discuss the Bastard in the room?'

Rose immediately chokes on her food, and I wonder for a few moments as she splutters and coughs whether I'm going to have to leap across the table and perform the Heimlich manoeuvre on her. Not that I really know how, other than what I've picked up from watching *Casualty*.

'Ummm . . . do we have to?' she says, once she's finally recovered.

'Well, no, we don't have to. But it's what we're here for. All of this was to set a mood, wasn't it? Not just so we can stuff our faces.'

I feel a flood of guilt wash over me as I see her blush, and lay down her knife and fork. She's taken that personally, and I understand why. The distance between us is like a field full of landmines, and I've just accidentally set off an absolute humdinger. Still, it's too late to take it back, and blustering on about what I did and didn't mean will just make matters worse.

'Right,' she says, gulping down half her glass of C at once. 'Well. What do you want to know?'

'Everything, I suppose. Within months of Disco 2000, you two were married, and not long after you were pregnant. It's always struck me as odd that while what I did merited being sent into the wilderness for the rest of my life, what he did resulted in you agreeing to marry him. I've never quite figured out why he got a second chance, and I didn't.'

I hadn't intended to say any of that, but it just kind of oozed out, my voice much calmer than I am actually feeling. Because it had hurt, so very, very much. I understood her banishing me – if I could have banished myself, I would; I totally deserved it. But her life with him had continued, and that made it all worse.

She chose him over me – a childish view, I know, but one I could never quite shake off. From the moment she met Gareth, in fact, I felt like she chose him over me, which was at least one of the contributory factors to what eventually happened.

Rose is gazing off into the distance, the candlelight flickering over her face and making her beautiful eyes glitter, as she tries to come up with an answer. I suspect she's about to be brutally honest, and I'm not sure I'm ready for it.

'I suppose,' she says eventually, her stubby fingernails tapping away on the tablecloth, 'that I was, like Mum says, under his spell. I can see things a lot more clearly now, but at the time, I couldn't. All I could see was him – this handsome, charming, successful man, who just made me feel . . . lucky. Lucky that he'd chosen me, when he could have had anybody he wanted. Everything about him was just, I don't know, magnetic. His energy, and his style, and the way he talked – like the world was his, and he'd chosen me to share it with him.

'It was the first time I'd ever been in love, and it was like a drug. I couldn't get enough of him. Every minute away from him felt wasted.'

'Is that why you dumped all your friends, and me,' I ask, 'because you thought we were a waste of time?'

It's a cruel question, and I feel a bit like I'm kicking a puppy in the head here, but it's valid. I need to ask it, and I need her to answer it.

'It didn't feel like I was dumping you all at the time,' she replies, quietly. 'It didn't feel like that at all. In fact, there was something about the way he affected me that somehow allowed me to blame everyone else . . . I thought I was trying to fit you into my new life, and you just couldn't accept it.

And I think part of that is true – you were jealous, Poppy, you know you were.

'You were at such a loose end, and the timing couldn't have been worse really. But . . . yes. He painted such a perfect picture of our future, and there only seemed to be space for me and him. He pretended to want to include you, and Mum, and my friends, but he didn't, not really.

'This is another of those things I've only realised since – that it started early, the way he used to try and control everything. He'd buy me clothes that I didn't really like, that weren't me, but he'd tell me how beautiful I looked in them and that made everything all right. He'd arrange nights out with his friends, but never mine. He told me my job in the lab was a bit of a waste of time; that it was beneath me . . . that I could do better. I suppose he told me things that I wanted to hear, so I went along with them.'

She pauses here, and we both drink some more, and I eat one languid runner bean. I feel like screaming at her, truth be told – because it might have taken her years to figure out, but I could see all of this about Gareth from the very beginning. I hated him with a passion – and yes, she's right, I was jealous. But I was also worried that he was eating her up one mouthful at a time. God only knows I had a shitty way of going about it, but I'd wanted to protect her.

'Okay,' I say, when her pause looks likely to stretch into a maudlin silence. 'I get all of that. And there are things I'd like to say here that I won't, because it might result in us both exploding – but after. After . . . the thing that happened. Why didn't you realise then that he was the world's biggest Bastard?'

'The thing that happened?' she echoes, bitterly, pointing her fork at me as though she's considering aiming it at my heart. 'You mean the thing where you had sex with my boy-friend, Poppy?'

If she's trying to hurt me with that, she's on to a loser. I've felt so bad, for so many years, that there is nothing more she can do to me. That one act – that one pathetic, sweaty, dis-gusting, drug-fuelled act – has consumed my entire life.

I have never regretted anything more, and I include breaking my mother's heart in that. I've said I'm sorry a million times; spent months writing her letters and trying to speak to her, begging her forgiveness – and I was always met with a stony silence. It was as though I simply ceased to exist, while they went on to play happy families.

'Yes. That . . . Lest we forget,' I reply. 'I didn't do it alone, you know.'

She slams her fork down, and gravy splatters across the tablecloth. She looks angry and tearful at the same time, and I am sure it is only the thought of Mum hovering around in spirit form that stops her from getting up and walking out.

I can practically see her counting to ten and breathing deeply as she tries to calm herself down. I sit opposite, sipping C, and undoubtedly looking cool as a cucumber even if that's not how I'm feeling. I can't blame her for hating me, for all kinds of reasons.

'I was hurt,' she says eventually, not meeting my eyes. 'Bloody devastated. But when the dust settled, when you'd run off back to Mum with your tail between your legs, he was still there. We still had a flat together. A bloody cat, for goodness' sake. You didn't know this, but he'd also persuaded me to hand in my notice at the lab just before New Year, so I didn't even have a job. My whole life was tied into his – and he grovelled. God, how he grovelled.

'He seemed just as devastated as me – even worse, in fact, because it was all down to him. He told me he was sorry, and how much he loved me, and how he'd made the biggest, most stupid mistake of his life. That he was off his head on drugs, that you made the first move, that he didn't even realise what was going on until it was too late. That he'd do anything to win me back and make it up to me. And then, after weeks of this, he came home with an engagement ring and proposed to me.

'I might not win any Feminist of the Year awards for it, but I wanted to believe him. I wanted to be loved, and adored, and looked after. I wanted to forgive him, and live the life he'd said we could live – so I did. We got married, we had Joe. It seemed to be what he wanted, at the time, but I know now it wasn't. It was like . . . well, like a game to him. He had to win, no matter what the cost – but once he'd got me, he wasn't that sure he wanted the prize.'

Part of me had stopped listening as soon as she said that one line: 'you made the first move'. That was so far removed from the truth that my blood was boiling, and I was furious – with him for saying it, and with her for never, ever listening to my side of what was admittedly a pretty sordid story. I realise that I am repeatedly stabbing a potato to death, and force myself to calm down.

'Go on,' I say. 'What happened after Joe was born?'

'Well, a lot of things happened after Joe was born. I had a mini nervous breakdown – I didn't have a clue how to look after a baby, and felt like a huge failure. I couldn't settle him when he cried, I couldn't breast-feed properly, I was exhausted, and I was depressed. It's like the whole world expected me to be euphoric – I was happily married, and had this gorgeous, healthy baby boy – but actually I wasn't. I was falling to pieces.

'And Gareth . . . well, Gareth suddenly became very busy. His career started to really take off, and he was out all the time. Having meetings, ruling empires, shagging secretaries – who knows?

'All I knew was that my reality had changed beyond all recognition – he'd come home, often near midnight, and I'd just be this huddled wreck of a woman, sobbing and gibbering. It went on for months, and it was awful. He seemed to love Joe, and made a show of supporting me . . . but it wasn't real. He'd do things like buy me a gym membership, because I couldn't shift the baby weight, but never be there to look after Joe so I could actually go to the gym. Then he'd make sarcastic comments about how the only pounds getting lost were from his bank balance.

'He'd want to have sex, but it was always when he was drunk after a night out, or when I was knackered – which was all the time. And after we'd done it, he'd just collapse next to me without saying a word, like he'd performed a bodily function rather than made love to his wife.

'Mum came up a few times, and when she was there, he was perfect – made a big show of doing the dishes, and ordering takeaway so I didn't have to cook, and saying he was considering "getting me a cleaner" – as though I was so incompetent I couldn't do any of those things any more, and he was the big man helping me through my rough patch.

'It got to the stage where I felt like I was living with a stranger – and, to be fair, he probably did as well. It wasn't all his fault. I lost interest in everything other than survival – getting through the sleepless nights, dealing with the mind-bending tedium of looking after a demanding baby, living on biscuits and a secret brandy bottle I kept in the nursery. Honestly? I was a mess – and the worse things started to get for me, the better they seemed to go for him.

'It was like there was only so much happiness to go round, and he had it all – constant promotions, trips abroad, winning awards, new cars. It got to the stage where I was too embarrassed to go to work parties with him, because I was definitely ashamed of myself, and he found ways to let me know that he was ashamed of me too.

'It started with little digs – he used to joke, all the time, about my weight, or my mumsy clothes, or living in leggings, or how my conversational skills had been reduced to "goo goo" and "ga ga".

'He did it in a way that made it seem funny – like he was just having a laugh – so I could never really challenge him on it. In fact I thought I was going mad – imagining it all. Because when we were with other people, he was the perfect dad, the perfect husband – so I came to the conclusion that I had to be imagining it. Even when I caught him staring at me with complete disgust while I slobbed out in front of the TV, I told myself I was just being paranoid.

'When he started calling me Fatty Dumpling – calling it a term of endearment – I told myself I was being too sensitive. And when the sex got even worse, until it was just a cold, horrible, painful thing, I told myself it was my fault – that I'd become so unattractive, no man would really want to sleep with me, and I was lucky Gareth was still interested at all.

'By that stage I had nobody around to tell me any different. I had no friends, no colleagues. I didn't have you. I pretended to Mum that everything was fine, although I'm never sure she believed me. My whole world revolved around Joe, and Gareth, and what Gareth thought about me – I saw myself through his eyes only, and his eyes really didn't like what they saw, no matter how hard I tried.

'I remember this one night, when Joe was maybe ten months old, deciding I'd make an effort. I cooked dinner, and did this stupid dress-up thing – greeted him at the front door dressed as a French maid, you know, with one of those frilly caps and an apron? It was meant to be fun, to try and put some sparkle back into things. He just looked at me, as if I'd gone completely mad, and said something like, "I think you should have ordered that one a few sizes up, don't you?"

'Nothing I ever did was good enough, and it almost came as a relief when he left, to be honest. Of course he swore there was nobody else, but I've discovered different since – there were quite a lot of someone elses.

'By the time he packed his bags and walked out of the door, I was a wreck. I begged him to stay, practically held on to his ankles as he went for his car keys, Joe screaming away in the background – but it was weird. Once he'd gone – once I'd stopped crying and wailing and snivelling – I realised that I was relieved. That I could be fat without anybody telling me off for it. That I could wear tatty old leggings and nobody would see. That I could have my meltdowns in peace.

'It was hard. It was horrible, being on my own with a toddler – and I hated myself so much by this stage that I couldn't do all the things I was probably supposed to do, that Mum suggested. Like join mother-and-baby groups, or go to coffee mornings in church halls, or make new friends at single mums' events.

'She kept saying I wasn't the only person going through this, that I should reach out – but I couldn't. And, you know, we got through it – I survived, Joe survived. Sadly Gareth survived, although these days he just sends me snarky texts and emails that imply I'm a bad mother, and I try not to let those get me down. But . . . well, Mum was right. I suppose she's always right – he just sucked the life out of me.'

We have both forgotten our dinner by this stage, and the candles are burning low, and I notice that we are both in tears. Her, understandably, for being forced to relive all of this. Me, for having to hear it.

I mean, I knew some of it – I hadn't lived in a bubble. Mum told me when he left. But the rest . . . the control. The slow character assassination. Basically, the emotional abuse? I didn't know all of that, and I suspect Mum hadn't either, or she'd have hired a hit man and had Gareth erased. That, I think, is still an option – it's never too late for revenge.

I love my sister. In fact at times I've probably loved her too much – needed to love her too much. I love her so deeply, so fiercely, that I've never been right since she kicked me out of her life. I've always known this – known that Mum was right when she compared us to three-legged dogs and tortoises stuck on our backs – but I have never felt it as strongly as I do now.

I am devastated for her, and by what she has told me. I am furious with him for doing it, and with myself for putting her in a position where she had to cope with all of that without me, and with the fact that it has taken our mother's death for me to hear the full story.

Everything I've heard about Gareth, everything I suspected at the time, backs up my belief that sooner or later, all of that would have happened, with or without me. I'd always known that he was a monster. I didn't create the situation – but I certainly exacerbated it, and put her in a position where it all sped up, steam-rollered over her, leaving her like a cartoon character, squashed and flattened on the floor.

And I left her to deal with it all alone – if I'd still been in her life, I'd have been there, at her side, fighting her corner. Looking after Joe, kicking Gareth in the balls when he played up, protecting her. Instead, I hurt her, and made her even more vulnerable.

Now, after hearing all of this, I have no idea what to say. How to console her without risking rejection. How to apologise yet again. How to express my regrets, and show her how I feel. I am frozen, sitting there at the old oak table in the Posh Room, an empty glass of Bolly and a cold Beef Wellington congealing on my plate in front of me.

'So,' Rose says, swiping tears away from her face angrily. 'Is this the part where you say "I told you so", and look even more smug?'

'No,' I answer swiftly, horrified but not surprised that she would expect that of me. 'This is part where I say I'm sorry, again – because, let's face it, Bastards don't have to be male, do they?'

Chapter 31

Rose

I wake up with sore eyes, a pounding headache, and a champagne glass lying next to me on the pillow, laid there like a boozy rose.

My first thought is: where are the paracetamol? And my second thought is: did we set the garden on fire last night?

After my long, drunken confessional session with Poppy, we basically decided that Mum was right (again) and that our lives needed more fizz. So we finished off all three bottles of the Bollinger, and avoided talking about anything too serious for the rest of the night.

She asked questions about Joe, tentatively at first, as though I might refuse to answer them – but she'd found my weak spot. Like most mums, I can't resist bragging about my brilliant boy and all of his amazing achievements. Every now and then, as I recounted some tale about his performance in the Year Six leavers' play, or the way he saved a certain goal, or how good he is at the guitar, I would remind myself of who I was talking to, and temporarily clam up.

It made for a weird stop-start conversation – a constant

flow of maternal pride and childhood anecdotes interrupted by stilted silences and awkward moments.

It was during one of these that Poppy suggested we should make an effigy of Gareth, and burn it in the garden. As I lie in bed now – staring at that bloody Boyzone poster – I wonder why on earth we thought that was a good idea. But then I remember that I've spent the night spooning with a champagne glass, and it all starts to make sense.

We'd found one of my old dolls in the Hideous Extension, and cut its curly blonde hair off with nail scissors. Then we'd swapped her dress for a pair of trousers from an ancient Rupert the Bear, to make it look like a man – although Poppy decided it didn't look male enough, and used a marker pen to draw a giant penis on its forehead as well.

Then we held a little ceremony in the garden, dousing it in petrol we found in the lawnmower shed and setting it alight in the barbecue. There may have been chanting, possibly dancing – and there was definitely too much drinking as we watched its already creepy plastic face melt in the flames. It was all a bit pagan, and I was half afraid we may have conjured up some kind of scorned-woman voodoo; that I'd check my phone and see that Gareth had died the night before in a freak chip-pan fire.

I roll out of bed, and grab my phone off the drawers. No. Nothing at all, which is a relief – because while I've often fantasised about Gareth getting bumped off, or at least moving to Australia, I wouldn't like to actually cause his death with my freakish supernatural powers.

I am still fully dressed from the night before, and groan as

I make my way downstairs. I am a little woozy, and have to hold on to the walls as I go. The creaky staircase makes so much noise it feels as if it's being piped directly into my head.

I am expecting to see carnage when I get down there, but am pleasantly surprised to see that Poppy has already been up, cleared the Posh Room, and washed the dishes. There's a smell of toast in the air, which I react to like a trained sniffer dog, following the trail to the back kitchen door.

I realise when I feel the heat of the sun on my face that it's not quite as early as I thought. In fact, I see when I bother looking at my watch, it's just after eleven. I've had an unintentional lie-in.

I see Poppy sitting at the wooden bench, a plate of wholemeal toast and a cafetiere of coffee next to her on the table. She's just nibbled the edges of the slice, as if it might be poisoned. She looks a lot fresher than I do, and is reading a book. I recognise it straight away – *Harry Potter and the Prisoner of Azkaban*.

I pause in the doorway for a moment, not sure of how to behave. Not sure of how I even feel. Last night was exhausting. Talking about Gareth always drains me, which is why I've made an absolute masterwork of avoiding it over the years.

It exhausts me because it is traumatic, and because, after all this time, he still has the power to make me feel bad about myself – except these days, it is different. These days, I feel bad about what I let him do to me. About not spotting the signs earlier. About not facing up to what he was before so much damage was done.

Talking about him is bad enough – but talking about him

to Poppy? The sister I cut out of my life so long ago? That is a double whammy of massive proportions.

She didn't react the way I'd expected. I could see her twitching, see her slow tears, see that she was desperate to reach out to me. To touch me and console me. I'm glad she didn't – it would have been too much, too soon – but perhaps . . . well, perhaps one day, things will be different.

For now, I decide on cautious civility as I walk barefoot over the grass to join her. For now, I'll try and carry on doing what our mother wanted, and see where it leads. It would just all be so much easier if she was actually here to act as a buffer zone, make us laugh, chivvy us along – if she was out here on this gloriously sunny day, chatting and eating toast and making plans. I miss her so much.

Poppy looks up as I approach, and I see a hesitant not-quite-smile hovering on her lips. Like she too doesn't know how to behave this morning. She folds her page over, and offers me a slice of toast.

'Thanks,' I say, taking a bite and sitting down next to her. We both stay silent for a few moments, watching the blue tits on the bird table and admiring the riot of colour of an English garden in full summer bloom.

'So,' I finally say, 'I'm not feeling awesome this morning.'

'You're feeling better than that Tiny Tears doll is,' she replies, pointing to a pile of melted plastic and ashes in the barbecue.

'Yes. We well and truly killed her, didn't we? Anyway, what does Mum have planned for us today . . . ? I hope it doesn't involve climbing up hills or going to a nightclub. I'm too old for all of this.'

Poppy nods, and doesn't dispute my oldness – the cow – before replying.

'It's D, and all I know is that it's some photos, and a video, which we can download from her account and watch on her incredibly clever TV. It has a catchy title, though.'

'Oh yes?' I ask, not sure what to expect. 'What's it called?'

'Daddy Issues. Sounds like a classic.'

Chapter 32

Andrea: D is for Daddy Issues

'Darlings – how are the hangovers this morning? I'm working on the assumption that you took me up on C at least. You wouldn't be my daughters if you let a single drop of champers go to waste, and I hope you did me proud.

'As you can see, I'm filming this one in the garden. Lewis is here, manning the camera, and we've just had a splendid little breakfast. It's one of the first properly warm days we've had this year, and I think you'll agree it's looking gorgeous. Lewis, pan round, will you? It means move the camera, you big lug! That's it – do a full turn, like a slow-motion ballerina doing a pirouette – yes, keep going, nice and steady, so we get a full shot of the place.

'Well done Lewis, we'll make a cameraman of you yet! I think the hydrangeas are going to be especially lovely this year, girls. I don't know what you'll be doing with the cottage – it's really up to you. Your lives are in other places, so I'll understand if you sell it – but if you do, please make sure it goes to someone deserving, won't you?

'Not just someone who has the money, but someone who

will love it like I have, and will take care of the garden for me. Someone who will keep the birdbath stocked and polish the garden gnomes and leave the animals' grave-markers in place.

'We spent many happy years in this garden when you were children, and I've spent many more here since. After Penny Peabody, when the roles were few and far between, I started to enjoy the gardening a lot more. Discovered my green thumb late in life.

'Anyway. I've got to go to hospital this afternoon for an appointment – don't worry, Lewis is taking me – and I suspect that is going to be a more and more common thing in future. I know you'll both still be reeling from the fact that I'm gone, and I'm not at all sure whether these little home movies will help, or make it worse – but once an old luvvie, always an old luvvie, my dears.

'As you can see for yourselves, I'm not in too shabby a state. My appetite isn't much to write home about, and I'd be lying if I said there wasn't pain, but I'm still here, still at home – where I plan to stay for as long as humanly possible. But when I need to decamp and take the nice medical people up on their offer of care and drugs, I will. I don't know when that will be – it's all so bloody uncertain – but for the time being, I'd rather be here, with the gnomes and all my happy memories, than anywhere else.

'I know, as you watch this, that everything will feel unreal to you. That you might have had a difficult conversation last night. That you might have headaches.

'That you still won't quite believe I'm gone. The loss of a

loved one takes a terribly long time to actually sink in. To start with, the pain of it is raw, and unpredictable, and all-consuming – but you hold it in and cope, at least until you get through the necessities, like the funeral.

'After that, I'm afraid it's something of a slow burn. You think you're doing okay, but as time passes, you realise that you're not. Something will happen – you'll hear a funny story in the queue at the post office, or see an especially beautiful sunset, or hear a certain song on the radio – and it will spark some memory, or some urge to pick up the phone and tell me about it.

'The real pain comes then – with the thousand tiny paper cuts of grief – the small things that make up a human life. The missed birthdays, or accidentally buying me a Christmas present even when I'm not here to receive it. The future losses will hurt as much as the current ones.

'I don't have any way of protecting you from that, my sweets, other than to do what I'm doing – trying to bring you back together again, so at least you won't be facing it alone. And also to assure you that it does get better, with time – you'll never forget me, but eventually, you will get through whole days and then whole weeks without bursting into tears. You'll move on, and I don't want you to feel guilty about that – don't scratch at the scab once you start healing. Allow yourself to feel the pain, but allow yourself to let it go as well.

'I'm sounding incredibly wise in my old age – but only because I've been where you are now, trying to come to terms with the death of my own mother, wondering how someone so strong and vibrant could be gone from the world, and how the world could go on without her.

'I had you two, which was both a blessing and a curse – a curse because I had a lot to deal with, and it's very hard changing nappies while weeping into the talcum powder. But a blessing as well, because I had someone to pour my love into, and so much to do that I was distracted from it all.

'Your grandmother only met you briefly, as babies – well, you were a very chubby toddler at that stage, Rose, so adorable, and you were a few months old, Poppy. I know you've seen those photos, in the album on the bookshelf, but I think I have an old one somewhere of me as a baby, with my parents. I'll root out a photo of her and leave it for you – she was a lovely lady, although very tough on the surface. They were often like that, women who grew up during the Second World War – life hadn't been easy, and they'd learned to cope with a lot.

'My dad died before you were born, when I was just a teenager, and that had a profound effect on me. It certainly explained some of my later behaviour – and it also brings me to the matter at hand: Daddy Issues.

'This isn't an easy thing to discuss for me and, even now, knowing that this might be my last chance, part of me wants to chicken out. Even thinking about it is making my head hurt.

'Now, I know you two always had questions about your dad – and that was only natural. I'm afraid I simply never handled it well, and always fobbed you off or tried to distract you. That worked when you were little, and I think as you got older you were both too kind to press the issue in case I went into some kind of drama-queen meltdown.

'That was unfair of me, and I apologise – but all I can say is that I did have my reasons, which may or may not become clear, depending on how you choose to proceed. Because you have a choice to make right now, girls – and it's a choice you both need to agree on.

'This is going to be, if all my plans work out, a bit like one of those books you had as children, where you could pick your own endings. Do you remember those? You'd reach a certain point in the story where you were asked what you wanted to do, which road to take, or which magic box to open, and it would take you to a different part of the book. You in particular loved them, Poppy, although you always cheated and read all the endings first.

'So, this is your choice – if you want to know more about your father, I will tell you. You simply have to carry on with our little A–Z, and you'll get there in the end. Round about P, in fact. I know that seems a while to wait, but it's a big deal, and I'd prefer it if you two were a little more robust by the time you got there. There's all kinds of lovely adventures planned before then – don't groan, now! – that will hopefully allow you to feel better about the world.

'But, and this is entirely up to you, you can also choose not to find out. I mean, you've gone the whole of your lives without knowing much about him, so you might decide that you're happy to let it go, and continue as normal. I would understand that – and believe me, choosing to know won't be without its complications. I can't predict what they will be, but I'm certain they'll exist.

'So, if you do decide to pass, and sweep the daddy issues under the rug, then you need to completely skip P and Q. I'll ask Lewis to package those up in such a way that you can't see anything from the outside – I don't know, perhaps he'll find some nifty crime-scene tape, like in the movies, or one of those biohazard stickers? He's very resourceful. If you don't want to know, then just throw them away. Burn them. Throw them into the sea tied to a stone. Whatever you like.

'Either way, it's up to you. I'm sorry I'm not there in person to answer all your questions, although not sorry enough, it seems, to actually contact either of you right now and say "hey, girls, why don't you come over for lunch and I'll tell you all about your daddy?" It seems that I am still chickening out, just a little bit – please forgive me!

'Anyway, I'm going to sign off for now – I'm sure I've given you plenty to think about. After our visit to the hospital, Lewis has promised to drive me up to Carding Mill Valley, and we're going to try and do that little walk to the reservoir. Maybe call at the ice-cream shop on the way home, if I'm feeling up to it. There's nothing like knowing your time is limited to make you relish a little bit of raspberry ripple, believe me.

'I know this is all a bit of an ordeal for you, so I've planned a bit of a treat with E, I promise – nothing heavy at all. In fact, it may make you giggle.

'So, my darlings, farewell for now – and please remember, always, how much I love you both.'

Chapter 33

Poppy

We've watched the video with the curtains closed, to block out the sunshine that was glaring off the screen, and now the room feels heavy and dark. The streaks of sun that are creeping in around the fabric are casting golden yellow stripes, like spotlights, filled with dancing dust particles.

We are both silent, and both, I suspect, confused.

First, we looked at the old black-and-white photos that had been left in the D envelope. Neither of us had seen them before, but the notes on the back told us they were of Mum, from the 1950s. There aren't many – I suppose photos were more of a luxury back then – and they are small and square and not very clear.

She is dressed in white, her hair a fuzzy blonde halo around her head, and she's sitting on the lap of her own mother, chubby knees poking out of what looks like a home-made dress.

My grandmother, who of course I don't remember at all, does, indeed, look a little bit stern, trying to smile but seeming uncomfortable with having her picture taken. My grandfather, who is a tall man wearing a lot of Brylcreem, is standing behind with his hand on her shoulder, with the same half-grimace on his face.

It's not quite got that frozen-sepia look that you see on really old pictures, but it's hard to imagine them as living, breathing people – the people who created my own mother. People she lived with and laughed with and loved and grieved for, just like we are grieving for her.

It made me sad to think about that, so I distracted myself with sorting out the video. It took a bit of messing around accessing the video sharing account – password MyGrubbyAngels999, which makes you wonder who MyGrubbyAngels numbers 1–998 belonged to – but we got there in the end, and sat back and watched as our dead mother graced the flat-screen in glorious technicolour.

Seeing her there – perched on the bench we'd just been sitting on, in the garden we'd just been enjoying – was surreal. As though if we looked out of the kitchen window right now, she'd be there, with a cup of tea, watching the blue tits.

I'm not sure whether we're lucky to have this final chance of spending time with her, or whether it is simply dragging out an already long and painful process. Even as I think it, I feel guilty – the amount of effort that she and Lewis have put into this project, at a time when most people would just be wallowing in self-pity, is staggering. She was even trying to help us as she approached death, and I know I'm being ungrateful to even consider not seeing it through.

But . . . well, this is hard. I'm not good at dealing with complicated emotions, which is why I've streamlined my own life to the point of non-existence. I don't have close friends, or serious relationships, or children, or even pets. I have my work, my shallow social life, and my mother. Or, I had her, at least. Over the years there have just been one too many knocks, and at some stage I suppose I gave up even trying to get up and fight the next round.

Now I'm being plunged back into the messy, mucky, extremely disorganised world of my family, and being asked to make decisions that I'd rather not have to make.

Rose is looking as shell-shocked as I am, slouched on the sofa holding a mug of coffee that I know must be stone cold by now. Her poor ankles look swollen from the heat, and her hair is like a wild animal around her head. I can tell she's feeling awful, probably on several different levels.

Last night, she was more open. More honest. More drunk, to be fair. But I can't keep her drunk forever, and this morning she's retreated back into her shell a little, as though she's worried about the repercussions of even one frank conversation with me.

That hurts, and when things hurt, I tend to block them out, and ignore them until they go away. Thanks to our mother, however, that's not an option here – which was all part of her cunning plan, I'm sure.

'So,' I say, switching the TV off and throwing open the curtains. She cringes as the light hits her, as though she's a vampire in a movie. 'What do you think?'

'I think it's weird,' she says, shuffling up the sofa to get out of the direct sunshine. 'The whole thing. I miss her so much, and want to talk to her so badly, and when she does those bloody videos, they feel so realistic that I think I can. The way she talks, as though the camera is actually us, and we're with her?'

'I know,' I say, sitting opposite her on the armchair. Mum's armchair, the floral fabric worn down and shining from all the times she laid her hands on it. 'It is weird, how she does that. But I don't suppose we should be surprised, should we? She spent her whole life acting – and this is just another type of it, I think. Another role.'

Rose frowns at me, and seems upset by something I've said. I have no clue what.

'I don't think that's fair,' she says. 'I think she means every word – she's not just following a script, is she?'

'That's not what I meant!' I reply, exasperated. It's so grating, the way we are both ridiculously quick to jump to the wrong conclusion about each other – it is starting to grind me down.

'What did you mean then?'

'I meant that she's doing it all very deliberately – she is ill when she's making these videos, isn't she? Really ill. But she's pretending not to be, putting on a show, throwing in a few funny lines. She wants us to do certain things, and she knows she's manipulating us into doing them, leading us in a certain direction. I'm not saying she doesn't mean it all – she obviously does. I just mean that she's not daft – she knows us so well, she is predicting how we will react to things, building in light and shade so we don't just get bogged down in it all. She's trying to make it . . . fun, as well as making it matter.

'And that way she talks to the camera? All isn't-this-marvellous-girls? That's her using her professional skills for a very personal goal. I'm not criticising it, I'm amazed by it. That, in her last few weeks, she chose to do this. For us. Because, like she keeps saying, she loved us so much. Does that make sense?'

I've explained it as well as I can, and if Rose still wants to interpret it as me being a cow, she's welcome to. I think part of her still wants me to be a cow, because then I'd be easier to ignore.

She nods, almost reluctantly, and sips some of her coffee, immediately pulling a face when she realises how cold it is. I should make her a refill – but we have a decision to make first.

'What do you think, then?' I ask, rubbing the worn fabric of the armchair as though I am trying to absorb any last traces of my mother's touch. 'About the dad thing? Do you want to know or not?'

She surprises me by answering immediately, and firmly: 'Yes. I really do.'

Some of my surprise must show on my face, and she gives me a little smile, as though she's satisfied to have shocked me with something.

'Because of Joe,' she explains. 'I mean, it's not as though I believe that our genetic make-up is the be-all and end-all of who we are – Joe is nothing at all like his dad, for example, even though I do sometimes worry that Gareth will rub off on him every summer when he goes and stays with him.

'But Joe has asked about my father, and I've never been able to answer properly because I don't know myself. And one day, he'll be in the same boat we're in now – when I'm gone, I mean. He'll be the one with the questions, and there's no way I'll be capable of pulling off one of these A–Z affairs. I'm not organised enough for that, or selfless enough – I'll probably spend my last weeks on earth eating cheesecake and pairing socks and watching box sets of *Poldark*—'

'I love *Poldark*,' I say, unable to stop myself interrupting. Her smile returns, bigger this time, as she replies: 'Who doesn't?

'Anyway,' she adds, leaning forward and looking at me intensely, 'you can't say that you've never been curious, can you? It was always odd – she was so open about everything else, but this one thing just foxed her every time we mentioned it. I always secretly wondered if our dad was somebody . . . you know, famous? Like maybe we were the illegitimate love children of Robert Redford or something?'

I bite back a giggle at that idea, but can't deny that similar thoughts had crossed my mind.

'I know what you mean,' I say. 'Except not Robert Redford – I think she'd have mentioned it, relentlessly, if she'd ever met him. But maybe one of those British actors she worked with back in the Seventies? Like Robert Vaughn, or Timothy Dalton before he was Bond, or Ian McShane?'

'She did always have a bit of a thing for Ian McShane, didn't she? Always looked a bit dreamy-eyed when *Lovejoy* came on the telly . . .'

'Or,' I say, pouncing on a new idea with what is probably far too much enthusiasm, 'didn't she do a stint in theatre with Richard Harris?'

Rose bursts out laughing, and her whole body is shaking

so hard that cold coffee is sloshing out of its mug, and splashing on to her thighs. I've not seen her laugh like this for so very long, and it is joyous to behold.

'What?' I say, grinning at her. 'What's so funny?'

She wipes the tears from her eyes – the good kind, this time – and takes a few deep breaths, trying to stifle her giggles.

'It was the look on your face, sis,' she says, 'the look on your face when you said that. I don't think I've ever seen you so excited. You do realise, don't you, that you've just suggested that Professor Dumbledore is our *dad*?'

Chapter 34

Rose

I honestly don't think I've laughed so hard in my entire life. Apart from maybe that time in the tent at Glastonbury, when I was a Stoned Rose and every word out of Poppy's mouth was absolutely hilarious.

This time, I'm not stoned – just a bit hungover. And this time, Poppy isn't my best friend – she's the person I've been holding responsible for ruining my life for all these years, even if part of me knows that's not entirely fair.

And this time, we're not joking about our mum sneaking into a festival as a blue-boobied yoga freak – we're on some crazy beyond-the-grave odyssey that she's sent us on; an insane journey of reconciliation.

None of this is funny at all – but God, it felt good to laugh again. And it felt good to see Poppy relaxed again, even if it was for just a few moments; the way her face lit up at the thought of being Dumbledore's long-lost daughter was absolutely priceless. Well, she has been reading *Harry Potter and the Prisoner of Azkaban* this morning.

That look – that genuine glee – meant that for a little while there, she lost control. She stopped being the perfectly poised Poppy she is these days, and instead became the imaginative, excitable little girl she always used to be. The way I remember her, before everything turned to shit.

I suppose, no matter what comes next, no matter what the ultimate outcome of Mum's bonkers spirit quest, we both needed that. We both needed to laugh, to let go, to relax.

Now, egged on by Mum's insistence that E is just a bit of fun, I decide we should press ahead.

'Okay,' I say, pointing at the boxes on the living-room floor, 'while I'm still half dead with this hangover, shall we see what E is? She said it was funny, but I'm not sure I trust her. This spirit quest business is a bit unpredictable.'

'Spirit quest?' Poppy echoes, unfolding the now slightly tattered printout of the A–Z index. I hope she has a copy, or we'll be screwed.

'You know. Like in films. This reminds me of one – like at some point, we'll be asked to sit in a teepee and smoke a peyote bong?'

'Like we're Kevin Costner in *Dances with Wolves*,' she replies, obviously getting it. Of course. She looks up, frowning at me quizzically, still looking much younger and much more innocent.

'What would your spirit animal be?' Poppy asks, kneeling down and rummaging in the rose-painted box.

'Oh, I don't know,' I reply, giving the issue some serious

thought. This is, after all, a perfect hangover conversation, right up there with, 'What's your favourite superpower?' and 'If you were a colour, what would you be?'

'Maybe,' I say, after a few moments, 'I'd be a Labrador. They're big and cuddly and like to eat and sleep. I don't think I'd mind being a Labrador.'

'Well, I can see what you mean,' Poppy says, producing a slim A4 envelope from the box and waving it triumphantly. 'But that wouldn't have made the cut in the movie, I don't think. Spirit animals are usually something clever, or magnificent, like a fox or a grizzly bear or a deer. Not the pet equivalent of a foot warmer.'

'This isn't the movie version, though. It's our version. And I think you'd be a seal.'

'A seal? Why a seal?'

'Because you're all . . . I don't know, sleek, and streamlined, and shiny.'

'Funny you should say that,' Poppy answers, double-checking the envelope and seeing a giant black letter E scrawled on it. 'Because I also happen to be an absolute genius at balancing a beach ball on my nose, and clapping my flippers.'

I laugh again. I can't help it. She always could make me giggle – even when I didn't want to. It feels weird, though – fragile. Like we've both somehow decided to call a truce for the time being, pretend we're not both so tense, allow ourselves a small break. It's only skin deep, and we both know that, but for now, it'll do.

'What's in the envelope?' I ask, pointing at it. 'And do we need to be wearing face masks when we open it?'

'I don't think so,' she says, sitting back on to her heels and looking at the index again. 'It says here it's a photo, with a note on the back. I hope she's right, and this one is fun – because I couldn't help looking ahead at F while I was at it. I know I'm not supposed to, but my eyes just kind of accidentally skimmed ahead, and it doesn't look like a barrel-load of laughs.'

'F is for Fungus?' I suggest, not quite wanting to let the easy mood die just yet. 'F is for Fibre? Does she want us to eat a bowl of All-Bran mixed up with magic mushrooms? I wouldn't put it past her . . .'

'Well, that would definitely help with finding our spirit animals, even if we did have to hold the pipe-smoking ceremony on the loo . . . but no. It's F is for Forgiveness.'

Poppy casts a nervous glance in my direction, and looks ridiculously vulnerable. She hasn't put make-up on yet this morning, and her hair is tied back in a slightly messy pony, and if I squint my eyes up a bit, she could be ten years old.

Ten years old, and asking me to forgive her for losing the lids to my felt-tip pens, or eating the last Curly Wurly even though she knew I was saving it, or spilling orange cordial on my maths homework. Asking forgiveness for any one of a thousand tiny childhood transgressions that are all part of growing up.

Except, of course, this time she's asking me to forgive her for a whole lot more – and I am nowhere near ready to do that. My lack of forgiveness is so deeply ingrained in me, I don't know if I ever will be.

Neither, though, do I quite have the will to look into that vulnerable face of hers, and say exactly that.

'Well,' I answer, ignoring her silent inquiry, 'let's worry about that one when it's time.'

Poppy nods, uses her long, perfectly shaped fingernails to slit open the top of the envelope, and out falls a photo. It's old, an 8 × 10-inch shot that looks as though it could have been used for some kind of promo. It's a bit crinkled, and curled around the edges, but is vivid in that gloriously glossy way of the Seventies.

She holds it up and looks at it, and her eyes widen in disbelief.

She turns it to me, and I see why. There, dressed in some kind of hideous hot-pants outfit made entirely of gaudy greens and golds, is my mother. The Seventies incarnation of my mother – all wild hippy hair and huge eyes and boobs.

She appears to be dressed in some kind of sexy mock Irish get-up, several buttons on her green waistcoat open to show off her cleavage, her tight green sequinned shorts ending inches above her bright gold thigh-high boots. She looks gorgeous, but ridiculous – like some kind of Playboy bunny version of a leprechaun.

That, however, isn't what is leaving us both speechless. We've both seen more amusing pictures than that of our mum.

What is leaving us speechless is the man next to her, his beefy arm slung around her shoulder, bloated face and bleary eyes smiling into the camera in a way that suggests he wasn't entirely feeling at his best.

The man she'd always claimed to have met, even though we were never quite sure we believed her. I turn the picture over, still shaking my head in amazement, and see that Mum has indeed left a handwritten note on the back.

Chapter 35

Andrea: E is for Elvis

Ha ha! Not to be smug, girls, but I told you so! I saw all your eye-rolling whenever I told you this story, but it's true – and here is the evidence! I thought I'd lost this, but Lewis has helped me empty the entire contents of the attic recently, looking for other things, and he unearthed this – for some reason it was being used as a bookmark in the manual that came with my Jane Fonda Workout, which probably explains why I never saw it again!

Anyway – here we are. Me and the King. I was very young here, in the States doing some awful show for St Patrick's Day, and he wasn't at his peak, poor man. But he was very sweet, even then. A real gent, even though we were all dressed like leprechaun strippers.

Good luck with the rest, girls – hope this made you smile.

Now, as Mr Presley might say, goodnight, and thank you, thank you very much!

Chapter 36

Poppy

When Rose comes downstairs the next morning, looking bleary-eyed and still tired, she catches me out with Lewis's index spread before me on my lap.

'You're skipping ahead, aren't you?' she asks, pointing at me accusingly.

I nod, and try not to look guilty. I'm a grown woman and she doesn't have the right to tell me off. At least that's what I keep reminding myself.

'She probably knew you would,' she adds, wandering into the kitchen in search of coffee.

'I know,' I shout through to her. 'It's like with those books with all the endings. I always cheated, and she knew I would with this – so it's all deliberately obscure.'

Rose comes back in, using the same mug she always used when she lived here – a giant one with a picture of Princess Diana on the side.

'Did you look at P and Q? And . . . well, do you even want to find out about our dad? I was only two when whatever happened happened, and I don't even remember him.

Sometimes I think I do, but I suspect I'm making it up. What do you think?'

I'm nowhere near as certain as Rose that I want to find my long-lost father. If he's even alive – there's no promise of that in what our mum has cryptically said so far. He could be dead, or in jail, or living on a small Pacific island creating animal-human hybrids in his evil-genius laboratory for all we know.

This whole thing with Mum, with Rose, feels like enough of a head-fuck to me – but if she wants to know, for Joe, for herself, for whatever reason, then I won't stand in her way.

'I do want to, and I did. But it wasn't much help. All P says is that we'll need our passports, and Q is for Questions. It's like the rest of the index – deliberately obscure, like I said.'

'What do you mean?' she asks, sitting down opposite me.

'Well, some of them say what the letters stand for – like D for Daddy Issues – but some don't. Some just have the letter, and a note about what to look for, and which box it's in. Others have little comments by the side, which I suspect are from Lewis – I think Mum was so caught up in this she forgot about real life.

'So he's helped out by giving us pointers, things like "will involve driving", or "pack for an overnight trip", stuff like that. It's like they shared one giant brain – she did all the wacky creative stuff, and he was all solicitor-like and sensible. It's weird that we don't know him better, isn't it? What did she tell you about him? I'm a bit freaked out that he seems to have been so important in her life, and we never even met him . . .'

She nods, grimaces as she scalds her tongue on the coffee, and says: 'I know what you mean. It doesn't exactly make me feel like a good daughter either. But I suppose that we're the ones who insisted on keeping our lives separate, aren't we? I've not been back to this place since . . . well, *since*. What about you?'

'I moved out when I got that job with the publishing company in London, and came back briefly after I got sacked.'

'You got *sacked*?' she says, eyes wide and tone incredulous. 'But why? You seem so . . . sorted. Although I did always wonder why you ended up doing what you're doing, for, you know, a dog food company.'

'Luxury pet supply specialist,' I correct, automatically. Understandably enough, she pulls a face.

'Yeah. Okay, luxury pet supply specialist. But it's not publishing, is it? I always thought that if you did go into marketing, it'd be for something creative, or arty, or important.'

'Pet supplies are important,' I insist, stubbornly clinging to my defence of a job that in all honesty I absolutely hate. 'To the millions of people who love their pets.'

She holds one hand up in the air, as though she is giving up, and concentrates on her coffee instead. We are both silent for a while, until I try and find the words to break it.

'I got sacked because I was a mess,' I say, simply. 'It was after everything that happened with Gareth, and you wouldn't have anything to do with me, and Mum was freaking out, and basically . . . I couldn't do the work. I missed meetings. I turned up late every morning, dressed like a bag lady. It was a competitive environment – lots of bright young things want

221

to work in publishing – and at that stage in my life, I just wasn't bright enough.'

I can see her churning this over in her mind, and am half expecting some kind of sharp rebuttal – a 'so, you're blaming me, then, are you?', or 'so you're saying it was my fault, your epic career fail?'

Instead, she chews on her lip, and twists strands of her frizzy hair around her fingers, something I always remember her doing when she was trying to be patient with me. When I'd stolen one of her tops, or accidentally locked her out of the cottage, or made some ridiculous proclamation, like 'science is rubbish, I don't know why you like it.'

'Right,' Rose says, quietly. 'I see. Well, shit happens. So when did you move out again? Mum always tried to tell me what was going on, but I wasn't in the mood to listen. I used to bite her head off if she even mentioned your name, to be honest.'

I can hear the regret and guilt in her voice, and know that Mum's video – the one with the You've Broken My Heart speech – has taken its toll on her as well as me.

'About a year later, when I started working for a ball-bearing firm in the Midlands. And yes, it was about as exciting as it sounds, but it did allow me to get the experience I needed, do my marketing qualifications, that kind of thing. I moved down to London not long after, and life got . . . well, busy. And the more I stayed away from here, the harder it got to come back. Everything here reminded me of you, and us, and how broken everything was – and I couldn't cope with that.

'The only way I could move on was to ignore it all, and

the cottage – Mum, our bedrooms, everything about this place – wouldn't let me. So I stopped coming – instead she came to me, or we had weekends away. I never made any declaration, or even a decision . . . I just stopped coming. I've not actually set foot in here for about twelve years. Maybe if we had visited, she'd have introduced us to Lewis, who knows?'

'Maybe,' replies Rose, looking around at the living room in that way we've both been doing for the last few days – like she can't really believe that she's here now, and that she's here because our mother isn't.

It's weird – the whole cottage is dominated by Mum; by her fragrance and her taste and her history. It's there in every little ornament, every framed picture on the walls, every book on the shelves, every singed cake tin in the kitchen. She's everywhere – but she's nowhere.

'I think,' Rose continues, 'that perhaps she liked having him to herself. We were both so tied up in our own problems, and we did that thing kids do. That thing where we don't really imagine our parents having lives of their own, outside of us. So perhaps she enjoyed having a whole side to her existence that we weren't involved in.

'She told Joe a bit about him, though – said he moved to the village about five years ago. He's basically winding down his business and decided to go into semi-retirement here. Anyway, he's looked after her, hasn't he? And helped her with all this. He's been a better friend to her than we were, and we should be grateful. Though I'm still a bit disappointed they weren't secretly bonking.'

'Yuk,' I reply, screwing my eyes up in disgust. That's

something I really don't want to picture, no matter how efficient Lewis's index-making skills are.

'So,' Rose says, gazing at Princess Diana's slightly chipped face, 'are we ready for the next one, do you think? I know we both needed some time off last night, but we might as well get on with it now. I'd ask how many more to go, but I'm guessing that's obvious.'

'I don't think anything about this is obvious,' I reply. 'She may have decided to skip some letters because they were awkward, or invented new ones purely to amuse herself. I think, though, that there are only a few left that we can do here – looks as though we're set to be on the move round about L.'

'She's sending us to ell?' Rose asks, deliberately mispronouncing it.

'Probably. She'll be there with a diamond-studded pitchfork, singing "Burn Baby Burn" and pelting us with garden gnomes made of cow pats . . . anyway. F is for Forgiveness, then. If you think you're up to it?'

Rose nods, and makes a 'move-it-along' gesture with her hands, like she's directing traffic and I'm illegally parked. She's getting tougher as this thing progresses, which may or may not be a good thing – I suppose it depends on who's on the receiving end of the toughness. I, on the other hand, feel as if I'm getting softer – more vulnerable, and more exposed. Being around Rose is like being emotionally exfoliated.

'Okay . . . here we go . . .' I say, fishing around in the box until I find the right packages. One is a big padded envelope, stuffed full of god-knows-what, with 'open me second, for F's sake' written on the side in our mother's handwriting. I put it to one side, and pick up the other.

It's a plastic bag – an ancient carrier from a shop that no longer exists – with a big letter F scrawled on the side. I scrunch it up and squeeze it, as though it's a Christmas gift and I'm trying to figure out what's inside.

'Is it a pony?' asks Rose, sarcastically. 'Please tell me it's a pony!'

I ignore her, and use my nails to unpick the knot that's been tied with the carrier bag's handles. Once I've done it, and broken a nail in the process, I empty the contents on the floor, where they scatter and clatter on the parquet. We both look down, a bit befuddled. It's a big mess of old-fashioned cassette tapes – C60s and C90s, some of them with writing on the paper stickers on the sides, some of them clear.

I root through them until I find a tape that looks a bit newer than the rest. Written on the side, in olde-worlde cursive script, are the words 'Play Me!'

'Wow,' says Rose, leaning down to get a better look. 'That's a bit *Alice in Wonderland*, isn't it? I didn't even know they still made cassette tapes . . . Joe wouldn't know what they were for. How are we going to listen to it? Even my car isn't so old it has a tape deck.'

'Never fear, Lewis is here . . .' I reply, reaching back into the box and hefting out an old machine. It's ancient, and I just about recognise it from our childhood. It's long and flat, and has a lift-up lid where you slide in the tapes, and big clunky rectangular buttons that only let you record, play, erase, and go backwards and forwards.

It was probably once the cutting edge of technology, but now it looks like something out of one of those really dated science-fiction programmes – like the 1970s version of The Future.

I look at Rose, and she just nods. I can tell she's nervous about what we're going to hear, about our mother's voice floating, disembodied, through the room, and so am I.

I slide the cassette in, close the lid shut with a clunk, and press 'play'.

Chapter 37

Andrea: F is for Forgiveness

'Darlings! I've gone old school – what do you think? Just thought I'd mix it up a bit. Or mix tape it up a bit, ha ha! I'm sure you're sick of seeing my ugly mug on the TV screen – goodness knows the general public was, by the time Penny Peabody got killed in that tragic boating accident, poor love.

'Anyway, I came across this old thing the other day, and thought it would be fun to record something for you. I've tested it out, and the quality is awful – but sadly I don't have a soundman around to fix it for me, so you'll just have to make do. Perhaps the crackling and echoing will add to the atmos – your mother's ghostly voice, rising up from the Great Beyond!

'Do you remember using this thing, actually? It seemed very cutting edge at the time, didn't it? I used it for work sometimes, so I could listen back to myself when I'd rehearsed lines for auditions – but we also used it together.

'We had a lot of giggles making recordings of us all singing, or doing little skits, and Poppy, there was one time when you were about eight, when you insisted on reading out "The

Owl and the Pussycat"? But you always used to get the first few lines mixed up, and said, very seriously, that they went to pee in a beautiful sea-green boat, instead of the other way round! You were very angry with me for laughing, I seem to remember, your little face all screwed up with indignation.

'I haven't been able to find many of those recordings, which is a great pity – not only because I'd like to pass them on to you two, but because I would love nothing better right now than to sit here at night, in my old age, and listen to them. It would be wonderful to hear your childish voices and your innocent giggles filling these rooms again, keeping me company and making me smile. Happier times, so full of laughter.

'I have a suspicion, Rose, that you taped over them all during that phase where you borrowed albums off your friends and recorded them. All those precious childhood sounds, wiped out for the sake of A-ha and Paula Abdul! There is no justice in the world!

'I found some of your old compilation tapes, though, which I've left in the bag for you – even the bag is an antique, from that little dress shop I used to take you to, remember? When you needed something special for a frightfully important event – school discos and the like – we'd go there and you were allowed to choose what you liked. I know the selection wasn't great, and you'd have preferred Top Shop but, being honest, girls, I only went there for one reason – they let me pay on tick and spread the cost out over the year!

'It's long gone now – I suppose everybody has credit cards these days instead. Anyway. I think the bag is a nice reminder, although goodness knows why I still have it. Enjoy the tapes as well – although I have to say I think some of your musical choices were a bit dubious. I enjoyed the rock history phase where you got into Bob Dylan and Joni Mitchell well enough, but I have to draw the line at New Kids on the Block.

'Right, I'm sure I've waffled on enough, and I'm feeling a tad on the tired side today, so I'll get to the point. I hope you enjoyed Elvis, and the cassette tapes, but I'm afraid this next one won't be a huge amount of fun. Because F is for Forgiveness, girls – and that is a tough nut to crack.

'The older you get, you know, the more you realise how important forgiveness is. I've learned to forgive certain people certain things – like you two, for being so obstinate all this time; and your father, for things that darkened my life way back when; even you, Poppy, for stealing that lovely little tobacco tin from the cabinet in the Posh Room – that belonged to my grandfather, by the way, so please take care of it.

'Forgiveness is always painted as a frightfully selfless act – full of virtue and nobility. But, truth be told, forgiveness is just as important for our own sanity as it is for the people we are so nobly forgiving. Holding on to old bitterness, to anger, to resentment – well, it drives you just a little bit mad, doesn't it? I'd suggest, if I may be so bold, that both of you are shining examples of that.

'Rose, you were never able to forgive Poppy for what she did – and Poppy, I don't think you've ever forgiven yourself. Or forgiven Rose for shutting you out of her life. You two darling girls, who should be so close, have built up this enormous gap between your lives, and filled it all up with anger.

'There does come a point, though, where you really have to let go – because if you don't, all that resentment will eat you up. Like a plague of emotional locusts, it'll strip the flesh from your bones, and leave you bare and exposed and brittle. Forgiving someone doesn't just save them – it can save you as well.

'So, this is your next task, and this one is aimed mainly at Rose – although Poppy, you have a big part to play. After the unpleasant events of that dreadful party to see in the new millennium, Poppy came back here in all kinds of pieces. Rose, you had your own ordeal to cope with. I was stuck in the middle, trying to mediate and getting nowhere. I look back now and wonder what else I could have done – if there is anything I could have said or written or yelled to stop what came next. If I could somehow have been a better mother, and sorted it all out for you?

'But of course that's pointless, and only serves to make me feel guilty – which I've decided not to allow. I did my best, and that's all I could do. I've begged you girls not to feel guilty about any of this, so I won't impose it on myself either.

'Back then, though, Poppy, you were desperate to make it up to your sister. To beg her forgiveness. To explain what had happened, and why it happened, and tell her how sorry you were. I saw you, for months on end, desperately making phone calls that were never answered, sending texts that were ignored, firing off emails that bounced back. That's when you started writing the letters – big, long, old-fashioned letters.

'You scribbled away in that big A4 notepad, filling pages and pages with your scrawl, bundling them into envelopes and sending them off to your sister. Every time I saw you lick a stamp, you had this awful, pathetic, hopeful look on your face – like this would be the one that made the difference. That this would be the one that made it right.

'The fact that they were all returned, unopened, devastated you – but you carried on writing them, for such a long time. Definitely while you were here, and I think while you were in London, messing up that publishing job.

'Every one – every single one – came back. It got to the point where the postman thought we were all mad, and I was starting to agree. I even wondered – because I do have a dramatic turn of mind, darlings, just in case you hadn't noticed – if Gareth had been intercepting them, keeping them from you somehow, Rose.

'But no – because when I asked, you simply said that you didn't want to hear anything that Poppy had to say. I know, of course, that it was your way of coping. Your way of dealing with it all – but it was cruel, my love. I suppose it was easier for you to just blame her – to ignore any of her pleas, to block out any defence, and cast her as the villain of the piece. It allowed you to take Gareth back, and plan a wedding, and build a life with him – because while it was all Poppy's fault, it couldn't be his, could it?

'Obviously, that wedding – that marriage – was a terrible mistake, and the only good thing to come out of it was Joe, bless him. But I also think that refusing to ever read those letters was a mistake, too.

'Once you decided to move down to London again, Poppy, I know you bagged them all up in a big black bin liner and threw them away. You were making a fresh start, and that was part of your process. But being the sneaky old coot that I am, I kept them – you always were lazy, so that'll teach you to leave putting the bins out to me! I kept them, tucked them away in the attic in the hope that, one day, Rose would finally be ready to read them.

'She never was, but recently, I read them.

'I should probably apologise for this invasion of your privacy, but I don't think I can. I'm a dying old lady and I have waived all claims on good behaviour.

'They were heartbreaking, those letters – all that pain and all that need, ignored and then cast aside. And I was furious – at him, mainly, but also at all of us, for letting this go on for so long. Now I can only hope that Rose might finally be willing to hear what you had to say to her, this sister who loves you so much.

'I can imagine, my loves, that you are both having a giddy fit right about now – Rose, at the thought of reopening these old wounds, and daring to entertain the possibility that you also played a part in this mess. And Poppy, I know, this will be a shock – you're probably very cross, and very unhappy at being asked to do this.

'Because I am asking – not telling. I have chosen some of those letters – not all of them, there were so many, and forgive me for being critical, but they were a little on the repetitive side, sweetie! – and I've put them in the padded envelope. Now, Poppy, this is up to you – I might have invaded your privacy by reading them, but now it's your decision whether you choose to let Rose read them as well.

'I know the Poppy in those letters is nothing like the Poppy you've gone on to create for yourself since then. These days, on the surface at least, you are every inch the elegant, successful career woman – and your emotions are as well managed as your horrible low-carb diet or your work calendar. Back then, you were very different – a cauldron of emotion! So, you might not want Rose to see them. You might decide that that part of you is dead and buried and good riddance to it – but I hope not.

'And Rose – I can't force you to read them. And even if you do, out of guilt or loyalty or simply wanting to do what your mother has asked, I can't control how you react. The spirit with which you respond.

'I can't control any of it – all I can do is hope.

'Anyway, I think that's plenty for now, don't you? I'm lucky I had a C90, I've banged on for so long . . . so, goodbye for now Rosehip, Popcorn. I love you both, very, very much.'

Chapter 38

Poppy: 17 February 2000

Dear Rose,

I'm so, so sorry. I've called and texted, but you just won't speak to me. You won't listen to me, and I know why, and I know I deserve all of this. But it's killing me, it really is. I just don't know what to do, so I'll keep writing and hope that one day you'll find it in your heart to forgive me, or at least tell me to my face that you won't. Even that would be better.

I'm at home, in your bedroom, where everything reminds me of you, and Mum is downstairs baking another cake. She doesn't know what to do or how to help. I'm supposed to be leaving for London next week, but I don't know if I can. I feel like my legs have been chopped off without you.

I love you so much, and I'm so sorry. I still can't believe I did it. The most disgusting thing imaginable, on so many levels. I can't stand Gareth – I'm sorry, I know you say you love him, but I hate him. I've always hated him. He's too smooth and too smarmy and he controls you like you're his puppet.

None of what happened can ever be justified, I know that, but I want you to understand some of why it happened. I've thought about nothing else since, I really haven't. I just keep going over and over it in my head, trying to figure things out and piece it all together. It's like a nightmare and there's no way out, because it always ends the same way.

I think part of me was just jealous – because he was in your life so much more than I was, and I'd always depended on you a bit too much. You'd always looked after me, and then suddenly it felt like you were gone.

I know it's pathetic. I'm a grown-up and there are no excuses. But as soon as you met him, it started – forgetting my birthday (which you did this year as well, not that I blame you), and cancelling weekends, and just never doing anything without him. It's like nobody existed to you apart from Gareth, and I just wasn't mature enough to deal with the change, because I'm a bit of a knob.

I was feeling awful at that party. I'd been doing nothing at home other than drink and go to the Tennyson's and lie around in bed, for months on end. I had my new job coming up, but even that felt like a failure – I never wanted to go into bloody marketing, for God's sake. I just didn't know what else to do.

On the night, you didn't seem to have any time for

me, and you couldn't see how much pain I was in. Writing it down now, I know how stupid I sound. Like a spoiled-rotten little girl, which is what I am. Like someone so selfish they wanted you all to themselves – which is just what I am accusing Gareth of, isn't it?

When I got there, that horrible old house on the hill was full of people I didn't know. A few old friends of yours, but mainly his, and Rose, they are such tossers! I still don't know how you tolerate being around them so much, when all they talk about is money, and they act like they're the kings of the fucking world.

I didn't know anyone, and you were off all night being a good hostess. Every time I saw you, it was like the real you had been swallowed up and replaced with some fake Rose, like aliens had taken over your body. The clothes you were wearing and the way you were behaving. It just wasn't you. And he was always there, hovering in the background.

I know you might find this hard to believe, but he was tormenting me, in his own way. It was like bear-baiting. I'd see him, draped all over you, and he'd give me a wink when you weren't looking, like 'look what I've got'. He'd pretend to be nice, and was always giving me drinks – all night, he'd find me, and give me more and more to drink. First it would be beer, then wine, then brandy, then Bailey's.

I'm not trying to defend myself here. It's not like he

held me down and shoved a funnel in my mouth or anything – the way I was feeling, I was more than happy to get drunk. But this was a whole new level of drunk. This was the most smashed I'd ever been.

Then, after the New Year midnight thing, I felt so sick I wanted to go to bed. I felt like I was on another planet, like everything was just a huge blur. I was bouncing off walls and falling over and couldn't even speak properly. I could see people dancing but wasn't even sure they were human.

That's when I saw him again, when I was trying to get up the stairs. That staircase was so big, and the steps all seemed huge, and I was trying to crawl up them but I couldn't even do that, so I gave up and just sat on them, about halfway up, clinging on to the banister. You know that feeling when you're drunk and you go to bed but you can't get to sleep, because every time you close your eyes the room spins? It was like that, even though I was awake.

Gareth came up to sit with me, and I was too far gone to even tell him to shove off. And he made a big deal of looking after me, and saying how much he wanted me to have a good time, and how he loved me because I was your sister, and then he said he had something to 'give me a little boost'. That's what he said – give me a little boost.

He said I couldn't pack in now because I'd spoil your party, and a bit of me thought he might be right, and mainly I was just so off my head I didn't know what I was doing. So I took the coke, snorted it all, and washed it down with some vodka straight from the bottle.

To be honest I was behaving like one of those people in an anti-drugs video, and I'm lucky I didn't drop dead. Right now I wish that had happened rather than what did, I really do.

After a bit I started to feel even more weird – like I was seeing everything through a big kaleidoscope. I know you've never been a drug girl, but basically it felt like the world was taking on a life of its own. Everything felt better, even the touch of the scrappy old carpet under my legs, and the wood of the banister. It was a big, giant, insane whirl of colour and sound. Like the trippiest music video ever.

He sat with me for a while, and then said he thought I'd had enough, and I needed to go to bed. I didn't really know what was happening, and he helped me up the rest of the stairs, and took me to my room. I thought he'd leave me there, and I could collapse and look at the ceiling swirling around or be sick or some-thing.

But he didn't leave. He started stroking my hair, and telling me how much I looked like you, and how pretty I was. It was so weird – part of my brain wanted to scream and kick him in the balls, but part of me, the part that was just totally fucked up on drugs and booze and neediness, was listening. You'd always said he could make a woman feel so special, and for once I was on the receiving end of it, at a time when I was feeling far from special.

He didn't force me into anything. I have to be clear about that. I'm not saying he made me do anything, I'm not. But I just felt like I couldn't stop it, I was so off my head. Or maybe that I didn't want to stop it enough to figure out how. I feel sick as I write that, but I'm trying to be honest.

He stroked my hair, and then he started kissing me, and . . . well, you know the rest. You found us like that, and even then I didn't really know what was going on – he ran off after you, and I fell down, and I couldn't even move again. Not for hours.

By the time I could, you'd gone, and he'd gone, and I couldn't get hold of you no matter how many times I called. The house was wrecked, and I was a mess, and I didn't know what to do. I couldn't stop puking up, and crying, and I ended up walking to the station in the snow. There were no trains, obviously, because it was New Year's Day, and I slept in the waiting room with all my clothes on top of me. I thought then it was the worst day of my life, but every day since then has just got worse.

I'm not blaming anybody but myself, and I'm not trying to worm out of it. I'm really not. I hate myself so much, more than even you could hate me right now. I'm so, so sorry – I don't know what else to say. I'm desperate to talk to you Rose – even if it's just for you to scream at me, or come home and beat the crap out of me, anything. I'll take any punishment you want to give – anything at all. Just please, please, please get in touch.

I love you so much and I can't believe I did this to you. I don't expect you to forgive me, but please at least call me – and let me try and explain. Please.

Poppy xxxxxxxxxxxxxxxx

Chapter 39

Rose

I stuff the letter back into the envelope with the rest, and stare at Ronan Keating's giant face on the wall.

I know what he'd say – he'd tell me life is a rollercoaster and you've just got to ride it. And I know what my mum would say – that now I know more about what happened, now I've seen another side of the truth, I need to forgive her.

And I get why she would say that, and she would probably be right. But it's not that simple, no matter how heart-wrenching those letters were. I chose to believe Gareth when he said she made the first move; I chose to listen to him when he begged for forgiveness, and I chose to ignore Poppy.

Partly I made those choices because they allowed me to go on living the life with Gareth that I thought I wanted. But partly, it was because the bigger hurt of the whole sordid affair was my sister's betrayal, not Gareth's. I could forgive him because he hadn't caused as much damage.

Poppy was my best friend, my ally in life, my little sis – Poppy was everything, and she'd destroyed me.

Knowing now, all these years later, that things weren't quite how he portrayed them isn't actually as much of a revelation as she might expect. Deep down, I think I always suspected something like that had happened, especially with hindsight and a clearer picture of the way my ex-husband operates. I just chose not to engage with it, because it was easier to shut her out.

I suspect one of the reasons that I returned all her letters and refused all her calls was to avoid exactly this feeling – it was simpler to heap all the blame on her. It felt as if she'd gouged out my heart at the time, and there was no way I was going to listen to mitigating circumstances. Nobody could blame me for reacting like I did, even her – it was completely justified, and I wasn't prepared to listen to her version of events.

I'm still not sure I am now. Because it's too big, and too nasty, and too difficult. I carved out a huge chunk of my life when I blanked Poppy, and admitting I might have been wrong means I'd have to face up to the fact that for all this time, I've been alone for no good reason. That we broke our mother's heart for no good reason.

I'm not ready for that, and I'm not sure I ever will be – because ultimately, no matter how much I can understand the truth of a lot of what she is saying, and how much I now see she was right about Gareth, it's still not much of an excuse for shagging your sister's boyfriend, is it?

We've all been drunk. We've all done stupid things. But this isn't on the same level as bringing home a traffic bollard, or doing a runner from an Indian restaurant, or tipping the cabbie with a snog. This is a world away from any of that, and it's not so easily forgiven.

I put the padded envelope aside, and decide I need to go downstairs. I've been up here for hours, and would quite like to stay here forever.

I pause in the doorway of my bedroom, go back, and tear that bloody Boyzone poster down from the wall.

When I emerge into the living room, Poppy is curled up on the sofa under one of Mum's vast collection of tartan blankets. She is pretending to be asleep, but I know better. She looks terrible – the worst I've seen her since this whole thing started. Her hair is greasy and flat to her head, her skin is taut and pale and dry, and I can see that she's been gnawing away at her usually flawless nails. It must be some kind of osmosis: a few days with me and even the most glamorous of women start turning into a frump.

'I know you're awake,' I say, sitting down on Mum's armchair. 'I can tell from the way you're breathing.'

She makes a pretence of waking up, yawning and stretching, and it almost makes me laugh, it's such a juvenile thing to do.

'Oh . . .' she says, wiping her eyes as though they are still full of sleep. 'Did you read the letters?'

'I did,' I reply, nodding. 'Although your handwriting was awful, and you clearly kept blubbing so much that loads of the ink was smudged.'

'And?' she asks, trying to sound tough but falling well short.

'And you were right about one thing you kept saying – none of it lets you off the hook. This isn't a film, is it, Poppy? It's not like we're in *Beaches* or *Steel Magnolias* or something, where I have some sudden rush of emotion and everything's immediately fine. This is real life, and it's a lot messier than that, and I'm just not ready to deal with F at the moment. In fact it can F right off. I'm not saying I won't be, ever, but . . . not right now. Even if mum's shaking her fists at me and doing her "we are not amused" face, it's not that straightforward.

'The best I can do is say that I'm sorry you went through all of that. It was your own fault, but I'm sorry – and I can see it's not as clear cut as I wanted it to be. I really don't want to talk about it any more, all right?'

Poppy scrabbles upright, the blanket falling to the floor as she moves, and refuses to meet my eyes. I don't know what she's thinking right now.

Maybe she secretly hoped I'd read those letters and rush downstairs and hug her. Maybe she's thinking I'm a nasty old cow. Maybe she's thinking none of those things – because this Poppy, the new Poppy, has become much better at hiding her feelings than the old one. Which suits me just fine right now – I can't deal with any more bloody feelings. I am already drowning in feelings, and it's making my eyeballs ache.

'Okay,' she says simply. 'Fair enough. Shall we move on with the A–Z? The quicker we do it, the quicker we can both get back to normal.'

I recognise her neutral tone as a classic self-defence posture, and go with it. Because she's right – we need to get through this, and both survive it. I know our late, great mother meant well, but at the moment, it feels as if it's doing more harm than good. It's opening up old wounds that might not stop bleeding, no matter how many plasters she tries to stick on from her celestial first-aid kit.

'Yep. Fine. What's next?' I ask.

She reaches for the index, which is now starting to tear where it's been folded and unfolded.

'Do you have a copy of that?' I say, frowning.

'Yes, Lewis sent a digital copy, plus I took photos of it, just in case. Anyway . . . G is an easy one. G is for "My Gorgeous Grandson", and there's one line next to it – it says "this is for Joe, and is none of your beeswax." I saw it earlier – it's in the roses box. Looks like it's another one of those British mammal cards. Maybe a darling deer or a beautiful badger. H is the next one for us, though. It's a theatre programme, and a note, and a . . . a DVD. Plus what she describes as "a load of odds and sods". I say "she" because I can't imagine Lewis saying anything like that. Do you want to do it now?'

'Might as well,' I answer, 'seeing as we're here. I'll go and make us some coffee.'

Poppy starts to rummage in the box while I walk through to the kitchen to put the kettle on. I realise as I do that I haven't eaten all day, and don't even feel hungry – for possibly the first time in about fifteen years.

Emotional trauma, it seems, has at least some side benefits.

Chapter 40

Andrea: H is for Hamming it Up

Hello my loves,

I'm writing this to you on a beautiful June evening. It's been one of those glorious days where you feel the long-forgotten sun on your skin, and everything in nature seems to be so glad to be alive. Do remember to top up the birdbath and the feeder while you're here, won't you? I wouldn't want my lovely little blue-tit family to think I'd abandoned them.

I've been to the hospital today, and it wasn't pleasant. They've been giving me some treatment that has made me feel absolutely ghastly, so I think that's the last time I'll be bothering.

It's only going to prolong the inevitable, and I've decided I'd rather spend my last weeks feeling at least human. There's a lot left for me to do, and I won't manage it with my head stuck in a toilet bowl, will I? And don't fret – Lewis was with me every step of the way. I practically had to kick him out so I could get some work done.

Anyway, on to business. I'm not sure how long I'll be able to keep going today, and I apologise now for the state of my handwriting. I've been spending so much time around doctors I seem to have started writing like one!

I am going to tuck this note inside one of my old programmes, and the subject of conversation tonight is unashamedly all about Me. Me, me, me, me, me. So there.

I'm taking a break from my emotional prodding, girls, to indulge in a good old-fashioned nostalgic wallow. I've so enjoyed getting all of this together, chatting to Lewis about it, and reliving a few glory moments. Old luvvies never die, darlings – they live on in celluloid heaven! I mean, Sir Alec Guinness might be long gone, but we still know these are not the 'droids you're looking for, don't we?

The programme I've chosen – from the many – is for *Grease*, and that run I had over the school holidays, playing Frenchie. I was exceptionally old to be playing a high-school student, but such is theatre, and it was great fun. You used to come along and sit in the box every night, and saw it so many times you knew all the words to that shama-lama-ding-dong song near the end. Plus you did the cutest ever little duet of 'Summer Nights' – you always insisted on being Danny, didn't you, Poppy?

That was a good time – but it wasn't always easy to combine my work with being a single mum. Rose, I'm sure you'll appreciate exactly how tough it was, now, after doing it yourself. I was trying to make life as stable as possible for you two, and that involved making a lot of compromises with my acting.

I tried to work during the holidays when you could come with me – all those days sitting on set with colouring books and dot-to-dots; what I'd have given for one of those Nintendo devices like Joe has! I had to turn jobs down, and of course I wasn't based in London, which is the centre of the known acting universe, so it wasn't always easy.

I had to balance the need to disrupt your lives with the need to earn money, and keep you two in Clark's shoes and fig rolls, as well as all those boring old things like paying the mortgage and the gas bill.

It was always a challenge, and I'm very thankful that Penny Peabody came along in my twilight years and rescued me from a life of cutting out food coupons and rationing my bubble baths. Still, no matter how challenging it was, it was a fabulous career.

I had so much fun, met so many interesting people; I travelled, and saw the world, and enjoyed pretty much every moment of it. I mean, it's not like a proper job, is it? I may not have hit the heights of some of my contemporaries, but I loved it – and somehow, with a nod and a wink from the big man upstairs, seem to have managed to combine it with raising two little girls on my own.

I've put together a little show reel for you, girls – it's on the video sharing thing that Lewis has set up, but it's also on a DVD too. I wanted you to have it like that as well so that you can pass it on to Joe without him having to see all the other, perhaps less fun, videos.

It's a collection of some of my favourite film and TV clips – and you'll get to see your dear old mama transformed before your very eyes into a collection of tarts with a heart, barmaids, sassy secretaries, yummy mummies, stern head teachers and, perhaps my most favourite of all, the nubile young victim of a dashingly handsome Count Dracula – that was before I had you two, and – if I say so myself – my bosoms in that peasant wench outfit are absolutely magnificent; they could have had a film of their own!

There are a few clips of some of my stage shows, and to prove I'm not a complete egotist, I found space on there for some footage of you two as well. Although you may not thank me for it – it's of you doing your 'Summer Nights' routine, and giving it loads of wella-wella-wella-uh!

In the package there will also be some more theatre programmes, a few old movie posters that have somehow survived the decades, and even some of my reviews. Only the kind ones, of course – the rest were ceremonially roasted over a fiery pit. I hope it's fun for you, and also helps you see me as someone other than your mother – because while that was obviously my most important role in life, it was far from the only one.

Now, while I'm at it, let's discuss the letter I. I'm going to ask Lewis to simply put it next to H and leave it blank, because to be honest, girls, I can't think of anything remotely interesting to go with it. So, I'm choosing I is for Inebriation – please tuck into that nice bottle of Amaretto I've left in the booze cupboard while you watch.

Happy viewing, and enjoy!

Mum xxx

Chapter 41

Poppy

'She was very, very good, wasn't she?' Rose says, slurring her words slightly around her amaretto glass. She's taken Mum at her word on the inebriation front – some instructions are simply easier to follow than others.

I don't mind. In fact, it's been perfect timing – things were ever so slightly tense after she read my old letters. I still don't know if I did the right thing in letting her or not. I guess if she'd come flying down the stairs in tears and we'd had an emotional reunion, I'd be more decided about it.

The reality is that they seem to have knocked her sideways a little, made her even more wary and cautious. I'm trying not to remember too clearly what was in them, and trying not to feel too bitter that she hasn't been willing to discuss them any further. Perhaps a tiny part of me had hoped that once she read my version of events, things would change – and that she'd realise how much all of this has damaged me as well.

As none of that seems to be happening – like she says,

this isn't *Beaches* – then the amaretto is some consolation. That and a very entertaining evening of watching my mother prance around the screen in a variety of outfits, using a variety of accents, and snogging a variety of men.

It was a bit of a rollercoaster for me, as I'm less drunk than Rose. Some of it was very, very funny – especially the nubile peasant wench falling under the mesmeric spell of Dracula's eyes as he fanged her. But I also found myself sitting there, the room dark apart from the flickering of the television, in floods of silent tears – seeing Mum there, on that huge flat-screen TV, but knowing that I'll never be able to talk to her about any of this.

Never be able to ask how she kept her face straight during the horror film; or how she managed to run away from that knife-wielding maniac in six-inch stilettoes, or why she had such a huge crush on Ian McShane. She's gone, and seeing her mature and change over the years on screen is just empha-sising how much I took her for granted while she was here, and how much I'll miss her now she's not.

'She was,' I reply, as we both politely ignore the clip of us pretending to be Danny and Sandy from *Grease* – it is unbear-ably cute and unbearably painful. 'She could have done so much more, couldn't she? If she hadn't been trying to look after us as well?'

'Yeah, but you can't look at it like that,' Rose says, trying to pour herself another glass and then looking confused when she discovers that the bottle is empty. 'She loved us, and she loved being a mum, and when you're a mum, it doesn't matter what you have to give up.'

'Really?' I answer, knowing that I'm looking less than convinced. Because I genuinely don't understand that aspect of Rose's life, or my mother's.

'Really. I mean, you don't know, you've never had kids . . . but that's how it works. I don't mind being a teaching assistant – it means I've been able to spend more time with Joe.'

'But weren't you supposed to find a cure for cancer?'

'To be honest, sis, if I found a cure for cancer, I'd probably lose it down the side of the sofa within minutes. After Gareth left, I could've gone back and carried on with my career – but it felt impossible, for all kinds of reasons. I wasn't exactly swimming in self-confidence, money was tight, and I had Joe to think about. I needed something stable that wasn't too challenging, and for ages, it worked perfectly. We can't all be hotshot career girls, you know.'

I bite back a snort at that one – because yes, while I have done well, and get to be the boss of my own particular universe, these days I'm seeing myself less and less as a hotshot and more as a saddo who's never done a day's work I'm actually proud of.

'What about now?' I ask, not wanting to throw mid-life career crisis into my current bucket of crap. 'Now Joe's older – you could do something else, couldn't you?'

She pulls a face, and uses her finger to scrape the last few drops of liqueur from her glass, licking it clean before she answers.

'I could. In fact I should. He's off to college, and it's not like I'm ancient or anything. I thought maybe about teacher training, but we could never afford it.'

'Is that the only reason?' I ask. 'Because there is that life-assurance policy Lewis mentioned; plus, well, you know, we might decide to sell this place. Mum would have wanted you to use the money for something like that.'

'Possibly. Although I can't think about selling this place right now. It'll make me cry, and possibly puke up. It's not just the money . . . I'm not sure I could do it. You need to be really organised to be a teacher, and really confident, and . . . well, I'm neither of those things.'

'That's bollocks!' I say, taking the glass out of her hand just as she starts sticking her tongue into it to try and lick a bit from the bottom. 'You're dead clever, Rose – you always were. You can do anything you want to do, if you set your mind to it.'

She pulls a face at me, but lets the glass go. I see her eyes drift in the direction of the kitchen, and know she's wondering what else is in the booze cupboard, the old lush.

'You sound like something off an American reality TV show, Poppy,' she replies. 'Like if I can dream it I can be it, and all that crap . . . it's not that simple in real life. Do you think she's got any gin left? I mean, she said I was for Inebriation, and I don't want to let her down.'

'I think you've already done her proud on that front. And I think you're just being a coward. Go to teacher training – you'll be brilliant at it.'

'Ha! Says the woman who always intended to write an award-winning book, and now writes advertising slogans for pooper scoopers . . .'

I stick my tongue out at her, and take the glasses through

to the kitchen. She may or may not be right on that front, and now is not the time to discuss it. Now is the time to go to bed.

'Let's do J,' she says, as I walk back into the room, clearly having other ideas. 'I'm absolutely shitfaced, and won't remember a thing about it tomorrow – so let's get another one out of the way. I've noticed she's trying to balance these things out – alternating the excruciatingly painful ones with the funny ones. And as we both almost wet ourselves laughing at that DVD, and we have all these lovely old cuttings to look at, I'm guessing that J will be an absolute bastard. Let's do it now.'

She's right, of course – that is what Mum's doing. Keeping us hooked, playing us perfectly, cranking up the tension and then deflating it. And I already know what J is. J is for Jealousy, and it's a list of things that made Mum jealous in her life – and our task is to talk about ways we were jealous of each other.

So while we really should go to bed – especially Rose – it's not an altogether terrible idea to get it out of the way while one of us is mildly tipsy, and the other is hammered.

'Okay,' I say, 'if you insist. I'm not going to argue with two-thirds of a bottle of amaretto, that's for sure. Give me a minute.'

I open up the box, and find the envelope marked with a J. As I do that, Rose shuffles off into the kitchen, and I hear the opening and slamming of doors, and the telltale chinking of glasses before she comes back in with two large gins.

'J is for Jin,' she says, grinning as she hands me a glass. 'If you spell it wrongly. I'd absolutely nail that teacher training, wouldn't I?'

'You would. Now, J is actually for Jealousy,' I reply, waving a laminated card at her while she throws herself back down on to the sofa so hard all the cushions whoosh as she lands. 'Shall I read it out to you?'

'You better had,' she says, sloshing the gin all over her T-shirt.

I flick on a lamp, and peer at the words. I'm not entirely sober myself, and am glad that this one has been typed so I don't have to decipher Mum's increasingly loopy scrawl. I know that the messier her handwriting gets, the more she was suffering, and that is an intolerable thing to have figured out. I wish I could un-think it.

'Okay . . . here goes . . .' I read. 'Darling girls, today we are going to deal with the dreaded Green-Eyed Monster, in all its many forms. Jealousy, envy, coveting thy neighbour's ass—'

'I covet my neighbour Simon's ass,' interrupts Rose. 'It's a mighty fine ass, let me tell you.'

I stay silent, and stare at her, until she makes an apologetic sound and mimes zipping her mouth up. I read on.

'Jealousy, envy, coveting thy neighbour's ass, whatever you like to call it, we've all felt it. Another one of the Big Nasties when it comes to our less attractive emotions. I've made a list of the things that brought out my green-eyed monster, and after you've read it, I'd like you two to discuss your own lists – specifically, the ways you were jealous of each other, both as children and now. That sounds exciting, doesn't it?'

'No,' says Rose, her face so sulky she looks like a teenager again. 'It sounds shit. Sorry . . . sorry . . . go on. Read the bloody list then.'

'Number 1,' I start, keeping my voice firm so she's not tempted to interrupt again, 'I was always jealous of Joan Collins. She had the most perfect bone structure I've ever seen, and it always made me want to give up.

'Number 2 – when Judi Dench was cast as M, I had an absolute fit, because it was one of my dream roles.

'Number 3 – I was always desperately covetous of Ian McShane – such a handsome man, brought out the beast in me! – and sickeningly jealous of all the actresses who got to appear in *Lovejoy* with him.

'Number 4 – I was secretly jealous of every perfect little couple in the village, especially when I had to see them at school events. Single mothers weren't as common then as they are now, and although I was happy with my choices in life, seeing their lovely little family units always made me want to scream.

'Number 5 – I was a tiny bit jealous of you two when you were teenagers, so young and perfect and with the whole world at your feet, just as my life felt like it was narrowing down to nothing.

'Number 6 – I was extremely jealous of people with money, and used to have fantasies about suddenly becoming rich, and being able to give you both everything in the entire world – plus have lovely shopping sprees in Harrods.

'Number 7 – my skin would practically turn a vivid shade of emerald every year when I stayed up late and watched the Oscars, knowing that I'd missed my boat on that front. I consoled myself by bitching about the dresses. Lewis helped with this one in later years, and is even more of a bitch than me.

'Number 8 – sometimes, and this is a nasty one, I was jealous of single people with no children, who could go out whenever they wanted and take exciting city breaks to Marrakesh.'

I finish reading the list, which ends abruptly – I suspect there was more, but perhaps she didn't want to admit to them, or perhaps she was just too tired to bother.

I'm glad that Rose let me get through it all without interruptions, and I sit back on my heels, waiting for her response. It wasn't as bad as it could have been, and I really can't begrudge Mum any of it. Much as we think parents are superheroes when we're kids – annoyingly bossy superheroes – she was only human.

'Is that it?' says Rose, looking at me expectantly. 'That's not so long, is it? And I still don't get the Ian McShane thing, do you? Anyway, what are we supposed to do now – discuss our *feelings* again?'

The gin is all gone from her glass, and her eyes are blinking rapidly, as though she's trying to get rid of her double vision. She is way too drunk for this.

'Yes, but we could do it tomorrow if you like . . .'

'No! I'll go first. I was always jealous of your legs. They

just go on forever, and you always made me feel like Stumpy McShortarse when I stood next to you.'

Hmmm. Fair enough, I think, deciding to reciprocate in kind.

'I was always jealous of your boobs. I didn't get any until I was sixteen, and even then they weren't the stuff of centrefolds. You were always so curvy, and you had perfect skin when I was covered in spots the size of power stations.'

'Yeah . . . you really did suffer with that, didn't you? Poor little Spotty Poppy. Well, I was jealous of your hair as well – yours has always been straight and shiny and easy, and mine is a nightmare.'

'Back at you. I always wanted your curls – it gave you this earth-goddess thing. And your eyes. You got Mum's eyes, and I, presumably, got lumbered with our absent dad's.'

She nods, bites her lip, and is clearly thinking of what else to add to the list.

'I hated the way you were so clever with words. You could do little rhymes, and make up limericks, and do improvised raps. All I could do was use Bunsen burners.'

I'm not so sure I'm pleased with the way this has slipped into 'hate', but there isn't much I can do about it. Rose is on a roll.

'Well, I was jealous of all your friends. People liked you much more than they liked me, even if I could rap,' I say. Which is true – she was always much more popular.

'And you were jealous of Gareth,' she adds, pointing one

unsteady finger at what she thinks is me, but is actually a few inches off to my left.

'Yes. I hated Gareth,' I admit.

'Well I,' she says, leaning so far forward I am worried she is going to topple off the sofa and land in a heap of wobbly Rose on the floor, 'hate your fucking face. The End!'

Right, I think, downing my gin in one. That went well.

Chapter 42

Rose

K, as it turns out, is for Karaoke. Poppy delved into the magical box to find that it was just a gaudy A4 flyer for a weekly night at the Farmer's, which I could tell deeply offended the marketing guru my sister had become.

'The apostrophes are in the wrong place,' she said, looking at it in disgust. 'Friday Night's are Singalong Night's. Uggh.'

Apostrophes, to be fair, were the least of my concerns. Mother dearest had simply written on top of the paper, in bright-red felt-tip pen: Go To This!

You really can't knock her sick sense of humour.

At least it was something we could do at night, which gave me the whole day to try and make myself presentable. I cracked open one of Mum's many toiletry gift sets, and given my hair a deep conditioning treatment to try and tame the frizz.

I plucked my eyebrows so I looked a bit less like a werewolf, and managed to squash myself into my jeans instead of my usual trackie bottoms. I fear my legs now resemble giant walking sausages, but there's not much I can do about that in the timeframe.

Poppy took one look at me and decided to give me a mini-makeover, which I endured silently, and with what I like to think of as a great deal of dignity. She trimmed my hair, and opened a few buttons on my top to flash some boobage, and did my make-up.

'You were always so much better at this than me,' I said, as she shaped and blended, a look of utter concentration on her face.

'I had to be. Spotty Poppy, remember?'

I do remember – not only that other people used to call her that, but that I said it to her myself the night before. I feel a blush of shame at the memory – she really had suffered.

When Poppy finished creating her masterwork of make-up, she gave my nose a little tap with the powder puff, just like Mum used to do, which threatened to tear me up and ruin all her magical mascara work.

I have to admit, though, that she did a good job, and I look better than I have in . . . well, years. She, naturally enough, just slipped into a tiny leather mini-skirt and swooshed her shiny hair out and became a supermodel. The cow.

Now, we are parked up outside the pub, and I really don't want to go in. I'm driving, as I am temporarily off the sauce after recent excesses, and Poppy is checking her lipstick in the passenger mirror. The mirror that is held on by silver duct tape. I keep several rolls of it in my boot, like a serial killer.

'Your car is a mess,' she says, once she's satisfied. 'It's like being trapped in a McDonald's recycling bin.'

'Thank you,' I reply, unhooking my seatbelt, 'we aim to please. God . . . I really don't want to do this.'

'Why not?' she asks, frowning at me. 'It's better than sitting in the cottage crying about the ghosts of traumas past, isn't it? Besides, you have a nice voice. It could be fun.'

'It's not that . . . I just don't want to see these people again. Look at this car park – it's packed. Everyone in the village will be here. And they'll all be, like, "look at those two little madams", and "they're only back now she's dead", and "God, she's put weight on, serves her right", and—'

'And I think you're overestimating how interesting we are, Rose. They have their own lives to worry about, without judging ours. And even if they do, who gives a shit? Once this is all done, we never have to see them again, do we? Now come on. Get into the groove, girl. It's show time.'

She gets out of the car, and teeters across the gravel with way too much ease for a woman in those kinds of shoes. Frankly, they look like she stole them from a prostitute.

I pull a face at her, but follow on behind, grimacing as we open the door to the pub. This is a place I've been to so many times. A place where I spent large chunks of my childhood, eating a bag of crisps and drinking a lemonade while Mum had grown-up chats and the odd gallon of G&T – but I am still gripped with uncertainty.

Once we're inside, I let my eyes adjust to the dim lighting, and try very hard to unhear the version of 'I Will Always Love You' that is being slaughtered on the karaoke machine.

I look around, and see that little has changed – still the same rugged stone floors; the ancient wooden bar; the horse brasses hanging from the wall. It's been painted, and it smells a lot less of smoke, but other than that, it's like stepping into a time machine. I almost expect to see my mother holding court in the corner that she always sat in, waving us over and sending us to the bar to get her a top-up.

Much to my relief, there's not suddenly a huge silence as we enter, while everyone in the village stares at us with hostility. In fact, all that happens is that a few people wave, and some of the farmers give their traditional effusive greeting of one single nod.

I head for a free table, and Poppy goes straight to get drinks. I sit nervously, twisting my hair around my fingers, and watch her. There's an exceptionally good-looking young man behind the bar, and they seem to be giving each other far more attention than it requires to order a white wine spritzer and a Diet Coke.

The mangled rendition of Whitney Houston finally comes to a stop, and I see as she steps from the makeshift stage area that Whitney was actually Tasmin Hughes, my old school friend from a million years ago. She's all dolled up, wearing a flimsy white frock that makes her look like Marilyn Monroe after she ate all the cakes in the entire world.

She's a big woman, but carries it in that proud, sassy way that makes her sexy – something I've never quite mastered. She pauses as she walks past, does a little double take as she sees me, and breaks out into a huge grin. I smile back, secretly hoping she'll move on, and struggle to keep it on my face when she sits next to me instead.

'I was hoping I'd see you around again!' she says, fanning

herself with a beer mat to cool her karaoke sweat. 'How are you, Rose? God, it's been an age, hasn't it?'

She doesn't wait for my reply, but instead reaches out and takes hold of my hand.

'I was so sorry about your mum,' she says, genuine sympathy on her face. 'She was a lovely woman, and we all miss her. Especially here.'

'Here? You mean the Farmer's, or karaoke night?'

'Both – she did a fabulous version of "Big Spender" every time. Had the old coots in fits, it did – she was one sexy mama when she wanted to be!'

I am momentarily thrown by this image, but once I squint at the stage, surrounded by disco lights, I can almost see it: Mum hamming it up, giving it some bump and grind, channelling her best Shirley Bassey and nailing it every time.

I burst into sudden and unwelcome tears, partly at that image, and partly at Tasmin's unexpected kindness. I'm not sure I'll ever get to grips with this emotional rollercoaster – one minute I'm coping, and the next I'm drowning in loss and regret.

Tasmin immediately produces a tissue from her cleavage, which I accept with a snotty gurgle, and says: 'It's all right, love, don't worry – I've been where you are, and I know it hurts like buggery. It'll get better, I promise. Just don't try and control it too much. Let it have its way with you and it passes quicker. Like sex when you're drunk.'

'Your mum died?' I ask, frowning as I try and remember if I'd been told. I remember Tasmin's mother well – she was big and brassy and managed a team of macho men at the chicken plant. She was what my mother always called a formidable lady, one of her highest compliments, usually reserved for Dame Joan Plowright and Queen Victoria.

Tasmin nods, making both her blonde curls and her chins wobble, and replies: 'About eight years ago. Breast cancer. They've told me I should think about getting mine lopped off as a precaution, but I'm still not sure I can bear to part with them.'

She gazes down at her glistening cleavage with adoration, and I find myself following her eyes and staring at her chest.

'Anyway. Losing your mum is a killer, no matter how old you are. Still stings. I still get those fits of tears like you're having now, only they come less and less often. Still miss her, always will.'

'I'm sorry,' I blubber, her gentle words only serving to make me cry more. 'I'm sorry your mum died. I'm sorry I'm crying. And I'm sorry I never visited you when you got pregnant.'

'Oh lord!' she says, throwing her head back and laughing. 'Don't worry about that one! You were only a kid yourself, and you weren't the only one – it was like everyone thought it was catching! Worked out all right, though, see – that's my Jake there, working the bar. Assistant manager, he is, la-di-da.'

I follow her finger, and see that she is pointing towards the good-looking guy Poppy is flicking her hair at. Jesus. He must be, what, 26, 27? Unbelievable.

'Are you still with . . . what was his name, Sean?'

'Miraculously I am, yes. Few ups and downs. The odd divorce, and the occasional death threat. But yes, still together, against all the odds – we have two younger ones as well, but obviously they're over at the Tennyson's. Is that your Poppy over there, talking to Jake, by the way?'

'I think "talking" is a kind word for what she's doing,' I reply, feeling my face flame up on my sister's behalf. 'She looks as if she's about to eat him for dinner. I'm sorry for that as well.'

'Again, there's no need to be sorry – do you ever do anything but apologise? Jake is a grown man, and I gave up worrying about his sex life a long time ago, once I'd drummed it into him that we didn't want any repeats of my circumstances. He lives in a soundproofed flat over the garage, and what I don't hear doesn't hurt me. What about you? You have a lad, don't you? Joe, isn't it? Your mum was so proud of him.'

'Yes. Joe. He's sixteen – so I suppose I'll need to start worrying about his sex life soon. And . . . thank you. For being so nice.'

'Why wouldn't I be?' she asks, looking confused.

'Because we've not been back here for so long. Because I thought you'd all . . . I don't know, think we were cows for not seeing enough of our mum.'

Tasmin puffs out a long, befuddled breath, giving Poppy a little wave as she finally starts to make her way back towards us.

'Don't be daft. Life gets complicated, we all know that. Your mum was happy here, and she never had a bad word to say about either of you. She was always full of her weekends away and her trips to see you, honest.'

I know she's trying to be kind, but I can't help being struck by the sadness of that – the thought of my mum sitting here, telling stories about her wonderful daughters and how well they looked after her, when the reality was so different.

Maybe she was trying to fool them, or maybe she was trying to fool herself, who knows? But the truth of the matter is that we broke her heart, no matter how many spa breaks Poppy took her on or how many roast dinners I cooked for her in Liverpool. She was forced to lead two lives – three in fact: one for me, one for Poppy, and one for herself – because of our stubborn refusal to put the past behind us. It is unbelievably sad, and I am feeling less like doing karaoke than ever.

I look around and see all the familiar faces from my child-hood, laughing and chatting in The Pub That Time Forgot, and know that this was a big part of Mum's life – and I chose not to share it with her. All that time, wasted.

Poppy places the drinks down on the table, and makes mindless small talk with Tasmin until she leaves, making me promise to stay in touch.

'I'm BigTas99 on Instagram,' she says, waggling her eyebrows at me. 'Don't be a stranger.'

Poppy has finished half her wine while she was at the bar cradle-snatching, and has also managed to get hold of a karaoke book that lists all the songs. She pores over it, appar-ently oblivious to everything around us that is making me feel so bad. Which I suppose is a good thing – life will be easier if we can alternate our nervous breakdowns.

'That was Tasmin's son you were chatting up,' I say, gulping my Diet Coke and wishing it had Jack Daniel's in it. 'He's only twenty-seven.'

She looks up at me, frowning.

'Well, that's a perfectly respectable age then, isn't it? He's nice. Got some good ideas about marketing this place, and he was also annoyed about the apostrophe issue. Plus he's fit as fuck. What are you going to sing?'

'"Big Spender",' I say, without even thinking about it.

'Cool. I can see that. Give it loads. I think I'm going to go for a bit of Girls Aloud. I love that "Sound of the Underground" song. You okay? You look a bit . . . soggy.'

I use Tasmin's boob tissue to wipe my cheeks, and try to pull myself together.

'Is it messing with your head, being here?' Poppy asks, closing the karaoke book and giving me her full attention. I nod, not really wanting to get into it with her. We're in this incredibly strange position where only the two of us know what the other is going through, but neither of us is quite able to offer comfort or consolation. We're still like prickly cacti, trying our best but constantly spiking each other by accident.

'I get that,' she replies, reaching out to touch my hand but thinking better of it at the last minute and snatching it away. 'It's hard. Being in all the places she's been, seeing her friends, finally being part of her life but doing it too late.

'It's like we're retreading her footsteps and she could appear at any moment, isn't it? I feel the same way – as soon as I walked in here, I remembered that New Year's Eve we had together . . . anyway. I can't deal with all of that right now. I need to switch off for a bit, if that makes sense, or I might spontaneously combust. I'm just planning on drinking and flirting my way through it tonight.'

I'm jealous of her ability to do either of those things, but am saved from further conversation by the arrival of Lewis, looming above us in all his bulk. He really is enormous, and still dressed in a suit and waistcoat, even in the pub on a Friday night.

'Ladies,' he says, nodding in greeting. 'It's nice to see you again. I'm delighted that you made it to K at least. I trust you're both keeping well?'

'If by "well" you mean "nervous wrecks", then yes, thank you Lewis, we're doing fine,' replies Poppy, raising her eyebrows at him, her tone slightly snippy. I still don't think she's forgiven him for giving me the keys to the cottage.

'Yes, thanks Lewis,' I add, hastily. 'Thanks for everything – for looking after our mother like you did. We really appreciate it.'

'There's nothing to thank me for,' he says, smiling. 'Every moment I spent in your mother's company was a privilege. I look forward to seeing your performances later.'

With a polite nod he ambles off, making his way through the crowds to sit in the far corner. The corner where Mum always used to sit. I'm probably imagining it, but I think he looks so sad, so lonely, sitting there on his own – as though the other half of him is missing.

'Right. I'm going to chat Jake up a bit more, get another drink, and start on the karaoke. Are you with me?' says Poppy, standing up and looking determined.

'No,' I say simply, 'but knock yourself out.'

She shrugs, and I look on as she shimmies through the pub, attracting admiring glances as she goes. Still gorgeous, like she was as a teenager – but these days, she knows it.

I sit mainly alone for the rest of the night, chatting to a few passing people who stop and express their sympathies, to Tasmin again, and to Gloria Lubbock, our old head teacher, who seems unbearably disappointed that I never gained my PhD. She was hoping for her first doctor, she says.

Poppy sings the Girls Aloud track, which brings the house down, and Tasmin does 'Like A Virgin', and even Lewis gets in on the act, doing a splendidly dignified version of 'My Way'. I manage to get through 'Big Spender' purely on adrenalin, acting it the way I thought my mother would act it, pretending I'm not me, but someone far sexier – someone farmers would like to watch waggling her huge hips.

It goes surprisingly well, and someone yells 'eat your heart out Shirley Bassey!' as I stagger back to my seat. Nobody has been hostile at all, everyone has in fact been incredibly kind, and somehow that is making me feel worse – like I don't deserve their kindness. Perhaps I'd feel better if they chased me on to the village green and whipped me with sticks.

After a couple of hours, I am desperate to go back to the cottage and pull the duvet over my head, but Poppy is feeling extremely merry and shows no inclination to end the evening at all. It seems to have become an unwritten rule of the A–Z that at least one of us must be drunk at all times.

'Can we go soon?' I ask, as she brings me yet another glass of Coke.

'Not yet, Rose . . . please? I've put us down for one more song. After that, I promise I'll come. Or you can go, at least, and I'll make my own way back.'

'By make your own way back, do you mean spend the

271

night with Tasmin Hughes's son and do the walk of shame through the village in the morning?'

'Maybe I do, and maybe I do . . .' she replies, grinning. She looks happy and, much as I want to resent her for it, I don't seem to have it in me. Progress of sorts, I suppose.

'One more song,' I say, like a stern mum relenting on one battle in a long war.

'One more,' she says, 'for Mum. We'll do "Summer Nights" – bagsy being Danny . . .'

Chapter 43

Poppy

When I get back to the cottage the next morning, I find Rose already up and about – unsurprising as it is almost midday – pottering in the garden, a duster in her hand.

'What are you doing?' I ask, walking barefoot towards her, sandals dangling from my fingers. 'Polishing the geraniums?'

She looks up at me, as though I've caught her out doing something sinful, and replies: 'No. I was dusting the garden gnomes' heads. You didn't walk all the way from the village like that, did you?'

'Nah,' I reply, collapsing on to the grass and stretching out. The sun is warm on my face, and the blue tits and their friends are tweeting away so much it feels like something out of a Disney cartoon. 'Jake gave me a lift to the end of the lane.'

I shield my face from the sun, and squint up at her. All I notice is her eyes – those big, beautiful eyes that are so much like my mother's. That image goes perfectly with her disapproving expression, and her stern voice as she asks: 'Did you have sex with Tasmin Hughes's son?'

'No,' I say, 'we stayed up all night listening to music, and just talked and talked and talked . . . it was so special. It's like we're soul mates or something.'

'Really?' she asks, sounding half hopeful, half disbelieving.

'Nope. We shagged each other's brains out. And just because he's Tasmin Hughes's son, it doesn't mean he's a child. I can assure you he comes with a fully functioning set of adult male bits.'

'I don't want to hear about his male bits, thank you very much.'

'Are you jealous?' I say, sitting up so I'm not quite so blinded. 'Because you sound jealous.'

She gives me a dirty look, and throws the duster at my face.

'Maybe I am,' she replies, sitting down next to me. 'In the spirit of honesty and transparency. It's been . . . well, a few years, shall we say. I'm not exactly fending them off with a shitty stick back in Liverpool.'

'That,' I say, throwing the duster back at her and hoping I haven't caught some rare form of gnome disease, 'is because you send out this incredibly unsexy old lady vibe. It's nothing to do with the way you look – it's the way you act. You need to get in touch with your inner Irene Cara.'

'What? Start working in a welding plant?'

'No, dummy, I mean you need to start feeling luscious again. Feeling like the world is going to remember your name. Do some sexy dancing through the garden sprinklers the next time your fine-assed neighbour is out mowing his lawn.'

'I don't think so,' Rose says, as she screws up her eyes and tries to imagine the scene. 'No, I just can't see that one working. Partly because we don't have sprinklers, I use a giant watering can I got in Home Bargains.'

'You'll have to improvise then,' I reply. 'I'll hold it over your head while you do it.'

'Thanks, but no thanks. Anyway. I took a look in the box.'

I feel momentarily taken aback by this, at her intrusion into what I have started to think of as my territory. I remind myself that Mum left those boxes for both of us, and that I can be a deeply unattractive control freak at times.

'I know we're on L, and I know that means we're moving on – but what is it, specifically?'

'Come on inside. I'll get us some coffee and you can see for yourself. Plus you need to pack. I'm already done, and I can't imagine it'll take you long to stuff all your lap-dancing thongs in a carrier bag . . . it's two photos, by the way – one of Mum at my house, and one of her in your flat. With some instructions written on the back.'

'Okay, okay, I'm coming,' I groan, as I drag myself back to my now quite sore feet. 'God, I'm tired . . . parts of me I never even knew I had are aching . . .'

'Don't. Want. To. Know.'

Chapter 44

Andrea: L is for Location, Location, Location

Hello darlings!

I hope you're both doing well, and my evil plan is working, even a little tiny bit. If you're reading this, then I have to assume it is, and that you're still at the cottage. I hope you both had fun at the karaoke night – did Lewis do his 'My Way'? He's such an old ham!

Anyway, not much room to write on these cards, so I'll make it quick – today, I'd like you to move on. You'll be visiting two places, both of which also begin with L, in a magnificent coincidence! Liverpool, and London.

I've stayed in both of your homes, and had wonderful times with you there – but you've never set foot on each other's turf, have you? Now it's time to throw off the sheltered environment of the cottage, and get out into the real world. Rose, you must stay a night at Poppy's flat; and Poppy, you'll also be heading North to see where Rose and Joe live.

This doesn't sound like much, but I think it's important. I don't want you to just go through this A–Z like a task you have to complete, then box it all back up without it making any difference. You need to see each other's real lives for the first – and hopefully not last – time.

Happy travelling, Rosehip and Popcorn – make sure you tell Lewis you're going so he can come and sort the blue tits out!

Lots of love,

Mum xxx

Chapter 45

Rose

A road trip with my estranged sister turns out to be not quite as much of an ordeal as I'd expected. We decide to go in her car, with our A–Z boxes packed in the boot.

Partly it's because I'm nervous about driving all the way to London in my duct-taped McDonald's recycling bin, but partly it's because I want to leave part of me behind. That way I know I'll have to come back, if only to get the car.

Over the last week, the cottage has somehow started to feel like home again. The initial shock of being there without my mother, and with Poppy, has scaled down to something bearable. More than bearable – comforting. I still find myself crying when I come across some precious Mum-related object – her nail scissors, in particular, set me off – but it is starting to feel like less of a trauma, and more of a consolation. Being here, and touching the things she touched, in such familiar surroundings.

The thought of leaving throws me off balance – as though

we have created a little bubble of unreality that is allowing me to function. I suppose that's why she asked us to move on, but I don't have to like it.

Locking the place up, insanely checking the lights are switched off over and over again, filling the birdbath to brimming, loitering in the hallway and tidying up her coats – it's all because I'm nervous. As though, if I leave the cottage, I'll leave my mother behind, and never be able to recapture her.

I think Poppy is feeling some of the same thing, and she tries to make it easier by giving me the old cassette player for the journey, along with the ancient carrier bag full of tapes.

Some of them are my recordings, and some of them are Mum's. A weird mix of Ultravox and Fleetwood Mac and Michael Jackson and a random Tracy Chapman album.

We settle on a few cassettes from about 1988, when I went through a phase where I used to record the Top Forty singles live off the radio on a Sunday. What can I say, I thought it was cool.

By the time we get to Islington, navigating our way through Oxford and the sprawling London suburbs, we've managed to not talk to each other at all, and instead have produced some very spirited singing along to 'The Only Way Is Up' by Yazz, 'Push It' by Salt-N-Pepa, and Guns N' Roses doing 'Sweet Child O' Mine'.

She parks the car in the underground garage, and I follow her into the lifts up to her flat. She's gone very quiet, and is jiggling her keys around nervously, her face all pursed up like a cat's bottom. She keeps pushing her hair behind her ears, and tapping her toes, and all of the carefree energy I've seen in her over the last few days seems to have dried up.

I'm not sure if she's so nervous because I'm here with her, if she's having one of those Mum-is-dead meltdowns that we both keep having at unexpected moments, or if she's simply slipping back into being London Poppy. If that last one is true, then I genuinely feel sorry for her, because London Poppy seems to be incredibly tense.

Her flat is in one of those old buildings that has been swished up for young professionals – all neutral colours in the hallways, and a gym in the basement, and about as much personality as a dead kipper. I'm sure it costs an arm and possibly both legs to live here, but it wouldn't be my first choice, and I find myself already judging.

I remind myself that that is not in the spirit of the A–Z, and that I have nothing to be judgey about – it's not like a small semi in the posh end of Liverpool is much to write home about either.

She unlocks the doors, and gestures for me to go in first, following silently behind and plonking her bags down. She picks up her mail, flicks through it, and immediately presses a button that makes the blinds swoosh open.

Sunlight floods in, and allows me to see the place properly for the first time. It's so neat and tidy that it looks like nobody lives here. All the furniture is black leather or chrome or a combination of the two, and the biggest single item in the room is a desk, where I presume she carries out work vital to the survival of the luxury pet supplies industry.

There's one framed photo of her and Mum – a really funny one of them both with green face masks and towel turbans – and one bookshelf, crammed with marketing manuals and that type of hardback non-fiction that's bought as much for the way it looks as what it contains.

This surprises me, as the Poppy I knew was a voracious reader – her bookcase back at the cottage was just as crammed, but there you'd find Thomas Hardy slumming it next to Judith Krantz, and Harry Potter getting intimate with Daphne du Maurier.

'Coffee?' she says, sounding business-like and to the point.

'Please,' I reply, gazing around at the flat, trying to imagine this as my once supremely creative sister's home and failing. It's got an open-plan design, and I see her walk into the kitchen and slam a few cupboard doors open before she pulls a so-annoyed-I-could-scream face.

'Sorry,' she shouts through. 'I ran out the night Lewis called, and I just kept forgetting to buy more . . . I have wine, or water.'

'What about bread and fish? Then we could invite the five thousand round and have a party.'

She frowns at me, obviously having had a sense of humour failure, and runs the cold tap for a while. She pulls one of those water filter jugs out of the fridge, and starts to fill it up.

I notice the old tobacco tin on her desk, and it makes me smile. I've not seen her smoking at all recently, so she must have given up, but it's nice to see it there – yet another blast from the past, one connection to the crazier Poppy of yesteryear.

Here, in this pristine environment, it's hard to imagine that Poppy existing – hard to envision her sitting in this room, with its walls in a million shades of beige, and its black leather and its chrome, rolling up a joint and actually relaxing.

I sit down on the sofa, which is actually more comfortable than it looks, and wonder what the hell we're going to do for the whole day and night. I'm feeling tense because she is, and I can't wait to get out of here and back to Liverpool – I just wish she wasn't coming with me.

'I don't have any food, I'm sorry,' she says, passing me a glass of water and perching on her desk. 'I just . . . well, I don't have any.'

'That's all right,' I say. 'We can order a takeaway, or go out. In fact, let's go out. We can get an early tea and have a drink. Are there any nice places round here?'

'Loads of nice places,' she replies, chewing her lip and frowning, 'if you're about twenty-five. I don't know . . . this feels weird, doesn't it? I've lived here for years, and it's only now, with you sitting there on the sofa, that I'm starting to feel a bit pissed off with it. With a lot of things.'

'What do you mean? It's really nice. It's a lovely flat.'

She laughs, but it sounds brittle and strained.

'It's a lovely flat, yes – but I should have outgrown it by now. I should have outgrown a lot of things. Like going out on the pull with women in their twenties, and never having any bloody food in the kitchen. I bet you never run out of food, do you?'

'All the time,' I reply, smiling gently. 'Because I rampage around the kitchen like it's an episode of *Man v. Food*, and eat it all. Apart from the quinoa salad. That always ends up in the bin because it's past its sell-by date.'

She taps the side of the glass with her fingernail, and the sound echoes around the sterile room. I hate this place too, but I'm not about to say it. I don't think Mum brought us here so I could put the boot in. Poppy seems to be doing a good enough job of that herself.

'I don't know, Rose. I felt different in the cottage . . . happier, even though we were there under bloody awful circumstances, and even though Mum was making us jump through all kinds of evil flaming hoops . . . it felt like home. This feels like . . . like a hotel.

'Like somewhere I should stay for a few nights while I'm at some business meeting, not a place where a grown-up woman should live. Not that I spend that much time in here – I'm usually at work. And when I'm not at work, I'm at that desk, doing more work. It's literally all I have in my life, apart from Mum . . . and, well. She's gone, isn't she?

'And I know you're trying to be nice – thank you – but I think perhaps I'm seeing this through your eyes. And it looks empty, doesn't it?'

'Well,' I say, not totally sure how to handle this one. 'It's tidy. My place is a dump, as you'll see. But perhaps you could just put a few more photos up? Buy some more books? Make a bit of . . . mess? You used to love a bit of mess.'

'I know I did,' she answers, managing a small smile. 'I was an absolute pig! But after I got sacked from that first job, and then decided to try again in London, I made myself change. I needed to be organised, and focused, and work hard. I couldn't let myself carry on being the way I was – mooning around after you, wallowing in my own filth, so chaotic I forgot to brush my own teeth half the time. I had to be different – and this is what I ended up with. It's definitely different. I'm just not sure if it's better.'

'Well, come on, it's not that bad, is it? I mean, you must have friends? Go out a lot?'

'Yeah, I suppose,' she replies, not looking too enthused about it. 'There's this girl Kristin I go drinking with. And this guy called Josh I met in the gym . . . but he's just a fuck buddy.'

I recoil at the phrase, and of course she notices.

'It's true, sorry if it offends your delicate sensibilities. We don't all live like nuns.'

I wave it away – it's none of my business what she does with her vagina – and ask: 'What else? Do you have any more nice photos we could frame up?'

She thinks about it, chewing on the skin around her finger, and pulls an uncertain face.

'Well, I have some of Mum. And . . . well, there are the pictures of the kids.'

'What kids?'

'I'll show you.'

She jumps up and dashes around to the other side of her desk, apparently filled with a new enthusiasm. She comes back bearing a black vinyl photo album, which she hands to me, hovering by my side as I open it.

The whole album is filled with smiling little faces – some obviously African, some Asian, all shiny teeth and big eyes. Page after page after page of them.

'Who *are* these children?' I ask, confused.

'They're my sponsor kids. You know, like in those adverts on the telly, where you pay X amount a month so little Jimmy can drink clean water, that kind of thing?'

'But there are loads of them!'

'There are . . . twenty-seven, I think. I get little letters from them, and photos, and updates about how they're doing, and I send them Christmas presents . . . it's nice.'

I flip through the pages, looking at brightly coloured scenes from the rural Third World, and shake my head.

'You sponsor twenty-seven children?'

She nods, not seeming to think it's weird at all, and I realise that this is one of her many coping mechanisms. The guilt, the pain, of the last seventeen years has taken its toll on both of us. I've dealt with it by eating, and throwing my whole energy into Joe's life at the expense of my own. She's been tidying up, working, finding fuck buddies and sponsoring children. It's absolutely insane.

I close the album, and stand up.

'Come on,' I say. 'We're going out. We both need a drink. I'm going to have a quinoa salad, and you're going to have

285

pasta, and we're going to at least try and enjoy ourselves, okay? Then we'll come back, and I'll spend the night pretending I'm in a posh hotel, and tomorrow we can go to Liverpool and I'll show you my humble hovel. How does that sound?'

'You had me at pasta,' she says, finding her smile again.

Chapter 46

Poppy

My self-pity party has well and truly ended by the time we pull up in the driveway of Rose's house on the north side of Liverpool. I've been given a commentary on the way there, and seen the Liver Birds, and the river, and the beach. She's chattering away furiously, because, I think, she's a bit freaked out by all of this. By bringing the enemy into home territory – letting the sniper through the gates.

I don't know if she'll ever feel any different, but I do know that Mum was well and truly an evil genius – she must have understood that this, this swapping of life experiences, confronting the realities we'd built without each other, was one of the biggest tests we would face. Bravo, Mommie dearest.

Rose switches off the mix tape as we arrive – Lisa Stansfield was at number one with 'All Around the World' – and we both sit and look at the house. It's quite small, with a patch of garden in the front, and it's in a nice neighbourhood of similar properties, all neatly lined up like Stepford homes. The cul-de-sac is quiet, and there are small kids out and about riding on their bikes, playing football, and chasing each other up and down the street.

There are grown-ups out gardening, and every driveway seems to have a mumsy-looking car parked in it, and grey wheelie bins waiting to be collected are lined up like plastic soldiers.

'Right,' she says, sounding determined. 'We'd better go in. I warn you, it's not like a hotel. Or if it is a hotel, it would have terrible reviews on TripAdvisor.'

She carries her bags up the path, and I follow her, staying silent.

She unlocks the door, and walks through. Within seconds, she is looking around, sniffing, her face screwed up. The curtains are closed, just enough sunlight creeping through to show a hallway with stairs leading to the bedrooms, and she seems slightly off balance as she leads me through to the lounge.

'What's up?' I say, looking around curiously. 'Have you been broken into or something?'

'Not unless the burglars decided to order a Domino's and get the beers in,' she says, pointing to an empty pizza box and scattered Heineken cans. 'I mean, I'm not the world's best housekeeper, but I didn't leave it like this . . .'

She stands, hands on hips, and frowns, trying to piece it all together, before walking back into the hallway and bellowing at the top of her voice: 'Joe! Are you up there?'

It's an impressively loud bellow, and done in that certain tone that only mothers seem able to pull off. Even I feel automatically like I've done something wrong.

'I thought he was at his dad's?' I say, opening the curtains so we don't feel like we're in a funeral parlour. The living room is small, and cosy, and not at all the hovel I was expecting, apart from the rubble on the floor.

'He's supposed to be,' she replies, stomping into the kitchen and automatically putting the kettle on. 'But my spider senses are tingling.'

She goes through the motions of making us a cuppa – and, predictably enough, she's not run out of coffee – while I mooch around. It's a lovely room, facing the back garden, with exactly the same levels of lived-in mess that our own mother used to surround herself with.

School letters are held up on the fridge door with magnets; a calendar on the wall shows all of Joe's various football matches and guitar lessons; the fold-out dining table is covered with a green polka-dot cloth.

'You're overdue for your smear test,' I say, pointing at the calendar.

'Ha! My one exciting social engagement for the month,' she replies, opening the fridge to look for milk. I notice some wilted quinoa salad alone on the shelf, and know it has a date with the bin.

'He's definitely here,' she says, pulling out a big semi-skimmed bottle, 'because there are five cartons of milk in the fridge. I forgot to cancel the milkman, obviously.'

'Is he hot?' I ask, trying to lighten the mood as she hands me my coffee.

'About as hot as Fred,' she replies. She pauses, then lets out another one of those tremendous bellows, shouting Joe's name. My eyes go wide, and I am fairly certain one of my eardrums has just exploded.

She leans her head on one side, listening out, and within seconds we both hear the sound of footsteps thundering down the stairs.

My nephew staggers into the room, ricocheting off the walls in a way that implies that at least part of his brain is still asleep. His long brown hair is tufting all over the place, and he's bare-chested, wearing fleecy pyjama pants with orange footballs on them. He appears to be even taller than the last time I saw him, super-skinny, and disconcertingly like his father.

'Mum!' he says, wiping sleep from his eyes. 'I didn't expect you back!'

'Clearly,' she says, leaning back against the sink, her arms crossed over her chest in a classic pissed-off mama bear pose. 'Why aren't you at your dad's? And did you drink all that beer?'

He looks a bit guilty, so I suspect he did drink at least some of the beer, but he stands up tall and tries to appear tough. Epic fail – the football PJs ruin it.

'It all got a bit messy at Dad's,' he says. 'Sylvie wouldn't let Amber and Ariel come – said they had chicken pox, but I suspect not. Plus him and Heather are . . . well, they're not exactly getting on. Heather's up all night with Charlie, and Dad just seemed really fed up and knackered, and . . . well, I decided to come home. He put me on the train from London yesterday. I was going to call you.'

'Why didn't you, then?' she prompts, her eyes flickering over him as though she's checking for damage.

'Lost my phone charger.'

'You could have used the landline.'

'Your number was in my phone, and I didn't know it off by heart, and I don't know Gran's landline number, and Dad said he was going to text you anyway.'

'Wow,' she says, trying to keep the smile off her face, 'you have an answer for everything, don't you?'

'No,' he says, grinning at her, knowing she'll forgive him anything, 'I don't know the capital of Uruguay.'

Rose walks over and gives him a gentle cuff across the head, followed by a hug. It's a long hug, and I can see him squirming slightly in her embrace. I stay quiet – this isn't my drama to intrude on, plus I have no idea who Sylvie and Amber and Ariel and Heather and Charlie are. Joe gives me a friendly nod over his mother's shoulder before he manages to escape.

'Sylvie is Gareth's second wife,' Rose explains, as though reading my mind. 'Amber and Ariel are their kids. Heather is the third wife, and Charlie is their two-year-old daughter.'

She turns her scrutiny back to Joe, who is sidling towards a cupboard full of chocolate cereal.

'What about the beer?' she snaps.

'Oh . . . well. That wasn't me, honest. Well, not all me, anyway. Simon saw the lights on last night and came round to check. He had a baseball bat and he scared the shit out of me – you know how hard he looks, even though he's dead nice. When he saw I was here on my own, we got the pizza, and the beer. And I only had one. Maybe two.'

He pours himself the world's biggest-known bowl of Coco Pops, and splashes on half a gallon of milk.

'He kept all the milk in his house as well – I think you forgot to cancel it . . . you look nice, by the way, Mum. Your hair's different.'

She half scowls, half laughs at his attempt to change the subject, and looks set to give him another telling off when there is a firm knock at the door. We all jump a little at the sound, but Joe recovers first.

'That'll be him now,' he says, wandering through into the living room and collapsing on a sofa that's seen better days, propping his bare feet up on the coffee table.

Rose looks slightly flustered, and does a thing with her boobs she probably doesn't even notice she's doing. She practically runs to the front door, and in comes the famous Simon – super neighbour and fine-assed lawn-mower.

He's a big man, dressed in working clothes, his hair shaved short and his face a little on the battered side. His eyes, though, are a vivid shade of blue, and look kind. The type of kind that would save your milk and look after your kid for you.

They walk through, and Rose introduces us. She looks flustered, her eyes constantly darting between me and Simon, as though waiting for something to happen. I realise with absolute horror that she is expecting me to flirt with him. Possibly screw him on the kitchen table. Because, after all, he's male – and that's what I do.

I can't say that I blame her for having some suspicions, but it still upsets me, the way she seems to automatically assume the worst. I know I don't have a good track record – the absolute worst, in fact – but I would never, ever do that. Not in a million years. I'm a different person now, and it cuts deep that she doesn't know that yet.

'Nice to meet you, Simon,' I say, politely shaking his hand. 'I'm just going to pop upstairs and freshen up. Then maybe Joe can give me a guided tour.'

Joe gives me a small salute in agreement, Coco Pops dribbling down his chin, and I disappear off towards the hallway. I need to get out of view, and quickly, because I suspect I am about to do some very ugly crying.

Chapter 47

Rose

I ring Simon's doorbell once, very briefly, half hoping that he doesn't hear and I can slink away again.

I've left Poppy and Joe in the house, after a day of showing my sister around the area. She feigned enthusiasm well enough, but seems far more interested in Joe than in me. In fact, the two of them are getting along so well I fear the house may burn down.

It makes me twitch, seeing them like that, side by side on the sofa, as though they've known each other forever. I love my boy more than anything in the world, and am worried about him setting foot in the toxic cauldron that Poppy and I seem to inhabit.

She's also told me about her Joe le Nephew savings account, and the frankly daft amount of money she's set aside for him. It's a kind gesture, but somehow I feel slightly threatened by it. By her incursion into my life. By all of it.

I needed to escape for a while, and Simon's seemed the sensible option. I wanted to thank him for looking after Joe, and looking after our milk, anyway.

He opens the door, and looks genuinely pleased to see me.

'Come in, come in . . . excuse the mess . . .' he says, as I follow him through into the living room. The layout of the house is exactly the same as ours, but the resemblance ends there. He only moved in last year, and it still looks as if he hasn't unpacked. Everything is perfectly tidy and uncluttered, the only sign of luxury being a mahoosive TV and some video games consoles.

The door to the kitchen is open, and I see one cup, one plate, one knife and fork laid out on the drainer, lined up with military precision.

'Were you in the Navy SEALs?' I blurt out, as he directs me to the sofa.

'Erm . . . no,' he answers, looking confused. 'They're American. I was in the Royal Marines.'

'Oh! That's . . . well, that's good. Anyway, I just wanted to thank you for looking after Joe like you did.'

'Not a problem,' he replies, sitting down opposite me on a chair that looks like it's never been used. 'How's it going? With your sister? And your mum's A–Z – Joe told me about it. Have you been all right?'

'Sometimes I'm all right,' I answer, honestly. 'And sometimes I'm not. Sometimes I just want to die, to be truthful . . . and, well, it's complicated, all this stuff with Poppy.'

'I can imagine. I was surprised to see her here.'

'I'm surprised she *is* here. I think she is too. But what can I say, our dead mother made us! What did you think of her? She's really pretty, isn't she?'

I have no idea why I am asking that. It is utterly ridiculous, and makes me sound like an idiot. It's as though part of me is probing, digging, wanting him to say 'ooh yes, she's gorgeous, is she single?' – so I can say yes, and he can ask her out, and those two can get married, and I can hate Poppy even more.

I remember what Mum said about picking at scabs, and suspect that's exactly what I'm doing – I want Poppy to behave badly so I can be justified in never seeing her again.

'I suppose,' Simon says, not playing to the script, 'if you like that kind of thing. I prefer a woman with a bit more meat on her bones.'

These, I realise as he says them, are words that are sacred to chubby women the world over, and I'd be lying if I said they didn't light a tiny fire down below. In a place where the fire has long ago gone out. I stare at him for a moment, unable to think of a response, so he carries on talking.

'Is this part of your A–Z, then, coming home?'

'Yeah,' I reply, looking around and not seeing a single photo anywhere in the room. 'L is for Location, Location, Location. I went to Poppy's yesterday. Next up is M, for Magical Mystery Tour, which seems to be some kind of treasure hunt. I don't know – my mother was never lacking in imagination.'

'It sounds like it. I'm sorry I only ever got to nod at her on the doorstep. So, how are things, with Poppy? Have you sorted out your differences?'

'Well, that's a tough question. Maybe we're trying to, I don't know. But she shagged Joe's dad, you see, which is a hard one to get over.'

He's silent for a moment, and I wonder if I've over-shared.

'Right. Well, that'll do it every time, I suppose. Anyway

– if you're off again, will Joe be staying at home? I don't mind keeping an eye on him if you need me to. Might even rope him in for some labouring work.'

'Thanks, but I think, if I can, I'll take him with me . . . I know he's sixteen, but . . . well. Thanks anyway. I'd better be getting back. Poppy and I need to go over the next one. And I need to stick my head in a bucket of cold water.'

He takes my rejection without a flicker – he is a hard man to read – and sees me to the door. I feel him watching me as I make the thirty-second journey to my own door, and assume he is making sure I don't get abducted by aliens or trip over a plant pot.

Inside, I find that Joe has gone up to bed, and Poppy is sitting on the sofa, legs tucked beneath her, flicking through one of our old photo albums. I notice a sad look on her face, like she's catching up on everything she's missed out on, but she seems to shut it down as soon as she sees me.

'You okay?' she asks, laying the album aside. I recognise it as one from when Joe was about five, his first year in school and super-cute.

'Yeah, fine,' I reply, collapsing down next to her on the couch. 'I'm just knackered. Joe being here threw me a bit, and I'm not exactly happy about his dad letting him come home on his own without telling me.'

'That is a bit off. Does Joe . . . what does Joe think happened with you two? I mean, I could see the look on your face when he told you why he'd come home, but you didn't say a word. Don't you ever want to just scream "your dad's an arsehole" at him?'

'Of course I do,' I say, flicking through the album and smiling at one of Joe dressed as a camel in his first nativity play. 'But that wouldn't help Joe, would it? I've always just told him that it was one of those things – that it was nobody's fault, we just grew apart. I didn't want him growing up hating his dad, no matter how I felt. It's my job to protect him, not traumatise him. And I think, as he's getting older . . . well, he's seeing stuff for himself, isn't he? At least that's always been my hope.'

'And what did you tell him about me?' she asks, quietly.

'Well I didn't tell him you screwed his father, if that's what you mean. Again, it's my job to protect him.'

I feel her tense next to me, and know she's upset. We're both upset. We're tiptoeing around each other, feeling the icebergs melt around us bit by bit, and both worried we might drown in the resulting deluge.

It's been so intense, all of this – losing our mum the way we did, finding out the way we did, getting through the funeral. We're dealing with grief, and loss, and a whole A–Z of shitty emotions.

I turn the page in the album, and point out one where Joe is brandishing one of his front baby teeth, looking proud as can be, the fresh gap showing in his grin.

'See this?' I say, smiling at the memory. 'He kept all his teeth in a little jar, every time one fell out. Didn't want the money from the Tooth Fairy – said he'd rather keep them than get a pound. For all I know he still has them upstairs.'

She smiles, and strokes the photo with one long finger, as though she's actually stroking a primary-school-aged Joe.

'I've missed so much . . .' Poppy says, almost in a whisper. 'And I know, before you say it, that I deserved to miss it. I'm not trying to make you feel bad. I just . . . well, I'm so sad about it. I should have been here, in his life – in your life. I wish I had been. I wish I'd been able to help you, Rose, and come to all these school plays, and see his tooth jar . . . I know it's my own fault, but I regret all of this so much. I'm grateful to know him now, but I'll never catch up. All this precious time, wasted.'

She looks exhausted. Completely drained. And God knows, that's exactly how I feel too.

'I think,' I say, after we've both been silent for a moment, looking at more pictures, 'that we might need a break, don't you? From all of this? I know we have M to deal with, and I'm definitely willing to do it – but perhaps we should have a few days off? What do you think? I could do with a bit of time at home with Joe, doing normal stuff, and I'm sure you've got a shedload of work to catch up on. Would that be all right? We're making progress, I think, but . . . God, I'm tired.'

Poppy nods, closes the photo album, and stands up without a word. I hear her go into the kitchen and get a glass of water, and by the time she returns, she is yawning and stretching in a completely pantomime 'I'm-really-sleepy' way.

'Good idea,' she says, back to being brisk and business-like. I appreciate that. Brisk and business-like Poppy is much easier to deal with than vulnerable Poppy.

'A few days off. I'll go into the office and make some people's lives hell. You see Joe. Then we can meet up back at the cottage for M. I looked at it earlier, and Lewis's notes say we'll need a couple of days. It's some kind of map in poem form. I bet it rhymes and everything.'

'Cool,' I say. 'Maybe it'll even be fun.'

Poppy nods, and walks towards the door into the hallway, where she pauses and looks back at me. I think there are tears in her eyes, but tell myself it is a trick of the light.

'And by the way?' she adds. 'Just for the record – I would never, *ever* shag your neighbour.'

Chapter 48

Andrea: M is for Magical Mystery Tour

1,
I'm curved and cool and far from poor,
I am a door, but not a door,
Climb my steps and take a dip,
But please be careful not to slip!

2,
My mouth is burned, oh poor me!
I'll cool it down, in the sea.
Maybe I'll dig up something old,
Then make my tongue feel nice and cold.

3,
Stretching out around the bay,
Candyfloss colours, all so gay!
Use my key, spend some time,
I'm glad it's not orange – that wouldn't rhyme!

4,
Inside me you'll find a kettle,
And a spade all made of metal,
Dig down deep and find out maybe,
What you wore as a baby.

Chapter 49

Poppy

'Nobody uses the word "gay" like that any more,' says Joe, staring at the poem again. He seems fascinated by it, and keeps touching it over and over. The poor thing is missing his granny, I think.

Mum has done a beautiful job on this one, using elaborate olde-worlde handwriting that I know must have taken her forever, and decorating the edges of the card with little pictures of flowers and birds. It's the very definition of gay – in the old-fashioned sense – and I think I might get it framed and hang it in the hallway.

'Grandmas do,' replies Rose, staring off out of the window and into the garden. She's looking at the neatly mowed lawn and the full birdbath and at the kitchen that has clearly been used, frowning. She is, I suspect, fast coming to the correct conclusion.

'Have you been staying here?' she says, her eyes narrowing, as though she's accusing me of sacrificing virgins at a Satanic altar.

'Yes,' I reply simply. 'I'd booked the time off work, and

decided I didn't want to disrupt things by going back. Is that all right with you, Mrs Bossy Pants?'

Joe looks from my face to his mum's, sizing up the likelihood of some kind of scrap, and decides to go off and explore the cottage. Wise boy.

'Well . . . I wish you'd told me, that's all. But there's not much I can do about it now, is there?' Rose responds, watching Joe's gangly figure disappear off towards the stairs.

I can understand, maybe, why she feels a bit put out. Like I've somehow done something sneaky, and managed to hijack the cottage from her. Used some kind of stealth to hide myself away here and do something deeply untrustworthy.

In reality, I hadn't planned it at all. I'd left her house in Liverpool feeling so downhearted, my car simply refused to drive back to London. I just couldn't face it again – the empty flat, the boring job, the bare cupboards. The overly jolly sponsor kids who weren't really ever going to be a replacement for real ones.

Ironically, it had been Rose herself who had pushed me over the edge. We'd stood on her doorstep and, as I prepared to leave, she'd hugged me. It wasn't a long hug or an especially affectionate one, but it was actual physical contact. And she had topped it off with the touching words: 'Don't crash, okay?'

It made me realise just how much I didn't want to leave her, and go back to the flat alone. It was different for her. She had something to stay at home for. She had Joe, and her cosy little house, and a hot Royal Marine living next door. I had nothing, I was starting to realise, and the only place I was likely to feel less miserable was at the cottage.

I've been here for the last two days, shuffling around, nosing in drawers and cooking and gardening, and, even worse (in her eyes), sleeping in Mum's bed. I hadn't planned that either, but somehow, it just felt right. My own bedroom – angst-ridden teenaged Poppy's bedroom – was too much of a reminder of a painful past, as was Rose's. Mum's, though – well, that suited Goldilocks right down to the ground.

I slept so peacefully in there, surrounded by her books and pictures, her clothes hanging in the lavender-scented wardrobe; nestled in sheets that still smelled of her perfume, resting my head on pillows she'd slept on. It was as if she was still with me, in the smallest of ways, and it helped me to think and to relax and to consider everything that had happened, and everything that was going to happen.

I needed the rest, and I'm not going to start apologising for it. Anyway, Rose is just narky because she came down by train at the crack of dawn, and because she hasn't eaten cake for two days. New health kick, she says, which from the look on Joe's face is something that happens with some regularity, and is not to be taken too seriously. I don't suppose it helped that I'd baked a huge cheesecake made with strawberries from the garden to greet her with.

'Nope. There's not much you can do about it now,' I reply, slicing up the dessert. 'Cheesecake?' I offer, knowing it's cruel but not quite able to stop myself.

'No. Thank you. Anyway. Joe's coming with us – I assume that's all right?'

'More than all right. We'll just have to make sure we behave ourselves, won't we? Shall we go in my car?'

'We better had. When shall we set off? I'm ready when you are.'

We both know where we're going because, despite our mother's magnificent attempt at being cryptic, it took us about one minute flat to crack her Enigma code. It does amuse me to imagine her gleeful little face as she tried to come up with cunning rhymes, though, trying to fox us.

We're going to Dorset, which is where she always took us on holidays when we were kids. It seemed like the most mysterious and exciting place in the world back then, but with hindsight, I realise that it was only a few hours away, and a lot more affordable than the package holidays to Spain and Turkey that our school friends were starting to go on.

I nod, and start to get ready. She already has bags packed for her and Joe, and it doesn't take long for me to get my stuff together either. Within an hour, I've texted Lewis so he can be on blue-tit patrol, and we're in the car heading for our first stop – Durdle Door.

Chapter 50

Rose

We are standing on the beach at Lyme Regis in Dorset, which is still one of the prettiest places on the entire planet.

It's early morning, and the only other people out are dog walkers and parents with toddlers who have clearly kept them up all night, tired-looking dads building sandcastles with one eye closed, mums sipping coffee from cardboard cups between their yawns.

It's already sunny, and the sea is a sparkling blue horizon stretching on forever. It's going to be a beautiful day, and I vow to myself that I won't spoil it.

I've been in a terrible sulk ever since we started our not-so-Magical Mystery Tour, and I need to snap out of it. Nobody likes a sulk, especially a 42-year-old sulk. I woke up this morning in the unfamiliar surroundings of a little guest-house, where we all stayed the night. Joe's snoring reached near-nuclear levels, and I am not exactly feeling refreshed, but today is a new start and I will try to be less of a pain in the arse.

It has been a weird few days – after living pretty much in

Poppy's pocket ever since the A–Z began, I expected to feel liberated as she left Liverpool in her Audi. Relieved. But actually I just felt a bit deflated and sad, which was altogether confusing.

Joe had been well and truly knee-capped by the card my mum left for him as well, refusing to tell me what she said but giving in to a very un-macho fit of tears after he read it. He's still got it, I know, folded up in his jeans pocket, that card with a picture of a fox on the front. I tried to comfort him, but what could I do? Tell him it'll all be okay? That it'll all get easier? People keep telling me that, and sometimes, depending on what mood I'm in, it makes me want to whack them round the head with a frying pan.

I think the best advice I got was from Tasmin – to just let the pain have its wicked way with you. When the tears come, don't fight them – because they will always win.

Despite the crying fit, Joe was excited about going back to the cottage, and seeing Poppy again, and possibly setting off on an A–Z adventure. I was less excited – especially when I realised that she'd been staying there.

It's mean spirited and petty to resent that, but I did. I felt like she'd somehow had more time with Mum than I had; laid claim to the place, put down roots. Become the better daughter. All very unattractive, but that, coupled with my sugar deprivation, didn't exactly put me in the best frame of mind for our reminiscent family trip.

Mum had obviously pictured some kind of emotional reliving of glory days past – trying to get us to remember those happy family holidays; playing barefoot in the sand, hunting for shells, flying kites on top of the cliffs. Simpler times.

She'd left a package for us as well as the poem, which contained a key with a number tag on it, and a pile of photos. The photos were all of us when we were kids, pulling faces and proudly showing off sandcastles and eating ice creams. It looked as though every day was blissfully sunny, and every beach was our own personal playground.

Joe was fascinated by them, and kept staring at me, and staring at Poppy, then staring at the pictures, as though trying to make it all line up in his brain. Kids never assume their own parents were little, do they? I felt the same when I saw that photo of our mum as a baby. Surely she'd arrived on the planet fully grown and ready to cook my tea?

We explained the rhyme to Joe on the way down – the first verse was about Durdle Door, a magnificent limestone arch that rises up from the sea off the coast of Dorset. There are about a million steps carved out of the cliff to get down to it, and by the time we arrived, it was after lunch and the place was swarming with people, crawling up and down the steps like little touristy ants. It was a gorgeously sunny day, and the shimmering sea was bobbing with kids paddling and dogs swimming and little rowing boats.

I struggled with the climb – both up and down – and noticed that both Poppy and Joe pretended to be struggling as well, stopping every few minutes and making a big show of being out of breath when I knew they were fine. I understood that they were trying to be kind, but it made me feel even more disgruntled. Like a depressed hippo trying to keep up with the graceful gazelles. All my own fault, and at least it made me more determined to stay on the latest health kick.

It's a beautiful place, but not quite like I remembered it. It's . . . fuller. With hindsight, I think Mum must have planned our trips to this part of the coast for the early morning or late afternoon, when there were fewer people around. Clever Mum.

Our next stop was Charmouth – the 'burned mouth' in the poem – a beach where you can dig for fossils, and eat ice cream, also referred to in Mum's dastardly clever rhyme. Another place we loved to go as children – we'd hire hammers from the local shop and chisel away at rocks, trying to unearth some rare belemnites. Mum would treat each find as a precious and amazing scientific discovery, and keep them all in little coin bags for us to take home.

Joe and Poppy got into the spirit of things, digging away and poking around on the cliff faces, both of them using their phones to take pictures of their finds, Poppy running off to the shops to get a carrier bag so Joe could store his fossils.

I was glad to see Joe happy – but not quite glad enough to jolt myself out of my sulk. If I'm honest, I still feel threatened by their relationship – Joe isn't daft, he knows something bad must have happened to break us apart, but he doesn't know what, and hopefully never will. His newfound Aunt Poppy is just a barrel-load of laughs as far as he is concerned, and I feel frumpy and boring and old in comparison.

After our trip to Charmouth, we ate fish and chips (I took the batter off, honest), and Poppy called round various places until she found us somewhere to stay for the night. I was keen to get it all done in one day, but she pointed out that it was getting late, and we wouldn't be able to go digging around a beach at night-time without potentially getting arrested.

Now, as I look around at the pastel-coloured shops just opening for business, and the crescent of brightly painted beach huts stretching around the curve of the beach, I'm glad I listened to reason. Yesterday might have been a fail on the happy memories front, but this place was always my favourite.

It's already quite warm, and I am barefoot on the sand, enjoying the feel of it between my toes as we stroll along the beach.

'So, I see what she means about the gay colours now,' says Joe, looking at an especially vibrant pink café. 'But I'm not sure about the orange?'

'It was a joke,' Poppy replies. 'Because orange is supposed to be the one word you can't rhyme properly, and also it's a fruit, like a lime – and this is Lyme Regis. Geddit?'

'I suppose. It's quite clever, but Granny wasn't exactly Ricky Gervais, was she?'

'Thankfully not,' I respond. 'That would just be weird, especially with the beard. Now, we're looking for number . . . what's on the key again, Poppy?'

She checks the tag, and points ahead. The beach huts are one of the loveliest features of this place, and we always used to hire one when we visited. People really love them, and paint them up, filling them with all of life's essentials for a

British seaside holiday – kettle, windbreaker, raincoats, umbrellas, that kind of thing.

We arrive at our particular hut, and find that it is an extremely cute shade of bright blue, almost exactly matching the colour of the sea. Poppy raises her eyebrows in a question, and I gesture for her to go in.

I am assuming that this was one of those field trips that Lewis mentioned, and I find myself wondering if Mum came with him. If she was well enough at that stage. If they drove down here together, and strolled along the Prom, and ate freshly caught crab and watched the sunset. I really hope they did.

Poppy opens the door to the hut, and we all crane our necks to see inside. Sure enough, there's a kettle, as promised. Canisters of tea and coffee. A couple of striped deckchairs. A pile of Mum's beloved tartan blankets. And – laid neatly out on a little wooden shelf – a vast collection of fossils, exactly like the ones Joe and Poppy collected yesterday.

I know that these ones, though, are antiques in their own right – these were collected by two brown-haired little girls in the 1970s and 80s, carried home in triumph and immediately forgotten about. Except she didn't forget – she never forgot anything. She kept our treasures, and cherished them on our behalf, and now she's trying to give everything back to us.

It's an unexpected sight, and it brings the sharp sting of tears to my eyes. I'm a mum myself now, and I know I do the same – I have hoarded the precious mementoes of Joe's childhood, the certificates and prizes and finger paintings, keeping them safe long after he's forgotten about them. My mum loved us like that, with that same steadfast dedication, and it's killing me that it took her death for me to finally appreciate it.

Joe gives me a little squeeze on the shoulders, and I blink the tears away.

Poppy looks at me, as if to check that I'm all right, then, when I nod, walks into the beach hut and emerges waving a huge garden spade. There is a luggage tag tied to its metal handle – one of those big old-fashioned cardboard ones, like Paddington Bear had – and she holds it steady in the morning breeze, so she can read it out.

'Can you dig it? Look behind the hut!' she says, frowning. She's gone without her make-up this morning, and her hair is loose and wild and unbrushed, and she looks a lot more like the little girl I used to play with on this beach than she has for a long time. Staying at the cottage has definitely relaxed her, and I'm ashamed of myself for begrudging her that time there.

Joe, who might think he is grown-up but is still a giant child in half-baked man form, is immediately thrilled at the thought of digging for treasure, and disappears off behind the hut. There's not much room, just a few feet, and he just about slips into the gap. Poppy passes him the spade, and he starts digging, in an awkward straight-armed motion because of his trapped position.

'This isn't as easy as it looks,' he says, scooping shovels-full of sand off to the side.

'I suppose she rented this, and put the stuff inside, and

then needed to bury whatever it is somewhere nobody else would go, or a dog wouldn't dig it up,' I say, trying to imagine the logistics of all this, and marvelling at how a woman dying of cancer could find the determination. Then again, my mother wasn't any old woman, was she? She was the late, great Andrea Barnard, darling.

Eventually, after Joe puffs away and we sit in the sun watching, there is a clunking sound, and Joe freezes mid-push. He looks down, and kicks aside some more sand, and says: 'I've found something! Shit . . . sorry, language, I know . . . it's a chest of some kind . . .'

He manages to contort himself enough that he can push the rest of the sand away, and tugs the chest from the ground. I have no idea how she managed this – she wouldn't have been well enough, and Lewis could barely fit *in* the beach hut, never mind behind it. She probably charmed some innocent passing fisherman to do it for her, flashing a Penny Peabody smile and laying on the feminine wiles.

Joe emerges at the front of the hut, and places the wooden chest down on the sand, where we all sit around it. For a few moments we just stare at it, as though it might belong to a chick called Pandora, until Poppy eventually reaches out and unhooks the clasp.

Inside, wrapped in pink tissue paper, is a supremely frilly garment that I immediately recognise from photos of Poppy and me as babies.

She reaches out and picks it up, holding the fabric in her hands and sniffing it, like she tends to do, before holding it up in all its glory.

'It's our Christening gown,' she says, eyes wide. 'The one Mum said had been passed down three generations of her family. We looked like little piglets wrapped up in silk in this, didn't we?'

Joe reaches out and touches it with one finger, a look of horror on his face.

'I didn't wear that, did I?' he asks, obviously feeling his budding masculinity under threat.

'No,' I say, shaking my head. 'Mum wanted you to, tradition and all that, but your dad's family had an equally disgusting sailor suit . . . wow. It's actually kind of pretty, in an evil Victorian doll way, isn't it?'

'I can't believe either of you two was ever that tiny,' says Joe, sounding awestruck. 'Maybe I can save it and, if I have kids, they can wear it. That'd be kind of cool. Or maybe, Auntie P, you'll have a baby and they can wear it.'

Poppy laughs, but it sounds a tiny bit brittle.

'No. I'm too old. I think that door has well and truly shut,' she says.

'Don't be daft,' replies Joe, nudging her, 'you're only, what, thirty or something? Plenty of time yet. Anyway. What do we do now?'

A wasp chooses that moment to make a beeline – or a waspline – straight for my leg, and I feel the usual chest-tightening anxiety kick in. At the exact same moment, both Poppy and Joe reach out and swat it away, then high-five each other. It seems I now have two fearless wasp warriors to protect me.

I look at them both, smiling and laughing with each other,

the sunlight reflecting off their shiny dark hair, and feel a sudden rush of warmth and happiness and . . . well, peace. The first peace I've felt for such a long time. A sense that everything will, against the odds, somehow all turn out all right.

My mum. The evil mastermind.

Chapter 51

Andrea: N is for Nudity

'Hello my darlings! Here I am, back on video, gracing your television or phone or laptop or whatever it is you're using. I haven't done a little film for you for a while, and thought you might be missing my smiling face.

'Lewis is here with me, partly to hold the camera and partly to make sure I'm a good girl and I take all the pills and potions the doctors have told me I need to take. I've had a couple of overnight stays in the hospital, but nothing too stressful – in fact it gave me a nice rest, and I feel much better.

'I hope you enjoyed your little trip to Dorset, and that it didn't turn into a Magical Misery Tour. Assuming, of course, that you managed to figure out those dratted clues! I had a lot of fun doing that, and visiting the hut, and burying your treasure. We've paid the rent on the hut for the rest of the summer, by the way, so feel free to visit again if the mood strikes you.

'Lewis drove me down there for the day, fussing like the old woman he is all the way, obviously convinced I was going to kick the bucket somewhere on the M5! But the bucket remained well and truly unkicked, and we had a lovely time. He indulged me by listening to my stories about our holidays there, and even took me for lunch in that lovely little restaurant at Lulworth Cove. He does spoil me, much as I mock him.

'I hope it brought back as many happy memories for you as it did for me – and although I always try and stay jolly for these little videos, girls, I must admit that it makes me terribly sad to think of not being there with you. Not being able to see you together again, on those beautiful beaches, enjoying those beautiful sunsets. I'd give anything to be there, to share it with you, to create a few more precious memories, but it's not meant to be.

'Anyway, I don't want to get maudlin about things. Or, if I do, I certainly don't want it captured for posterity – because that's the thing about film, isn't it? It simply never goes away, especially in the quite bonkers digital age you young people live in.

'I discovered that quite recently, much to my amusement, which is why I decided to make N stand for Nudity. Now, as an actress in the Seventies, quite a lot of flesh was flashed – but I only did one nude scene. Please don't recoil in horror, it was all very tasteful! Actually, it wasn't . . . but hey ho!

'I was playing a young girl who was suffering from amnesia after being attacked by a hammer-wielding lunatic at a funfair. She was lucky to survive, but couldn't remember a thing about her life, even her own name. She ends up in a kind of residential home that is a tiny bit like a loony bin, and every night, she sleepwalks, going back to places she knew, leaving a trail of clues for the handsome young doctor who is obsessed with solving her mystery . . . I know, it sounds wonderful, doesn't it?

'Now, for some reason, the director thought it made perfect sense for our young heroine to go about her sleepwalking business absolutely starkers. And for some even stranger reason, I agreed – what can I say, I was only nineteen, and quite pleased with my body, thank you very much. So there I am – in my altogether – stalking hospital corridors and knocking on the doors of derelict buildings and even on one occasion riding a fairground carousel horse in a dream sequence!

'It was very arty and low budget, and I genuinely never thought I'd see it again – until just recently, after mentioning this to Lewis, he managed to find a clip from it on YouTube! Honestly, there are some strange people out there . . . anyway, it is, of course, the dream sequence carousel scene, and I admit to both laughing and crying a little at seeing it again.

'Laughing because it is so bloody funny – those Seventies art-house movies did tend to take themselves seriously – and crying because it was odd, seeing myself there, like that. So young and strong and fit and healthy, which is pretty much the opposite of how I feel these days.

'But I promised not to be maudlin, so I won't be. The link to the clip is on our account, so if it takes your fancy, feel free to look – if you can handle it!

'Now, I'm being a little lazy here, but I couldn't think of anything fabulous to do for the letter O – no rude jokes, please, Lewis, I can see that naughty schoolboy look on your face! I'm a bit tired today, truth be told, and I think that perhaps you need to speedily move on to P – if, of course, you've decided to go in that direction.

'So I'm going to keep O simple. O is for "Oh My God, Is That My Mother's Bare Bottom Riding a Carousel Horse in a Dream Sequence?"

'And the answer is yes – it most certainly is! Happy viewing, girls!'

Chapter 52

Poppy

She didn't look brilliant in that last video – the modern one, not the nude one from the 1970s – and the sadness of that is sitting like undigested food in the pit of my stomach.

Despite her attempts at jollity, you could see that she was in pain, and her casual references to hospital stays were heartbreaking. We should have been there, helping her through it. It's like watching a replay of a horrific car crash, knowing what is going to happen but being unable to stop it.

We're at Euston Station, sitting up on the balcony looking at the departures board, waiting for Joe's train to Liverpool to be announced. Then the two of us are off to St Pancras to get the Eurostar to Paris – because it's time for the most mysterious letter of all, P.

I'm feeling extremely nervous about it all, and I suspect Rose is too – because she is wittering on like a mad woman, making sure that Joe knows all the house rules, has enough money, remembers to eat, goes to bed on time, and doesn't burn the street down. He, to be fair, is looking resigned and tolerant in the face of her tirade.

'Simon says he'll pop round tonight, and keep an eye on you. Plus you can actually go and stay at his if you prefer.'

'I know, Mum,' says Joe, doing an awesome job of not rolling his eyes, 'you've already told me. I'll be fine, honest. I'll ignore any knocks on the door, and won't invite drug dealers round, and make sure I take my vitamin pills. I'll be okay, don't worry.'

'I think,' I say, half an eye on the board and half on my sister, 'that Simon likes you.'

'Well, yes,' replies Rose. 'He's a nice bloke, he probably likes most people.'

'No, I mean he *like* likes you.'

'*Like* likes me? What are you, sixteen?'

'Excuse me!' interrupts Joe, holding his hand up in the air. 'I'd like to point out that I am actually sixteen, and even I wouldn't say that. But . . . I think she might be right, Mum. It makes me a bit sick in my mouth, but Simon does look at you in a like-like way.'

Rose gapes at us both for a moment, then shakes her head so hard her curls bobble around her face.

'Rubbish. And anyway, I'm too old for that kind of stuff.'

Joe gives me a look, finally doing the eye-roll, as if to say: 'See what I have to put up with?'

There is a sudden movement in the herd of people down below, a group exodus towards a platform that lets us know that the train has been announced, and we all stand up and grab our bags.

We walk with Joe to his train, and Rose insists on staying until the very last second, until its bright-red Virgin logo has disappeared off into the distance. She has tears in her eyes, and I'm not sure it's only about her son leaving us.

After we stopped laughing at the YouTube clip, the one of mum prancing round stark-bollock-naked on the fairground horse, we were both a little melancholy.

'It was *quite* tasteful,' she'd said, after warning Joe not to look unless he wanted his retinas burned out by his bare-butted Granny. 'The way they draped her hair over part of her boobs?'

'Yeah,' I'd replied, looking through the comments section and recoiling in horror at how much of a fan base my own mother had in certain circles, 'she looked a bit like the Khaleesi from *Game of Thrones*, didn't she? I bet she'd have been in that if she'd still been acting. She could have nailed that Diana Rigg part.'

'But . . . the other video. She didn't look too well in that one, did she?'

'No,' I'd replied, feeling the same myself. 'She looked . . . vulnerable. I don't think I've ever known her to look vulnerable before. It wasn't nice to see. Maybe it was the thought of doing P that was getting her down as well. That must have been difficult.'

So difficult, in fact, that in the end she'd chickened out yet again – not of telling us, but of telling us herself. Instead, she'd passed all the information on to Lewis, who had typed up a series of notes and memories to get us started. And being Lewis – my mother's sworn protector – he'd added his own spin on it all.

We've read the letter, which has shaken us both up – I

know I was only just about holding it together for Joe's sake, and I was 100 per cent sure that was the case for Rose as well. There were some uncomfortable truths in there, and I'm beginning to think that a fantasy version of our father might be altogether less distressing than the real version.

Now we have our journey to look forward to, and a new cassette recording full of answers to our questions – or at least the questions that Lewis, an elderly gay man, thinks we might want answering.

We're going to have to listen to the tape on an ancient Walkman Rose has dredged up, sitting next to each other on the train with one headphone each, just like we did when we were kids and Mum could only afford to buy one between us.

That invariably used to end up with us punching each other. I can only hope the same doesn't happen while we're on our way to Paris, to potentially meet our dear old dad. Rose hasn't said as much, but after reading Lewis's letter, she must also be wondering if this might be a terrible mistake.

We amble towards the exit, irritating the commuters with our slow pace, pulling our wheelie cases behind us as we start the walk to St Pancras.

'Poppy,' says Rose, as we emerge into the noise and bustle of Euston Road.

'Yes?' I reply.

'You do know, don't you, that that letter means our dad definitely isn't Dumbledore?'

I nod. She's right, sadly. Not unless there was a much darker side to Dumbledore than we all suspected.

Chapter 53

Lewis: P is for Paris

Dear Rose and Poppy,
    Your mother isn't feeling too well today, partly because of her illness, which is now taking a thorough hold of her, and partly I think because she is worried about this particular entry in her A–Z.

She wasn't feeling up to a video; I'm sure you'll have noticed she wasn't at her best in the last one. We tried making a cassette recording, but she broke down in the middle of it. As you know, this is quite unlike your mother, so I persuaded her to let me handle this one instead.

Her concerns, I think, are double-fold – she is upset that she is leaving you alone to deal with this situation, wanting still, even in her darkest hour, to protect you both. She is also ashamed of certain elements of the past, although personally I see no reason for her to be – everything she did, she did for you two. It's vital to remember that.

She's talked to me many times about your father, and

from those conversations, I will piece together what you need to know. I will also, in a separate package, leave some photographs, and his last known address – although as a disclaimer I must point out that both are many years out of date, and neither of us truly knows where he is, or even if he is still alive. I offered to hire some kind of private detective to discover more, but even the thought of it visibly shook her – as though if she poked that particular wasp's nest, she'd be stung to death.

Anyway, your father's name is François Henri Martin, although I believe he went by the stage name of Franky Martin. His grandparents were French, and your mother met him during a production of *Romeo and Juliet*. They toured to Paris with it, and that is where their romance seems to have blossomed.

From what I've heard, and seen in pictures, he was a very handsome man, deeply charismatic and charming. Your mother, who was several years his junior, fell head over heels for him, and rushed into what became her first serious relationship.

After what sounds like an idyllic and passionate honeymoon phase, during which you were conceived, Rose, your mother started to see the flaws in Franky's make-up. His public persona was one of a cool 1970s man-about-town, but secretly he was consumed by insecurity and became increasingly bitter at what he perceived to be a lack of recognition within the industry. When he failed to get parts he auditioned for, he became angry and resentful, and sought solace in narcotics.

From what your mother has told me, this was initially recreational, in the way of the era – marijuana, and LSD, to start with, both of which were very fashionable within certain circles. But as their relationship went on, she began to realise that it was more than recreational for Franky – it was an addiction.

She tried to cope with the situation as best as she could, and eventually you came along, Poppy. She had hoped that the increased responsibility and the joys of father-hood would help straighten him out, and even supported him through a phase of what we would now call detox.

However, like many addicts, he was unable to stop – and, shortly after your birth, Poppy, he also discovered heroin, which was starting to make its way into the country, especially through their American show-business friends.

I'm sure this isn't pleasant for you two to read, but I remain convinced it was even more unpleasant for her to go through. Your mother, as you know, is an incred-ibly strong and loving woman – but she was also young, trying to build her own career, and caring for two small children single-handed.

I believe the crisis point came around the same time as her own mother died, and Andrea made the decision that she still believes saved your family. She used her small inheritance to put down a deposit on the cottage, moved you all to the countryside, and shut Franky out of her life. And, of course, out of your lives as well.

This has always resulted in very conflicted emotions

on her part, but I trust her enough to believe that she made the right choice. I hope that you trust her enough to believe that as well.

She has asked me to help her compile a set of questions for the next letter of the A–Z, believing, rightly I am sure, that you will have many. She wants it to be personal, but in my belief is too fragile to be filmed, so I will attempt to do it via the cassette recording device. I will ask her the questions, and she will provide the best answers she can.

They might not completely satisfy your understandable curiosity, but they will simply have to do – I would remind you at this point that perhaps things might have worked out differently if you two had been around more, and she had felt you were strong enough to hear this rather unpalatable part of her history in person.

I will be as thorough as her health will allow, and try to anticipate your questions – but I must say that I will not push her further than I think she can bear. While her loyalties lie first and foremost with you two, mine lie, and always will, with her.

If you are heading to Paris, then I wish you luck. You might like to listen to the questions before or after your trip, I will leave that up to you. Just please, always, understand that your mother loves you more than I have ever known a human being love anyone before – it has been a revelation. She is going through so much pain, so much personal turmoil, and yet your wellbeing is still of paramount importance to her.

I would hope that any unanswered questions, or lingering doubts on your part, will be offset by the knowledge of that sacrifice.

With all kind regards,

Lewis Clarke-Smith

Chapter 54

Lewis and Andrea: Q is for Questions

Lewis: So, perhaps we could start with some basics. Why is François Martin not listed on the girls' birth certificates?

Andrea: Goodness, Lewis! You are going full-on Jeremy Paxman, aren't you? Been watching a little too much *Newsnight* with your cocoa, have we? But . . . fair enough. It's the obvious point for a solicitor to start with, I suppose. The first time – with Rose – it was mainly out of anger. On my part.

Franky was out at a casting – something to do with one of those cop shows at the time; it might have been *The Sweeney*, I can't quite recall – and I'd arranged to meet him at the registry office. We'd both been up all night – me with the baby, and him with a bottle of Jack Daniel's.

I got there in time for our appointment, and he just didn't show up. I was stuck there in the waiting room, trying to deal with a two-week-old baby on my own, and it was all so humiliating.

I later found out it was because he didn't get the part, and went straight to Soho to meet his alleged friends. Forgot all about us. That wasn't unusual, especially as time went on, but just then it stung. Badly.

I was so in love with my darling little girl, you see, and it hurt that he couldn't be bothered to even officially claim her. So I left him out, in a fit of pique. With Poppy . . . well, by that time, things had become unbearable, to be honest. His life was one long, morbid party – the drugs had completely taken hold of him, and I was starting to realise that everything was going dreadfully wrong. So that time, it was deliberate.

I had no idea if he'd even be alive by the time she grew up, never mind still in our lives. I felt like . . . like it was going to be down to me to raise these girls, and he didn't even deserve a mention. Gosh. That makes me sound like the bitter one, doesn't it?

Lewis: Not at all. It makes you sound human. Now, moving on, tell us a little about how you met – and what his good qualities were.

Andrea: Excellent question, Lewis! Because I don't want you girls to think that he was an unremitting loss – of course he wasn't! He was partly responsible for creating you two!

Well, obviously he was handsome. Quite irresistible, with his big brown eyes and moody French cheekbones and hair that was fashionably long. A little like a young

Alain Delon, which he played on. But he was such fun as well, he really was – full of charm and humour. He was one of those men who made you feel so special, like you were the only woman in his world.

He was frightfully clever, and a wonderful actor. We met when he was playing Mercutio, and I was Juliet. The chap playing Romeo was most definitely not interested in girls, I have to say – you'd have loved him, Lewis! Anyway, we were doing a regional tour, with a week in Paris, and by the end of the run, we were a couple. It was marvellous to start with, no matter what happened later. It really was. No man has ever taken my breath away in quite the same fashion.

I still remember, so clearly, him showing me around Paris, so handsome and strong . . . holding hands under the Eiffel Tower, drinking coffee by Notre-Dame . . . it was like something from a film, to be honest. Perhaps that's why it didn't last, I don't know . . . but I loved him, so much. And I have to believe that he loved me – and no matter what eventually became of us, that love was such a precious thing. I might not want my girls to have the same unhappy ending, but the love? That, I very much want for them – both of them.

Lewis: Of course you do. Now, fill us in on where you lived, and how your life together looked.

Andrea: We had a little love nest in Notting Hill. It wasn't quite as fashionable then, but it was all we could afford. To begin with it was all very boho – we hung out with an arty crowd, and there were lots of lovely soirees and nights out. It was very sociable, very lively. The Seventies were like that. I can leave the address as well, Lewis – pass it on to the girls, will you? Then if they want to, they can go and visit. Anyway, things were already changing by the time Rose was born – I don't want you to think you caused any of it, girls. The rot had well and truly already set in.

He was out later and later, often not coming back for days on end, and when he did turn up, I was never sure which Franky I'd be getting. Sometimes, he was wonderful – he genuinely adored you girls, when he was on form, he was such a doting dad! He'd come back into our lives like a whirlwind of energy, and for days at a time, we'd have trips to the park, and breakfast in bed – all of us – and lovely walks, and it would be so nice.

The problem was that he wasn't on form for that much of the time . . . he was hanging round with a wild crowd, and the drugs were considered normal. Of course they might have been for somebody else – but his personality, that moodiness I used to find so dazzling, meant that for him it was a disaster. For all of us. I tried to help him, but I couldn't. I think even if he'd won every role he went for, won Oscars and BAFTAs, he would still have been a little bit . . . broken. I don't know why. Perhaps a more mature woman could have figured him out, but I was far from mature. I still don't think I am.

Lewis: You are perfectly mature, my darling, but only when you want to be! See, a case in point – your mother is sticking her tongue out at me, girls! Anyway. Moving on. Why did you finally decide to end things?

Andrea: Oh . . . oh my. This is harder than I thought it would be, you know. I'm feeling a bit tearful. This all feels like ancient history, but at the same time it's still so vivid, it's like it happened yesterday . . .

Lewis: Do you want to stop? Take a little break? You're due some more painkillers any time now . . .

Andrea: No! Let's rip the plaster off, shall we? Well, it was after my mother died. Her illness was long and drawn out and deeply unpleasant. I was an only child, so all of the pressure fell on me, and I'm afraid I felt rather sorry for myself. It's one of the reasons, as I've mentioned, that I've chosen not to tell you about my current predicament. I have Lewis, bless him, and there's simply nothing to be gained by dragging you into it as well.

But anyway . . . that's neither here nor there. I always tried to take you both with me when I could, to sit with her and visit her, but it was very difficult at the end. A deathbed is no place for babies. So, on the day she finally passed away, I'd left you at home with your father. He'd been on his best behaviour for a while, trying to be a good soldier while I was going through my ordeal. That's the thing about Franky – he was never a bad person, girls. Never malicious or cruel – the only person he didn't like was himself; he didn't really have a mean bone in his body. He was just weak. So weak that he couldn't last that long without a little chemical assistance.

I came home, that day, utterly drained – you can imagine how I felt, I am sure, my darlings, as you're going through something similar yourselves. Grief can be so bloody exhausting.

When I finally made it back, desperate to see you, and Franky, I found the two of you basically looking after yourselves, while he was sprawled on the couch. Rose, you were only two, but you'd tried to feed Poppy by pouring milk into her mouth! You were both covered in it, and soaking wet because no nappies had been changed all day, and screaming the place down. He was just lying there, listening to Led Zeppelin full blast, to drown it all out.

That, I'm afraid, was the last straw. I suppose I was grieving, and traumatised by Mum's death and all the run-up to it, and I just couldn't cope with anything more. I knew, right then, that this man was never going to change – or at least not change enough for it to be safe for us to be around him. And a few weeks later, we were gone. I can't say that it was easy on my own, and part of me really did miss him, but . . . well, it had to be done.

Lewis: Were you ever in touch again, after that?

Andrea: Well, I'd hear about him, on the grapevine, you know? Mutual friends, our old set. I'd see him pop up on the telly every now and then. I used to wonder if I'd ever bump into him on the occasions I was down in London working, you two in tow – but I didn't. From what I heard, things got a lot worse before they got better, and he ended up doing a teensy, tiny amount of jail time. Then, round about 1982, 1983, something like that, he did get in touch – passed a letter on via my agent. He said he'd moved to Paris, cleaned up his act, was doing some French theatre and rebuilding his life. That he was sorry for everything, and that he'd love to know how his girls were getting on.

Lewis: And . . . what did you say to that?

Andrea: Eventually, I wrote back. It took me a couple of weeks to make my mind up, but life's too short, isn't it, to hold grudges? It's not like I was inviting him to move in, or sending the girls there to tour the Louvre with him – so I replied, letting him know how wonderful they were, and sent him an up-to-date photo. But . . . well, I never heard back. I don't suppose he was quite as clean as he said, or maybe he never got the letter. I don't really know. That was the last I ever heard from him.

Lewis: And why didn't you ever tell Rose and Poppy about any of this – when they were older, at least?

Andrea: Oh Lewis! You know why! I was . . . I was embarrassed. And ashamed. And worried that they'd resent me, and I simply couldn't stand that. I also . . . well, I've never been a great believer in nature over nurture, but I suppose part of me was worried that if I exposed them to the truth, to his lifestyle even, then it might damage them in some way.

Poppy, darling, forgive me for saying this, but over the years I have had my concerns about you . . . and Rose. Well, you had your own addictions, didn't you? But now, I think, I have to say that I'm so proud of you both – and although you might have inherited some of his looks, and some of his traits, you're nothing like him, really. Just like Joe is nothing like Gareth.

I'm sorry, though, you know . . . I'm sorry it all ended like it did. I'm sorry for you two, growing up without a father, and I'm sorry for myself, for being forced to do it all alone. And I'm sorry for him most of all – because he missed out on you two.

Lewis: I think that's enough now, Andrea. You look exhausted.

Andrea: No, no, I'm fine . . . I could go on all day!

Lewis: No, you couldn't – and I won't let you. It's time for a nap, and it's no use arguing – don't make me spank you again . . .

Andrea: Don't say that, my daughters will think I'm into S&M . . . okay, okay . . . I give in . . . goodbye girls. I tried to love you enough for two – please forgive me if it didn't quite work . . .

Chapter 55

Rose

I have no idea how I'd imagined my long-lost father would look, but it certainly wasn't like a 50-year-old prostitute dressed as Rihanna.

Although, after listening to that heartbreaking question-and-answer session my mum did with Lewis, nothing would shock me. She'd tried to be kind about him, but you could still hear the pain in her voice as she talked about that time in her life.

I'd barely coped on my own with one baby – my mum had two children; her mother was dying and she was dealing with a drug-addict partner. I've always thought of her as a strong woman, but I'd had no idea quite how strong. Leaving him had taken its toll, but she'd done it anyway – and raised us beautifully.

None of her answers had made for easy listening on the train, though, and neither Poppy nor myself is exactly full of *joie de vivre* as we emerge into Paris.

We have a couple of photos, and one of them is especially poignant – an old Polaroid, taken of the two of them with the Eiffel Tower in the background. Our father had written on the back of it: '*Andrea, je t'aime!*' – and it is so easy to imagine them here, young and in love.

We cross the city in silent awe, wandering through the broad boulevards and pretty side streets and walking along the bank of the Seine to our hotel in the Marais.

It's just as hot here as in the UK, and the place is crammed with backpacked tourists. By the time we reach the third arrondissement, we are both hot and overwhelmed.

Poppy seems to know the city well, navigating our route with ease, but it's the first time I've ever been, unless you count a weekend at Disneyland when Joe was eight.

After checking into the hotel and eating lunch in a street-side café, she leads me into the noise and crush of the underground Métro system. I follow her like a lost sheep, marvelling at how well she fits in here – she even looks French, with her long dark hair and stylish clothes and big brown eyes.

We emerge again into an area that is part tourist dream, part nightmare, walking from the Abbesses Métro stop to see places I've only ever seen in films – Sacré-Coeur, Montmartre, the Moulin Rouge. There are cobbled streets and quaint squares and artists with easels in front of them; glorious views of the city, tiny cafés selling even tinier cups of coffee; the sound of chatter and laughter and live music.

But there are also, as we wander into the Place Pigalle, sex shops and theatres advertising nude shows and women of all ages and types loitering on corners. It's one of those fascinating areas where you can walk for two minutes and be in a different world, leaving behind arty Bohemian splendour and entering a seedy landscape of sex and commerce.

Unsurprisingly, perhaps, the address we have written down for our father is in the latter area, and we enter a tree-lined side street that could be described as 'shady' in all kinds of ways.

We have to ring the buzzer for the flat several times before we finally hear footsteps thundering down the stairs inside, along with a flow of words that are annoyed in any language. I am so nervous my tongue is sticking to the roof of my mouth, and I am gripping and ungripping my fists, leaving little nail prints on my own skin.

Poppy, though, looks super cool. I'm familiar enough now with Present-Day Poppy to understand that just because she looks it, she doesn't necessarily feel it, and I'm sure she's just as tense as I am. I mean, it's a big deal, meeting your father again for the first time since you used to wee in your own pants. I feel a tiny bit like I might be about to do that right now.

When the door opens, it is clearly not our father. Not unless he has undergone some radical changes, like gaining a pair of double-D boobs, losing one of his front teeth, and gaining a fright wig.

The woman on the doorstep stares at us with hostility, all kinds of fleshy bumps and lumps pouring out of the hip-hop party outfit she's squeezed into. She lets off a volley of rapid-fire French, and I'm relieved I don't have to translate. Poppy, she explained earlier, spent six months working here for the European division of her pet supply company, and is more equipped than me to deal with this on every level.

The two of them engage in an unintelligible exchange of information, with the woman eventually softening to something less frightening, and to something more human, more sad, to be honest, presumably as she begins to understand why we are here and who we are looking for. Every now and then, amid the flurry, I hear words that sound English – papa, detox, photo.

There is a lot of hand waving, and nodding, and she eventually disappears back up the stairs. The smell of spices and cooking vegetables drifts out of the building towards us, making me immediately hungry despite the situation.

'What's going on?' I ask Poppy. 'Is he dead?'

'No,' Poppy replies, shaking her head and glancing at her watch. 'But he's not here. He moved out about three years ago. He used to live here, with Anne-Marie and a couple of others, but left because he wanted to clean up his act.

'She knows who we are, and says he used to talk about his daughters back in England all the time. She even knew our names. He had a photo of us – one from school, must be the one Mum sent him – that he carried everywhere with him. She's trying to find some information right now about where we might find him.'

'Is he still in Paris, then?'

'No,' says Poppy, flashing me a grin. 'But it does have a tower. She thinks he's in Blackpool. He used to work here doing street theatre for spare change, and says he got a pitch doing something similar back in the UK.'

Anne-Marie reappears and presses a crumpled piece of paper into Poppy's hand. She's effusive now, obviously glad to have been able to help us, but that doesn't stop her accepting the 20-euro note that Poppy passes over. I suppose a girl's got to pay them bills. I make pathetic attempts at *au revoir*-ing, and we leave, waving as we go.

I don't know if I am relieved or annoyed. Part of me assumed the worst, that he'd have gone the way of addicts the world over and died an early death – and really, would that be so very terrible? Are we just reopening wounds that are best left closed, for all of us? Our mother had very good reasons for keeping us away from him, and they may all still be valid. Plus, why should we assume that after all this time, he would even want to see us?

But part of me, if I'm honest – the part of me that is perhaps still just a little girl wondering why she doesn't have a daddy – anticipated some kind of wonderfully touching reunion. I mean, we are in the City of Light, and it all looks a bit like a movie set anyway. Perhaps I have been infected with sentimentality.

Oh well, I think, as we head back into the less scary streets of tourist Montmartre. Paris was a bust. But Blackpool will probably be just as good – if we decide to go.

Chapter 56

Poppy

We have made our decision, and it doesn't involve a trip to Blackpool. I think this was easier for me than Rose, because my heart is definitely not 100 per cent in this whole long-lost-dad thing.

Maybe I'm just nastier than her – or maybe it's because I'm softer, who knows? But my overwhelming feeling right now, as we crack open a bottle of wine in our hotel room, is one of relief. I am barely coping with losing my mum, and introducing a dad into the equation would feel like a step too far.

I've lived without a dad for so many years, he doesn't really exist in my mindscape. Hearing our mum sound so broken-hearted about it all on the cassette tape, talking about the tough decisions she'd had to make, didn't exactly make the whole reunion idea any more attractive.

I just wished that she was still here, so I could tell her it was all okay – that she'd made the right choice. That she'd protected us. That she'd been the best mum ever, and definitely had loved us enough for two.

There is no way that he could ever replace her and, in all honesty, I am angry that he is still alive, and she isn't. Our mum did everything right, and is gone. He did everything wrong, and is still here. It feels wrong on so many levels, and my only real wish is that they could swap places.

We have, though, looked him up online. Anne-Marie had given us a website address, and we were able to locate Cranky Franky with relative ease. As we waited for the page to load on my phone, we had no idea what to expect – but the reality was even weirder than we could have imagined.

We are confronted by the image of a tall man wearing a clown outfit, with the tragic whited-out, teardrop-stained face of a classic picture-book Pierrot. There is a drooping plastic rose in his clown jacket pocket, a frilly red ruffle around his neck, and he is wearing shoes in the shape of baguettes.

Wow, I think, gaping at him. Our dad is quite literally a sad clown.

'I'd like to meet him, one day,' says Rose, gazing at the picture with a mixture of pity and longing. 'When all of this is done. Give him a chance, at least.'

As the A–Z is all about second chances, I can't really object – but I'm not feeling it. I shrug, and drink, and say nothing.

I flick away from the website and into my photos. We called at the Eiffel Tower on the way back here, and recreated that picture of Mum with Franky, from all that time ago. He's part of me, I know, just as Mum is, and my sister is. But not necessarily a part I want to connect with. Not just yet, anyway, and maybe never.

It's hard to describe to my sister, but I feel a little like my armour is leaking. There is too much emotional rain getting in, and it's making me soggy.

So I deal with that the only way I know how – by pretending it's not happening.

Chapter 57

Rose

'You don't want to?' I ask, topping up my own wine and studying her. Poppy has put her phone away, and is very quiet, rooting around in her suitcase.

We brought the next couple of instalments of the A–Z with us, just in case. It felt wrong taking it from its flower-strewn cocoon in the Special Things Box – we're on to the one with the poppies now – but that isn't an easy thing to lug around on international travel.

I know Poppy has never been as intent on this Daddy Issues mission as me, and want to understand why. She, however, seems more interested in getting drunk, and opening the next envelope.

'I'm . . . ambivalent,' she finally says, screwing up her face as though trying to decide if that was the right word or not.

'Okay. Well, you don't have to come with me.'

She simply nods, and I'm not sure what she's thinking. She's putting her Face on – the one that says nothing bothers her. The one that says I Am Fine, Screw You Very Much. The one she used to wear all the time when we started this adventure; the one I always wanted to punch.

Now, though, I know better. I know it means she's upset, and trying not to show it. Because showing it – around anyone, but perhaps especially me – makes Poppy vulnerable, and she hates being vulnerable.

Ironically, the Face now makes me want to hug her instead of punch her, and for once I don't fight the realisation. Not so long ago, every time I had kind thoughts about Poppy, I'd replay sins past, and shore up all my anger and bitterness to keep them at bay. Now – after all of this – I simply don't have it in me.

My mum is dead, and my dad is a sad clown with a drug addiction and a wasted life. They are both proof that everything passes by far too quickly – and that there are more than enough sad moments to go round without seeking them out.

'But you can come if you want . . .' I say, pushing the issue, even though I can tell from her body language that she doesn't want me to.

'Maybe. Probably. Look, I don't know, okay? I just . . . well, I'm not thinking especially kind thoughts, not right now. I keep thinking I wish he'd died and Mum was still alive. I know it's not his fault, but it's the way I feel. I know I'm a horrible person, and I'm trying to be better, but . . . I don't want to lie and go all gooey-eyed about the thought of meeting our long-last dad, all right?'

'All right. I get it. I suppose I just feel . . . sorry for him, to be honest. It doesn't look as if his life's been a laugh a minute, does it?'

'And I know I should feel sorry for him, too. More than I do, anyway – but I keep thinking about Mum, and the way her voice was cracking on that cassette tape, like she was trying not to cry, listening to everything she'd gone through. Everything he'd put her through. It feels somehow like I'm betraying her if I forget all that and start playing happy families.'

'Mum said she'd forgiven him,' I respond, frowning at the ceiling. 'And she'd want us to as well, I think.'

'Well, Mum wanted us to forgive each other too, didn't she – that's what F was all about – and I'm not sure that's happening . . . anyway. Ignore me. I'm being snipey because I'm tired, and I've had too much coffee. It's best not to pay me any attention when I'm in a mood like this – I try not to. Right. I have R here. It says R is for Rhonda, and it's a photo with a note on the back.'

Poppy holds the picture up, and it's of a chubby, smiley-faced blonde woman wearing a blue medical uniform.

'It says this is Rhonda, and she was Mum's Macmillan nurse . . .' Poppy mutters, frowning as she tries to decipher our mother's increasingly scrawled handwriting. 'She wants us to buy her a bunch of flowers, and "pop a few bob in the collection box", it says here. Yet another person who did more for Mum while she was dying than we did.'

She throws the picture down on the floor, and collapses on the bed in a pile of long limbs and tangled dark hair, her arms folded across her face. She's struggling, I can see, and kicks her shoes off so hard they bang against the wall.

I reach out from my bed to hers, and take hold of one of her hands. She responds tentatively at first, but then twines her fingers into mine and holds on tight. I suspect she's crying beneath her shield, and I let her have a few moments.

'It'll all be okay,' I say, quietly. 'We're almost done now. The A–Z will be finished, and we can get on with normal life.'

This seems to make her even worse, and I hear a heaving sob get stifled.

'That's what I'm afraid of!' Poppy says, eventually, her voice jagged and raw with pain. 'I don't want to go back to my normal life. I *hate* my normal life. You'll tootle off to Liverpool and I'll probably never see you and Joe again, and I'll be supervising jingles for scratching posts, and our dad will be collecting coins in a bucket on the bloody pier in Blackpool . . . and Mum will still be dead. It's all so messed up.'

She used to get like this when we were kids; all inconsolable drama and tears. She has a lot more justification for it now, but it still half amuses me. I do what I always did back then – make comforting sounds and wait for the storm to pass.

When it finally does, she emerges from her nest of hair with damp eyes, and an embarrassed expression.

'Sorry,' she mutters, sheepishly. 'Just being a twat. You want to do S? We're here for the night anyway, and it looks like a good one. It's another video. We could watch it on my phone.'

'What is it?' I ask, hoping it's not another heavy task, and suspecting from the smirk on Poppy's now-calm face that it's not.

'S,' she announces, grandly, 'is for Sex.'

Chapter 58

Andrea: S is for Sex

'Let's talk about sex, baby! Ha ha, remember when that song came out, girls, and I thought it was a bit rude? I used to make you sing "six" instead!

'Well, you're both a lot older now, and there's no need to be embarrassed – though I secretly hope you are. I'm feeling pretty poorly now, truth be told, and when I'm not woozy and drugged up to my eyeballs, I'm in pain. It's not pleasant, and anything that gives me a giggle – such as the thought of you two wincing while you watch this, wondering if I've left you a dog-eared copy of the *Kama Sutra* – is very welcome, thank you.

'Poppy, thankfully you have never confided in me on affairs of the heart – or other body parts – but I suspect that you don't live like Mother Teresa. I'm not an idiot, I've seen the way you behave around men, you slattern! So, well done you – just try and remember that there is more to a relationship than what fits where and how fast you move it. Life would be a poor thing without love, and it's never too late to find it, sweetheart.

'Rose, you're a different matter entirely. I know you had that disastrous online dating thing a few years ago, with the chap who said he was a detective inspector and turned out to be a lollipop man, but I don't think you've had many escapades since.

'This is a shame on many levels, as you are a woman in your prime – much as you like to pretend you're some dried-up post-menopausal crone. Your forties are a wonderful time for your sex life – I shan't go into details for fear of giving you a heart attack, but mine were splendid!

'So – this is your mission, should you choose to accept it. I'd like to add that this message will self-destruct, but I fear that would be too much for even the resourceful Lewis to arrange. Girls, go out on the pull – doll yourselves up, drink a few glasses of vino, and let the world know you exist!

'I don't know, at this stage, if you chose to go on a foreign adventure to seek out your father – or whether you found him, and how that went for you both. Well, I hope – please think as kindly of him as you can. He's a flawed human being, but I have moved on from those old wounds, and hope that you can too. Either way, I thought you might need cheering up – and what better way than a night on the town with a little gentle flirting thrown in for fun?

'Happy hunting – and, as ever, much love, Mum.'

Chapter 59

Poppy

Rose couldn't look more nervous if she tried. She also looks great – I've seen to that – but her hands are shaking and her breath is coming in panicky little wheezes. It's so sweet; she's like a teenager on her first night out.

'It's easy,' I say, leading her into the crowded bar, the noise levels so high I have to shout. 'We'll just give fake names, and make up fake jobs. I do it all the time. I usually pretend I'm a nurse – men go nuts for nurses. Just listen to what I do, and play along.'

She glares at me, her made-up eyes sparkling, and I suspect that if she had biblical powers, I would just have been turned into a pillar of salt.

We decided, after laughing and cringing our way through Mum's last video, that she was right – we did need cheering up. We'd travelled the world, made steps towards meeting our estranged father, and I'd had a mini-meltdown. Then, after all that, we'd had to watch as our visibly wasting-away mother pretended to be jolly for our sake. This was bloody hard going, and we both needed to take the Alcohol Cure.

The bar is dark and hot and throbbing with life. The music is R&B with occasional French hip-hop beats thrown in, and I smile as we are enveloped in the warmth and potential. These places are my natural environment – but poor Rose looks terrified.

'I don't speak French,' she'd said, lamely, as we were getting ready. 'Apart from stuff I know from song titles.'

'That's fine. In fact, that's even better – nobody will expect much of you. Anyway, these are French men, Rose. They're genetically hard-wired to flirt with any woman they encounter.'

I'm not sure whether my pep talk helped, but the three glasses of wine she'd downed certainly had. I hand over an extortionate amount of euros in return for some more, and look around until I spot a table. There's one that's almost full of men, men who have clearly come here straight from the office and are letting off steam. There are two chairs free at the end, and I stride towards them.

I don't bother asking if the seats are taken – that's a very English tradition – and instead simply sit down, smiling widely at the group. There's a mix of ages, from early 20s through to mid-50s, and they're all pretty drunk. Perfect.

'*Salut, tout le monde!*' I say, greeting them. '*Je m'appelle Millie.*'

It's a fake name I've used before – Millie is a nurse on the paediatric unit – and one I feel comfy with. I look at Rose expectantly, raising my eyebrows at her in a prompt. She visibly jumps, as though she's just remembered that she has to talk, and says: '*Je m'appelle . . . er . . . Vanilli!*'

I blink my eyes, and try not to laugh. Which is more than can be said for our new pals, who clearly think this is the funniest thing they've ever heard. Even Rose, once she realises what's she's done, starts to giggle.

It turns out to be perfect, and breaks the ice in a way that no amount of stories about my imaginary time on the children's A&E ward could have done.

Within seconds, we are all chatting. Well, to be precise, I'm chatting. Rose is grinning like my simpleton sister, and drinking. A lot.

One man in particular seems very taken with her. Or at least certain parts of her. He's probably in his later thirties, and has chocolate-drop eyes and deep-brown hair and a borderline weird goatee. Truth be told, he looks a bit like an off-duty magician – stick a cape on him and hey presto.

His name is Patrice, and he can't take his eyes off Rose's chest. He's definitely much more drunk than we are, and tells me in French that she has beautiful boobs.

'What did he say?' asks Rose, whispering in my ear. 'I heard "beautiful". Was it my eyes? Does he think I have beautiful eyes?'

I giggle, then bite it back. She sounds so excited.

'Yeah, let's go.with that, shall we? Anyway . . . look around. This place is full of potential S partners. Maybe it's time to use some of your French?'

'But I'll sound stupid!'

'No, they'll appreciate the effort. And Mum is watching. Come on, finish that glass, then go and get us some more. Make it a bottle. And on the way, talk to some men, all right?'

She downs almost a whole glass of wine in one go, and gets to her feet. She's slightly unsteady, but looks determined as she makes her way through the crowds. I keep my eye on her, ready to leap to her aid if necessary, and grin as she encounters a large gaggle of guys.

I can't hear what she's saying over the din of the music, but the group lets out a huge whoop of delight, and cheers as she goes past. One of them accompanies her to the bar, and I suspect that she is not paying for her own drinks.

By the time she gets back to us, she is flushed bright red, but looking slightly triumphant. The men are waving at her and she is waving back.

'What on earth did you say?' I ask, genuinely intrigued.

'Well . . . you know how I said I only know French from song titles?'

'Yes.'

'I used one of them.'

'Which one?' I say, not able to keep the grin off my face at her shocked expression. I'm not sure if she's shocked at their reaction, or her own behaviour.

'I said . . . *voulez-vous coucher avec moi, ce soir.*'

That's it for me. I'm out for the next five minutes, laughing so hard I have tears streaming down my face and feel on the verge of some kind of stroke. Absolutely perfect.

'God Rose,' I finally manage to mutter, 'that's . . . brilliant. Where have you been hiding your inner slapper for the last few weeks?'

'The last few years, to be honest. And that was fun, I have to say. Plus they all said yes, apart from one who looked like

357

he might not be keen on lady parts in general. So, what next?'

'Try it on him,' I say, gesturing to Patrice, who is now chatting to his friends – probably about the crazy English girls pretending to be a 1980s boy band.

'I'm not sure I want to,' she whispers, glugging down another half-glass of *vin rouge*. 'He looks a bit like Dynamo's Dad.'

'Well you don't have to actually *coucher* with him, do you? It's just for fun!'

She nods, and tucks her curls behind her ears, and sticks out her boobs. She taps Patrice on the shoulder, and he immediately turns round. She leans in, and murmurs to him, and the response is instant. He stands to his feet, and offers her his hand in a 'let's go' gesture that leaves her utterly terrified.

It's so stupidly funny – the look of delight on his face, the look of horror on hers – that I fear I may never breathe again. Rose, though, is staring at me in desperation, obviously needing a rescue.

'*Un moment, s'il vous plaît,*' I say to Patrice, who is still waiting. His friends are grinning away, and clearly having the French equivalent of a 'get your coat you've pulled' conversation.

I lead a furiously blushing Rose towards the ladies, where we immediately collapse in giggles, leaning against the sinks and gasping for breath.

'Oh no!' she says, once we've calmed down. 'What do I do now?'

'Well, do you want to shag Patrice? I'm sure he'd be happy to show you his magic wand!'

I touch up my lipstick as I wait for her to think about it. I don't have to wait long.

'No!' she squeaks, looking shocked. 'Of course not! I've only just met him!'

'Well that's kind of the point, isn't it?' I say, frowning at her in the mirror. 'Mum wanted us to go out on the pull.'

'Well, we have pulled. She didn't say we had to shag them as well. It's . . . not me, Poppy. Never has been, probably never will be. It does feel good to think that someone under the age of eighty might actually *want* to shag me, but . . . no. Thank you.'

'Okay,' I reply, stashing my make-up back in my bag. 'No problem. It's not a big deal, either way.'

She looks completely flabbergasted, but I'm not sure why. I am struck again by how different our lives have become – this kind of thing is normal for me. It happens most weekends, although admittedly not usually in Paris. For her, though, it's all a bit of a revelation. Perhaps, between us, we make one normal human being.

We sneak out of the loos, and hide behind the pulsating crowds of dancers as we edge our way to the door. Rose, who seems to feel maternal even towards grown men, is worried that we will hurt Patrice's feelings, but I assure her he'll get over it.

'So,' I say, as we emerge back out on to the street. There are people standing around smoking and chatting, and the air is still warm. Summer in Paris. Divine. 'I'm glad you had a good time. And I'm glad you asked a whole bar-ful of French men to sleep with you. Mum would be proud. Any regrets?'

I'm clearly feeding her a line, and she gets it straight away.

'*Non*,' she warbles, creditably in tune and attracting some strange looks from the smoking crowd, '*je ne regrette rien!*'

I raise my palm to Rose, and she gives me a hefty high-five. We start to stroll along the pavement – going in completely the wrong direction – but enjoying seeing the city at night.

'It was good, wasn't it?' she says, linking her arm into mine. 'Being out, and not doing something heavy and serious?'

'I know what you mean,' I reply, thinking back to my earlier melodrama and feeling a bit embarrassed about it. 'And I'm really sorry I went all Teenage Angsty Mutant Poppy on you earlier.'

'It's all right,' Rose says, patting my hand. 'I kind of miss Teenage Angsty Mutant Poppy. She's more authentic than Perfectly Poised Poppy. And you know what you said, about me going back to Liverpool, and never seeing me and Joe again?'

'Yeah?'

'Well, I really hope that's not true.'

I squeeze her fingers, and say a little prayer that she's right. That all of this turns out all right in the end.

'Okay. Good. I hope so too. Do you want to go anywhere else?'

Rose ponders it, then replies: 'I don't think so. If I drink any more wine, I'll be embarrassing myself in the gutters of Gay Paris.'

'Well, in that case, you know what it's time for, don't you?'

She shakes her head, still grinning.

'It's time for Joe le Taxi . . .'

Chapter 60

Rose

We are back at the cottage, which feels like coming home in a way I'd never imagined it could. We've been to the village to stock up on supplies, bumping into Tasmin Hughes and Fred the Milkman, and are now fully prepared for a lengthy stint finishing up the rest of the A–Z.

I've called Joe to check that he is still alive, and spoken to Simon, who assures me that he is. I've even sent a brief email to our father. It's a tentative first step, and I've no idea what will eventually come of it.

I'd like to get to know him, and perhaps for Joe to have him in his life – but before any of that happens, I need to be sure that he is well and truly free of his past demons. Joe has had enough messing around from father figures – we all have – and I don't want to bring any more chaos into his world.

I don't think Poppy shares my enthusiasm for getting to know our dad, and I have to accept that. Maybe it's the fact that I'm a parent myself that makes me more open-minded – he's missed out on his daughters' entire lives, and doesn't exactly seem to be living the dream, working as a sad clown in Blackpool.

Maybe it's because I think, deep down and buried under layers of more recent events, that I still have some residual memory of the time when he lived with us, and she doesn't.

I was only two, but I feel like it's there – a ghost of a thing, an intangible sense of someone who used to bounce me on his knee until I laughed, and jump in muddy puddles, and tuck me in at night, and smell of spices. It might not even be real, and if I try too hard to capture it, it disappears off around a bend in time. It's like seeing something from the corner of your eye.

Whatever it is, I feel more of a connection to the man than my sister does, and I hope he gets in touch.

Poppy has spent the morning firing off work emails and frowning at her phone as though it's Satan's spawn, mumbling under her breath and occasionally swearing, very loudly. For once I'm glad that I don't have a high-flying career – nobody would miss me even if I took a month off during term-time, never mind in the summer holidays. Being an anonymous worker ant has its advantages.

Eventually, she throws the phone on to the sofa, hard, where it bounces for a few seconds, then disappears off down the side, between the cushions and the arm.

'You'll have to stick your hand in and fish around for it, like you did for loose change when you were a kid,' I say, pointing at the couch. 'We used to find all sorts down there, didn't we? Mum said it wasn't a sofa, it was a black hole.'

'Yeah. I remember. I once found a copy of one of those

racy erotica books from the olden days down there – Black Lace, was it? I asked no questions. Anyway . . . the way I'm feeling at the moment, I'm not bothered if I never see it again. I've had it up to my eyeballs with work. I never wanted to do marketing in the first place . . . I think I'm going to get them to make me redundant.'

'Really? How will you manage that?'

'I have my ways . . . maybe I'll go and live on a desert island and eat coconuts and seduce dusky young men. Or maybe I'll come and live here, and write that book I always said I was going to write.'

'But how will you support your many sponsor children?'

'The flat is worth a fortune. And I can bash out a bestseller. I'll set it in Paris, and it can be about a beautiful heiress who's a bitch in the boardroom, and the bedroom . . . I don't know. This whole thing – Mum dying, us being together again, the A–Z – has been awful in a lot of ways. I don't know about you, but I feel like a burns victim right now, I'm so raw. But it has at least made me do some thinking, about my life, and what I want from it.'

I'm not sure how I feel about the thought of Poppy living here, forging her fresh start, and when I force my feelings to stop squirming around and look carefully at them, I realise that I am slightly jealous – but not unmanageably jealous. I mean, it's not like I can move – Joe's friends, his education, his whole life, are all firmly rooted in Liverpool. So why shouldn't one of us stay on?

'Well, I wish you luck,' I say, and leave it at that. I'm worried that the jealousy part will sneak out and ambush my voice, and we are both still hyper-sensitive to any negative comments from the other.

'Shall we do T? It says it's another letter, and that we need to listen to David Bowie singing "Time". I'll find it on my phone, as yours seems to be otherwise engaged. I think the A–Zs are getting shorter, don't you? I suppose she was trying to do them as she was getting more and more poorly.'

There is silence for a few moments, as we both ponder that hideous thought, interrupted only by the sound of emails and texts landing on Poppy's buried phone.

'Do you think it would stop if I set the sofa on fire?' she asks, sounding half serious.

'I think you might burn the whole cottage down. It'll run out of juice eventually. Anyway, I've found the song – let's just play *Aladdin Sane* really loudly so we don't hear it. We can sit on the sofa and read the letter together at the same time.'

I place my phone down on the side table, and the music starts. The haunting, melancholic voice of the late, great David fills the room. Time, he tells us, is waiting in the wings . . .

Chapter 61

Andrea: T is for Time

I hope you're listening to the song, girls – poor David! When this album came out, I was just a girl really. I was so in love with him, and all his weirdness – he was like the ultimate misfit king. I couldn't believe it when he died, and so young. Now I find myself – even younger – facing the same situation, and listening to these old tunes to try and take the edge off.

First of all, apologies – I know my writing is getting terrible. I'm struggling to hold the pen now, and struggling to stay awake for long periods of time, and struggling with the whole death thing, to be honest.

I've tried to keep this A–Z as upbeat as I possibly can, but I find that tonight, I'm running out of steam, and I've most definitely misplaced my smile. Perhaps it's down the side of the sofa? Anyway, U is up next, and I couldn't dredge up any enthusiasm for a long lecture about Understanding, or how Unbearable it's been to see you two tear each other apart. So I'm making it U for Upping Sticks – because tomorrow, girls, I am leaving the cottage to go to the hospital, and realistically speaking, I know I won't be back.

I have just packed my bags, and it was very tricky. How on earth do you plan an outfit for the end of the world as you know it? And how can it be that I will end my life with just a few odds and sods thrown into a wheelie case – how can I reduce everything I will need to a few random possessions? It makes me feel so small, so insignificant – like all the work, all the striving, all the battles I've fought, come down to nothing at all.

Anyway, I've tied up as many loose ends as I can, and hopefully not left anything embarrassing around the house to shock you with. I know Lewis will help me through the rest of this project, and I know he'll look after my blue tits, and I know he'll be with me through everything that I have left to face. He is my loyal and wonderful friend, and the day I met him was probably the luckiest day of my life. He's like my guardian angel in tweed, and I know he'll take care of me.

But still. Still, I find myself almost intolerably sad right now. I've missed my evening painkillers, because I want to be fully conscious for my last night here, in this place where I've built so many memories. I've sent Lewis home, because I want to be alone with those memories – to say my goodbyes. I suppose I had some drama-queen image of myself floating around the cottage looking ethereal, reliving past glories, making my peace with my future.

But for once, my drama queen has let me down. It's

hard to look ethereal when you're tied up in knots with pain, and I simply can't make my peace with it. I can't say goodbye with any sense of justice, or fairness, or calm. I don't want to go, girls. I don't want to leave. I'd like to cling on here, to just go to sleep on the sofa and never wake up. If I was brave enough, perhaps I'd do just that.

They've offered to set me up at home, those lovely Macmillan ladies, but I can't face that either. This cottage has seen its share of sadness, but I don't want to turn it into a hospital ward. I want to leave it for you two, as a refuge, a safe haven. A reminder of what we all once had together. I don't want it smelling of death and disinfectant; that would soil all that it has been to us.

So, I've wandered around the bedrooms, and had the longest bath, and now I'm sitting here, alone, in my dressing gown, listening to David and feeling about three hundred years old. Three hundred years old, and yet still a child – because my time has run out, and I have no idea what happens next, and for once, I am scared.

I'm scared and I'm in all kinds of pain, and I feel so very lonely. I know it's not fair to say that to you, but I'm not feeling very fair right now. I'm starting to wonder if this whole A–Z – this Grand Dame nobility of mine – hasn't just been a folly. The foolish conceit of a dying old woman, who still thinks she can control the world. In reality, I can't even control my own body – and perhaps, I think, I have made a mistake. Perhaps I should have told you.

Perhaps I should have sent for you both, and had you here with me now, for one last goodbye. One last hug. Even one last argument – anything, to get another chance to see your smiles; hold your hands; hear your laughter. Stroke the soft skin of your faces, just as I did when you were tiny children, and the world was a simple place.

If I close my eyes, and let my mind drift, I can almost hear your childish laughter echoing around the room, listen to the sound of your feet running around upstairs playing a game. Hear one of you counting while the other one hides. I know they're just ghosts – ghosts of all those carefree days when we were whole.

It's selfish, but I miss you both so much – my precious girls. I wish you were here with me, now, holding my hand and looking after me and telling me it'll all be all right, even though we know it won't. I don't want to be alone, and yet I am.

But perhaps I'll feel differently tomorrow. I don't know. I'm consumed by a fit of the black dog and can't seem to shake it. This cottage has been my home – our home – for so long that it has become part of me. Leaving it tomorrow will feel like I'm accepting the inevitable, and it is breaking my heart. The unimaginable is starting to become real, and I feel weak and old and useless.

I'd give anything to have more time. More time here, more time in my garden. More time with you girls. More time with Lewis. More time on this beautiful, beautiful earth. I feel like my whole life has been so insignificant, so meaningless, and I don't have any more time left to change that.

So, my darlings, please don't make that depressing thought come true. Give it some meaning. Make the most of your time – because, before you know it, it will all have slipped through your fingers.

I love you both, more than I could ever put into words,

Mum xxx

Chapter 62

Lewis

I didn't intend to be here, at Andrea's cottage. I didn't intend to be standing outside, like a Peeping Tom, watching those two young women go through their own personal hell.

I didn't intend any of it. It just happened. I was out walking with Betty, a sad and solitary affair without Andrea, and my feet seemed to bring me here of their own accord. It's happened a few times now – it's as though I enter some kind of fugue state, and when I emerge, I find that I am here, outside her front door. Looking through the windows at a life that is no more. At a home that has lost its heart.

Betty, as she is doing now, knows that this is a special place – a place where her human friend will open the door and give her a cool bowl of water and, just possibly, a nice sausage as well. She is whining and scrabbling at the gravel in the driveway, keen to get inside and curl up on Andrea's sofa. Much like myself, Betty hasn't yet quite come to terms with the fact that Andrea is no longer here.

At first, I'm not quite sure what has happened to provoke the anguish I can see through the window, until I catch the mournful sound of that David Bowie song she loved so much. And then I know. They are on T, and that heartbreaking letter she scrawled to them the night before she left the cottage for the last time.

She'd wanted to take it out the next day, replace it with something more cheerful – 'T for Tom Cruise, darling, they could watch *Cocktail* and throw drinks around the kitchen! That would be so much more fun!'

But I'd insisted she leave it in, and did my Firm Lawyer face until she finally agreed. I felt it was important. That they needed to know – to know how much she was suffering, and to understand how hard all of this was for her. They needed to know that it wasn't all about their own pain – but about hers, as well.

Now, as I gaze nervously through the glass, I see the end result of that knowledge. The two girls – grown women, I know, but always girls to me – are huddled together on the sofa, their arms wrapped around each other like small children cuddling, weeping uncontrollably. Their misery, their distress, is so tangible you could practically reach out and touch it. I am a voyeur, intruding on their private pain, a spectator of their agony, and I cannot quite tear myself away.

They're strangers to me, and yet they are part of Andrea – and I am on the outside looking in, watching them sob, unable to help.

I feel sharp tears sting my own eyes, and let them come. I'm old enough and ugly enough to let my emotions take over at times like this. Times of such pain, and such loss, that all we can do is roll over, legs in the air, and surrender.

I wonder if I should knock. Call in for a cup of tea. See how they are getting on. I wonder if we could console each other, us poor lost souls trying to rebuild a life that Andrea's passing has devastated.

But no, I decide. Not right now. They are consoling each other, or at least sharing their unhappiness – and that is, after all, what Andrea had wanted. Seeing them there like that, faces raw and twisted with grief, doesn't feel like much of a victory – but I realise, in a way, that it is. And that they have a few more steps to take yet.

The A–Z, I know, becomes altogether more random towards the end. She was running out of energy, out of time, out of everything, and I found myself often answering the door to delivery men bearing boxes of movies and other strange items. Those last few days were terrible, just terrible – how she managed to rally to make that final video, I still don't know. Sheer bloody-mindedness on her part.

And love, of course. That was always her motivating factor – the love she felt for these two sobbing women; her precious grubby angels.

I put Betty back on her lead – it will be the only way to get her to move – and walk on as quietly as I can, hoping they don't hear my feet crunching on the gravel. I'm sure they won't – they are lost in their own moment.

As I leave, I am still crying, the tears streaking through the dust that our walk has left on my cheeks. I feel as though I might never stop crying, and yearn to be back out in the hills, where I can be alone with my memories.

My life feels so dull without Andrea's light to illuminate

it, and I am clinging to the forlorn hope that all of those stories I was told as a child are true.

That, when my time is done, and this useless old body finally catches up with my mind and decides that it's had enough, we will be reunited.

Chapter 63

Poppy

A whole day passes before we feel able to move on to the next letter, even though it is cheerily marked as V is for Victory.

That letter – her last night in the cottage – destroyed us both. I know how guilty I feel, and know that Rose must feel the same. Mum had made her views on guilt very clear earlier on, but neither of us was at all capable of saying no to it after that. And I don't think we deserved to.

The fact that we weren't there with her wasn't completely our fault. But the fact that she had been put in this position – unable to reach out to her own daughters – was.

I still don't know how we would have reacted, if she had made that phone call. If we'd both been told that she was dying, and that she wanted us at home with her.

I like to think that we'd have both risen above our petty differences, called a truce for her last days – but I'm not 100 per cent sure we would. More likely, we'd have faked it, badly, and she would have seen that, and it would all have been so much worse. We're a pair of absolute arseholes, and we are both right to be ashamed of our behaviour.

The one positive to come out of that letter, to come out of our mother's anguish, was the way we reacted – the proof that her A–Z was working. That it hadn't all been wasted, or meaningless, or insignificant.

In the middle of all that pain, all that guilt and regret, we had turned to each other, and we weren't alone. I had Rose, and Rose had me. That much, Mum had achieved.

Drained and battered, we are now both ready for round 22, which comes with a mysterious package and a note. It's another British mammal card – a darling deer, this time – and I can tell from the slightly clearer handwriting that she is feeling a lot better than she did when she wrote T and U.

I find myself stroking the cardboard, and sniffing the ink, as though I can somehow find a trace of her there. A trace that I can hug, and comfort, and care for. Because, right now, I am sick of thinking about myself, and even about Rose – I just want my mum.

I want my mum, so I can tell her how much I miss her, and how much I love her, and how very, very sorry I am that we all ran out of time.

Chapter 64

Andrea: V is for Victory

Girls, I can only apologise for that last letter. I'm sure it was a difficult read, but the ever-wise Lewis insists that it stays.

I was feeling very down, and I hope you'll forgive me. I'm all set up in hospital now, and it's really rather nice. The staff are so kind, I have some superb drugs flowing through my system, and as much jelly as I can eat. Not bad!

There isn't much space here, although I can use the back of the card as well, so onwards with V – and Victory. There are four items in your package. Two are medals – I'm so sorry they're plastic, they were described as 'party favours' online and came in a pack of six. I've given the others to Lewis and Rhonda and myself, and left one for Joe. We are champions all, just like that delightful Mo Farah.

Also in the package is that lovely leather-bound copy of *The Secret Garden* that you won in high school, Poppy, for the Creative Writing prize. Such a clever girl. And

Rose, you were named Forest Hills Young Scientist of the Year in 1991 – and here's your prize, a paperback of *A Brief History of Time*. I can see that you read it, from the dog-eared pages and the notes you left in red pen, as though you fully intended to quiz Stephen Hawking at some later point.

I was so proud of you both back then, and I still am today. I know you've probably long forgotten these small victories, but I kept them, of course. I loved those little plates inside, with your names and your achievements written on them in fancy letters.

I fully expected you to go on and be a writer Poppy – you were always so good with words – and for you to carry on with your science, Rose. You've both made careers for yourselves, and there is nothing wrong with either of them – but I don't sense a great air of Victory around the two of you when you talk to me about your jobs.

I know I've asked a lot of you both throughout this whole A–Z, but now I am being cheeky and asking even more. Put on your medals, and be proud of who you are – but also ask who you *could* be. Are you living the lives you should have led? Are you happy going in to work every day? If not, it's never too late to change – and being happy in your work is one of the biggest victories of life.

Personally, I was always devastated never to have won an award. Penny Peabody came close – I was nominated for Best Supporting Actress in a British Drama by some cheesy TV magazine – but alas, it wasn't meant to be. Perhaps there will be a film set in heaven, and I can chalk up an Oscar there!

Anyway. The card is full, and I am tired, so I will bid you a fond farewell.

To victory!

Mum xxx

Chapter 65

Rose

'She's right, isn't she?' I say, swooshing my huge hair over the nylon medal necklace. The plastic disc hangs low, perched on my chest. Poppy is wearing hers, too, and I suspect we both look ridiculous.

'Of course she's right,' replies Poppy, who is already looking through the illustrations of *The Secret Garden*, stroking them as though they might come to life beneath her touch. 'She always is.'

'My job is boring,' I say, Stephen Hawking nestled on my lap. 'In fact my whole life is boring. I'm going to do that teacher training.'

Poppy looks up at me and smiles. So much of the underlying enmity between us has been drained away by that letter of Mum's, by David Bowie, by the uncontrollable sobbing on each other's shoulders. It feels so much easier to be around her, like a particularly nasty boil has been lanced and can now start to heal.

'And I'm going to write that bloody book,' she says. 'We've both done all right, but somewhere along the line, we've also both been knocked off track – and we can't keep blaming other people for that. We can't keep blaming Gareth, or each other, or stuff that happened a million years ago – if we want things to change, we have to make them change. We have to make Mum proud again.'

'We will,' I say, forcefully – because I really believe that is true. I believe that I can try and become a Biology teacher, and I definitely believe that Poppy can write 'that bloody book'. She might not be here with us, but our mother is still an inspiration. She is still making me feel as if I might emerge from life victorious, in exactly the same way I always tell Joe he can be whatever he wants to be as long as he works hard enough.

We've cracked open a new bottle of very nice gin, and I raise my glass.

'A toast!' I say, holding it towards Poppy.

'To our mother, crazy old lush that she was – and to us! To victory!'

Poppy chinks her glass against mine, and we both down our drinks in one, barely blinking as a double measure of gin goes down. That, I think, as I pour us the next, is genetics at work.

Chapter 66

Poppy

I'm not entirely sure that *Homes & Gardens* would recommend redecorating while completely off your head on gin, but we're pushing the envelope here. We should probably get a double-page spread: Interior Design – the Tanqueray Way!

W has turned out to be for 'Wonderwall', and now neither of us can get that song out of our heads. It also explained why Mum had taken down those family pictures of hers, leaving one wall dotted with spooky bare patches and faded frame outlines.

She'd managed to somehow get a copy of the Oasis single – possibly from my bedroom, as I'd left a stash of vinyl in there when I moved out – and glued a circular note on the middle section. The note is written in a spiral, in tiny writing that gets smaller as it curls inwards. A strange mix of her usual *Alice in Wonderland* tendencies, and Britpop classics of days gone by.

'Create your own Wonderwall, my darlings – and tend to it! Keep it alive like it's a garden of our history. And remember: all the roads we have to walk are winding . . .'

Along with the single was a huge brown file, crammed full with photographs. The albums on the bookshelves are still stocked, so she must have had copies made – or, more likely, Lewis had.

The pictures cover vast amounts of time, and flicking through them is a bittersweet experience – because like most trips down memory lane, there are a few ruts in the road, and a couple of muggers waiting to threaten you at knifepoint and steal your emotional handbag.

There are a few more of our own mum as a baby, with her serious-faced parents, and one of her father in his Royal Navy uniform. There's even a much older one, of our great-granddad, also in a Navy outfit, with sleeked-back hair and a face like Errol Flynn. He's grinning at the camera in a way his son never seemed to manage, and looks quite the character – he's also holding the very tobacco tin I stole from the Posh Room, although it looks shiny and new in the picture.

There are a couple of Mum as an impossibly cute toddler, with bundles of blonde corkscrew curls, wearing those frilly knickers that they seemed to like back in the day. One of her as a schoolgirl, early 1960s I'd say, spoiling her studied pose with the fact that one of her socks is pulled up to her knee and the other is sagging around her ankle.

After that, as Mum pursued her acting career, they all become a bit more glamorous. Mum's headshots through the ages; pictures of her with the famous and semi-famous, photos taken on sets and in dressing rooms, drinks glasses jostling for place with pansticks and clouds of smoke puffing up from huge glass ashtrays.

There's one of her with her own mum, early 1970s from the state of the boot-length Afghan coat my mum is wearing, in what I recognise as Piccadilly Circus – the same, but with bright Cinzano ads and Ford Cortinas and mini-skirts. My grandmother looks a bit awkward, overwhelmed by it all, and I'm so sad I never got to meet her. So sad that our own mum had to deal with her death all alone, much younger than we are now, and without any family to help her. Without a crazy A–Z to get her through it.

Our father features in a few pictures – one of them together in a bar, again shrouded by smoke and barricaded in with a table full of empty glasses. She looks young and vibrant and completely loved up as she snuggles against him; he is a little more aloof, with a now retro-cool 1970s beard, a cigarette drooping from his mouth. They look impossibly young and stupidly glamorous.

There is one of her while she was pregnant – with Rose, I suspect – doing the traditional side-on pose to show off her bump, and pictures of her and our father with us as newborns. I've never seen these before – only the ones that show her alone with us – and again, it's a melancholy thing.

It should have been the happiest time of their lives, but on the one with me especially, Rose's podgy face beaming away next to my bald head, Mum just looks so tired. Defeated. Like some of the life has been sucked out of her. Dad's even smoking in that one, and I am amazed at the thought of people being able to puff away on maternity wards.

The bulk of the photos, though, are of us. Me and Rose as kids, a full range of time-machine snapshots: holidays in

Dorset and paddling pools in the garden and walks with Patch and first days at school and Christmas plays and birthdays with number balloons doing their floaty helium dance above our heads.

I recognise our different stages, and it feels odd, like looking at a picture montage of somebody else's life. There are blessedly few of me as Spotty Poppy, because I'd learned to avoid cameras like the Artful Dodger by that time, and not so many once we were older – when we were both off at university.

She has, wisely, edited Gareth out of existence, and the last one of us all together was taken months before that hellish night at Disco 2000. We'd both come home for Mum's birthday, and she'd asked a waiter in the restaurant to take a photo of all three of us. The last-century version of me is looking a little sullen, and Rose is smiling and radiant.

Mum, of course, looks wonderful. Being a professional poser, it was hard to catch her unawares in a bad position, but this one is especially lovely. She'd been asked for her autograph while we were out, which had made her particularly smug, and she just looks so happy, squashed there between the two of us.

The change after that is sudden, and devastating. There are pictures of Joe as a baby, pictures of her and Rose, pictures of her and me. But never any of us all together. As we root through them all, oohing and aahing and laughing, it is one of my biggest regrets that we never added to her collection. To her stash of memories of us together, healed and whole and strong. She deserved more than we gave her, so much more.

We can't change that now, but we can at the very least create our own Wonderwall – she's even left us two pairs of scissors and a giant packet of Blu-Tack to make it easy on us.

After a brief debate on how to organise it – chronological, in order of size, in a square or in a spiral – the gin makes the final decision, and we simply both start cutting and sticking pictures on the wall at random.

One of Joe ends up next to one of Lewis dressed as Hamlet; one of Rose as a teenager ends up next to Mum on the beach in a bikini; one of Patch ends up juxtaposed with one of our grandmother staring silently into the lens; one of Rose's graduation is flush with my Mum and Elvis.

By the time we are finished, much of the wall is covered. It will probably look bloody awful in the morning, but to two drunk ladies, it is an awesome creation of stylish design.

We stand back and admire our handiwork, making complimentary comments about each other's choices, and it strikes me how far we've come. How far Mum has brought us. When we started this whole thing – this A–Z madness – we could barely stand to be in the same room as each other. Even at our own mother's funeral.

And now? All these letters later; after all the road trips and arguments and bad karaoke and treasure hunts and brutal, tear-jerking honesty, we can stand side by side, and I can say to Rose 'you were the fattest baby in the world' without it starting another round of hostilities. Our Wonderwall is truly wonderful.

We take a few more snapshots on our phones, vowing to get them printed out along with our Eiffel Tower shots so we can add to the collection, and then stand back and look at it all some more. We even take photos of the photos, we're so pleased with it.

Rose is staring at one particular picture with a frown on her face. I follow her line of vision, and see that it is of Mum and Lewis, on Stapeley Hill. It's obviously been taken by Lewis holding his long arms out, a senior-citizen version of a selfie, and they are both grinning like very naughty children.

'We should invite him over,' says Rose, biting her lip. 'I mean – look at them. He was such a good friend to her. He was with her when she died, and he helped her arrange all of this, and now he's alone. He doesn't seem to have family, definitely not any kids, and now he doesn't even have our mum. She'd want us to look after him, don't you think?'

I nod, and look at all the photos of Lewis that are scattered over our Wonderwall. There are more of him and his dog than our grandparents and our father combined.

'You're right. We should. Maybe we could try and cook him something. Or at the very least get a Chinese in and some plonk. On the A–Z list, X is for Movie Night. I know that could mean anything in Mum's universe, but maybe we could ask him round for that.'

'As long as it's not X for X-rated movie night, and Mum doesn't have a whole sideline in adult films she never mentioned to us . . .'

I shudder, physically, at the very thought, and hope that's not true. Seeing our mother's bare bum on a carousel horse was quite enough, thank you, without discovering she was also known as Peaches McMuff or Trixie-Belle Nipples as well. Although they do sound like they'd make interesting characters in my new book.

'I'll text him now,' I say, 'while we're too drunk to change our minds.'

Chapter 67

Rose

Lewis enters the cottage with his dog, the famous springer spaniel Betty. Or at least I feel as if she's famous now, after sticking so many pictures of her up on the Wonderwall.

She's a beautiful old lady, with huge, round brown eyes and rust-red colouring on her soft white fur. As soon as she is through the door, she scampers around, ears back, sniffing the air, as though she is furiously searching for something.

Or, I think sadly, someone. Poor Betty is on the list of creatures who are desperately missing Andrea Barnard, purveyor of fine A–Zs and even finer sausages. Eventually, she seems to give up, and jumps on to the sofa, where she circles three times before settling into a ball with her muzzle tucked beneath her tail.

'Ah,' says Lewis, presenting me with a bottle of wine that looks far too good to accompany the roast dinner that we've managed to produce in his honour, 'she's looking for her, isn't she? I must admit that I find myself doing the exact same thing with alarming frequency.'

'I'd like to see you curl up in a ball with your nose touching your tail, Lewis,' replies Poppy, standing on tiptoe to kiss him on the cheek to take any potential sting out of her words.

'Alas yes, I think those days are behind me . . . anyway. I was delighted to receive your invitation to movie night, ladies, although knowing a bit more about it than you, also slightly concerned.'

'Yeah. I think we all are,' I reply, looking at the contents of our A–Z package for the letter X. It is in two parts – a bundle of DVDs, and a huge dice, the type people would use for games in the garden.

Mum has covered each numbered side with glued-on paper, and each face of the dice shows a different film beginning with the letter X. The whole thing is covered in multi-coloured rainbow glitter, bits of it falling off constantly, leaving the table and everyone who comes into contact with it sparkling like a contestant on *Strictly Come Dancing*.

Lewis nods, and reaches out to stroke the dice, almost without seeming to notice his own actions. It's a familiar gesture, and one I've seen in Poppy and myself as well – the urge to touch objects that she touched, as though she may have left some magic in them, a trace of all she meant to us.

'She was struggling a little, by this stage,' he says, taking off his tweed jacket to reveal a tweed waistcoat and a tweed tie. Even on a night off, he looks every inch the respectable lawyer. I wonder, idly, if he has to get all his clothes tailor-made, just to accommodate the sheer size of his bear-like body. He wipes his hands down his sides, and his waistcoat immediately starts to shimmer.

'She had considered making X for exes – as in former

partners,' he says. 'But eventually she decided against it. I think I remember her exact words: "we've already given over too much of our lives to romantic disasters – it's time to put those behind us." And then she started to get creative with the craft materials – nothing seemed to make her happier than a glue stick and some glitter . . . horrible stuff, that. I spent several days looking as if I'd been to a Disney Princess party. Anyway. Something smells good?'

'Well, it'll probably taste terrible, so make the most of it,' says Poppy, who, I notice, is also looking a little bit Disney Princess with her sparkle-smeared cheeks. 'We've set up in the Posh Room – we thought perhaps we could eat, and then see what the Dice of Fate hands out for us to watch?'

'Wonderful,' replies Lewis, following us through. 'I so hope we get *X-Men*. I'm quite an admirer of that Wolverine chap. I did try and talk her into that *Magic Mike XXL* film about the male strippers, and suggested we watch it purely for research, but she said it was too much for my old ticker . . .'

I bite back a giggle as we settle around the table, Betty taking up an alert position beneath it, obviously hoping for some scraps. Poppy serves up the meal – slightly over-cooked roast lamb, slightly under-cooked carrots, and perfect roast spuds, which we bought frozen and just warmed up. Even we couldn't ruin those.

I pour the wine, and Lewis, the perfectly polite guest, proclaims himself delighted with every single morsel of what is, in all truthfulness, a decidedly under-par meal. We chat about the A–Z, and tiptoe tenderly around each other, all scared of breaking the magical spell of civility and provoking tears – because it happens so easily, and often so unexpectedly.

I find I can sit and think about my mum, remembering our last conversation and doing that thing she warned us against, picking at wounds, deliberately trying to make myself suffer, and still I remain dry-eyed and in control.

Yet the smallest of things – like being in the queue at the Post Office and seeing a postcard of the village that she once sent to me; or going into the Hideous Extension and seeing that ridiculous ab-crunching device she bought and never used, or remembering her rehearsing her Penny Peabody lines down the phone to me – can set me off into spasms of incoherent sobbing.

When it happens, it's not pretty – I need to find a private place, and wail like a wounded animal, and am completely unable to move or speak or function, the pain is so raw.

I don't want to do that tonight, and I'm pretty sure nobody else does either. So we are polite, and Poppy is sharp and sarcastic but in a funny way, not a mean-girl way, and Lewis tells us stories about village life, and asks questions about Joe, and together – with some effort – we all get through the dinner without stabbing ourselves with a butter knife.

Of course, the evening would have been a lot more fun with my mother there, and I am full of regret that we never did this while she was alive. I'd have loved to have seen those two sparking off each other – it would have been all aboard the banter bus, as Joe would say.

As we finish our dessert – which may be over-stretching

it for a tub of Ben & Jerry's Chunky Monkey – Lewis leans back in his chair, his magnificent belly stretching the buttons of his waistcoat, and dabs delicately at his jowls with a napkin, looking like a Roman emperor who's just enjoyed a fifty-course banquet.

'So,' he says, after a small pause. 'Have you discussed what you might do with the cottage at all? Obviously, there's no rush, and the only reason I ask is that . . . well, if you do decide to sell, I would appreciate first refusal. I find that I simply can't bear the thought of strangers living here, which I know is ridiculously sentimental.

'I have the funds, and I can't think of anything better to spend it on now; I was planning on asking your mother to accompany me on a round-the-world cruise as soon as I was fully retired, but . . . well, that wasn't meant to be. It would be a kindness if you would consider me as the new owner. If you do want to sell, that is.'

Poppy is chewing her lip, her glittery face a little twisted up in the candlelight. She gives her ice-cream spoon one last lick – she seems to have completely overcome her aversion to carbs and sugar – and lays it down in her bowl with a small clatter.

'Lewis, that's a lovely thing to suggest,' she says, and I am relieved to hear a gentle tone of voice emerge from her mouth, 'but I don't think we'll be selling.'

Both Lewis and I look at her and raise our eyebrows. I knew she'd been considering changing her lifestyle, but we've not properly discussed it. I feel a sudden niggle of uncertainty, and realise that, as far as we have come, I still don't 100 per cent trust her. Perhaps we will always be works-in-progress, who knows?

'I know we've not talked about it much, Rose,' she says, obviously sensing my hesitation, 'but if it's all right with you, I want to stay. Work has been harassing me to death even though they know why I'm on leave, so I don't think I'll have any problems making a case for some kind of severance package, and I have a lot of cash tied up in the flat, and . . . well, I can do it. I'll pay you your half, you won't be left out of pocket, honest. I just . . . I want to stay.

'I know it sounds weird, and I probably shouldn't be making big decisions like this when my head is all messed up, but it feels right. I want to stay here, and write, and learn how to cook properly, and look after the blue tits, and . . . just *be*. Does that make sense?'

She sounds desperate, pleading, almost exactly like she used to as a little girl when she wanted me to play Monopoly with her, or was begging to tag along on one of my big-sister adventures. I could rarely resist it then, and I find I can't now.

I nod, and smile, and reply: 'That would be good, Poppy. I think Mum would like it if one of us was still here. And then Lewis can visit as often as he likes.'

'And you,' she says hastily, reaching out to grab my hand. The sudden movement alerts Betty, who stands up and sniffs in search of food. I notice that the dog is also looking a little bit sparkly – one of us must have stroked her after touching the glitter dice.

'You and Joe,' she continues. 'I'd like you two to visit as well.'

Lewis is silent throughout our exchange, but I swear I see a glassy sheen in his eyes as he watches us.

'We will. I promise.'

Poppy nods, and puffs out a long breath, as though a weight has been lifted from her shoulders.

'I think that's a splendid idea,' says Lewis, pouring us all another glass of wine. 'And she would indeed be delighted.'

He looks pleased, even though we've just rejected his offer to buy us out, and I suddenly decide that right now would be the best time to ask him a question I've been dying to ask – but have been too scared to until now. I don't think I could have handled the answer any earlier.

'Lewis,' I say, one hand going down to scratch Betty's ear, as though I need to be doing something else while I even think about this. 'Do you mind me asking about . . . about the day Mum died? I know this is really hard for you, and we're both so grateful for everything you did for her, for us, but . . . was it peaceful? Was she in pain? I know she had good reasons for not telling us, but I feel like I'll never be able to move on from it unless I ask.'

I hear Poppy gulp down half a glass of wine, and Betty licks my hand, as though she is reassuring me, and Lewis blinks away the tears that I most definitely hadn't imagined.

'Strangely, it was,' he replies, after a few moments. 'Very peaceful. For her at least. Earlier in the day, not so much – she was so focused on getting through the last video, she insisted on refusing any drugs for hours. But after she'd done that, and she knew the A–Z was finally finished . . . well. Yes. She seemed so much more at rest.'

'The staff were wonderful at controlling her pain, and in the end . . . well, she seemed to simply go to sleep. She woke from her slumber a few times, but that's basically what it was like.

'She was as peaceful as she could be, knowing that she'd tried her best to help you two, and that she'd told you how much she loved you. The only thing that could have given her any more peace would have been seeing this – seeing you two here, together, behaving like the loving sisters she told me you once were. And I like to think, somehow, that she is seeing it – and that she knows she succeeded.'

I nod my thanks, and realise that I am crying. I glance at Poppy, and see that she is also crying. I return my gaze to Lewis, and he has given up the battle, and has tears streaming down his round cheeks. All three of us are glitter-faced, weeping wrecks, and eventually, after staring at each other in horror, we begin to laugh. Because we all look ridiculous – even the dog. Minutes later, we are still crying – but this time with amusement.

This, I think, looking around the table at my sister, and at the man my mother loved so much, listening to our slightly manic giggles, is also what she would have wanted.

'Right,' I say, once I can speak again. 'I think it's movie time. Poppy, clear a space, and we'll roll the dice . . .'

Once the plates have been taken away to the kitchen, along with Betty, who is following the trail of leftover gravy, we all stand up in preparation. I hand Lewis the dice, and indicate that he should do the honours.

There are six movies listed on there – *X-Men*; *The X-Files* film; something called *Xiu Xiu* that I assume is Chinese; that xXx film with Vin Diesel in it; *X-Men: First Class*, which I think is a bit of a cheat, but does have the added bonus of James McAvoy, and *Xanadu*. I'm really hoping it's not *Xanadu*. I don't think I could endure Olivia Newton-John in a roller disco – it's more than my fragile mind could take.

Lewis makes a fine performance of blowing on the dice like they do in gambling movies, which results in him smearing glitter all over his mouth, and rolls it across the tablecloth. It leaves a shining trail, as though a disco snail has crawled past, and eventually bumps its way to a standstill. We all peer at the result that's left face-side up.

Fuck. It's bloody *Xanadu*.

We all look at each other in disgust, and Lewis finally breaks the silence.

'Best out of three?' he asks.

'Definitely,' replies Poppy. 'It's what she would have wanted.'

Chapter 68

Poppy

'Y,' I say, reading from the now almost-disintegrated A–Z index, 'is for Yesterday. And it's a letter, together with some diaries.'

'Okay,' replies Rose, frowning at me. 'Do you really think we need to do it today? I spoke to Joe earlier, and he's fine. In fact he sounded brilliant. I thought . . . I thought we could have a bit more time, and that then perhaps he could get the train down for the last bit of the hols. If that's all right with you.'

'Of course it's all right with me. That'd be brilliant. But . . . well, we've been putting this off for two days now, haven't we? And I think we both know why.'

She nods, and twists her hair around her fingers, and looks sad.

'It's because we're getting near the end,' she says. 'And neither of us wants to get to the end. Because when we get to the end, it's all over, and we go our separate ways, and everything goes back to normal.'

Hard as it is to believe, she's right. At the beginning of all of this, we couldn't stand the sight of each other. Rose preferred to tear the flesh from the side of her nails than to look me in the eye, and I acted like the world's biggest bitch just to hide how vulnerable I felt.

Since then, the A–Z has stripped us bare. It's knocked us down, trampled on us, and built us back up. Our mother has guided us over so many hurdles, dragged us out of pitfalls, pulled us from the clifftops of our self-destruction. And along the way, she's made us laugh, and cry, and eat, and play, and get to know each other, and ourselves.

The thought of it all ending – of reaching the dreaded Z – is almost too much for us to bear. Because after that, it's up to us, isn't it? Then, we have to play our own roles, without Mum there to direct us.

'I know,' I say, reaching out to hold her hand. She is physically trembling, and I squeeze her fingers. 'It's a horrible thought. While we've been doing this, it's like she was still with us in a way. All those photos, and videos, and everything else she left behind – it's been like she's not actually gone. But she wanted us to do this, and I don't think we should chicken out at Y, do you?'

Rose looks as though she wants to disagree with me, but reluctantly nods, sinking down on to the sofa in defeat.

I smile, trying to make it look more encouraging than I feel, and pull the note out of the A–Z box. It is accompanied by a hefty package wrapped in brown paper and tied with string, like a parcel in a black-and-white movie.

I open the envelope marked Y, and together, sitting side by side, we read.

Chapter 69

Andrea: Y is for Yesterday

Hello my darlings – Mother here! This will be my last note, so I'll try and make it a good one. My pain levels are under control right now, which makes everything easier, doesn't it? I can only hope that yours are under control as well. At least I have morphine, darlings – you only have gin!

Yesterday, I spent most of the afternoon making a glittery dice with the names of movies on the side. I hope you enjoyed that game, and cheated as many times as it took until you got *X-Men*. I would expect nothing less, and would have done the same myself. Hugh Jackman, yum.

Yesterday, I also had a visit from a frightfully handsome young doctor from Ghana. Lovely man, though sadly not a miracle worker.

Yesterday, I threw caution to the wind and had lime jelly instead of strawberry – I know, I know, how crazy of me!

And yesterday, after I'd done my dice, Lewis took me

out in my wheelchair for a little walk. We didn't go far
– just to the park – but it was wonderful to feel the sun
on my skin, and see the beautiful weeping willow trees
draped over the grass, and to listen to the children
playing on the swings. He brought Betty, and we had a
good old slobbery cuddle. Darling dog.

So, all things considered, not a bad yesterday at all.
But now, it's gone – and a new day has started. The
possibilities are . . . well, I'd like to say endless, but as
I'm on a drip and wearing a nightie right now, maybe
not!

The point, though, remains the same – our yesterdays
make us who we are, but our tomorrows make us who
we will become. That sounds suitably wise, and is my
way of saying – girls, are you ready to say goodbye to
yesterday? Are you ready to throw out the rubbish, to
leave all of the pain and misery behind? Are you ready
to move on?

My goodness, how I hope so. I hope that you have
forgiven each other, and forgiven yourselves. If you have,
then say so – because just thinking it doesn't count.
Look each other in the eye, and say goodbye to those
nasty old yesterdays. Do it for yourselves, if not for me.
And, while you're at it, get rid of something else – those
horrible guilt lists I asked you to write, what feels like
an age ago now. The only reason I asked you to write
them down was so that you could throw them away.

And when you're done with that, the package contains
a little gift for you. It's a collection of some of my diaries,

from over the years. I always wanted to be a good journal keeper, but never really had the self-discipline, so I was always a little hit or miss. There are some years where I write most days, others where there are only a couple of entries.

Some are funny, some are sad, and some, I am horrified to say, are just plain boring. These diaries are not for you to read now – now is the time to focus on your own lives. They're for the future. For when you need to feel me close, and can't pick up the phone.

For when you find yourself in a situation and wonder what I'd think . . . well, I can't guarantee the answers will be in there, but at least something will be in there. Even if it is just me mooning over Ian McShane or complaining about the short shelf life of goldfish.

The diaries are a little bit of me, for you two to keep forever. I hope they bring you some pleasure, some comfort, and some consolation – I may not be there in person, but I can at least be on your bookshelves!

Anyway, as I said, I had a busy day yesterday, and am feeling a snooze coming on. Morphine, delicious as it is, doesn't make extensive periods of lucidity especially easy. Enjoy the diaries, girls – and don't forget. Talk to each other.

With love, as always,

Mum xxx

Chapter 70

Rose

Poppy, sharing my mother's flair for the dramatic, has insisted on a midnight ceremony. I am counting myself lucky that she hasn't insisted we dress up in pagan robes and smear our faces with golden syrup.

I'm also a bit tired, truth be told. I stayed up late last night reading one of Mum's diaries. I know she said not to bother with them right now, but, well, what's she going to do about it? I curled up in my teenaged bed, and spent hours enjoying her first-hand accounts of her show-biz exploits.

The diary I read covered the Penny Peabody era, and was perfect – not too much turmoil, not too much hand-wringing and trauma, just a lot of very amusing anecdotes about life on set, and actors who played tough guys insisting on having exactly the right blend of aromatic oils burning in their dressing rooms, and who was bonking who.

She has such a witty and engaging style, I have no doubt at all that, like Poppy, she could also have been a writer. Maybe we'll edit her diaries and publish them; they could easily be cult classics. All those perverts who watched her nude carousel horse scene would buy them.

I know all the diaries won't be so much fun. I know some of them, in fact, will be extremely painful – but that is a journey for another day. For now, it's nice to imagine her healthy and happy and enjoying her twilight years.

Poppy has been in the mower shed again, and emerges brandishing a plastic petrol can. She pokes the ashes in the barbecue, and pulls a face.

I don't blame her. The contents are pretty revolting – the half-melted face of our Tiny Tears Gareth effigy, distorted into horror-movie form, chubby arm folded over her head as though trying to ward off the flames.

Tonight, she has decided, we are going to get rid of our Guilt Lists in style.

It's a pleasant night, the countryside sky draped with the kind of dazzlingly clear stars that you just don't see in the city. I can hear an owl hooting, and the cows from the nearby farm, and it's incredibly peaceful.

The lights from the cottage are casting a glow over the garden, and the gnome collective looks magnificently eerie – like they might come to life at any moment and frolic over the lawn, with their fishing rods and watering cans and little red hats.

'So,' says Poppy, grinning at me in the moonlight. 'We're all set. I have my list – do you have yours?'

I nod, and tug the huge wad of memo-pad notes from my pocket. It feels like a different lifetime, that night when I sat, destroyed, sobbing over all of my perceived crimes, still not quite believing that my mother had gone. I was in shock, and none of it felt real. Some of it still doesn't.

'Shall we read them?' I ask, glancing at Poppy's single piece of paper in curiosity. I wonder if there is anything on her list, or on mine, that will damage us – that will take us back to our pre-A–Z world, when we could barely function in each other's company. I hope not, but I don't think we can ever be 100 per cent sure – our relationship, like all relationships I suppose, will always be a work-in-progress, and maybe that's not a bad thing.

She nods, and we silently exchange papers. I unfold hers, and see one word staring out at me, written in bold capital letters: EVERYTHING. Well, that's straightforward enough.

It takes Poppy a little longer, obviously, to decipher my scrawl, and plod through the pile of crumpled squares. I see her smiling at some, frowning at others, and finally, looking up to meet my eyes when she comes to the very last entry. The one I didn't even want to write: that I never gave Poppy a second chance.

'Well,' she says, handing the pages back to me. 'I don't know what to say about stabbing Yoda in the eye, but that last one? About me? I'm well and truly ready to burn that one, Rose. Because you have given me a second chance – even if it was only because Mum made you.

'You could have said no. You could have walked away from all this, and gone back to Liverpool, and we probably would never have seen each other again. Instead, we're here, together. And maybe . . . maybe you have forgiven me?'

I suppose, at heart, that all of our mother's frantic planning and scheming and plotting has always been leading up to this. To this one moment – to us standing here, in her garden at midnight, listening to the owl chorus and wondering what comes next. Only one letter of her A–Z might technically have been called F for Forgiveness, but the whole thing has basically been about that one issue.

Do I forgive Poppy, knowing everything I know now? Looking back on the whole affair with hindsight, under-standing how she felt? After losing our mother, and getting each other through the A–Z, and taking the first tentative and terrifying steps back into each other's lives?

'I do forgive you, Poppy,' I say simply. 'Forgetting won't be as easy, for either of us – but I do forgive you. I love you. I've missed you. And now . . . well, I can't imagine life without you. If you can forgive me for the way I reacted, I can forgive you for what happened. D for Deal?'

She reaches out a hand, as though to shake on it, and instead pulls me in for a hug. I wrap my arms around her, and feel her snuffling away in my hair. I suspect she's crying, and I pat her back to console her.

'Okay – let's do this,' she says, when she eventually pulls away. There is a real fizz about her tonight – a sense of bound-less energy. She's practically bouncing on her bare feet as she takes the petrol can, and pours a splosh on to the barbecue.

I stand back – the splosh looked a bit on the generous side – and wait until she lights it. With a small wooshing sound, the flames leap up, dancing gold and red in the dark night sky. There is a crackling noise, and the smell of burning plastic as Tiny Tears disintegrates even further.

She looks at me, little flickering flames reflected in her wide brown eyes, and I nod.

At exactly the same moment, we both throw our Guilt Lists into the fire, where they crinkle and crumple and turn quickly into a small pile of ash.

Chapter 71

Andrea: Z is for Zapplebums

'Hello Rosehip, hello Popcorn! I hope you are both splendid today – although perhaps, like myself, you're feeling a little blue. We have reached Z, and we are at the end of our last adventure together.

'This will be my last recording for you, and I've decided on the good old-fashioned tape recorder again. I have one more video to make, so I'm saving all of my screen presence for that – it will be an important event, and I don't want to fluff my lines. Because while it is the end of the A–Z for me, it will be the beginning for you – and I'm planning on giving the performance of my life.

'I have no idea where you are, right now, or what you are doing, or how you're feeling. This whole project has been created in a vacuum – for all I know, as I record this, you could have given up by now. Or not even started.

'All those envelopes could have remained unopened, and you might never have even seen that photo of me with Elvis . . . I like to think you did. I *have* to think so. I have to cling to my belief that you're still here, still trucking as they say, still listening.

'I have to believe that this has all made a difference. That your future will be healthier because of it. That all my wishes and all my prayers have been answered, and that you two are together again. The not-knowing is killing me – or is that the cancer, ha ha! Sorry, gallows humour . . . anyway. I have to accept that I will never know what effect all of this has had on you – it's like the ultimate cliff-hanger. At least for me.

'I hope you've enjoyed yourselves, or at the very least not murdered each other. For me, it's been quite the mission – an A–Z of all my dreams. I realise that some of it may have been odd, or upsetting, or downright bewildering at times, but it wasn't just about healing your relationship, girls. It was about me, saying goodbye.

'We all know that we won't live forever. We all know that the time will come when we leave our loved ones, and look back on our lives knowing that the end is nigh. That there will be no more chances, no more choices, no more anything.

'But knowing it in theory and facing up to it in reality – knowing that life is finite, and every minute you have left is being measured out like grains of sand in a giant egg timer – is very different. At the start of this, I had no idea how much time I had left, and whether I'd even get to the end of it. If fate hadn't been kind, I could have left you hanging at H, I suppose!

'Lewis thinks, and he is usually right, that I am simply too stubborn to let go until all of this is complete. Until I feel as if I've done the best I can – and perhaps that is the case. I'm certainly relieved, in a way, to get to Z – even if it is the end. I don't have too much left in the tank, truth be told.

'It's all very strange, isn't it? It is to me, at least. Lewis, at my insistence, has gone home for the night, and I am lying here, in my hospital bed, recording my voice for my daughters to listen to after I'm dead. It really doesn't get much stranger than that – knowing that everything I leave behind, all of these messages and videos and letters, will be all that's left of me.

'It's more than most people get, but I know that for you, it will never be enough – no matter how many questions I have answered, how many thoughts I have provoked, none of this will ever be enough. It's simply not the same as having me around, is it? Believe me girls, if I could pull off that particular miracle, I would.

'I've done the next best thing with all of this, and I've done it with so much love. It's been tricky at times, and I'm finding, as I lie here, alone, that this is one of the trickiest of all. Because it's my final chance – my final attempt to leave you stronger than I found you. I can hear the nurses chattering outside, and I can imagine Lewis getting home and pouring himself a big glass of port, and I can imagine you two, going about your normal lives with no idea of what is about to happen to you. The shock of the phone call I know you'll be getting before very long now.

'I can imagine all of that, but I can't quite imagine how all of this will finish – for any of us. I've started a story that I will never be able to quite end. Will you two become sisters again? Does Heaven exist, and if so will I be heading that way? And how *will* Lewis cope without me?

'I've suggested a lot of answers throughout this A–Z, but

these last few have got the better of me. I suppose I will simply never know – unless the answer to the Heaven question is "yes", of course!

'I'm wittering on, I know – but I find that I am so reluctant to press that big "stop" button. It feels ominous somehow, glaring at me in the half-light – like if I press stop on the recording, I'll be pressing stop on my life. Pressing stop on my contact with you two. Letting go – and I really, really don't want to let go. I want to hold you both so close to me, snuggle you up in my arms and kiss your faces and keep you safe.

'I know you're grown women, but in my mind, you're still my babies. My darling little girls. You're my whole life – and I so want to protect you from what is to come.

'I can't do that, sadly. Nor can I come up with a truly satisfying Z to end all of this with. It's really very annoying that after all this effort, the last letter of the damned alphabet is such an awkward one. Lewis left me a very handy dictionary for inspiration, and I did come up with some great finds – for example, did you know that "zwitterion" is a real word? No? Me neither! It sounds wonderfully exotic, but is actually something to do with ions and chemistry. Frightfully dull.

'And did you know that in India and Iran, the part of a house set aside for women is called the zenana? Or that a ziggurat is a type of tower? That a fence of thorns is known in Sudan as a zareba? I'm not quite sure how useful any of this is to me now, but I suppose it's never too late to learn.

'Anyway, I suppose all I really need to tell you is that I love you both in a zillion different ways. I love you so much, in fact, that it surpasses all known language, and, I think, needs a brand-new word. I have decided that word will be "zapple-bums". The definition of "zapplebums", in case you were wondering, would look like this in the dictionary: *zapplebums: adjective – word used to describe the ultimate in love, adoration and pride.*

'That, my darlings, is the way I feel about you two. Feel free to alert the nice people at the Oxford English Dictionary.'

'And now, I fear, I must finally press "stop". I can only hope that it isn't too literal. I shall end with something I also plan to start with, if the God of Tape Recorders allows me one more day. I shall end by asking you both to always remember this one simple thing: I love you, and I know that you love me.

'So for now, darlings – my gorgeous, grubby angels – goodbye. My love for you is zapplebums.'

PART THREE

The Final Curtain

Chapter 72

Joe: The Reviews Are In

It's a nice place, this. Up on the hills, really pretty country-side all around us. We've come down for Mum's birthday, and Aunt Poppy made us a cake.

The cake was pretty disgusting – I suppose she's still learning – but we all pretended it was lovely. Especially Lewis – he talked about that cake like it was the best thing he'd ever eaten.

Now we're out here, with him and Mum and Poppy and Betty. It's the middle of October, and the sun is still shining, but it's a bit chilly. The apple trees in the cottage garden are drooping with fruit, and there was a frost on all the gnomes' heads this morning when I woke up and looked out of the window of Poppy's old room.

That's my room now, when I come and visit, and she's said it's fine if I want to leave stuff there, or get rid of her things. I quite like it though – there's a lot of books, and the other day I found a packet of Rizlas hidden inside a copy of *Bridget Jones's Diary*. I can't take the mickey out of her for it, though, because then I'd have to admit I was reading *Bridget Jones's*

Diary in the first place. And, knowing Poppy, she'd post that on my Facebook page, and that would be social death.

Poppy and Mum have gone on ahead, and are dancing around the stone circles singing some kind of chant. I can't hear what it's about, but it seems to involve a lot of arm waving and jumping.

Mum started her teacher training this term, and she seems to be enjoying it. The house is full of files and colour-coded charts and highlighter pens, so I guess she means business. She also seems to mean business about her new health regime, which is great. She's even been coming to the gym with me and Simon.

I'm starting to think maybe she's doing other stuff with Simon as well, but that's none of my business. He's certainly round at the house a lot more, and they've had a few nights out at the cinema and the pub quiz. She goes a bit giddy when he's in the room, which is weird. But, I suppose, nice. Simon never looks giddy – he probably had it trained out of him when he was in the Marines – but he definitely looks happy when he sees her. Hey, maybe I'll have a new stepdad one day, who knows?

I'm not so sure about a new granddad though – she's been emailing him in Blackpool, and they've talked about meeting up, but it hasn't happened yet. It's a good job I'm already used to strange-shaped families.

Poppy is still at the cottage, where she tells me she is writing a 'bonkbuster'. I didn't ask too many questions about that – I'm a bit scared she'll answer them. The boxes – the ones covered in pretty flowers – are there too; Mum said it was their spiritual home. I'm not so sure boxes have spirits, but these are pretty special boxes.

Lewis is lagging behind us, further down the hill, mainly because of Betty, I think, who moves about as fast as a snail. It's nice that he's here, though. I think he's been a bit lonely without Granny, and I get the impression that Poppy has kind of adopted him. They're really rude to each other, but in that way that says they like each other?

I catch them up, close enough to hear that they're going on about goddesses and Mars Bars. Nutters.

I still miss Gran myself, but I think she'd be made up to see this. In that card she left me – the one with the fox on the front – she told me how much she loved us all, as well as giving me some advice. She said I should learn to recognise true gold when I saw it, and to treasure the things that matter in life.

It was all a bit heavy for me – I'm still trying to get my head round Physics A-level – but I won't forget it. I still have that card, and I always will.

I miss her. I wish she was dancing round those stones with Mum and Poppy. It feels weird that she's not here – that all this stuff has happened without her being here to see it.

Though who knows, really, I think, looking at the way those two are hugging that giant stone – the Witch Stone. Maybe she is?

Acknowledgements

This book has been quite an A–Z for me as well as Rose and Poppy – mainly H for Hard Work, and T for Tearing My Hair Out. But there's also been a lot of S for Support along the way, and as ever I have people to thank.

Kim Young, Charlotte Ledger and the team at HarperCollins have been with me all the way, so big hugs to them. Also to my agent Rowan Lawton – welcome to the crazy train!

There are also several individuals who have helped me in various ways – often involving beer, always involving laughter – who I'd like to give a shout out to: Sandra Shennan, Pamela Hoey, Jane Murdoch, Jane Costello, Milly Johnson, Jane Linfoot, the Barbacoa Quiz Gang, and Vikki Everett.

On a very personal note, my family have, as always, been brilliant. My lovely kids Keir, Dan and Louisa keep my head out of the clouds, and where it belongs – washing their PE kits, looking for lost keys, and remembering that it's swimming on Tuesdays. Big thanks also to my handsome, clever musical genius of a husband (did I get that right Dom?), for listening to me ramble on about fictional problems, letting me watch

Supernatural, and tolerating a lot of take-aways. Love you all to infinity and beyond.

My extended family, the Crazy O'Malleys, as ever, need a thank you – especially my mother-in-law, Terry, whose showbiz stories most definitely helped me create Andrea Barnard.

One of the main themes of this book is grief, and how we deal with it. Sadly, I've lost too many good people from my life in recent years, as have several of my friends. Perhaps we are simply at the age where we say more goodbyes than we used to. So my final message is to all of the loved ones we have lost: we still love you; we still miss you, and we still think about you every single day.

Meet
Debbie Johnson

1. What was your inspiration for The *A–Z of Everything*?

The initial idea actually came from the title – I was lying in bed at night thinking, as you do, and the *A–Z of Everything* came to me . . . then I created the story around it, based on lots of my own experiences, seasoned with imagination! I lost my own mum a few years ago, and my father as well, and I was raised as an only child (I have a very weird-shaped family which I won't bore you with!) so sometimes, I feel like I have nobody to turn to to ask a question. I'll try to remember someone's name from childhood, or wonder about something my mum mentioned to me in passing when I was only half listening, and realise that I have no way of answering those questions. It's quite a lonely thing – and I would dearly love to have an A–Z of my own from my mum. I think anybody who has lost someone close to them will understand that urge, that desperate yearning for one more conversation – and as this is fiction, Rose and Poppy got to have it!

2. What are the key themes in the book and why did you decide to write about them?

I'd say there are three big ones – love, grief, and redemption. The obvious one is grief, but that sounds so morbid, and I hope that the book is, ultimately, uplifting. The flip side of grief is the fact that in order to miss someone so very much, you were very lucky to have had them in your life at all. The amount we grieve is proportionate to the amount we loved, and love is to be celebrated. Life is to be celebrated and the A–Z is as much about that as death. It's not just about two women missing their mum – it's about two women rediscovering their mum, and each other, and themselves. The other big theme really is redemption. Nobody gets through life without doing a few things they shouldn't; sometimes things that we are deeply ashamed of and which scar us and those around us. The way that Poppy and Rose rebuild their relationship is about redemption – second chances, forgiveness. Realising that the important things in life are not guilt and anger and sticking to your guns – but being willing to love each other, warts and all.

3. This book is a departure from your previous romantic comedies. Your warm sense of humour is still apparent throughout, but did you enjoy writing something different and more emotional?

Very much, yes. My Comfort Food Cafe books had taken a step in that direction, they had humour and romance but also dealt with some very real and painful issues. This was a step further – and although I know it might not be quite what people have come to expect of me, I hope they enjoy it too. I think it's the first book I've ever written without a sex scene in it, now I come to think of it . . .

4. Andrea refuses to let her girls know that she is dying in order to bring them together after her death. Do you understand Andrea's motivation for secrecy?

Completely. On a personal level, I was with both my parents at their death beds – just me and them. That was unbelievably hard, and in all honesty I still feel a bit traumatised by it. I know others will feel differently, and see it as a privilege, but for me it was extremely awful, both times. I have to say I'm with Andrea – I'm not sure I'd want my children to go through that, thinking they had to sit there for my sake, as though they'd let me down if they left? I think I'd rather encourage them – and myself – to live our lives in a way that leaves us all in no doubt about how much we love each other, how much we care, and how much we'll be missed. Andrea didn't want all the emphasis to be on her death – she wanted it to be on her life, and on her daughters' lives, and I think that is a noble and brave thing. I understand why Poppy and Rose felt a little cheated and angry about it, but I think Andrea's motivations were pure.

5. Which of the characters in the book do you identify with most? Are any of them based on people you know?

I have to say I'm a bit of a Rose! None of the things in this book, apart from losing my mother, are based on any events or people from real life, but when I was reading it back I realised how much of myself was in Rose. Her struggles with weight and health ring true to me, and I'm sure a lot of other women – sometimes we are so busy looking after other people we seem to be incapable of looking after ourselves. On a more light-hearted note, my other-in-law was a model and actress in the Seventies and Eighties and tells us lots of amusing stories that seem to get bigger every time – so there was definitely a spark of that in Andrea's tales as well!

6. Who is your favourite character and why?

I can't answer that! I love them all. I identify most with Rose, but I adore Poppy's feistiness, and love Andrea's wit and joie-de-vivre. Lewis is great fun, and Joe is adorable . . . plus, you know, the guy next door is pretty tasty too!

7. Where do you see Rose and Poppy's journeys heading after the book has finished?

That's always one of the weird things about writing a book — you finish your story, but the characters still exist in your head. I wrote a book called *Pippa's Cornish Dream* in 2015 — a sweet rom com — and every now and then I find myself wondering what Pippa's up to these days! I like to think that Rose will continue to build her self-esteem, and her new career — we saw the signs of that happening, and I think she'll get there in the end. She will also get it together with her neighbour, and by the time Joe goes off to university, her life will look very different than it did when we first met her, when she was binging on chocolates and feeling sorry for herself. Poppy . . . well, I like to think that Poppy writes her best-seller, and lives a brilliantly eccentric life in the cottage — that in some ways she becomes the new Andrea! I was wondering if she should find love, maybe have the child she always secretly wanted — but ultimately I think Poppy's journey is all about a love affair with herself, and reaching her full potential. She becomes best pals with Lewis, and I like to think they have many adventures together! And — most importantly of course — Poppy and Rose stay firmly in each other's lives.

8. If you made your own A–Z of Everything, which letters would be easiest to fill first and what would you fill them with?

I've actually thought about this . . . well, not an A–Z exactly, but perhaps about writing down every daft little detail about myself that I can remember — my childhood, my parents, that kind of thing. Not because I'm that egotistical to think it's interesting, but because I know that at some point (hopefully in the very distant future), my own kids will have to say goodbye to me. They will be the ones with questions — and even if they don't find me especially fascinating right now, they will once I'm gone! I think if I was going to A–Z it, the big one would be L of Love — I genuinely had no idea how much you could love your own children. The oldest of my three is 19 now, and it is still a revelation to me. Like

Andrea, I think I would also want them to try and avoid the big nasties – Guilt and Jealousy are so destructive. I'd probably make D for Dogs . . . I love Dogs. Or maybe Daniel Craig, depending on what mood I was in . . .

9. Where's your favourite writing place, and do you have a particular routine?

I write on my sofa, on a laptop, usually with two old dogs lying next to me snoring away – which they are doing right now! I drop the younger kids at school, come home, write, and then pick them up again. Either side of the school run is delightful chaos – the bit in the middle is where the work gets done. I'm really, really lucky to have been able to build a lifestyle that allows me to both work, and put in my 'mummy' time as well.

10. Who are you favourite authors or books and have they had an influence on your writing?

I have so many favourite authors! I love crime fiction and fantasy, and certain authors just delight me every time. Nora Roberts I adore, when she is writing as Nora or as JD Robb, and I think she has been an influence – she's a great example of how style and humour and romance can be combined with a fast-moving plot. Her characters are always so vivid as well, no matter how many books she writes. I think Sue Grafton's Kinsey Millhone books have influenced me – I love her strength of character, Kinsey is as real to me as someone I actually know. I love John Connolly – he has a great sense of humour blended into the crime and supernatural themes. I like books with a strong sense of place, which I've been told mine also have – like Philip Kerr's Berlin stories, or James Lee Burke's Louisiana tales. Mine are in places like Dorset, which isn't quite as glamorous I know, but I do like the idea of transporting someone out of their daily existence. If I had to Desert Island one series though, it'd be the Belgariad books by David Eddings. They're just totally perfect little fantasy adventures, which I read as a teenager and my son has since read – in fact the first copy of the first book recently literally fell to pieces, we've read it so many times!

Find out more about Debbie on Twitter: 🐦 @debbiemjohnson
and Facebook: ⬛/debbiejohnsonauthor

Discover
Debbie Johnson's
bestselling romantic comedies

'A sheer delight'
— *Sunday Express*